The SEAL Series

JACK SILKSTONE

The characters and events portrayed in this book are fictitious. Any similarity to real persons, living or dead, is coincidental and not intended by the author.

Published by Jack Silkstone

ISBN: 9781983240027

This book is dedicated to the Military Working Dogs who
have served, loyal and steadfast, alongside their handlers
in the world's deadliest conflict zones.

TABLE OF CONTENTS

SEAL of Approval

Chapter One

Special Warfare Operator Mike Saunders placed the two halves of his M4 carbine on his desk and glanced at the Belgian Malinois working dog that sat at his feet. Reaching down he ruffled the hound's ears and was rewarded with a snuffle from a wet nose. Smiling, he returned to cleaning his weapon and watching the video playing on his battered laptop.

Tall, with broad shoulders, Mike looked as if he had stepped out of a SEAL recruiting poster. The twenty-eight year old had a square jaw, slate gray eyes, and short blonde hair. A cheeky smile and an easygoing attitude topped off what most women called a 'complete package'.

His dog, Axe, was an equally handsome specimen. Smaller and leaner than the related German Shepherd, he had a dark face with intelligent brown eyes and alert ears that jutted from the top of his head. That is, except for the very tip of his right ear which drooped forward like a wilted leaf.

Mike finished cleaning a component and scanned the SEAL team room. Richard 'Rick' Anderson and Javier 'Ernie' Ernesto were also working on their weapons in a space resembling a football locker room. The men, and Axe, were team-mates, SEALs on standby at their base in Coronado, ready to leap into action, at a moment's notice.

"Hey Mike, how's that lady of yours doing? She launched her modeling agency yet?" asked Rick, a muscular African American who was the squad Corpsman and a notorious ladies man.

Mike snorted. "The party's tomorrow. And before you ask, you're not invited."

"Bro, you're killing me. What's the point of knowing someone who owns an agency if you're not allowed to meet the girls?"

"Meet, is that what you call it?" added Ernie from the bench seat where he was cleaning his pistol. The short, athletic Mexican was the squad's communications guy, happily married, and a father of two.

Rick flexed his bicep against the fabric of his camouflage combat shirt. "Hey, it's not my problem ladies can't resist, the Rick."

Mike finished assembling his carbine. "Did you seriously just refer to yourself in the third person?"

"Rick Slade gets all the ladies."

"The only thing Rick Slade's going to get is herpes," quipped Ernie.

Mike snickered. "Burn!"

At that moment a craggy-faced, barrel-chested SEAL with short gray hair barged into the room and bellowed. "Grab your panties ladies. We've got a hit on Barbosa. Wheels up in ten."

Chief 'TJ' Lines was their squad leader. Mike guessed his age at mid-forties but no one actually knew how old he was. He'd been a SEAL for longer than anyone could remember.

The men sprang into action, fitting their weapons together and grabbing their gear. Camouflage body armor covered with pouches was thrown on over their fatigues along with backpacks and their night vision equipped helmets.

Mike snapped his gun belt around his waist and checked his pistol was secure. "Where's he at?"

"Location of interest on the outskirts of Puerto. We've got approval. The platoon's launching and we're on point. I'll give orders in the air."

"Nice, going after the top dog," said Rick as he grabbed his medical kit.

"Only way we roll," added Ernie as he finished donning his own gear and made for the door. "I'll see you boys in the hangar. I wanna grab some extra batteries."

"I'll come with." Rick followed the comms guy out of the team room, leaving Mike and TJ with Axe. Mike finished fitting the dog's harness then rechecked all the buckles were closed. As he snapped on a lead, his laptop started chiming. He glanced at the flashing icon on the screen.

His girlfriend, Stacey, was calling. He locked eyes with a frowning TJ. "It'll only take a minute."

"You've got thirty seconds." The Chief continued preparing his equipment.

As the call connected Mike looked down at Axe's intelligent eyes staring up at him. "Just a second, bud."

The call connected and an attractive blonde appeared on screen. "Michael, where are you?" Her high-pitched voice crackled through the speakers.

He fought the urge to grimace and braced himself as he delivered the bad news. "At work babe, 'bout to head out the door."

Stacey's heavily made-up face screwed into a scowl. "What do you mean you're heading out? Where are you going?"

"Honey, I can't tell you. You know how it is."

One perfectly manicured eyebrow arched. "Really, you're going to play that card. You do realize that my agency launch is tomorrow?" She flicked her hair to emphasize the point.

"Of course, look I'm going to do my best to get there but–"

"But? All I ever hear are excuses, Michael. I'm beginning to think that you've got zero interest in this relationship."

"Hey, you know that's not true."

"Then make sure you're here tomorrow night." Her face disappeared as she terminated the call.

Mike glanced down and took in the concerned expression on Axe's dark face.

"Yeah, I know bro." He took up the dog's lead.

"Walk with me, Mike," grunted TJ from the doorway.

The three of them, two operators and a canine, left the SEAL's training facility in the direction of the Naval Air Station hangars.

"You might not know this, Mike, but when I first joined the teams, I was married." The old SEAL had a voice that sounded like gravel being tossed in a steel drum. "It didn't last very long. You know why?"

Mike could guess why. "No, tell me."

"Because she was a narcissistic princess. A lot like that pretty little lady you're fooling around with. Bud, SEALs and girls like that don't work... not long term."

At a loss for words, Mike remained silent.

"Yeah, they're fun and she's probably a great lay, but that's it. You can't count on them. They're about as reliable as a cheesecloth condom. Soon as things get tough, they're going to cause you heartache and headaches. Isn't that right, Axe?"

At the sound of his name, the dog glanced up at TJ and licked his chops.

"See, even Axe agrees."

They entered a cavernous aircraft hangar and joined the rest of the squad. Rick and Ernie had organized their parachute rigs and other equipment. Behind them, the rest of the SEAL platoon, another ten men, also prepared their gear.

"That lady of yours doesn't look or sound like the sort of woman a SEAL should be dating, brother," continued TJ as he found his rig in the line of parachutes.

Rick laughed as he adjusted his harness. "The old man giving another one of his infamous lectures?"

"Hey, I'm just trying to look out for our boy. That's what brothers do."

"I get it, TJ, and I appreciate your advice, but I think you're wrong about Stacey. She's a good person. She's just got a lot riding on this agency." Mike adjusted his own chute, checking the suspension hooks that would hold Axe across his chest.

Rick snorted. "She may be hot but, that woman's crazy with a capital C."

Mike frowned and turned to Ernie for support.

"Whoa, brother, don't bring me in on this." Ernie tossed Mike a *Starburst*, his favorite. "Who you choose to date is completely up to you." He lowered his eyes to his equipment. "But *essè*, the bitch is crazy. I mean, who the hell hacks their boyfriend's email account."

"She's a little insecure," said Mike as he unwrapped the candy.

"Bro, she chooses what you wear," added Rick. "And then, when you don't wear it she refuses to go out with you. That girl is all about herself."

Mike chewed the *Starburst* as he glanced down at Axe sitting at his feet. "What about you bud, you like Stacey, right?"

The dog gave a whine as he lowered himself to the floor and covered his snout with one paw as the others broke into laughter. Mike shook his head in disgust.

TJ gave him a friendly slap on the back. "Hey, like I said, bud. We're just looking out for our team-mate. Now, let's get this show on the road."

***

On the other side of town, at the Iron Canyon Veterinary Clinic, Alison Taylor was finishing her final consult for the day. Chloe, a beautiful Golden Retriever sat on her examination table. It had been a last minute walk-in to the clinic. Chloe had chased a squirrel over an embankment and badly sprained her hind leg. Faced with an injured dog and a distressed owner, Alison had been unable to turn them away.

With the dog bandaged and her owner placated, the pretty veterinarian glanced at the clock on the wall, as she washed her hands.

"Oh crap!" It was already ten past seven. She was late for her date.

She slipped out of her scrubs and fished a flowery summer dress from a sports bag in the corner of her office.

Throwing on a pair of black flats with the dress she turned and faced the mirror on the back of the door. She grimaced. The face looking back at her might have been pretty, if it wasn't for the bags under her eyes. She pulled her long brown hair into a ponytail, applied color to her full lips, traced liner around her green eyes and dusted her cheeks with a touch of concealer. She was far from ready. But, it would have to do.

Her assistant caught her on the way out. “Have a good time.”

The restaurant was a short cab ride from the clinic. On the way, she checked her phone. She had three missed calls from Brian, her date. The banker would not be impressed by her tardiness.

A smartly dressed maître d' led her to the table where Brian was waiting. The handsome investment banker was dressed in a three-piece suit and wore a frown. She noted he already had a starter in front of him and a glass of wine.

She felt his gaze on her as she approached.

Smiling, she reached the table. “So sorry I’m late. I had a last minute consult.”

Brian remained seated. “I took the liberty of ordering you the salad.”

The waiter pulled her chair out and Alison sat. “Oh… thank you.”

The banker frowned. “I hope that’s alright. I mean this is a two star restaurant and I didn’t want to offend them by not ordering.”

Alison managed a thin smile. “No, it’s fine. A salad is perfect. I can always get the steak for entrée.”

“I did tell you it was a two star restaurant didn’t I?”

“A number of times, why? Is there a problem?”

He exhaled. “It’s just… Look, the owner is a client of my firm and…”

Alison’s face suddenly felt warm. “Go on.”

He leaned forward and whispered. “And, well you didn’t put very much effort into your presentation.”

It took every ounce of her strength to refrain from taking his glass of wine and throwing it in his face. Instead she whispered back. “Like I said, I had a last minute consult.”

He chuckled. "Please, I'm sure the dog's sprained ankle could have waited."
She grabbed her glass of water and drank to hide her disgust.
"Look, it's OK," he continued. "Just, for future reference, it's appropriate to wear heels to a restaurant like this."
The waiter appeared with a bottle of wine and Brian inspected it. "So, I had quite the hectic day today."
Alison didn't hear the rest of the words coming from his mouth. Her mind had wandered back to their first date. A casual drink at a bar, it had gone reasonably well. In direct contrast to his current behavior, Brian had been attentive, engaging and somewhat charming.
"Alison!"
She turned her attention back to him.
"Did you hear anything I said?"
She shook her head. "I'm sorry. Look, I'm not feeling very well. I might slip out to the ladies room. I'll also fix up my makeup."
He nodded. "Good idea."
"Excuse me." She rose from the table and made her way to the foyer. Instead of entering the restrooms, she ducked out of the restaurant and hailed a cab. Climbing in, she slumped into the back seat and fought back tears.
The driver glanced at her in the mirror. "Where to, Miss?"
She gave him her address and reached into her bag for her phone. The number she wanted was at the top of her favorites.
Her sister Leonie, answered. "Hey sis, I thought you were on a hot date."
"Things didn't turn out the way I expected."
"Are you OK? What happened?"
Alison gave her a run down on the brief encounter with Brian.

"You're kidding me? He actually said that? What an A-grade asshole."
"Yeah, I'm beginning to think I attract them."
"No babe, there's just a lot of them in the world. Look, where are you now?"
"On my way home."
"Screw that. Meet me at the *Cold Stone* at Rancho Del Ray. Triple choc ice cream will make you feel better."
Alison managed a chuckle. "Fine, but I'm telling you now. I'm done with men and I'm done with dating."
"Good, ice cream it is."

***

Mike rested a gloved hand on Axe's head and ruffled his ears. He could feel the animal's excitement; a bundle of barely contained energy pressed against his leg. The two of them, and the three other members of the squad, were hidden in a tree line a few hundred feet from the walls of a gated hacienda. If their intelligence was correct, and it so often wasn't, then one of the most wanted men in Mexico currently resided inside the lavish mansion.
Vicente Barbosa, or as his men called him, Barbosa the Butcher, was a Sinaloa Cartel kingpin responsible for the death of hundreds, possibly thousands, of Mexicans. However, that wasn't why he'd made it onto the target deck of the SEALs. It was for a far more personal reason as far as the United States Government was concerned.
Six months earlier, the CIA had linked him to the abduction and murder of a US citizen, a teenage girl. She also happened to be the niece of a high-ranking American Diplomat. With that act Barbosa earned himself the undivided attention of Predator drones, surveillance satellites, and teams of analysts at both the CIA and NSA.

An elusive target at the best of times, the outcry over the murder had driven him underground. Finally, they had isolated his location to this multi-story, walled estate deep within Sinaloa Cartel territory. And now, justice was going to be served.

Mike had parachuted, along with the rest of his platoon, from a C-130 transport aircraft with Axe strapped to his chest. It was the veteran working dog's tenth operational jump and it had gone off without a hitch. Highly trained, Axe was a vital component of the squad and couldn't be left behind. His sensitive nose detected hidden booby traps, tracked fleeing targets, and with his razor-sharp teeth he could dissuade most bad guys from putting up a fight.

From the darkness, he heard Rick's whisper. "How long till we get this rock show on the road?"

Mike turned his head so he could see the Corpsman through his night vision goggles.

"We keeping you from a hot date, gunslinger?" growled TJ from behind them.

"Nah, we're just giving the Butcher plenty of time to slip away."

Ernie lifted his head from the glowing radio panel. "Some of the other squads are having problems getting into position. The scrub around the back is pretty thick. Going to be at least another twenty."

"Always waiting," mumbled Rick, leaning back against his medical pack with his weapon held across his knees.

Mike gave Axe a reassuring pat, turned back to their target and scanned the walls of the hacienda. At least ten feet high, they posed a significant obstacle. Fortunately, the solid metal gates that guarded the entrance were wide open.

"Ghost One is reporting no significant activity on the target," whispered Ernie.

Ghost was the call sign of the Predator drone that was watching the compound from above.

"Yay, Intel probably fucked up again," said Rick.

"Regular ray of goddamn sunshine tonight, aren't you?" said TJ.

Rick snorted. "Well, I've got nothing to look forward to now, do I Mike? Stacey's party was going to be the highlight of my month."

Mike sighed. He'd managed to suppress all thoughts of Stacey and her threats, but now she was back on his mind. It had been almost six months since he'd met her in a bar in town. Vibrant, bright and sexy, the chemistry between them had been explosive. Now, he was forced to admit their relationship was almost purely physical. Yes it was fun. Hell, it was intense. But, once out of the bedroom the lack of connection left him empty. Worse still, TJ's assessment was spot on. She wasn't a team player and that wasn't going to change anytime soon.

"Ghost One's spotted movement." Ernie's voice snapped him back to the task at hand.

"Are the cut-off teams in place?" asked TJ.

"Negative, Ghost has eyes on five people gathering around a vehicle in front of the hacienda."

"The Butcher's about to leave the building," hissed Rick.

"The boss wants us to roll now," added Ernie.

"Roger. Mike, you and Axe are on point," ordered TJ. "We'll take down the targets at the car and then move inside."

Mike unsnapped the lead from Axe's harness, releasing him. He felt the dog tense with excitement. "Axe, wait." Gripping his carbine tightly, he waited for TJ to tap him on the shoulder.

***

As Mike moved through the front gates of the hacienda, he spotted a group of men clustered around a black SUV. The car's doors were open.

"Hands up, hands up!" TJ bellowed.

The men went for their weapons and Mike fired. His carbine bucked against his shoulder as his target dropped. Why did they always try to fight, he thought as he engaged another gunman. "Axe, down," he ordered as an AK blasted. The dog dropped to his belly.

Ernie and Rick made short work of the other cartel thugs. Then, as a team, they moved forward and checked the bodies.

"Vehicle's empty. Butcher must be inside," said TJ.

With the Chief off his shoulder and Axe by his side, Mike crept up the stairs. "OK boy, search."

The dog wagged his tail. Trained to locate, and if necessary, neutralize any potential threats, he trotted forward.

Weapon held ready Mike followed him into the foyer. Axe ignored the staircase that led to the second level and stopped in front of a heavy wooden door. Halting beside his partner Mike scanned the ornate fixtures and whispered, "Guy sure likes to throw some cash around."

"Perks of the business." TJ leaned across and checked the door handle. As it turned a gun fired. Bullets punched through the wood next to his face. "We've got a live one."

As Rick and Ernie joined them in the foyer Mike returned fire. "Need a breach!"

"Heads up." Rick tossed him an explosive charge.

He caught it and stuck it to the door. "Take cover." He yanked the initiator. As the fuse spluttered he pulled Axe back and placed his gloved hands over the dog's ears.

The explosive charge detonated with a loud bang. The doors flew open with a blast of smoke and debris.

"Axe, hunt." The dog dashed into the room, closely followed by TJ. Readying his weapon, Mike charged into the room on their heels.

TJ's suppressed weapon snapped. An armed gunman took a bullet to the face. Mike spotted another man behind a desk. The Butcher. His pistol was aimed at them. His head filled Mike's sights.

A flash of fur and teeth flew through the air. Axe clamped onto the cartel boss's arm, dragging him to the ground. The Butcher screamed as the dog bit down, hard.

TJ was the first to reach him. He jabbed the suppressor of his carbine in his face and yelled, "Shut the fuck up!"

Mike kicked the pistol clear. "Axe, release."

"Roll over. Face down," ordered TJ.

Reluctantly, the overweight Mexican rolled onto his front. Every time he lifted his head Axe snarled, savagely.

"Keep that beast away from me," whimpered the Butcher.

Mike checked the Mexican's arm as he cuffed him. Axe had left puncture marks but hadn't drawn blood. "Shut up or I'll let him eat it."

Ernie stuck his head into the office. "TJ, we've got a problem. Bravo squad has spotted two vehicles inbound on our position."

"They didn't intercept?"

"Negative, they're still short of the cut-off location."

"Shit, what about Charlie?"

"They're moving to our location now, ETA five minutes."

The Butcher laughed. "You've bitten off more than you can chew *culero*, my people are going to kill you all."

"Axe, guard."

A low rumbling growl silenced the Mexican.

TJ removed his helmet and rubbed his scalp. "ETA of the vehicles?"

"Under a minute."

"I say we hit 'em from the front door and hold them off till Charlie gets here," suggested Rick.

"Axe can guard the Butcher," added Mike.

"Let's do it." TJ fastened his helmet as he dashed back out into the foyer. He knelt a few feet from the open doorway and aimed his weapon at the front gate.

Ernie and Rick followed suit. The Corpsman smashed out one of the tall windows that framed the doorway so he could fire through it.

"Axe, guard." Mike poked the corpulent cartel boss with the toe of his boot. "I wouldn't move if I were you. He'll tear out your throat."

The dog gave a blood-curdling growl as if to emphasize the point.

Joining the others, Mike swapped out the magazine on his carbine. They'd killed the lights to hide from the approaching vehicles.

Ten long seconds later a black Chevy SUV roared through the front gates, skidding to a stop on the manicured lawn. The SEALs hit it with a devastating fusillade of fire. Windows shattered as their bullets shredded most of the occupants.

At least two men managed to escape. They returned fire as the second SUV shuddered to a halt behind the first. Mike switched his aim and pumped a half dozen rounds into it. His bullets skipped off the glass without penetrating. "Number two is armored."

An AK barked and bullets hit the doorway forcing TJ back as men spilled from the new vehicle.

"Fall back!" TJ yelled.

Ernie went first, followed by Rick. The pair took up positions at the door to a study, allowing TJ and Mike to move back to where Axe guarded the Butcher.

"Where the hell is Charlie?" screamed Rick as he covered them from the doorway.

Bullets smacked into the hacienda as the men outside unleashed everything they had on the SEALs.

"They're close, real close." Ernie wrenched open a door at the back of the study. "We can get out here."

"Grab the Butcher," said TJ.

Mike hauled the Mexican off the floor. "Axe, with me."

A volley of bullets shattered one of the office's windows. The Butcher broke free of Mike and dove through the opening.

"Oh shit." Mike hurtled through the window after him. As he crashed onto the gravel footpath, his weapon was flung clear and the Butcher sprinted away.

Stumbling to his feet, Mike spotted two men headed toward him, guns raised. Snatching up his carbine, he fired, hitting one of them. Time slowed as he realized that the second man had the drop on him. He looked directly into the gaping black muzzle of the man's pistol while he tried to bring his weapon to bear.

A flash of brown fur leaped from the hacienda. Axe hit the gunman, his jaws snapping closed on his arm as they collapsed to the ground. The pistol roared. Axe yelped.

Struggling to his feet, the shooter pushed the dog clear. As he raised his pistol to finish Axe, Mike fired. The carbine bucked in his shoulder. The gunman toppled over, dead.

Oblivious to Charlie squad's arrival, and elimination of the remaining gunmen, Mike sprinted to Axe's side and focused on the gaping gunshot wound in his partner's hindquarter. Tearing a field dressing from his pouch, he pressed the pad against the bloody hole. "Stay with me Axe. Stay with me boy."

The dog looked up at him with trusting eyes.

Mike struggled to control his emotions as he fought to stem the flow of blood.

Rick knelt next to him and dropped his medical kit to the ground. "Keep the pressure on." He pulled a razor-sharp knife from his vest and shaved a patch of fur off the Axe's front leg. He injected a painkiller and inserted an IV line in the exposed vein. Handing the bag of fluid to Mike, Rick inspected the wound. "OK, we're going to need to plug both sides before we can move him. "Ernie, what's our ETA on the chopper?"

"Ten minutes out. How's he doing?" the comms guy replied.

Rick nodded and dove back into his medical kit for another bandage.

As Mike stroked Axe's muzzle he noted the dog's eyes were glassy from the combined painkiller and blood loss. He ignored the SEALs from Charlie as they ran past to secure the perimeter. The beat of an approaching helicopter's rotors barely registered. It wasn't till Axe was in the hands of a USAF MEDEVAC team and the SEALs were extracting that Mike turned to TJ. "What happened to the Butcher?"

"He got away."

"Damn it, I messed up."

The Chief grasped his shoulder. "Not at all, bud. The guy who shot Axe, the one you slotted, that was Juan Barbosa, the Butcher's brother and right hand man. You and Axe took down a high value target."

"Yeah, let's hope Axe makes it." Mike wiped his eyes with his sleeve.

"He's a goddamn frog dog brother, he'll make it."

Chapter Two

The sun had barely crept above the horizon as Mike watched the USAF medical staff unload Axe from the C-130 cargo plane. The dog had been unconscious since Rick had sedated him and Mike had not left his side.

He handed his weapons and ammunition to TJ, before joining the dog in an ambulance. It was a short ride from Coronado to the veterinary facility at Marine Corps Air Station Miramar. Upon arrival, the staff were ready and waiting.

A nurse dressed in green scrubs blocked Mike from following the stretcher into the operating room "Sir, you can't go any further than this. You'll have to wait out here." She must have read the grief on his face as she added. "I'll have one of the girls get you a coffee. And as soon as he's stable I'll bring you in, OK?"

Mike nodded and collapsed into a seat in the waiting room. He sat quietly for a moment. Then it hit him, he was still wearing his body armor and helmet. Stripping off the items, he dumped them onto the seat next to him.

A young civilian receptionist offered him a cup of hot coffee.

"Do you need anything else?" she asked softly.

He shook his head and accepted the coffee gratefully.

"They're going to be in surgery for a few hours. So, you might want to duck away, grab a shower and a change clothes."

Mike glanced down at his uniform; it was covered in dried blood, Axe's blood. "No, I'm staying here till he's out."

She smiled, gave him a knowing nod and returned to behind the counter.

Finishing the coffee, he leaned back, trying to get comfortable in the hard plastic chair. He glanced up at the wall clock and noted the time. It was five after seven in the morning. Twenty minutes, he'd only been in the surgery for twenty minutes. It felt like Axe had been in there for hours.

Exhaling, he closed his eyes and tipped his head back against the wall. He really should give Stacey a call and let her know he was back. No, he couldn't deal with her right now. He hadn't slept in over twenty-four hours and she would be focused on her launch.

A gentle nudge woke Mike. His eyes snapped open and he jolted upright.

"Hey, brother," said TJ.

He checked the clock. Shit, it was nearly ten. Somehow, despite the stress he'd managed almost three hours of sleep. Spotting Rick at the counter talking to the receptionist, he leaped out of his seat. "Is he out of surgery?"

Rick turned to face him. "Not yet, bud."

"It shouldn't be much longer," added the receptionist.

The door to the waiting room opened and Ernie joined the rest of the squad. He handed Mike his cell phone and a takeout box. "Thought you might want some breakfast. Any news?"

Mike forced a smile as he took the items and resumed his seat. "Thanks, no news yet, he's still in surgery." He checked his phone; thirteen missed calls, all from Stacey. Before he could call her back, the smell of the food in the box hit him and his stomach growled. He hadn't realized he was starving. Opening the container revealed a breakfast burrito. Stacey had waited this long, what was a few more minutes.

As Mike devoured the spicy Mexican food, Ernie grinned. "Maria dropped them round."

"That woman is an angel," added TJ as he took a seat.

"An angel who gave birth to devil spawn," grunted Ernie as he took the chair opposite Mike. "You know what they did last night?"

"No, what?" he asked before taking another bite.

"They cut the TV power cord and set the sofa on fire."

TJ frowned. "They OK?"

"Of course. They're the spawn of Satan. So, yeah, they're fine."

TJ winked. "I think that might be the influence of their father."

Mike wiped his chin. “Hey, thanks for coming down guys.”

“Bro, Axe is our team-mate too,” Rick said, abandoning his pursuit of the receptionist and taking a seat facing Mike.

As he tossed the empty box in the trash his phone started ringing. He glanced at the screen. It was Stacey. He answered it. “Hey babe, look–”

“Don’t ‘hey babe’ me. Where the hell are you?”

“At the base. Axe has been–”

“You’re at the base! Have you forgotten this is the most important day of my life?” she shrieked.

Grimacing, Mike angled the speaker away from his ear. “Babe, babe, listen to me.”

“No, you listen to me, Michael Saunders. You get yourself over here now or we’re finished.”

“Stacey, please. Axe has been shot, he’s in surgery.”

There was a pause. “Michael, he's a dog. This agency is my future. And what I'm hearing is that you think a dog is more important than my future?”

Sighing, Mike placed a clenched fist against his forehead. “I can't leave until I know he's going to be OK.”

“Then you and I are done.”

“Stacey, don't be like that… Stacey?” Mike checked the phone. She had terminated the call. He glanced at his team members. All of them were looking away, pretending not to have listened. “She just broke up with me.”

Before anyone could respond a man strode into the room wearing bloodied scrubs.

Mike dropped the phone to his side and rose. “Is he going to be OK?”

The veterinarian nodded. “The short answer is he’ll live.”

“And the long answer?” asked TJ.

“I’m not sure if he’ll ever walk properly again.”

Rick leaned forward. “But, he's out of danger?”

“Yes, he’s waking now.”

Mike fought back tears. “Can I see him?”

The vet glanced at TJ who wore a stern expression. “Yes, but only for a moment. He needs to rest.”

Mike followed the vet through to the recovery room. Axe lay in a wide cage with the door open. His rear leg had been shaved. The angry red wound had been stapled shut.

When the dog saw him his ears rose and he attempted to sit.

"Axe, down, stay." Mike squatted and patted the dog. A tear ran down his cheek as he ruffled the ears. "I thought I'd lost you boy."

Axe lifted his head and licked Mike's hand. Then he lowered his head and closed his eyes.

"He's lost a lot of blood and needs to rest," said the vet.

Mike kissed the dog's head. "I'll come back soon." Blinking hard he gave him one last pat before returning to the waiting room and the concerned expressions of the rest of his team.

"All things considered… he looks good," said Mike as he reached for his phone.

TJ clasped his shoulder. "Who ya calling, slick?"

"Stacey. If I rush, I can still help her set up for the function."

"Nope. Not happening." TJ snatched the phone from his hand. "You're heading back to the team room for a shower. Afterward, we're running through a debrief. You can have your phone back when we're done."

Lacking the energy to argue, Mike followed the team out to the parking lot. Spotting Ernie's SUV, he climbed in the back. TJ was right. The op had been a cluster fuck, a debrief might provide insight as to why.

***

Hot water streamed over Mike's head and down his aching back. Bracing against the wall he let the warmth soak into every muscle. Finally cleansed of the grime and fatigue of the last twenty-four hours, he dried himself, dressed in shorts and a T-shirt, and joined the others in the team room. "We gonna do this debriefing or what?"

TJ lifted a cooler onto a bench seat and opened it. He pulled out a can of *Coors* and handed it to Mike. "Debrief can wait. We need to lift a beer for Axe."

He offered one to Rick, but the Corpsman waved it away. Instead, he opened his locker and rummaged inside. "If we're raising a drink for Axe it should be something a little stiffer." He revealed a bottle of *Pyrat Rum* and four empty 40 mm grenade casings. "Our boy deserves the best yeah?" He placed them on the bench next to the cooler.

Mike nodded. "The best for the best. Although, I'm going to chase that with one of TJ's beers."

Ernie added a bottle of *Gran Dovejo Reposado Tequila* to the mix. "Not before you have a shot of this."

"I didn't realize I was rolling with a squad of alcoholics," TJ said as he splashed rum into each of the metal casings and all four men lifted them toward the ceiling.

"For Axe, the best sidekick a SEAL could have," said Mike.

"A goddamn frog dog through and through," added TJ.

"Axe!" they echoed.

They downed their shots, then Mike took a swig from his beer as TJ refilled the casings with a healthy slug of tequila.

"I've got a toast," said Rick.

"Fire away," said TJ.

"To Mike and his freedom. Welcome back to single life, brother."

Mike frowned as he downed the tequila shot. "TJ, I need my phone back. I've got to call Stacey."

The grizzled Chief shook his head. "You don't wanna do that, bud. She's not right for you."

Mike contemplated the statement as the alcohol warmed his stomach. "I guess not. I mean, she dumped me because I couldn't make her launch party."

Rick sloshed more rum into his 40 mm casing. "Dude, your partner got shot. It's not like you didn't want to be there. You tried your best, brother."

TJ nodded. "Any woman who dates a SEAL needs to know, when you're on the job, the team comes first. Women like her… self-absorbed 'n' all. She's never going to understand honor, courage and commitment."

Mike took a sip and savored the burn as it slid down his throat. "Yeah, you know, she's kind of selfish, right?"

The other men laughed as they drank.

"Good looking," said Rick, "but a total bitch."

"Total bitch," echoed Ernie.

"You know boys," TJ added reflectively.

"Helmets on." Rick chuckled. "Here comes another war story."

"Shut the hell up, Rick. This is important." The Chief took another swig from his beer. "You know what the problem with women is?"

"They nag you about everything?" said Ernie.

TJ scowled. "Your wife's an angel, Ernie. Most men aren't that lucky."

"I'll drink to that." Rick charged their 40 mm casings with rum. "My ex-wife was a goddamn nightmare. Whereas, your wife, Ernie, is patient, dedicated, smart, an awesome mother and she's beautiful. She's way too good for you."

The men all toasted Ernie's wife, Maria.

Mike reached for his beer and chased the rum with a healthy swig. He was starting to feel the effect of the booze. Aches and bruises were forgotten along with Stacey. "TJ, what were you saying?"

The Chief squinted in thought. "Oh yeah, I was going to explain the difference between SEALs and women." He finished his beer and cracked a new one. "Rick, why is it that when a newbie joins the squad you know you can trust him?"

"That's easy, bro. It's because he's been through BUD and SQT. He's a goddamn frogman."

"That's right. He's been selected for the right attributes, trained in the basic skills, put through the wringer and as a result you know he's good to go."

Mike snorted beer from his nose. "TJ, are you saying what I think you're saying?"

"Damn straight. If you want to make sure you've got a good woman, you've got to run her through a selection process, just like BUD."

Rick laughed. “I don't wanna date a woman who can pass that shit, bro. Did you see Demi Moore in G.I. Jane? That chick had bigger guns than Mike.”

“Hey, come on. Mike’s are pretty massive.” Ernie chuckled as he poured another round of tequila.

“Not BUD, you thick sons of bitches,” TJ continued. “A selection process especially for women. One that reveals who they really are, a woman, no, a girlfriend selection course. That's it, a Girlfriend Selection Course.”

Rick nodded as he downed another shot. “Golf, Sierra, Charlie. I love it. We test Mike's next girlfriend to make sure she's not a narcissistic, princess, cow.”

“Hey, what about you?” said Mike.

“Bud, I love narcissistic, princess, cows. I'm just not about to marry another one. You're the dude who falls for princesses and wears his heart on his sleeve. Hell, you’re a walk over boy. Girls have you eating out of their hands on the second date. You’re a goddamn dream boat.”

Ernie nodded in agreement. “It's true, *essé*.”

“So that's that.” TJ lifted his 40 mm casing. “The next time Mike gets serious, we're gonna run a selection course. Boom!”

Mike frowned. “Guys, I'm not sure about this.”

TJ sloshed more rum into his casing. “Brother, this is for your own good.”

Chapter Three

Head aching Mike pushed the vet's door open and strode to the counter. Lifting his sunglasses, he shot the receptionist a weary smile. "Hi, I'm here to see Axe."

As she opened her mouth to respond, he heard a loud bark from behind her. "That would be him now," she managed as the aggressive barking continued.

Hangover forgotten, Mike pushed open the door to the recovery area, entered the room and stood dead in his tracks at the sight before him. The Army veterinarian was perched on a steel examination table. Axe had made it half way out of his cage, barking with his hind legs dragging behind him.

Mike approached slowly. "Hey, easy boy, easy."

Axe's demeanor changed instantly. His ears rose and he stopped barking. Instead he tried to scrabble across the floor to Mike.

"Axe, stay!" He knelt and lifted the dog back into the cage. Axe gave a soft whimper and licked his face. Mike did his best to make the dog comfortable, stroking his muzzle as he adjusted the bedding. "Hey, it's OK, buddy. I'm here, everything's going to be fine."

The vet climbed off the table and hid behind Mike. "He wouldn't let me check the wound. Went crazy as soon as I touched him."

"I think he's a little stressed from the incident. He should be fine now I'm here."

The vet squatted alongside him and reached in to check the bandages around the dog's hind leg.

Axe gave a low growl and bared his teeth.

"Axe, no!"

The vet backed off, raising his hands in the air. "I give up. I can't get close to him. You're going to have to change his bandages."

"No problem." Trained in combat first aid, Mike didn't have any difficulties inspecting the wounds. He checked the flesh around the surgical staples for tenderness and infection, there was none. The vet handed him fresh bandages and he changed the pad covering the wound. Then he sat with the dog, ruffling his ears. Axe's eyes never left the vet. "What's the prognosis, doc?"

The vet leaned against the stainless-steel table watching Axe warily. "The bullet missed the bone but it destroyed a lot of muscle and ligaments. I'm not sure how it'll heal. Then there's his attitude. If I can't get close to him I can't treat him."

"I can come in every day."

"That would help."

Axe nuzzled Mike's hand prompting him for another pat. The dog sighed, relaxing, and finally took his eyes off the vet.

"Do you think he'll work again?"

The vet shook his head. "No, his days of chasing down bad guys are over."

Mike continued to stroke the dog's ears. "You hear that, boy. Looks like it's going to be all ball-chasing and lying in the sun from here on." In spite of his words, Mike felt empty. The idea of going to work each day, and not having Axe by his side, would take time to come to terms with.

Remembering work, he checked his watch. Crap, he was going to be late. He gave Axe another pat. "I've got to get going, buddy, be good for the doc."

"That would make a nice change," said the vet.

Mike closed the dog's cage. As he rose Axe whined while glancing up at him with sad brown eyes. "Hey, none of that. I'll be back this afternoon." Mike gave him one last pat through the mesh and followed the vet out into the waiting area.

"He's a good dog, Mike. But, if we can't turn his temperament around we're going to have problems."

Mike shook his hand. "He'll be fine." Then he ducked out of the door to his pickup. As he drove across town to Coronado, he couldn't help but worry that Axe's attitude change might be permanent.

***

Mike pulled up to the twenty-five yard shooting range and joined the rest of his squad for training.

He spotted TJ at the ammunition point, loading magazines from a box of cartridges. The Chief looked fresh despite a heavy night's drinking.

"Hey bud, how's Axe?"

"He's OK, the wound looks like it'll heal." He found his weapons in the squad trunk and laid them on the ground before joining TJ to fill magazines.

Already at the firing point, the other squad members were shooting their suppressed carbines at paper targets.

Mike and TJ worked in silence for a few minutes before TJ spoke again. "You wanna tell me what's eating at you?"

Mike dropped a half-filled magazine on the bench. "He won't let the vet near him. I've never seen him like this, TJ, his entire temperament has changed."

"Bud, I've seen the same thing in operators. They take a big hit like that and suddenly they're jumping at shadows and snapping at their closest friends. Sounds like your boy's got post-traumatic stress disorder. When are they going to let you bring him back to work?"

"They're not. Vet says he's done."

"Shit bud." TJ reached out and grasped his shoulder. "I'm sorry, he was a great working dog."

"Hey, what's up?" asked Rick as he and Ernie joined them.

"Axe is going to be retired," said Mike.

"Ah crap. I'm sorry, dude," said Ernie.

"That's shit bro, he's an amazing dog," added Rick.

Mike sighed. "The big problem isn't his leg. He won't let anyone near him, except me. TJ thinks he might have PTSD."

Rick nodded. "Yeah that makes sense. Getting shot messes with the best of us. But he'll be OK in the long run. You'll keep him, right?"

"How can I? We're out on jobs every second day and I can't leave him with just anyone."

"I'd take him," added Ernie. "But with the kids…"

"I understand," said Mike.

"Look, if you need to take some time off I can talk to the Skipper," said TJ.

"Yeah, I might have to." Mike picked up his magazine and went back to loading it. The others did likewise.

"Ernie, that little rat dog your mother has," said Rick. "I remember it being a total shit head. Who sorted it out, when her neighbor's mutt tried to eat it?"

Ernie scowled. "That 'rat' was a pedigree Chihuahua, you idiot. Yeah, someone did help her. My brother found a vet out near Iron Canyon who specializes in traumatized dogs."

"And she fixed your Mom's Chihuahua?" asked Mike.

Ernie nodded. "Allegedly, she's Dr. Doolittle or something."

Mike managed a laugh. "I think Axe needs something a little heavier duty than a Chihuahua whisperer."

Ernie shrugged. "Maybe, my brother said she's real pretty."

It was Rick's turn to frown. "What the hell, bro? You never told me about a pretty vet."

"She's not your type."

"Not hot enough?"

"Too smart."

Laughing, the team moved down to the firing point. For the first time today, Mike managed a smile. It felt good to be surrounded by friends. Finding a spare target, he racked the action on his carbine and readied himself. Then, as he was about to squeeze off a round, his phone rang. Fearing the worst, he pulled it from his pocket and answered.

"So, you're finally going to answer my calls, Michael," snapped an angry voice.

Stacey, he mouthed to TJ. "Hey, look I'm–"

"I don't care!" she screamed.

Wincing, Mike held the phone at arm's length as she continued to rant. Suddenly, a gloved hand plucked it from his grasp.

"Standby!" TJ held it in the air. Stacey's voice still screeched from the speaker.

"Ready!" echoed Rick and Ernie, their weapons held tight.

"Up!"

The phone arced high in the air. Rick and Ernie's weapons spat suppressed rounds as they tracked it. Mike flinched as his smartphone disintegrated in a hail of lead.

"Nice shooting boys," said TJ. He turned to Mike and winked. "You need to change your number."

***

A few hours later Mike and the others were back in the team room when there was a knock at the door.

"Come in," bellowed TJ.

One of the headquarters' administration staff stuck his head inside.

"Hey Mack, what's up?"

The sailor gave TJ a nod. "The old man wants to see Mike in his office."

Mike frowned. "Just me?" It was rare for the commander to request the presence of an individual SEAL without their platoon chief.

"Yes."

"I'll get into a clean uniform."

"No need, boss just wants a chat," said the sailor. "I tried to call you but your number's disconnected."

Mike scowled at TJ. "Yeah, my phone's shot. I've got to get a new one."

Five minutes later, Mike waited outside Commander Conner's office. As he waited, he wondered why the 'old man' wanted to talk to him. The last time he'd spoken face-to-face with Team Five's C.O. was when he'd marched into the unit three years earlier. The thirty-five-year-old commander was a busy man, who rarely had the opportunity to spend individual time with the hundred-odd operators in his SEAL Team.

The door opened and the C.O. appeared. "Mike, come in and take a seat."

He stepped into the spacious office and sat in the chair opposite the commander. In the few seconds it took Conner to return to his desk Mike scanned the room. The walls were adorned with a handful of framed photos and plaques, but there were fewer than he expected for a ranking officer. In the corner, on a wooden stand, hung the commander's combat vest and helmet.

"Mike, I wanted to personally break this news to you. I know how important Axe is to you and your squad." He frowned as he pushed a piece of paper across his desk. "The veterinarian has submitted his report. The Navy has chosen to discharge Axe."

Mike nodded as he scanned the document. The information wasn't surprising. Axe was incapable of working and the Navy had no use for a Military Working Dog that couldn't work.

"There's more."

Mike glanced up. The commander continued, "Mike, the Navy is going to have him put down."

The words hit like a punch to the chest. "What? Boss, they can't do that. He saved my life. Axe is a goddamn hero."

Conner exhaled. "I know Mike, but it's out of my control. The Navy can't risk retiring a dog that may attack someone. The vet submitted his report and the decision was made well above my pay grade. I tried to convince them otherwise, but they won't be swayed."

Mike swallowed hard. He wasn't about to shed a tear in front of his commanding officer. If the Navy had decided his dog's fate, there was nothing the C.O. could do.

"If you need any time off, Chief Lines will look after it. I've already spoken to him."

Mike nodded grimly.

"Son, as far as I am concerned that dog and you are both heroes. I wish there was more I could do."

Mike left the commander's office fighting the urge to punch the walls and scream with rage. Instead, he decided to confront the vet who had condemned his best friend to death. If he could convince him he wasn't dangerous, then maybe he could have the order revoked.

"Where you going, bud?" TJ's gravelly voice caught him by surprise.

Glancing left he spotted the Chief, Rick and Ernie waiting for him.

"They're going to kill Axe," said Mike.

TJ nodded. "We know."

Mike noticed the men were carrying black equipment bags. "What's going on?"

Ernie gave his bag a pat. "We grabbed some gear for tonight's job."

"What job?"

TJ wrapped an arm around his shoulder. "Operation Lumberjack. We're going to recover the Axe."

"We never leave a man behind, brother," added Rick. "Compared to hunting cartel douche bags this'll be a walk in the park."

"You do know he's being held on a Marine base?"

TJ chuckled. "Goddamn Taliban, Al-Qaida, Sinaloa, and Libyan bastards couldn't stop me. What makes you think a pack of Jarheads are gonna do any better?"

Chapter Four

Car headlights swept the parking lot of the veterinary facility. A vehicle pulled into a driveway on the opposite side of the street. It was three in the morning; late for a serviceman to be out on a Tuesday night.

Drunken singing carried on the night air. The driver helped her rather intoxicated Marine from the car up to the front door and they disappeared inside. A moment later the first-floor lights came on.

Mike's radio crackled as Ernie reported in. "Drunk leatherneck is home. We're all clear."

"OK Rick, let's do this," whispered Mike from where they hid in the trees at the edge of the parking lot. A dozen feet away Ernie lay in a thicket, where he kept watch on the road to the clinic. TJ waited in a minivan, parked up the road ready to make the pickup.

Rick led as they strolled casually from the trees, across the parking lot to the front door of the facility. Mike removed a lock-pick kit from his backpack. After inspecting the door, he chose the appropriate tool. Then, as he made to insert it, Rick slid a key into the lock.

"Where the hell did you get that?"

Rick flashed one of his signature smiles. "From Veronica." He pushed open the door and they slipped inside.

"Who the hell's Veronica?" asked Mike as an alarm gave a warning beep. He spotted the panel and made his way toward it.

"You know. The receptionist."

Mike stopped in his tracks. "You've been seeing the vet nurse? Bud, you talked to her for like three minutes."

He strolled nonchalantly across to the security panel and punched in a code. "Hey, what can I say? Ladies love the Rick."

The beeping stopped.

"She gave you the code?"

"Yeah, once I let her know how heartbroken you are about Axe. Told her you were weeping like a little girl. You should have seen it. Heart melted in about five seconds flat."

"Does TJ know about this?"

"Of course he does. Gramps knows everything. Now let's find that crazy mutt of yours and get the hell out of here."

Mike held up his hand. "Wait, so what happens when Axe is discovered missing and there's no sign of a break-in?"

Rick winked. "I've got a plan for that."

They crept through the foyer, down a short corridor into the recovery room. Mike eased the door open. "Axe, it's me buddy." Using a flashlight he located the cage and opened it. The dog gave a single excited bark.

Rick gave Axe a pat. "Hey bro."

Mike scooped the dog out of the cage and cradled him against his chest as he would a child. "Right, let's get out of here."

As they made their way back to the front door Rick contacted TJ on the radio. "We're ready for pickup, Pops."

The radio crackled. "You're ready for a punch in the face."

Rick laughed as they paused at the door and waited for the minivan to pull in to the parking lot. Once it stopped at the entrance he slid open the door and they loaded Axe inside.

Mike waited as Rick reactivated the alarm and locked the front door. Then TJ passed a wrench through the driver's window. Rick used it to smash one of the windows. As he leaped into the van a siren wailed.

"That's your plan?" Mike asked.

As TJ drove the van out of the parking lot Ernie jumped in through the open door and Rick slammed it shut. "Damn straight. And might I add it's pretty much the best plan ever."

"Not bad, Rick. Now shut your pie hole," snapped TJ.

Rick whispered, "He doesn't like his call sign."

Mike cradled Axe's head on his lap. "Guys, you're the best."

"You're not going to cry are you?" asked Rick.

"Rick, shut your pie hole," Mike said.

Twenty minutes later, Axe was sleeping on a duvet at the end of Mike's bed as the men discussed the dog's future over a beer in the living room.

"What's your plan now you've got him here?" TJ asked as he sucked back a *Coors.*

Mike let his shoulders drop as he sat on the couch. "I guess I'm gonna have to do something about his temperament or I won't be able to leave him with anyone when we're on jobs."

"So you're going to keep him?" asked Rick.

"I can't trust him with anyone else."

"You need to take him to the vet I told you about. She'll sort him out," said Ernie.

Rick grinned. "Any luck–"

"Pie hole, Rick," said TJ.

Laughter filled the room as Mike took a swig from his beer. For the first time since Axe had been shot he felt hopeful. "OK, I'll take him in to see her first thing tomorrow. TJ, do you mind if I'm a little late for work."

"Take the day off."

"What about us?" Rick asked.

"Ernie can have a late start. You and I are going running, got to burn off all that pie you've been shoving in your hole."

***

"Well, this is it, bud." Mike opened the passenger door of his pickup and lifted Axe out. He carried the wounded dog across a dusty parking lot into the waiting room of the Iron Canyon Veterinary Clinic.

A female receptionist looked up and smiled. "Hi."

"Hi. We're here to see Doctor Alison Taylor."

"Perfect timing. Her last patient finished up early so you can take him straight through."

"Thanks." Mike pushed the door open with his foot and carried Axe into the examination room.

Doctor Taylor greeted him with a bright smile. "Hello. You can put him down over there." She gestured to a table.

Mike saw immediately why Ernie's brother thought she was cute. A brunette with a button nose, lush mouth and green eyes, she wasn't what he'd call a stunner but more the girl next door. He judged her height at around five-foot-six. Not short, but by no means tall. And, while she wore baggy scrubs, they couldn't hide her curvy figure. Not really his type, but then this wasn't about him.

"Mike, isn't it?"

"Yeah, you must be Alison."

She nodded as she washed her hands. "On the phone you said he was shot?"

Mike kept a close eye on Axe as the dog surveyed the room, every muscle tense. "Correct, he's a Military Working Dog. Discharged as a result of the injury."

"And it was a little over two weeks ago?"

"Yes, he's recovering well but–"

"His temperament has changed?" Alison added as she dried her hands.

Mike nodded.

"I see that a lot with heavy trauma. I get a lot of dogs with PTSD from being hit by cars or attacked by another animal." She approached Axe. "OK handsome, let's have a look at you."

The dog's ears flattened against his skull and he bared his teeth.

"Axe, no!"

Alison lifted a hand to silence Mike. "It's fine. He's just letting me know he's not happy. You'd never bite me would you, Axe?"

Her question was answered with another savage growl.

Mike frowned. "Axe! Look, I'm not so sure about that. I wouldn't–"

"No, it's OK. Mike, it might be better if you waited outside. Axe seems to be taking a lot of his cues from you."

His eyes narrowed. "What are you saying?"

"I'm saying you've been as traumatized as he has. You're tense and worried. Totally understandable, but your energy isn't helping the situation."

"Now hang on a second. I'm a qualified dog handler. We've been working together for three years. If anyone understands how he feels, it's me."

She nodded. "That's exactly my point. Listen, I don't mind if you stay. But I want you to sit down over there and keep quiet." She pointed to a chair against the wall.

He slumped into the seat and crossed his arms.

"Let's try again, Axe." The vet took a liver treat from a jar and extended it on her open palm. "Are you going to be a good boy?"

The dog glanced at Mike but he ignored him.

Alison took a step closer. "Good boy, Axe." Slowly, inch-by-inch, she made her way closer. The dog's nostrils flared as he inhaled the scent of the dried meat. When she was close enough, his tongue shot out and scooped it off her palm.

"Tasty isn't it?"

Alison was now standing less than a foot from the dog. He eyed her suspiciously as he chewed the snack.

Mike bit his tongue as she reached out to pat his head. He saw the dog's lip lift in a half growl.

She displayed no fear, instead ruffled his ears. "Hey now, none of that."

Mike watched with growing disbelief as Axe let the vet inspect his wound without growling. "I'll be damned," he murmured.

The dog remained silent but watched Alison's every move.

"You're healing well, handsome man," she patted his head again. "Mike, can you put him on the ground so I can see how he walks."

He shook his head. "He can't walk, he's still wounded."

The vet's lips thinned. "Has he tried?"

"Look, I'm not a complete fool. I've had a few years experience with dogs and I don't think he's ready."

She raised her eyebrows. "And I guess my seven years of study and five in practical experience counts for nothing?"

Mike rolled his eyes. "Fine." He gently lifted Axe from the table and placed him on the floor.

The dog lay still on the tiles, his injured leg extended at an awkward angle.

Mike slumped back in the chair. "See."

Alison shook her head and took another treat from the jar. Squatting a few yards in front of Axe, she offered it to him. "Hey buddy, do you want this?"

His ears angled forward and his tail thumped the floor. His floppy ear bounced up and down.

Mike smiled. "Come on boy," he murmured.

Axe glanced at him, and then at the treat, and back to his partner. Then, with little effort, he climbed to his feet, walked forward and gently took it from her hand.

Mike didn't miss how he kept the wounded leg hitched high.

"Good boy." Alison ruffled his ears again. "Now let's go for a little walk." She took a lead from a hook on the wall, clipped it to his collar and led him slowly around the room.

Mike caught the dog's eye as they turned and walked back toward him. "Traitor," he mouthed. "So what do you think?" he asked gruffly, folding his arms.

"I think he's a beautiful animal who needs a little care. But most importantly, you need to stop treating him like a person."

It was Mike's turn to frown. "I don't treat him like a person."

"Listen, I know you've been through a lot with Axe. But he doesn't need your sympathy. He needs your leadership. He needs you to be strong, to tell him what to do."

Mike slumped back in the chair and closed his eyes. For a split second, he was transported back to Mexico, back to the moment when Axe was shot. If he had moved a little faster, he might have been able to save the dog from being wounded. It was a moment he had relived repeatedly since that day.

"Mike, Mike."

Alison's voice snapped him back to the present.

"Are you alright?"

"Yeah. Sorry, I spaced out. Yes, I hear you." He focused on Alison and realized she was watching him closely.

"Mike, how would you feel about Axe staying here at the clinic? Only for a week or two. You seem to have a lot on your mind and he would really benefit from intensive therapy. You could come and see him every day."

Mike nodded. "That would be good. I've got to work."

Her beaming smile instantly made him hopeful. Things would work out. Axe would be healed and maybe, just maybe, they'd be a team again. He said his farewells to the dog, then set up an account with the vet's assistant on his way out. As he pushed open the door to leave, he almost ran into a middle-aged blonde and two young children. "Morning, ma'am." He held open the door as the family passed through, then was on his way.

"Who the hell is that?" Leonie asked Alison when she joined her sister in the waiting area.

"Just a guy with an injured dog. How have you been?"

"I think you mean 'a total hunk' with an injured dog. You should definitely hit that."

Alison laughed. "Can you get your mind out of the gutter?" She glanced out the window as Mike climbed into his truck.

"Not when it's led there by an ass like that. So what's his story?"

"He's arrogant, over-confident and military. Not my type at all." She squatted to embrace her nieces.

"Handsome, fit, confident and a dog guy. No, you're right. He doesn't sound anything like your type."

"He's got issues, Leonie. Now, where do you want to go for brunch?"

"Perfect, you're always saving strays and you could do wonders with him."

She tucked one squealing child under each arm and hoisted the toddlers off the ground. "I'm a veterinarian, not a psychologist."

"Oh please. Men and dogs have so much in common. All they need is a pat, good food and–"

"Enough, you don't recall the date with Brian? Like I said, I'm staying the hell away from men."

Leonie grinned. "Come on, I mean a celibate nun would make an exception for that fine looking piece of–"

"Enough already, I'm starving."

***

As Mike drove through the security checkpoint at Coronado Naval Base his new phone chimed with a message. He pulled into the parking lot in front of the team rooms and glanced at the screen.

The old man wants to see you…TJ

Exiting his truck, Mike ducked inside and put on a clean uniform before heading over to the headquarters building.

"He's in his office," said Mack from behind his desk.

Mike continued down the corridor and knocked on the commander's door.

"Enter."

As he stepped inside, the CO glanced up from his computer and gestured to the seat opposite. Mike sat and prepared himself for the bombardment of questions regarding the abduction of Axe.

"How's things, Mike?"

"You know how it is, sir."

"Yeah, well I'm afraid I've got bad news and good news."

More than a little confused, Mike frowned. The commander was smart enough to recognize he was involved in the kidnap. Hell, until Doctor Taylor, Axe hadn't let anyone else near him except the squad members. Mike swallowed hard and met the commander's steely gaze.

"I'm not sure if you've heard but last night there was a break-in at the Miramar vet clinic. Kids looking for drugs busted in and now Axe is missing. That's the bad news."

Mike didn't know whether to feign surprise or anger.

"Did they catch them?"

Conner shook his head. "No, but the Jarhead Commander of the base assures me they'll find Axe. I wanted to let you know before you heard any rumors."

"Appreciate that, sir."

"The good news is with Axe missing we've got more time to appeal his discharge and destruction. I've nominated him for a heroism award. That should assist the process. Now, if he could just stay 'lost' for a week or three that should give us enough time."

Mike wasn't sure what to say. He swallowed the lump in his throat and fumbled for words. "Sir, I–"

"It's all good, son. As far as I'm concerned that dog's as important as any of my SEALs. In fact I'd swap him for half of Bravo Platoon. Their antics have caused me nothing but grief this week. Now, get out my office so I can sort out this shit storm."

As Mike left the headquarters and walked back to the team room he was filled with hope. Between Doctor Taylor, his squad, and now the commander there was a good chance Axe would be fine. Hell, if Conner had his way, the dog would become a decorated hero.

Entering the team room he found TJ and the others inspecting new marksman rifles.

Rick greeted him with a grin. "Hey brother, did you hear the news?"

"Yeah, allegedly Axe escaped from death row." Mike smiled.

"Our furry friend's going to be a decorated war hero," added TJ.

Mike blinked back tears and cleared his throat. "The only reason he's still alive is because of you guys. In fact this is the second time Rick's saved him."

"Don't mention it, he's a team-mate. Now, how about you give us the details on this sexy vet?"

He shook his head. "Always thinking with your dick, Rick. She knows her stuff. Axe is going to be staying with her for a few weeks."

Rick grinned. "Damn, she must be hot if you're letting her look after your dog."

"She's attractive, but not my type."

"Not your type," said Ernie. "You mean she doesn't have fake boobs and she's not going to steal all your shit?" He and Rick burst into laughter.

TJ handed Mike one of the marksman rifles. "OK, enough shit talking. Let's get these bad boys down to the range."

Chapter Five

Spots of rain fell from a gray sky as Vicente Barbosa leaned over his brother's coffin and gently straightened the dead man's tie. "I am alive today, Juan, because you saved my life. I swear on my soul that I will find the man who took yours. I will tear his heart from his chest and grind it under my boot." He wiped a tear from the corner of his eye before turning to face the crowd that had come to pay tribute to the brother of the Butcher.

Maneuvering through the people he shook hands, while forcing a smile, and nodded as they offered their sympathies. Once clear of the mourners, he weaved through the tombstones to the convoy of black SUVs parked at the edge of the cemetery. A dozen heavily armed guards waited for him. Until vengeance was his, Barbosa wasn't taking any chances. If the Americans wanted to kill him they would need to send more than a handful of SEALs.

"Where is Raul?" he asked as he reached the convoy.

His head of security rounded one of the SUVs. "Here."

Barbosa glanced at a vehicle climbing the track toward them as he reached into his jacket, withdrew a handkerchief and wiped the raindrops from his aviator sunglasses. "Do you know who killed my brother?"

Raul shook his head. "No, we're still reviewing the CCTV footage."

The approaching vehicle pulled in behind his SUVs. A moment later five men dressed in dark suits and sunglasses exited. Barbosa's security detail eyeballed them as they approached and positioned themselves a few yards away.

He glared at his head of security. "They're with us. You've had eight days and still nothing?"

"We know they're SEALs."

The corner of Barbosa's lip curled into a snarl. "I told you that, you idiot." He reached into his jacket again as the party of suits arrived.

One of the men stepped forward, removing his sunglasses. His jet black eyes locked on to Barbosa's. The thin mustache crowning the man's upper lip trembled as he struggled to contain his mirth at the situation. "Mr. Barbosa."

He gave the man a curt nod and turned to his men with his hand still in his jacket. "This is Ramirez. He will be avenging Juan."

Raul scowled. "You're letting an outsider handle our business? Boss, that's–"

Barbosa drew a suppressed pistol and shot him neatly in the heart. His former head of security was dead before his body hit the wet grass.

He glared at his men. "Raul failed me. He wasn't there when my brother was killed, and then couldn't find me the man who murdered him." He spat at the body. "Failure will not be tolerated. Ramirez, if you please." He gestured to his armored SUV and his guards opened the door.

As they sped away Barbosa drummed his fingers against a leather armrest, eyeing Ramirez. "What have you discovered?"

"I've examined the CCTV footage and the man who shot your brother is a SEAL. A member of Team Five. They're based at Coronado, California."

"How do you know that?"

"A number of them wore patches on their shoulders." He held up his fingers in the V for victory symbol. "The Roman numeral five."

Barbosa took his pistol from his jacket and removed the suppressor. "Where exactly is Coronado?"

"Across the border in San Diego."

"And you have people there?"

"Yes."

"Good." He slid the weapon back into its holster and placed the warm suppressor in his pocket. "I want you to find the man who killed my brother. Then, when you do. I want you to kill someone he loves… before you bring me his heart."

Ramirez nodded. "This type of work is what I do best, Mr. Barbosa."

Chapter Six

Mike visited Axe every afternoon. Slowly, day by day, as the week progressed, he noticed a change in the dog's temperament. He'd gone from intermittently growling at Alison whenever she approached to allowing her to manipulate his injured leg with barely a whimper. By Thursday afternoon, Axe greeted Mike at the door of the recovery room with his lead in his mouth.

Alison gave him a smile. "He's been ready for the last hour. I think he wants you to take him for a walk."

Grinning, he took the lead from Axe's mouth, then shot her a concerned look. "You sure he's alright to walk outside?"

Stepping closer she placed her hand on his elbow. "Mike, Axe isn't a child. He's a dog. He'll be fine."

He smiled sheepishly. "I know, he's also my best friend. Makes it easy to forget." His eyes lingered on hers for a moment. Then she realized that she was holding his arm and blushed.

"You guys have fun."

As he walked Axe down the corridor, to the exercise yard, the dog kept glancing back at Alison. "You really like her don't you?" It wasn't something he could ever say about Stacey. Axe and the former model had been standoffish from day one.

The dog paused at the door and looked back at the recovery room.

"Come on, we'll see her again in a bit."

Once in the yard they strolled along the fence. Axe responded well on the lead but still protected his wounded leg. Ernie's Mom was right. Alison was a miracle worker. It had been barely two weeks since Axe had been shot and here he was walking.

After a few laps of the tennis court-sized yard Axe had warmed up and tentatively tried using his injured leg.

Remembering what Alison had said about leadership he began running him through the drills they used at work.

He started simple, walking backward with the dog staying by his side. Then he removed the lead and allowed Axe to wander the yard by himself.

"Axe, freeze."

The dog stopped instantly.

"Axe, come."

He limped to Mike and sat in front of him. He slapped his thigh and the dog walked clockwise around him and sat alongside his left leg.

"Good boy." He bent, ruffled his ears, and fished in his pocket for a treat.

"You two work so well together," said Alison from the back door of the clinic. "Coffee?" She held out a mug while sipping from another.

Mike turned and flashed a smile. "Um, what have you done to my dog?"

"What do you mean?"

"He's changed completely. He's back to normal."

Axe barked excitedly and walked toward the veterinarian.

Mike followed the dog and took the coffee that Alison offered him. "OK, so aside from being in love with you, he's back to normal."

She leaned and tussled Axe's ears. "It's nice having the attention of a handsome man like you."

Mike smiled as he sat next to her on the stairs. "So where to from here?"

"We've still got a bit of work to do. While his leg is healing well, the PTSD has a little way to go. Isn't that right, handsome?"

Axe was looking up at her admiringly with his long tongue lolling out of the side of his mouth.

"Hey, cut that out. You're going to give me a complex." Mike took a toy from his pocket, squeezed it and threw it across the lawn.

They watched Axe limp after it.

He took a sip of the coffee and held the mug with both hands. "Hey look, I was a bit of a jerk earlier this week. I want to apologize for that." He turned and looked at her.

"Don't worry about it. I know I came across a little harsh."

Their gaze locked over their mugs and Mike noted how pretty her green eyes were. There was a kindness about them that he hadn't noticed before. His gaze dropped to her supple lips and he imagined kissing them. Then his eyes flicked back to hers. Her intensity confirmed a similar thought was on her mind.

Then, as he considered leaning across and kissing her, Axe dropped the now slobbery toy directly onto his groin. "Thanks, bud." He laughed as he recovered the slimy ball. "As much as I hate to, I've got to get going." He finished the coffee with a single gulp and climbed to his feet. "Do you want me to take him inside?"

She shook her head, tossing her long brown hair. "No, I'll stay out here with him for a little longer. We'll see you tomorrow."

He patted the dog. "Be good, bud. I'll see you later." With a final nod and a smile he entered the clinic and made for the front door.

As he reached the waiting area, he heard, "Hey, Mike."

"Yeah." He turned to face Alison.

She looked as if she wanted to ask him a question but fumbled her words. "Umm, I just wanted to know what time to expect you?"

He smiled. "I'm hoping to finish up work early. If I can, it will be around fifteen hundred."

"That's three, right?"

"Yeah, three."

"See you then."

As Mike left, Alison slapped her forehead with her palm. Feeling Axe push past her leg, she glanced down at him. "You didn't see that, did you?"

He sat and stared at her.

"Oh, you did. Well that's even more embarrassing. Come on. Let's get you something to eat."

***

Early the next morning, Mike joined his team-mates at a training facility. Located on the outskirts of San Diego and run by civilian contractors it was a state of the art shoot-house that allowed, low risk, and highly realistic indoor training.

He spotted TJ and the others standing behind one of the black minivans they used to transport equipment and personnel around town. The squad had almost finished gearing up for a session in the 'house'. They wore protective chemical warfare suits and were now strapping on their combat vests. As he approached, TJ broke away from the van and headed toward him.

Mike gave him a nod. "Hey, Chief."

"Morning, Mike, once you're ready grab the clowns and I'll see you inside."

"Roger." He continued across to the van where Rick and Ernie were preparing. "Good morning." Grinning he retrieved his gear bag from the trunk.

Rick met his smile with a scowl. "What's good about it? TJ's got us running drills in gas masks and suits. Gonna be sweating our asses off for the next five hours."

Mike pulled his protective clothing on over his T-shirt and shorts. "Yeah, but Rick it's a beautiful day."

"How's our boy doing?" Ernie asked as he opened a weapons crate and took out his carbine.

"Great. He's coming along well. Alison has done wonders with him." He slung his armor on over the protective suit. As he reached for his weapon, he caught both Rick and Ernie grinning at him. "What?"

Rick shot him a broad smirking grin. "So it's Alison now, is it? That's why you're so damn happy. You're hitting that aren't you, bud?"

Ernie's eyes narrowed. "My brother said she was hot."

"What? No. No, it's not like that. She's not my type." Mike avoided eye contact with his friends as he attached his weapon to the clip on his rig. "You guys ready?"

Picking up his gas mask, he walked in the direction of the shoot-house.

Rick yelled after him. "I call bullshit. Why else would you be so damn happy? Only time I'm wearing a shit-eating grin like that is after a night of hot, sweaty sex. Oh shit, you're not back with Stacey are you?"

Mike waved him off and pushed open the door into the training facility.

Already inside, TJ had his gas mask on and his weapon ready. "Game faces on boys. We're running room clearance drills."

Mike let his rifle hang and adjusted the straps on his mask. "Not everyone's a sex-crazed maniac like you, Rick. Some of us are high on life."

"You fuckers better mask up or you're gonna be high on tear gas," yelled TJ as he hit the gas release button.

A rotating red light flashed. A hissing noise filled the air as they fitted their masks.

"You like her though, don't you?" Rick wheezed through his respirator.

Mike inserted a magazine of paint cartridges into his weapon and cocked it. "She's cooler than I initially thought."

Gas was now visible inside the room.

"Just call me cupid," Ernie said, using his carbine as if it were a bow.

"I'll call you mother-fucking stupid," added Rick. "Boy needs to tap that, not get into another relationship."

"Wrong!" TJ bellowed through his mask. "You dimwits need to tap some goddamn targets otherwise I'm going to keep you in these suits all day."

Ernie readied his weapon. "No need to be like that."

"We're just looking out for our boy, TJ. I mean, we don't want to have to run a girlfriend selection course, just yet."

"What the… Are you in love, Mike?" demanded TJ.

"Negative, Chief!"

"Good, if that changes, let me know." TJ racked his weapon. "Now, let's put paint on paper. On me!"

***

Alison's favorite café was an eclectic establishment only five minutes from her clinic. A converted garage, the Spanner Shop now housed a four-head espresso machine and the best sandwiches and muffins in a ten-mile radius.

As she pushed the door open, a bell clanged. The twenty-something barista glanced up from the machine and smiled from under his handlebar mustache.

"Hi, Simon." Glancing around, she spotted her sister sitting at a table.

"The usual, Ali? Your sister has already ordered."

"Thanks. That would be lovely."

She wound her way through the rough-hewn benches and ambushed her sister with a hug and a kiss on the cheek. "Hello, beautiful lady."

"Beautiful?" Leonie returned the embrace. "I feel like I've been hit by a eighteen-wheeler."

Alison sat on the bench opposite.

"Whatever you do," continued Leonie, "don't have children. Especially not daughters, and in the name of all things sane, do not volunteer to help out at a damn ballet camp."

"Is that where the girls are?"

A waiter arrived with their coffees. "Here's your quad and a latte." He placed a gargantuan mug of coffee in front of Leonie. The smaller tumbler looked like a shot glass next to the bucket of caffeine.

"How many shots are in that?" Alison asked.

"Four," replied the waiter. "Enjoy."

"Leonie, you're going to give yourself a heart attack."

"Trust me when I say it will be welcomed." She wrapped her hands around the mug and took a sip. "God I needed this. Now, tell me what's been happening in your life?"

"Work, work and more work."

"Any more hunky Navy SEALs been to visit?"

Alison shrugged as she sipped.

"Oh, he's been back hasn't he?"

"He kind of has to, Leonie, I'm treating his dog. He comes in every day to visit Axe."

Her sister smirked. "I don't think I could handle that. I would have torn those jeans off him by now and had my way with him on every horizontal surface in the clinic."

Alison snorted coffee from her nose. "You're out of control." She reached for a napkin.

"No, you're out of control. Big hunky man who looks like he's straight off a *Calvin Klein* poster comes in and you do nothing. You have to hit him up for a date."

"You want me to ask him out?"

"Um yeah, this is the teens. Or whatever the hell they call this decade. You know what I mean. We're all empowered and shit now. You can ask any guy out if you want to. Hell if you want to bang him on the first date that's completely up to you."

As she wiped coffee from her chin, Alison caught the annoyed glance of another patron. "Shh, I want to come back here." She giggled.

Leonie shrugged. "I'm just saying it's OK for you to ask him out. Hell, bring him here and have a coffee. Or, are you still hung up on him being a jerk."

"Well–"

"God, Ali, you don't have to shag his personality just that rock solid body."

"No, it isn't that. He's actually turned out be a decent guy. Yeah, he's a little stubborn and full of himself. But the way he is with Axe is really very sweet. He's so gentle and kind, yet also stern. The two of them work perfectly together, like a finely-tuned machine. He's also a really good listener–"

"Wow, you're already in love with the guy. You should just get down on one knee and SEAL the deal," Leonie said between chuckles.

Alison blushed and lifted her coffee, hoping it hid her flushed cheeks.

"Don't be shy, sis. If you like the guy, ask him out. Hell, make it about the dog if you want. Get to know him and then…" She made a circle with her fingers and inserted the opposite hand's index finger. "Uh huh. Oh yeah."

"You're shocking."

Leonie cocked her head to one side. "And you're in need of a good lay."

She checked her watch then downed the last of her coffee. "Sorry this was quick, but I've got to get back to the clinic. I've got a client coming in to check on a dog. Let's do something together, real soon." She jumped up and gave her sister another hug.

"You're leaving me for him, aren't you?"

She kissed her on the cheek and started for the door.

"Fine, run off after your handsome Navy SEAL and leave me to cry into my bucket of coffee," Leonie yelled across the café.

"Oh god, I'm so sorry," Alison told the barista. "Please, put it all on my account and I'll fix it up when I'm next in."

"Good luck," he said winking.

She paused. "I'm going back to work."

"Sure you are."

***

Alison's assistant glanced up from her computer as she entered the clinic. "He's already out back with Axe. He's been here for the last hour." She pointed to a bright bunch of flowers on the counter. "And he brought these in for us."

"Really?"

"Alright, they might only be for you."

Alison suppressed her smile until she entered the corridor, then it burst free. She gathered herself, before stepping outside. In the exercise yard Mike and Axe were playing ball. She watched them for a few throws and noted the dog was still guarding his injured leg. Catching Mike's eye she called out, "He's definitely improved, but he still has a long way to go."

He flashed her a smile.

Alison caught herself staring. Mike was wearing a tight T-shirt that did little to hide his muscular build. His biceps strained at the thin fabric sending a shiver up her spine. Her sister was right. The tall, blonde-haired SEAL looked like he had stepped straight from a *Calvin Klein* shoot onto her lawn. The driver's license he'd used to open his account said he was 28. However, his slate gray eyes told a different story. They'd seen more than their fair share of pain and suffering.

He smiled, revealing a dimple, and she knew he'd caught her ogling, probably almost drooling.

"The improvements are all because of you. Two weeks ago the Army vet told me he might never walk again and couldn't be trusted around people. Now, look at him."

Axe lay on the grass, the ball still in his mouth as he watched them.

"Hey, what can I say? He's a special dog." Alison stepped closer, drawn in by his smile.

"You're an amazing vet, Alison, I'm so glad we found you and I don't think either of us will ever be able to thank you enough."

"Please, call me Ali, and the beautiful flowers are a great start."

He glanced down at his feet. "I… I just wanted to say thanks for taking such good care of my best friend."

Her heart lurched at his shyness.

They sat together on the rear deck.

Mike stared out into the distance. "He saved my life you know."

Glancing sideways at him, she spotted a tear in his eye as he watched the dog chew the ball.

"Guy got the drop on me, would've killed me. Axe took the bullet." He turned to face her. "That's not something you can ever repay. That's just one reason why I couldn't let them put him down."

She reached over, grasped his hand and squeezed it gently. "No one's going to hurt him now, Mike. He's safe here."

Sensing his distress, Axe abandoned his ball, walked across, and put his head on Mike's knee.

"See, there isn't a person in the world he trusts more than you."

He scratched behind Axe's floppy ear. "Even after everything I've put him through?"

"You guys are definitely a team."

"Yeah, well this team-mate has to get going." He gave her a heart-melting smile. "Thanks again, Ali. I guess I'll see you tomorrow?"

"I look forward to it."

He gave the dog one last pat, rose, and made for the door.

"Mike!"

He turned. "Yeah?"

She took a deep breath. "Tomorrow, after you visit Axe, would you like to grab a coffee or something?"

The corners of his mouth curved in an easy smile. "I'd like that. I'll be here around two. Does that work for you?"

"Don't you mean fourteen hundred?"

"It's a date." He disappeared through the door.

The dog looked up at her with intelligent eyes.

"You heard him," she gushed. "It's a date."

Chapter Seven

Ali's gaze met Mike's over their coffees. The pair had spent the past hour exercising Axe, then left him in the care of her assistant. Now they sat in her favorite coffee haunt, the Spanner Shop. She traced her finger around the lip of her cup. "So, why a SEAL?"

Mike shrugged. "My dad was a Navy guy. Always said it was the best time of his life. So when I left college, I decided to enlist. The recruiter was a team guy, and well, the rest is history. What about you, why a vet?"

"I grew up on a farm in the Midwest and always loved animals. There was no way I would or could do anything else."

He smiled. "Well, Axe and I are pretty happy you didn't take a different path."

Ali melted at the sight of his dimples. "I'm glad you found me. Axe is a wonderful dog. I'm enjoying working with him."

He held his mug in both hands and peered over it. "Uh huh."

She blushed. "Well… it's been nice getting to know you, too."

"I'm enjoying it." He lowered the mug. "So, why doesn't an intelligent, attractive woman like you have a man in her life?"

"What is it with you men? You all assume I want and need a man in my life. Why doesn't a hunky SEAL like you have a partner… or do you?"

He shook his head. "Nope, just me and Axe."

She laughed, tucking a stray strand of hair behind her ear. "I'm just messing with you, Mike. I've had a few relationships. But none of the guys hang around. I guess they don't like competing with dogs for attention."

"Hardly an even competition, is it?"

"What do you mean?"

"Well, dogs are loyal, steadfast, always happy to see you, no matter what. No man can compete with that."

"Are you saying I should date a Golden Retriever?"

"No, maybe just a man who has things in perspective."

"Oh." She raised an eyebrow, suggestively. "And do you have things in perspective, Mr. Michael Saunders?"

He smiled into his coffee. "Maybe. Oh, before I forget, is it alright if I take Axe out tomorrow?"

"He's your dog. You don't have to ask my permission."

"I just thought that, as his doctor you should be consulted," he said, his expression matching his serious tone.

"Well then, as his doctor I should probably know exactly what it is he'll be doing."

"Ah, that part's a surprise."

She frowned. "Well then, how can I know if it's suitable for his condition?"

He grinned. "Well, I thought you could supervise."

She set her coffee down. "Sounds like you're trying to sneak in a second date."

He leaned across the table, stopping when their lips were less than an inch apart. "That's exactly what I'm doing. I've got to run, but I'll pick you up tomorrow at ten."

"Yes, sir," she murmured, fighting the urge to kiss him.

"I'm not an officer, Ali. You don't have to call me sir."

She pursed her lips seductively. "What if I want to?"

"Now, that's a different matter altogether." He settled back in his chair and downed the last of his coffee. "I really do have to run. I'll pick you and Axe up at ten hundred sharp."

"I look forward to it."

Ali's gaze followed his every movement as he went to the counter and paid the bill. Her eyes were fixed on his buttocks. Damn, they looked good in the tight jeans he wore. He glanced back at her before disappearing through the door. She sighed as she finished her coffee. Crap, she hadn't asked Mike what to wear. A ten o'clock pickup with Axe suggested something physical, she hoped. Because the last thing she wanted to do was turn up in heels and a skirt when they were going on an adventure.

***

Outside the café, as Mike approached his truck, he spotted a white sedan across the street. His eyes narrowed as he studied it. The car was familiar. Too familiar, right down to the dented front right fender. He swore he had seen it earlier today, parked outside Ali's clinic. As he eyeballed the car, trying to make out the driver, it pulled out into traffic.

He drummed his fingers against his thigh as he watched it disappear behind a sixteen wheeler. Shaking his head he opened his truck and climbed in. The coffee had left him a little edgy. Not to mention he hadn't been sleeping well since Axe was shot. He managed a smile as his mind turned to the date he'd planned. Now at least he had something to look forward to.

Chapter Eight

Ramirez located Barbosa perched on a bag of coffee beans, smoking a cigar at the rear of the rusted warehouse. A number of heavies stood in a semicircle around the elderly, battered, man crumpled at the Butcher's feet.

He didn't trouble himself with the victim. That wasn't his business. He was being paid to find Juan Barbosa's killer and exact revenge.

The cartel boss exhaled a mouthful of smoke into the face of his victim, before looking up. "You got something for me?"

Ramirez's eyes narrowed behind his aviator sunglasses. "Can we go somewhere private to talk?"

"No. I am comfortable here."

"That's not what concerns me."

Barbosa laughed. "Oh, don't worry about Pedro. Where he's going there's no one to talk or listen." He prodded the body with his shoe. "Isn't that right, my friend?"

Ramirez shrugged. "In that case, I've found your man."

"Who is he?"

"His name is Michael Saunders. He's a Petty Officer with SEAL Team Five. My people are gathering intelligence. When we have enough information, we'll strike."

Barbosa rose from his perch and signaled for Ramirez to walk with him, between shelves stacked high with fragrant coffee beans.

"I want you to find what this man loves. Gather every detail of his life and find what he lives for. Then, when you have done that, I want you to take it from him." Pivoting, Barbosa turned and placed a hand on his shoulder. "I want him to feel loss like I have felt. I want him to grieve like I have grieved. Then, when he begs for his life, I want you to kill him."

Chapter Nine

The next morning at 1035 hours, Ali sat beside Mike as he drove his pickup across a cattle guard and up a dusty road. Ahead, a gleaming white mansion materialized from behind a line of trees.

Ali thought it looked like a temple, more at home in ancient Greece than California.

"Please tell me you haven't brought me to a country club when I'm wearing sneakers and leggings," she lamented as they approached the multi-story, white-pillared structure.

"Nope, you're good." Mike turned onto a track that weaved through the freshly mowed lawns and lush green gardens that skirted the mansion.

Ali twisted her head to look back at the house. "What is this place?"

"It's a country club for rich jerks. A buddy of mine's old man owns it. He lets me use the facilities."

The landscape dramatically turned from manicured gardens to the harsh, rocky canyons that Southern California was renowned for. The road snaked its way up a narrow valley for another half-mile before he parked the truck. "We're here."

Exiting the air-conditioned cabin, Ali inhaled a deep breath of warm, clean air, and surveyed their destination.

The valley was pristine desert with cactus, rocky outcrops, and stunted desert plants pockmarking the steep walls. Turning, she inspected the area behind the truck as Mike dropped the tailgate. It had been cleared out to about fifty yards, at which point there was a tall mound of sand.

"Mike, what is this place?" She joined him as he was unloading stakes with targets attached to them. "Ah, now it makes sense."

"Yep, we're going to do some shooting." He opened the rear doors of the dual-cab truck and lifted Axe from the bench seat to the ground. The dog immediately limped around to the tailgate and sat next to Ali. "Buddy, I'm beginning to think you prefer her over me."

"Well, I have been feeding him and you know that's the quickest way to a man's heart."

"So I've heard."

Stroking Axe's head she watched as Mike set up two targets, twenty yards from the pickup in front of the wall of sand. Then he took a locked box from the cabin and opened it, revealing a black handgun. "You ever fired a pistol?"

Ali shook her head. "No. My dad wasn't really a gun kind of guy."

"That's cool. It takes all types." Mike took up the pistol. "This is a Glock nine millimeter. It's the most common pistol used by police and military. Easy to use and very safe if treated with respect."

He spent the next fifteen minutes explaining how the pistol worked and how to manipulate the controls. Then using an empty magazine, he taught her how to load, cock and position herself to shoot. When she was confident he took a live magazine, loaded the pistol and positioned her facing the targets.

"Don't be afraid of the weapon, Ali. Treat it with respect and never forget that you're the one in complete control."

She held the pistol in both hands, how he had shown her, and aimed at one of the paper targets. Squeezing the trigger, she flinched as the weapon fired. Dust spurted from the ground below the target. She lowered the pistol to her side. "I'm afraid I'm not very good at this."

"Hey, it's your first time." Mike turned and nodded at the truck where Axe was sitting calmly with his tongue lolling. "Axe, thinks you're doing OK."

Ali turned and checked the dog. "He's not afraid. That's a good sign."

"Not as tense as you. Now, let's try again." Mike stepped in behind her as she raised the handgun.

As he wrapped his arms around her and placed his hands on hers, a tingle of excitement raced across her skin. His body was hard and muscular and he smelt like sweat, oil, and aftershave. She swallowed and concentrated on the pistol's sights.

"See how you've got your arms locked out. You're all tense. You need to relax more."

That was verging on impossible, she thought. His mouth was directly next to her ear and she could feel his breath on the side of her face. A tremor of desire rippled through her as his lips gently brushed her lobe. She exhaled, tried to relax, and gently squeezed the trigger.

Dust spat up from the mound, slightly to the left of the target.

"Nearly there."

Yes I am, she thought. She forced herself to relax, trying to ignore the sensation of his body pressed against hers as she aligned the pistol with the target.

"You want to focus on moving just your finger tip," he said softly.

"You're making it kind of hard to concentrate." She squeezed the trigger and the pistol jumped. "Where did that go?" she asked, lowering the gun.

"On target." He took the pistol from her, cleared it and they walked downrange.

She joined him as he examined the paper. "I can't see where it hit."

"In the black." He pointed to a bullet hole half an inch under the bullseye. "Nice one, sharpshooter, you're a natural."

She leaned forward and poked the mark with her finger. "Woo hoo." Straightening she turned and found herself looking directly into Mike's eyes. For a moment they gazed at each other and for a split second, she thought he would kiss her. Then he faltered and turned his attention back to the target.

"Do you want another go?"

She nodded. "Yes."

As they walked back to the firing point she wondered if Mike was suffering similar emotional wounds to Axe. It made sense, considering the bond between the two. She noticed the dog watching his every move as he thumbed cartridges into the pistol's magazine.

He handed it to her with the pistol. "This time I want you to try it by yourself."

She took them tentatively and turned to face the mound. "Make sure I don't do anything wrong." She inserted the magazine and pulled back the slide, as he had shown her. A smile confirmed it was correct. Then she took careful aim and squeezed the trigger.

"On target."

She fired again.

"OK, so you've definitely got the hang of this. Most people take at least an hour before they're hitting the paper."

Smiling she lowered the pistol. "I put it down to a great instructor."

"Nope, you're a natural." Mike loaded another magazine and handed it to her. "Must be the doctor's steady hands."

She fired off another four magazines before calling it quits.

"I've got something to admit to you," Mike said as they walked back to the truck.

Ali's eyes narrowed. "Is this where you tell me you're married?"

He laughed. "No, nothing like that. It's just… It wasn't my intention to only teach you to shoot." He lifted the truck's tonneau cover and hauled out a picnic basket and a cooler. "I planned on wooing you with champagne and fine food."

She smiled. "And here's me, swooning after one bullseye. I really should learn how to play hard to get."

Mike spread a blanket on the ground. As he laid out the food he shot her a worried look. "Now, we've got cold chicken and a selection of salads. I hope that's OK. I asked your assistant what you liked and if there was anything you didn't eat. She said you love fried chicken. That was OK, wasn't it?"

Dumbstruck, she nodded. "Are all SEALs so thoughtful?"

He grinned. "No ma'am, we just like to be prepared. Time spent on recon is seldom wasted."

"Well, I think it is exceptionally sweet."

Their gazes met and held as Mike moved closer and placed a hand on the side of her hip.

She closed her eyes in anticipation.

With an excited bark, Axe nudged them both with a wet nose.

Mike let his hand drop. "I think he can smell the chicken."

She managed a weak smile. "We can't have him going hungry."

***

Mike sat in the web seats of a C-130 transport and adjusted his parachute leg straps. It was Monday morning and the squad was conducting free-fall insertion training. Decked out in camouflage uniforms they wore bulky parachutes, heavy packs and their weapons were strapped to the sides of their bodies.

The roar of the aircraft's engines almost drowned out Rick's voice. "How was the weekend, brother?"

Mike shot him thumbs-up. "Good, real good."

"Did you bang the vet?"

"Rick, she saved the life of a team-mate. Show a bit of respect." He returned his attention to checking his equipment.

"You totally did, didn't you?"

"Rick, have you ever heard the expression 'a gentleman never tells'?"

"Bro, you're a SEAL. So that's clearly not you. Cough up the details. Was she a rocket?"

Mike shook his head. "You're a child, Rick. Ali's more of a woman than you could comprehend."

"He's got a point there," added Ernie from where he was conducting his own checks. "You've got simpler tastes, Rick."

"Whatever, we all know Mike's hitting it."

"How about you clowns keep your minds on the job," bellowed TJ from where he stood next to the controls for the aircraft's ramp. He lifted two gloved fingers. "Two minutes out."

"You totally had a dirty weekend with her, didn't you?" Rick continued.

Mike fastened his oxygen mask and pulled his goggles over his eyes. The others did the same and they joined TJ at the ramp.

"Stand by," he transmitted over their internal frequency. "Oxygen on."

They turned their tanks on. A moment later, the ramp lowered with a whine. Icy cold air ripped into the cargo hold.

"Thirty seconds," said TJ.

"I bet Mike didn't last that long," transmitted Rick.

"Pie hole, Rick." TJ held up his hand.

They readied themselves. "Go, go, go!"

Mike leaped off the ramp into the thin air, alongside the Chief. Rick and Ernie were close behind.

As they tracked across the clear sky Mike stabilized himself. At close to thirty thousand feet, San Diego bay was a sparkling jewel. The bright, blue water stood out against the golden beaches and slate-gray cityscape.

"Hey, Mike," Rick transmitted.

He turned his head and was faced with the sight of Ernie in an all-fours position with Rick behind him, one hand behind his head and the other on Ernie's hip.

"Is this how you did it, bud? Doggy style with the vet."

Mike couldn't believe what he was seeing as the two veteran SEALs pretended to fornicate while free-falling at an altitude close to twenty-thousand feet.

"Seriously, show a bit of respect guys."

"What the hell are you clowns doing?" transmitted TJ. "Tighten up the formation."

Mike shook his head as the pair abandoned their pantomime and joined him and TJ in a diamond shape.

"Mike," transmitted TJ.

"Yeah?"

"Things getting serious with this girl?"

He didn't respond as they plummeted through the atmosphere at 120 miles per hour.

"You know what's got to happen if it is, brother. Approaching two thousand."

Mike checked his altimeter. As the needle hit two thousand feet he pulled his chute. The canopy expanded overhead, the harness wrenching at his shoulders. Then, as he leveled out, he checked that the rest of the squad was safely under silk.

"OK, form up on me," ordered TJ.

He steered his chute in behind the Chief.

"Mike, you didn't answer the question. You serious about this girl, or what?"

Mike didn't respond.

"Silence is damning, isn't it TJ?" Rick said.

"You wouldn't know, Rick. You can't keep your pie hole shut. Now, what's the deal with this girl?"

Mike drew on his right toggle, banking to follow the Chief. "Yeah, I like her. She's done wonders for Axe. She's also nothing like any other woman I've met." Their drop zone on the beach was rapidly approaching.

"Good for you. Keep us posted on how it's progressing."

Mike flared as the sand rose toward him, and touched down gently a dozen feet from TJ. He pivoted and watched Rick and Ernie make their landings.

"Good work guys," TJ bellowed. "Now let's dump these chutes and hit the range."

Chapter Ten

Ramirez was sitting with his family at the dinner table when his phone rang. He pulled the device from his pocket and inspected it.

"You know the rules. No business at dinner," his wife said.

"This is important."

She frowned, but dismissed him with a wave of her hand.

"Thank you, darling." Leaving the dining area, he answered the call as he entered the living room. "Speak!"

"Boss, it's me, Eduardo."

"What have you got?"

"I've been following this guy for a week now. Every day he goes to a veterinary clinic in Iron Canyon."

"Why?"

"I think he's seeing the woman who works there. They've been spending a lot of time together with a dog."

Ramirez grabbed a packet of cigarettes from the coffee table. "So, our target has a woman. That's good."

"It would be easy to grab her."

He tucked the phone between his shoulder and ear, and tapped a cigarette into his palm. "Not yet. Keep watching. I need to get our people in place."

"You got it, boss."

Terminating the call, he scooped a lighter off the table and strode outside to smoke. Lighting up, he gazed out over the wide expanse of desert dusted with saltbush and cacti. Sunset bathed the harsh landscape in a soft orange hue that masked its true nature. He exhaled. It was a lot like the happy family life he maintained with his wife.

As he smoked the howl of a coyote filled the air. Within a matter of moments another joined the first animal's call. He smiled as he listened to their chorus.

Once he finished the cigarette, he flicked it off the porch into the sand and punched a number into his phone. "Pedro, we're going to need two vehicles, eight men and clean passports with US visas."

"What's the mission?"

"We're going to take care of a problem for our good friend."

"So, it will pay well."

"Of course. I want the best we have."

"When do you need them ready?"

He stroked his mustache as he considered the question. "Twenty-four hours."

"Done."

Terminating the call, he considered another cigarette when a voice startled him.

"Are you going to finish dinner with your family?"

His wife's tone implied it was not a question. "Yes, my dear."

"What was the call about?" she asked as she led him back into the house.

"Business, darling. I may have to leave, later in the week."

"How long? Remember, your son's football final is this weekend."

Ramirez took his seat at the head of the table. "A few days at most. It's a simple in and out job."

***

Wearing a one-piece swimsuit, Ali stood in the portable rehabilitation spa set up in the yard. She watched as Mike led Axe, in a bright yellow vest that resembled a lifejacket, toward the spa.

"Ali, I'm not sure this is going to work."

"Why?"

"He hates water."

She placed her hands on her hips and cocked her head. "That information would have been useful yesterday."

Mike smiled but his eyes never left her curvaceous frame. The plain, one-piece suit did little to hide her curves.

"Hey sailor, how about we focus on rehab and not the merchandise."

As he lifted his gaze back to hers he caught the smile on her lips. With a grunt he picked up the dog and lowered him into the spa. "Your call. But, he's not going to like it."

Growling, Axe laid his ears flat and struggled.

Mike stepped back from the water and put him down on the grass. "See. I told you."

Ali folded her arms and arched an eyebrow, her lips pressed firmly together.

"Mike, he's a dog. He doesn't get to decide what's good for him, that's your job."

"Fine."

He lifted Axe over the lip of the spa and placed him in the warm water. The dog's legs cycled as they broke the surface, his ears flat against his skull as he paddled frantically.

Ali held him as he attempted to swim for the edge of the pool. "It's OK, Axe."

Mike leaned against the tub. "So what's this supposed to achieve?"

"He's guarding his damaged muscles resulting in atrophy. This will let him exercise them to their full potential, without weight."

"Making them stronger?"

"Yes."

Axe looked anything but strong as he panicked and tried to hook his legs over the side of the tub.

"I think he would be more comfortable if you held him." Ali struggled to keep him inside the hydro bath.

"I told you."

With a scowl, she snapped, "Michael, get in the tub."

"Yes ma'am." He stripped off his shirt.

It was Ali's turn to gawk. She knew SEALs trained hard but this was ridiculous. Every inch of his bronzed body looked like it had been chiseled from rock.

Climbing into the tub in his shorts, he stood alongside Ali in the warm water. Grasping Axe's vest, Mike pulled him back from the lip of the spa, forcing him to float. "Hey bud, it's OK."

Axe fought the water for a moment then adopted a powerful swimming stroke. Mike struggled to keep him in the middle of the tub.

Ali gave him a pat. "Not so bad, is it handsome.'

"Yeah, it's alright."

She glared sideways at him. "I wasn't talking to you."

He grinned. "Oh, my bad."

They stood side by side in the water as Axe continued to swim powerfully. It took the two of them to stop him reaching the side of the tub.

"Damn, he's strong," Mike grunted.

"This will make him even stronger."

Together they held the dog as he paddled at a steady pace.

"Is Axe your first military dog?" she asked.

"No, I had a dog before him…"

"And?"

"He was an explosives-detection dog. We were on a mission in Afghanistan. When we made entry on a Taliban stronghold he sniffed out an IED. He saved a lot of lives that day." Mike swallowed. "Most of us got clear, but when the bomb went off, Captain was on top of it."

"I'm so sorry," whispered Ali.

A tear ran down his cheek. "Two dogs have saved my life, Ali. I couldn't save Captain, but I can save Axe."

The compassion in her face was not something he'd ever seen in any of the women he had dated, certainly not in Stacey. Leaning over he kissed her gently on the lips. She responded tenderly, their mouths pressed softly together.

Mike's anguish was washed away in a sea of passion as her mouth opened slightly and he nibbled gently on her full, lower lip. He released Axe and slid his hand behind her head as the kiss gained in intensity. Their tongues touched and everything outside the kiss ceased to exist.

A bark quelled their passion. They broke apart, laughing as Axe barked again.

Mike turned his attention back to the dog. He ruffled Axe's ears. "I guess he thinks he should be the center of attention."

She smiled. "He seems to be pretty comfortable in the water."

"Well, technically he's a SEAL."

"Look, Mike," she said softly. "I've been hurt before–"

Mike grasped her around the waist and pulled her close. Pushing a strand of hair from her face, he kissed her again. There was no warm up this time. For a precious few minutes, he felt like he was a teenager. Then, Axe once more, voiced his displeasure.

Mike pulled back slightly. "I think he might have had enough." He gave her one long final kiss. Then, grateful that his shorts hid his excitement, he climbed out of the tub. Together they managed to lift the waterlogged dog out of the spa and onto the grass. Then, when he removed the float vest, Axe snorted and shook, covering him in wet strands of fur.

"Thanks, now I smell as bad as you do." He laughed as the dog rolled onto his back and wriggled like a furry worm. Then he jumped to his feet and trotted around the yard. "He looks better already."

Ali climbed out of the pool. "A few more sessions and you'll see a different dog." Wrapping a towel around her hips, she asked, "Do you want to have a shower before you go?"

He shook his head. "I'd love to. But, I've got to run. I'll get into clean clothes at work." He caught the flash of disappointment on her face. "Hey, I was wondering if you're free for dinner tomorrow night."

She wrinkled her nose. "Are you asking me out? Because I don't want things to get weird between us."

He grinned. "Yes. Yes, I am. Although, technically it's our third date. Look, I really like you Ali and I want to see where this goes. We can take it slow."

She returned the smile. "That sounds good."

***

Mike was making adjustments to his equipment when Rick joined him inside the submarine lockout chamber. He glanced up and gave the Corpsman a nod. Like Mike he was dressed in a black wetsuit, scuba tanks, and a combat vest.

"You're spending a lot of time with this girl, brother. You telling me you still haven't squared her away?"

"I'm not telling you anything."

Rick adjusted his equipment. "Come on, Mike, we're supposed to be a team."

"Quit it. I'm not going to kiss and tell." He checked that his dive mask was secure around his neck.

"You hear that? Our boy's in love," Rick announced as TJ and Ernie joined them in the chamber.

"You falling for the dog doctor, *esse*?" asked Ernie as he spun the handle that sealed the men in the chamber.

"Guys, Ali's cool, I like her. But for now that's it."

TJ fixed him with a questioning look. "Like! That sounds awfully close to love, Romeo."

Mike shook his head. "I give up. You guys are out of control."

The three members of his squad burst into laughter.

"Commencing flood up and equalization," said Mike as he hit the button for the valve that released seawater into the chamber. "Watch your ears."

The men were still laughing as salt water rose rapidly to their knees.

"I'm in love. Boom, I'm all shook up," sang Rick until he had to stuff his regulator into his mouth. He continued humming until the water rose to the ceiling.

Mike gave all three men thumbs-up before he turned the locking arm and opened the outer door. They finned out onto the sleek black hull of the Virginia-class attack submarine and hovered in the water. Then, when they were ready, TJ gave them the signal to move off and they swam in single file behind him.

Bringing up the rear Mike was happy to follow the others through the murky green water. He was completely preoccupied with thoughts of dinner with Ali.

***

Mike lifted his glass and flashed a smile at the gorgeous woman sitting opposite him. "To Axe, his recovery and his match-making skills."

Ali touched her glass to his as their eyes locked. "To Axe."

Sipping his champagne, his gaze lingered on her. She wore a black, slim-fitting halter neck dress that showcased her elegant throat and ample cleavage. With her hair up and only enough makeup to emphasize her full lips and hazel eyes, she was stunning.

"I wanted to thank you for how much time you've spent with Axe. You've worked wonders for him… But, that's not why I invited you out to dinner."

She took a sip of champagne. "Really, then what's the reason?"

He leaned forward and whispered. "I'm trying to seduce you."

Eyes sparkling she pressed her lips together and swallowed. "Well it's working."

"Sir, your entree."

They both jumped at the waiter's voice.

Ali blushed as he placed their dishes in front of them and refilled their glasses.

"How did you find this place?" she asked once the waiter had left.

"A buddy of mine raved about it a few months back. I thought it was worth a try."

Ali finished a mouthful of the scallop. "Well, if the starter is anything to go on I think he was understating. If the meal is this good, I'm not going to have room for dessert."

"I know a great little café around the corner that serves an amazing pecan pie." He smiled suggestively. "They're open late."

She put on her best southern accent. "Why, Michael Saunders, you do know how to show a girl a good time."

As the lovebirds made eyes at each other another pair was watching them closely. Rick stood outside the French restaurant with a curvaceous blonde on his arm.

"Come on Ricky, you promised me dancing and a good time?"

"Damn it woman, give me a second." He could see that his boy Mike was completely smitten. He assumed that the pretty brunette was the veterinarian and it was clear that Romeo more than 'liked' her.

"Are you checking out that girl?" the blonde asked indignantly.

Rick scowled. "No, I only like hot pieces of ass like you." He reached around and grabbed her buttocks. "Come on, let's get out of here."

As they walked down the street he sent a message to TJ.

Our boy is out to dinner with the vet and he's all loved up… Time for selection?

A moment later a reply hit his phone.

We'll get to the bottom of this tomorrow.

Chapter Eleven

Yawning, Mike dumped his gear bag on the bench in the team room and stretched his neck. He smiled to himself as he opened his locker and searched for a stick of deodorant. Last night was the most fun he'd had in months and all they'd done was talk.

He and Ali had left the restaurant at closing and continued flirting in a local café. They'd remained there till the early hours of the morning when the staff had forced them to leave. Only then, had Mike hailed her a cab then walked home.

He'd finally reached his apartment at four in the morning. Two hours was all the sleep he'd gotten before reporting for duty.

Rick entered the room. "Late night, brother?"

"Yeah, I could murder a cup of coffee."

"There's a pot in the briefing room. I'll grab one with you."

"Sounds good." Mike closed his locker and followed Rick into the lecture room they shared with the other squads. As he stepped through the doorway he spotted Ernie and TJ sitting side-by-side. Rick took the seat next to them. All three sat facing an empty chair.

He frowned. "Hey, what's up?"

"Take a seat, Mike." TJ nodded to the empty seat.

"What's this? Some kind of intervention?"

"You could call it that."

Mike turned the chair backward and straddled it. All of them, even Rick, sported stern expressions.

"Where were you last night?" TJ asked.

"Guys, seriously, what's this about?"

"Are you in love?" snapped Rick.

"Jesus, Rick, you couldn't interrogate a chimpanzee with a fist full of bananas," growled TJ.

Mike laughed. "So that's it?"

"You've been spending a lot of time with this Ali chick, brother," said TJ.

"Guys, she's been treating Axe. It's been kind of hard for me not to spend time with her. Why, is that a problem? You boys getting jealous?"

TJ shook his head. "Given your track record with women and relationships in general, we're concerned you're heading for another train wreck."

"Oh come on. I've only been on three dates with her."

TJ's eyes narrowed. "Rick, tell him."

"I saw you at the restaurant last night, Mike. I saw how you were looking at her. This is a bit more than a hit it and quit it."

Mike clenched his fists on his knees. "Fine, you got me. I really like this girl. There, I said it."

"Rick thinks you're head over heels in love with her," said TJ.

"He wouldn't know what love was if it punched him in the dick."

Rick let out a raucous burst of laughter. "Did I just get dissed on love by the guy whose last girlfriend was a psycho? Oh, and didn't the one before that steal all your shit when we were in Afghan?"

Mike scowled.

"This is for your own good," added TJ.

"What exactly is this?"

Ernie rocked back on his chair. "You remember, *essé*. The 'selection' course."

"Guys, that was a joke. You don't…"

All three men frowned.

"If she passes, we'll embrace her as one of our own," said TJ.

"But, if she fails," added Rick.

"Then she's out," finished Ernie.

Mike paused in thought. "Look, this girl isn't like the others. She's stable, compassionate and grounded. I don't think–"

TJ interrupted with a shake of his head. "Your track record suggests you don't think, slick. Trust me. This is for your own good."

Mike sighed. "OK, where do we start?"

"Tomorrow. It's Saturday. You're going to invite her on a hike with you up Mount Otay."

"What if she doesn't want to go?"

Rick laughed. "Then last night wasn't as special as you thought."

***

"So why the sudden urge to go hiking?" Ali asked as Mike pulled his truck into a parking lot at the base of a rugged mountain range.

"You mentioned you liked the outdoors and I thought it might be a good chance for us to get to know each other."

"Good idea, I like it." She pushed open the door and jumped out. "Come on. Let's do this."

Mike grabbed his backpack, locked the truck and led her through a camping ground to the trailhead.

As they climbed a narrow path up the side of a canyon, she turned to him. "Have you been up here before?"

"Once or twice."

"You bring all your girls up here?"

"No. Most of the women I've dated wouldn't climb into my truck much less a mountain."

"Really? Have you always dated princesses?"

Mike laughed. "Yeah, I guess I have. Let's just say you're nothing like them."

"I'm not exactly sure how to take that."

He smiled. "Trust me, it's a good thing. You're the best thing that's happened to me… and Axe, in a long time."

They reached the crest of the canyon and paused to take in the scenery. Mike dropped his pack on the ground and handed her a water bottle.

"You know, I could be a total princess. You'd have no way of knowing."

"That's what we're here to find out," said TJ over the covert communicator lodged inside Mike's ear.

Given the tiny device only had a range of a few hundred yards, he glanced around hoping to spot him. However, TJ was an experienced sniper and a master of camouflage, he wouldn't be seen.

Mike glanced at his watch. It was a little past midday. "You OK to step it out? We'll make the peak in time for sunset and be back down before it gets too dark."

Smiling, Ali glanced back over her shoulder. "Sounds good." She held up the bottle of water. " You sure you don't want me to carry something other than this?"

"Nah, I'm good."

"Big strong SEAL and all that."

"Not at all. I'm just happy following your butt up the hill."

Mike's comment was rewarded by a puking sound in his ear. Clearly his flirting didn't impress TJ. Ali rolled her eyes and powered up the hill, leaving him in her dust. "OK, so that was cheesy," grunted Mike as he stepped off after her.

"No shit," added TJ over the radio.

***

It took them nearly three hours to climb to the peak of Mount Otay. When they finally reached the top they were greeted with a spectacular view across the Mexican border. Mike wiped the sweat from his brow as he dropped the heavy daypack on the ground. Ali had set a surprisingly fast pace up the mountain and, carrying the gear TJ had given him, Mike worked hard to keep up. His T-shirt was drenched in sweat and his legs were aching from the steep ascent.

"Wow. You can literally see for miles." She pointed at the spectacular vista stretched out before them. "That's Mexico, right?"

Pulling a fresh bottle of cold water from his pack he tossed it to her. "Right. I've gotta say, you're fitter than half the guys on team."

She snickered. "As if. But, do I pass the princess test?"

Mike raised an eyebrow. "What do you mean?"

"Come on." She shot him a cheeky smile, stepped closer to him, put her hands on his hips, and kissed his sweaty cheek. "It's pretty clear that you bought me up her to test my mettle. You're not looking for another princess, are you?"

"Not a chance." He covered her lips with his.

"You guys are making me sick."

This time it was Rick's voice that startled him, transmitting through the tiny radio lodged in his ear.

Mike made a point of prolonging the kiss for the observer's sake. When they finally broke, he scanned the terrain around them with a critical eye.

"What are you looking for?" asked Ali.

"Squirrels, sneaky squirrels."

Rick chuckled in his ear and whispered. "That's sneaky, secret, squirrel to you Romeo. And don't bother looking you ain't gonna find me, bro. I'm like a ghost."

"We need somewhere to set up our picnic and wait for sunset." He pointed to a rocky outcrop with a flat patch of sand in front of it. "How about over there?"

Mike hadn't had time to inspect the pack TJ had given him that morning. The Chief had assured him it contained everything he needed for a romantic hike. He took out a blanket and a cooler bag filled with a selection of cold meats, biscuits, fruits and cheeses.

As he offered her a cracker with a slice of cheddar, she whistled. "Wow, I'm impressed, sailor."

"So am I," he mumbled.

"OK Romeo, time to initiate phase two of the operation," said Rick in his ear. "I need you to excuse yourself for a trip to the little boy's room and head twenty yards down the hill, due east."

"Fine," he mouthed.

Ali was gazing at the horizon as she ate.

"Hey, babe, I've got to duck off to the little boy's room."

"You mean the little boy's boulder."

"Right," he said with a chuckle. Circling the outcrop, he started off into the scrub. After what he estimated was twenty yards, he stopped. "I'm here. Where are you?"

He nearly leaped out of his skin when a bush in front of him materialized into a figure. It was Rick, dressed in a shaggy sniper suit.

He grinned, revealing brilliant white teeth through the camouflage. "Hey, bro."

Mike shook his head. "Seriously, you guys are children."

"I know, isn't it awesome." A packet of *Starburst* appeared from under his camouflage and he offered one to Mike.

After the uphill climb, sugar was exactly what he needed. He took the candy, unwrapped it and chewed. "So, what the hell's TJ got planned now? I think Ali's proven she's no princess."

"Eh, so she climbed a hill. Let's see how she goes with sleeping rough on a mountain."

"Why in god's name would she do that?"

"Because you're going to feign an illness."

Mike shook his head. "She's a vet bud, which is a type of doctor. She'll see right through it."

"Not when you've got real symptoms."

He frowned. "Rick, what do you mean by symptoms?"

"You know, fever, stomach cramps, dizziness."

"And why would I have them?"

Rick grinned sheepishly. "Don't blame me, this one's on TJ."

Mike glanced at the *Starburst* wrapper he was rolling between his fingers. His stomach gurgled. Suddenly he didn't feel well. "You sneaky motherfucker."

"Bro, it's for your own good."

"You're a dead man."

"Hey, at least this way you don't have to pretend, because pretending is lying, Mike. And that's bad."

"Mike, are you alright?" Ali called out from behind him.

He turned to see where she was. When he looked back, Rick was gone. "You guys have taken this too far."

"Don't worry. We'll be here watching over you like guardian angels, *essé*," transmitted Ernie, confirming that he was also part of the conspiracy.

"Hell's Angels more like it." As Mike ascended the slope he spotted Ali standing near the peak wearing a concerned expression.

"There you are."

As he got closer she frowned. "Mike, are you OK?"

His vision went blurry. He collapsed to his knees "No, I'm not feeling–" Projectile vomit spewed into the sand and he slumped to all fours. "Screw you, Rick."

***

The next half hour was a blur of throwing up and shivering as Rick's concoction played havoc with his intestines. Thankfully, Ali wasn't put off and helped him back to their picnic site where she propped him up against a rocky outcrop. She never left his side as she tried to get him to keep down water. After half an hour he was feeling slightly better but still couldn't stand. He wanted to curl into a ball and die.

"Mike, did you eat anything dubious in the last twenty-four hours?"

"Define dubious," he croaked.

"Seafood, dairy or chicken?"

"Um, all three." He managed to sit up and drink some of the water she offered him.

Ali found a medical kit in the backpack and handed him two aspirin. "This will help with your fever."

He took the pills before checking his watch. "It's getting late. I don't think I'm going to be able to get off the mountain before dark."

Ali wore a concerned expression as she glanced up from her phone. "Mike, I don't have any cell coverage. Do you?"

He managed to hand her his phone without vomiting.

She checked. "No bars. Do you want me to run down now and get help?"

He shook his head. "No. The path is treacherous and it'll be dark before you get halfway. Plus, I'm terrified of the dark, so there's no way you're leaving me here by myself."

Ali laughed. "Come on warrior, you're not afraid of coyotes and wolves are you?"

His eyes went wide. "You're shitting me. There are wolves out here?"

"Of course. I get at least one dog a week that's been badly mauled." She rose and started collecting dried branches from the surrounding bushes. "We'll make a fire. It'll keep them away."

He struggled to get to his feet and help. Another bout of dizziness and vomiting hit him.

"Hey, you need to rest up. If we have to spend the night here, that's fine. The temperature won't drop very far this time of year. Plus we've got a space blanket and plenty of water." Ali made a fist-sized pile of dried grass and placed the sticks she had collected next to it. "Do you have a lighter?"

Mike shook his head and groaned. "Is there one in the pack?"

"No."

He watched her open the medical kit and inspect the containers inside. "We do have potassium permanganate though." She continued rummaging through the kit. "If there's something with glycerin in it, we might be in business. Ah, huh. Jackpot!" She held up a bottle of hand sanitizer.

"What are you going to do with that?"

"Watch and learn." She opened a dressing and placed it on the ground. Then she tipped some of the potassium on it as well as a squirt of hand cleaner. Using a twig, she blended the two compounds. The mixture erupted into flame and she added kindling to it. In no time she had a small fire burning.

"Where did you learn that?"

"I went through a survival show phase. It was a bit of an addiction."

Mike's laugh turned to retching. "Seriously, I'm impressed, and a little bit emasculated."

"Hey, you rest up. When you're feeling better we'll walk out." She wandered a few yards from the fire to collect more branches. "Oh and who's Rick?" she asked over her shoulder. "When you were sick you kept abusing some guy called Rick."

"He's a buddy of mine. I'm pretty sure it's his cooking that did this to me."

"So we've got Rick to blame for a night out under the stars with you and the contents of your stomach."

"It would seem that way."

As the sun dipped below the horizon, Ali snuggled in next to him with the space blanket wrapped around their shoulders. With their little fire crackling in the cool evening air, they were actually very comfortable.

"It's so pretty out here," said Ali as the first stars appeared in the sky. "I don't think you should be so harsh on Rick."

"Yeah, we'll see about that." Mike slipped his arm around her back as he scanned the mountain landscape for any sign of his team-mates. "You're all in the shit," he mouthed.

"You're welcome," responded Rick from the darkness.

Mike subtly pried the device from his ear and buried it in the sand under him.

"You OK?"

"Yeah, I had a bug in my ear."

"You're not having a great time up here, are you tiger?" She passed him a bottle of water.

He rinsed his mouth. "It's not that bad. I've got you here with me."

She patted his cheek. "You're so sweet when you're not puking all over the place."

"Oh, you had to bring that up."

Ali laughed. "I see what you did there.

"I'm sorry, it just came out."

She snorted. "Right, no more. Topic change, how many kids do you want?"

"Wow, trap a man on a mountain and hit him with the big ones."

"That's right, handsome. You're a captive audience."

"Well, I definitely want kids. But not while I'm still in the SEALs. I'm not missing out on them growing up, like my dad did."

"You said he was Navy?"

"Yeah, I didn't get to see much of him." Mike took another sip of water. "Don't get me wrong, he was a great father, when he was around."

"Is he still alive?"

"No, cancer got him." He handed the bottle to her. "What about you? Want kids?"

"Three, a boy and two girls."

"You've got all this worked out, haven't you?"

"It's a girl thing."

They sat silently gazing out over the mountains. The stars shone brightly in a cloudless sky, the lights of Tijuana sparkling along the coast.

"You sure you didn't plan this?" she asked, snuggling into him.

He was thankful the darkness hid his face. "No, why would you ask that?"

"Because this is about as romantic as it gets."

Chapter Twelve

The squad was already assembled in the briefing room when Mike finally arrived at work. In the corner of the room, stood a whiteboard with his name on one side and Ali's on the other. Under her name they'd written a list of attributes: flexible, endurance, problem solving, nurturing, not a princess.

Under his name they'd written a single phrase: pukey whiner.

Rick was the first to spot him. "Morning, Bear Grylls, how'd you sleep?"

His lip lifted in a snarl. "You know exactly how I slept, douche bag."

Ernie snickered. "Looked pretty cozy, all snuggled up with your princess charming."

"Yeah, she rode in on her big white horse and saved your ass," added Rick.

"You guys are bastards. I'm going to pay you back for this, and when I do–"

"Hey, Romeo," interrupted TJ. "There's no harm done. In fact, not only have we tested the mettle of your future wife, but we also brought you two closer. The crucible of adversity has forged a bond between you that will not easily be broken. What more could you want?"

Mike, Rick and Ernie all stared at the craggy Chief in silence.

"What the fuck, TJ. Have you been reading some Tony Robins shit or something?" asked Rick.

Mike sighed. "As much as I hate to say it, he's right. Last night Ali really came through for me."

"Steady on, brother. She's through the first gateway, but we're a long way from bashing a trident on her chest," said TJ.

Mike slumped into a chair. "What's next then?"

"A subject close to my heart," said Rick.

"Let me guess; some kind of gold digger test?"

"Correct."

TJ flipped over the whiteboard to reveal a detailed list of actions and reactions. "Listen up, whelps, this is how it's going down."

Mike held up his hand. "Stop. Can I please have one night off to take her out for dinner? You put her through hell, and she deserves a break."

"You sure she's the one who needs a break?" asked Rick.

Mike glared at him.

TJ turned to Ernie, who nodded. "OK, tonight the GSC is on hold. But the day after, we're back on schedule."

Mike nodded. Small wins were all that he was going to get at this stage.

"Where you going to take her?" asked TJ.

He shrugged. "I haven't thought that far ahead."

The Chief fixed him with a stare. "You like this girl, right?"

"Um, yeah."

"OK, an old buddy of mine owns a pretty good restaurant over in Little Italy. It's called Just 'n' Thyme. I'll give him a call and get you a table. He's also got shares in the Old Ken cinema. Take the girl to see something nice."

Mike was a little taken back. TJ had just dropped the name of one of the most exclusive restaurants in the city. He knew that because Stacey had wanted to go, but they'd been booked solid for six weeks. "Thanks, TJ."

"No problems." The veteran SEAL cracked his knuckles. "OK, so back to the plan. Mike, tomorrow night you're going to cook for her, and then take the following day off."

Mike's eyes narrowed. "There has to be a catch."

TJ grinned. "It's a selection course. Hell yeah, there's a catch."

***

As TJ briefed the squad on the next phase of the Girlfriend Selection Course the subject of their planning was chatting with her sister in the veterinary clinic's waiting room.

Leonie handed over a large coffee. "So, what the hell happened last night?"

"You're an angel." Ali took a sip. "Where do I start?

"At the beginning." Leonie took a seat.

"So, Mike took me on a hike up Mount Otay."

Her sister grimaced. "Really, that sounds about as romantic as dinner with Donald Trump."

"No. Actually, it was amazing. He packed a lovely picnic. The view was beautiful."

Leonie's eyebrows rose. "And let me guess, you stayed on the mountain all night making love under the stars."

"Not exactly."

"Oh god, what happened?"

She sighed. "Mike got hit with a bad bout of food poisoning. He was vomiting and dizzy, the works. We had to spend the night out in the wilderness."

"What a nightmare."

"Not at all, it was kind of nice. I lit a fire and we talked until he fell asleep. By morning everything was fine."

"So, you nursed him all night. What can I say. Honey, you're a sucker for a wounded critter."

"I got the feeling that the whole climbing the mountain thing was a bit of a test."

Her sister grinned. "And you passed it with flying colors. So what's next? When are you going to see this super stud again?"

"Well..." Her eyes sparkled. "Tonight, he's taking me out to apologize for the mountain fiasco."

"Oooh, where you going?"

"Just 'n' Thyme."

"Get out of town. How'd he get a booking at such short notice?"

She shrugged. "I have no idea. Then we're going to a rom-com at the Ken Cinema."

"Girl, this boy is pulling out all the stops. You're going to get yourself some sweet loving tonight, and I want all the juicy details."

"You're incorrigible." She took another sip of the coffee. "Now, what's going on with you? How did the girl's camp go?"

Leonie groaned. "Let's not talk about that. Tell me all the details of this new man. I bet he's got a massive…" She wiggled her finger suggestively.

Ali snorted into her coffee, dribbling it down the front of her scrubs. "Leonie, I haven't slept with him."

"Yeah, but I bet you've felt it through his jeans all thick and throbbing."

"Leonie, we're not having this conversation."

"Oh, we just did baby. That one's going straight in the double click bin."

"The what?"

"You know. The place I store mental images for when I double click the mouse."

She raised her hand. "Enough. I love you sis but that's too much information."

"Not at all. By the way, I'll be here tomorrow for all the juicy details."

"I won't be here. I'm taking the day off and, Mike is too."

"Ooh, a lazy day of sex… that's even better."

Standing she kissed her sister on the cheek. "Get the hell out of here. I've got work to do."

"Is that how you order your SEAL around?"

"Out!"

"Fine, I'm going. But tomorrow, I want all the details."

Chapter Thirteen

Mike wrapped his arm around Ali's shoulders as they left the Ken Cinema and walked the dark streets of the city. Despite the late hour she felt safe nestled against her SEAL. "What did you think of the movie?"

She felt him shrug.

"Ah… It was good."

"The truth please."

He chuckled. "OK, I thought it was a little cheesy."

Ali laughed. "It's a rom-com. What did you expect from Sandra Bullock and Ryan Reynolds? It's meant to be cheesy. That's the point."

Mike dropped his hand to her waist. "I have to admit, I've always liked Sandra Bullock."

She smiled. "Oh, really. Here's me thinking you're more of a Reece Witherspoon kind of guy."

"No way, Bullock is sassy and seriously sexy. I've seen everything she's in."

"Me too. Which one's your favorite?"

"You mean, apart from the Proposal?" He winked. "I loved her in Miss Congeniality."

"You're kidding?"

"Nope, I really like that movie."

She snuggled in against his arm. "Me too. I must have watched it at least fifty times."

"Let's dig it out on a rainy day," said Mike as they turned into a park and walked along a gravel path. "Although I'm not watching the sequel, it was crap."

"Yes it was."

"Ali, I hope tonight's made up for the debacle on the mountain."

"Are you kidding? It's been perfect. I've never had the chef hand deliver his signature dish before."

"And I'm sure he's never had someone ask to take the bones home in a doggy bag."

She shot him a frown. "I bet he's never met a dog like Axe either."

Stopping, he stepped in front of her, ducked his head and kissed her. "And that's why Axe… loves you."

"Just Axe?" she murmured.

As he kissed her again he expected to feel panic at her words… but he didn't. He'd never been with a woman who made him feel so elated yet at the same time content. It was the piece that had been missing in all his relationships. "He's had more time with you."

She smiled. "This is true."

As they continued along the path Mike reflected on the date. TJ's contact had pulled out all the stops for them. If he didn't know better he'd suspect that the Chief was setting him up for some kind of test.

Pausing, Mike scanned the park ahead of them. His eyes darted across the dim landscape. He could see a jogger in the distance and someone walking a dog. Nothing that suggested trouble, and yet he couldn't shrug off the feeling that something wasn't quite right.

"You OK?"

His eyes snapped back to her. "Hey, yeah I'm good." Almost instantly the feeling of uneasiness was replaced with something else. Exhaling softly, he took a moment to appreciate her beauty. Her eyes shone in the soft glow cast from the park's lights. Tipping his head, he pressed his lips against hers and wrapped his arms around her waist. She responded eagerly and seconds turned into minutes as they embraced.

"Hey, pal."

The voice was slurred.

Mike spun toward the figure approaching them and stepped protectively in front of Ali. "How can I help you?"

"You can give me your wallet, asshole," the man hissed, pulling a knife from under his grubby jacket.

Ali gasped.

Mike quickly assessed their assailant. His hair and beard were matted, his eyes bloodshot. The stench of body odor filled the air as he approached. When he wasn't talking his jaw was clenched and grinding. "Let's not do anything stupid."

"Listen, punk," the mugger slurred.

Mike sprung into action. One hand clamped down on the wrist of the knife hand, the other further up the arm. Wrenching the man's wrist backward he forced him to his knees. The knife clattered on the sidewalk and he kicked it clear.

"Stop, it hurts," he wailed as Mike forced him onto his stomach and locked his arm behind him. Only then did he check on Ali. "You OK?"

She stared at him with wide eyes. "Yeah, yeah I'm fine."

"Can you call 9-1-1?"

She fumbled with her purse. "Of course."

A patrol car responded in a matter of minutes and in no time the perp was cuffed and detained inside. Mike gave the officer a statement before they continued their walk.

"I'm really sorry you had to see that," said Mike softly.

Ali stopped, grabbed his face and kissed him. "You're amazing. I feel so safe when I'm with you and now I know why."

They broke and he smiled. "No, you're amazing and I've got a dog that can walk now to prove it."

"Shall we go see him?"

"It's your night, babe. I thought you might like to grab some gelato for dessert."

Her teeth flashed, a cheeky grin. "I've got some in my freezer."

"Sounds good."

Mike glanced over his shoulder as they left the park. He couldn't shake the feeling they were still in danger.

***

Ali lived in a quiet, semi-rural suburb on the outskirts of San Diego. It was a short drive from the clinic where they'd stopped to feed Axe the remains of Ali's T-bone. Then, bidding goodnight to the dog, they had driven to her townhouse.

As Mike killed the engine, she faced him smiling. "Thanks for a wonderful evening."

"An absolute pleasure." He leaned across and planted a long kiss on her. Lifting his head, he said, "Let me get your door."

As he made his way around to her side of the truck, Ali smiled to herself. Say what you would about military guys, but they were gentlemen. Or at least Mike was. One look at her tight dress and heels and he had taken it upon himself to lift her in and out of the truck. That was fine with her. His hands on her waist and the scent of his cologne sent her heart racing, every time.

A moment later he opened the door. "Here you are, little lady."

She stepped onto the running board and kissed him again as he wrapped his hands around her waist. He was hard against her as they pashed. Leonie was right, she could feel how large he was.

"I think we should take this inside," she managed between bouts of passion.

He cupped her buttocks. "You sure?"

"Yes, I'm sure." She moaned as he lifted her out of the truck. Pushing the cab door closed he carried her across the lawn to the porch. Somehow, between kisses, she found her keys and he unlocked the front door. "Where to?"

"Second room on the right."

He swept down the hall into the master bedroom. As he lowered her gently onto the bed he kicked off his loafers. In the soft light from the street lamps outside her window she caught his cheeky smile.

"What?"

"Damn you're sexy."

She moaned as he lowered himself on to her, his lips traced her ear lobe and she shuddered with delight. All thoughts of playing hard to get were out the window as she unbuttoned his shirt.

"So, we're not going to take this slow?"

"Are you kidding me?" Her voice was husky. "I've wanted your hands on me all night."

"I've made a good impression then?"

She managed to completely undo his shirt exposing his chiseled abdomen. "You could say that."

Mike slid his hand under her dress and ran it up her leg to her waist as he kissed her. His touch was electric. She arched her back as his hand slid to her inner thigh.

"I want you now," she gasped as he redirected his attention back to the lobe of her ear.

"I've wanted you since we first kissed."

His warm breath sent her into overdrive. "Not before then?"

"OK, maybe when you hit that first bullseye." He bunched her dress up on both sides of her hips and slid it over her head. Kissing her neck, he unsnapped her bra and freed her breasts.

She bit her lip as his mouth found her nipple and he took it gently between his teeth. His hands roamed her body, stoking the fire that burned inside. "Promise me I'm not just another notch on your belt," she said as he kissed her neck.

He paused. "I like you, Ali, I like you a lot."

Her full lips formed a smile. "Then why are your clothes still on?"

Mike slid off the bed and out of his pants in one smooth maneuver. Noticing that the curtains were open he reached across to close them. Glancing out the window he spotted a white sedan parked across the street.

Ali let out a sigh. "Are you teasing me on purpose or just giving my neighbors something to look at?"

Mike pushed the car from his mind as he turned. Laughing, he climbed onto the bed and lowered himself on top of her.

She gazed up at him with lustful eyes. "I hope you weren't planning on sleeping tonight."

Chapter Fourteen

Mike slipped through the door to the briefing room. The unit's intelligence officer had already begun his presentation to the platoon. Ducking into the back row he took a seat next to Rick.

"Where you been?" whispered Rick. "TJ ain't happy you weren't in for the run this morning."

"I slept in. What have I missed?"

Rick's brow shot up. "You slept in?"

"Yeah."

Grinning, Rick lifted his hand. "High-five, brother."

Mike left him hanging. "Anything new on the Butcher?"

"Nope. He's gone to ground."

"Damn."

At the front of the room the intelligence officer paused and advanced his slides. "That concludes the latest target updates. What I'm going on with now is the assessment from Homeland Security."

"This ought to be good," mumbled Rick.

Among the SEALs, Homeland Security had a reputation for releasing alarmist reporting that they usually ignored.

"The latest assessment indicates that, due to recent successes against the Mexican cartels, there may be an increased threat to military personnel in the San Diego area. Although the Butcher has gone to ground, Homeland thinks he might be looking to conduct a revenge attack stateside. Team Five has been identified as a potential target."

One of the SEALs thrust his hand in the air. "Hey, sir."

"What's up, Dean?"

"If Barbosa wants revenge won't that make him easier to target. I mean he's got to coordinate that shit, right?"

"True, but it also means we need to be vigilant. Guys, you need to report any suspect behavior. When off base make sure you maintain a low profile. That means no military style training shirts, no Oakleys and no cargo pants. Remind your wives that dressing kids in cammo or SEAL branding is a bad idea."

Rick lifted his hand. "What about Team Five limited edition assless chaps. Is Mike still allowed to wear them?"

The officer chuckled. "Rick, what you and Mike wear in the Blue Oyster is completely up to you. OK, if there's no other questions, we're done here."

As the SEAL operators filed out of the room TJ rose and made eye contact with each of the squad. "Alpha, we're staying." He waited till they were alone. "Mike, good of you to join us."

Rick slapped Mike on the shoulder. "He slept in."

He shook his head. "Thanks, bud."

"Well, I hope you're all rested up because we're moving into the final phase of the selection course."

Mike sighed. "Come on guys, Ali–"

"Still hasn't passed," shot Rick. "Bro, you made a promise. You gonna break a promise to your team-mates?"

He shook his head.

TJ fixed him with a steely gaze. "Good, because tonight is stir-Friday."

"Except it's Thursday, *essé*," corrected Ernie.

"Yeah, it's a joke," said TJ.

Ernie snorted. "Not funny, you shouldn't tell jokes, Chief."

"You know what is funny?" TJ said. "Beach running in waterlogged dive masks."

"OK, I take it back. It's funny."

"I thought as much. Alright, tonight Mike is going to cook for the lady."

"Yeah, we went through it yesterday, I've got it," said Mike. "I make the pasta and you guys run the mission. Look, this might be nothing but I keep seeing the same white sedan around town."

TJ frowned. "You think it might be related to the Homeland assessment?"

Mike shrugged. "It could be nothing."

"It could be something, you get plates?"

"Negative, there wasn't one on the back. I haven't seen it from the front."

"Well, let's keep an eye out and if it turns up again we'll check it out."

***

Later that evening, only a few miles from Coronado, Ali arrived at Mike's fifth floor apartment. He gave her a quick tour, before returning to the preparation of their dinner. It was pretty much exactly as Ali expected a military guy's place to look. Sleek, clean and with the exception of a few photos, completely devoid of personal effects. With a glass of wine in hand, she checked out the balcony and the view. Even at night it was spectacular. She could see all the way out across the parklands to the USS Midway museum.

"Great place and a killer view," she said, reentering the apartment.

Mike turned from the stove. "Thanks, I don't get to spend as much time here as I'd like. Although, I'm thinking I'll have to move. Once Axe is better he's going to need a yard."

Leaning against the bench top she watched him chop fresh parsley. "They won't let him go back to work?"

The knife paused, mid-slice. "Do you think he'll be physically able?"

"In time, yes. He's made great progress in the last week."

"That would be awesome. However, I'd need the Army vet to retract his original assessment."

"I could definitely help with that. I can be very persuasive when I need to be."

Mike rinsed his hands in the sink and dried them on his apron before leaning across the counter and kissing her. "Don't I know it."

"So what exactly are you cooking?" she asked as he returned to preparing food.

He dipped a wooden spoon into the pot and tasted the contents. It's an Italian dish that my mom taught me to make. I hope you like pasta."

"Love it." She watched him open the oven, letting steam escape into the room. The rich smells of chocolate and whiskey flooded her nostrils. "Oh, my god, what is that smell?"

"That's the *piece de resistance*. My mom's Mississippi mud cake. It's a secret family recipe." Taking a baking tin from the oven he placed it on the bench top and draped it with a clean dishcloth. "Now, all that's left is to cook the pasta and we're in business. I hope you're hungry."

Ali slid around the granite island and stood behind him as he reached into an overhead cupboard. "Yeah, about that." She kissed the back of his neck and slipped her hands around to his hard stomach. "I was kind of hoping we could take a few minutes to work up an appetite."

Mike abandoned his search for the pasta. Turning his head, he muttered against her lips, "That sounds like a good idea."

As she pressed her breasts against his back, her fingers slid beneath the waistband of his jeans. "I thought you might like it."

He moaned as he tensed against her. Then, turning, he scooped her off the ground so she was straddling him. They kissed as he sat her on the bench and she wrapped her legs around him. "You have all the best ideas," he managed, sliding off her T-shirt.

Her jeans followed a moment later, tossed into the corner of the kitchen.

"You better turn off that sauce or it's going to burn," panted Ali.

He reached out and flicked the cooktop off. "We can always eat cake."

"Sex and cake? You're possibly the sexiest man I've ever met." She ripped off his shirt as he dropped his pants.

"Yeah, well I'm not letting you leave. For the next twenty-four hours you're mine."

***

Ali relaxed in a deck chair on Mike's balcony, enjoying her coffee and a bowl of cereal. She and Mike had spent the morning in bed. He'd made breakfast, then dashed out for a run while she took the opportunity to check her emails and grab some sun.

A thump on the door startled her. She shrugged a bathrobe on over her underwear and walked across the apartment. "Who is it?"

"Delivery for a Michael Saunders."

She opened the door, but left the security chain in place.

The man on the other side stuffed a letter through the gap. "Where's Mister Saunders?" he demanded.

Ali could see the guy was big and middle aged. She put him in his late forties, possibly fifties. He had gray hair, a weathered face and intense gray eyes.

"Can I take a message?"

"So he lives here. Good. Give him this letter and tell him this is a courtesy call. If he doesn't pay up, we're going to take his truck."

She took the letter.

"You understand?"

"Yes." She closed the door and slid the bolt shut. Examining the letter, she walked across to the bench where she had previously spotted a pile of mail. As she added the envelope to the heap she noticed that most of the open documents in the pile were overdue bills. It looked as if Mike was in financial trouble.

She returned to the balcony and was about to sit when there was another knock at the door. "Are you serious?" she murmured.

"Mike, Mike, I know you're in there!" a female's high-pitched voice yelled.

Ali frowned. Who was this woman and what the hell was she doing at Mike's door at eleven o'clock on a Wednesday morning?

"Mike, you can change your number but I know you haven't moved!" she screamed. "Baby, come on, let me in. I know you're there. I know we can work this out."

Ali padded quietly across to the door and looked through the security peephole. The woman outside was pretty, very pretty in fact. Her hair was honey blonde and her lips a slash of bright red lipstick. Vision through the hole was limited, but she could make out a black singlet and what she hoped were fake boobs. Mike wasn't kidding when he said Ali wasn't like any of his ex's.

"I bet you didn't make it up Mount Otay, did you sweetheart?" she whispered.

"Fine, you know what, fuck you, Mike. I was the best thing that ever happened to you and you completely screwed it. You chose that stupid dog over me. Now you can sleep alone at night."

Ali tried not to laugh as the woman stomped off in her high heels. "So that's the infamous Stacey." Mike had told her about the ex and what had happened after Axe had been shot. One thing was for sure; Ali would never make him choose between her and the dog. Axe had saved Mike's life. For that reason alone she would never begrudge his feelings for the dog. However, the whole issue with his finances was something that concerned her.

She pondered the issue for half an hour before the sound of a key in the lock signaled his return.

Shirtless and coated with sweat, he bent and kissed her. "Hey, you."

Ali exhaled as she drank in his lean muscular frame.

"I'm going to grab a shower. You want in?" he asked dropping his shorts and standing naked in the living room.

She rose, letting the bathrobe slide off her body revealing her underwear. Unclipping her bra, she released her breasts and stood with her hands on her hips and watched him grow. Their talk about his finances could wait.

***

An hour later, still damp from the shower, Mike prepared a chicken salad. He served it with a slice of mud cake, drenched in cream.

"So, your ex dropped by while you were out."

He stopped slicing tomatoes and turned to her, with a scowl. "Stacey? What did she want?"

"I think she was trying to make amends. I didn't let her in. She's got quite the potty mouth."

"I'm so sorry you had to experience that."

"Kind of reflects poorly on you, Michael."

He looked up from tossing the salad. "How do you mean?"

"Well, she definitely wouldn't have made it up the mountain, so clearly you were thinking with your dick not your brain. You've got to tighten up your testing process, Mike."

He swallowed nervously as he placed bowls on the island. "Testing process. I'm not sure I know what you mean?" Head bent, he returned to the salad.

"Babe, are you OK?" she asked.

"Huh, sorry no, I'm just a little preoccupied with something."

"Do you want to talk about it?"

"No, it's nothing for you to worry about."

She sighed. "Look, Mike. You had another visitor. A debt collector who told me to give you this." She reached for the letter from the pile next to her. "He said if you don't pay they'll take your truck. If you're having financial problems, Mike, you can talk to me about it."

His jaw clenched as he read the letter. "It's nothing I can't handle. Got a little behind on a few things because I was away. I'll get them sorted this week." Scrunching the note into a ball, he tossed it in the sink.

"Alright. But if you need a hand, just let me know. I'd be happy to waive all of Axe's medical costs."

He turned to face her. "You'd do that for me?"

She nodded. "You're a good guy Mike and–"

"Go on."

"And, I more than like you."

He wiped his hands on a dishcloth. "Why haven't I ever met a woman like you before?" he asked, rounding the counter.

She arched an eyebrow and shot him a smile. "We covered that."

Mike wrapped his arms around her waist and kissed her gently. Her mouth met his eagerly and the kiss gained intensity as his hands caressed her. “You’re the most amazing woman I’ve ever met,” he whispered breathlessly.

***

Ali sat on a park bench with her sister watching her nieces playing in a sandbox. The toddlers hadn’t spotted her yet. They were completely enthralled with the plastic spades and buckets that she’d previously bought them.

Stretching her neck, Leonie enjoyed the escape. “So give me the sordid details.”

Ali shook her head. “The sex is great and that's all you're getting.”

Her sister feigned horror. “Oh, come on. You've got to give me more than that. Seriously, do you know the last time Steve and I had sex? I can't remember the last time he got up close and personal with my vagina.”

Ali grimaced. “T.M.I.”

“Come on, don’t be a bitch, Ali.”

She laughed. “Enough. Fine, all I’m going to say is that it’s the best sex I've ever had. His body, god, it's carved from granite. He seriously looks like an artist sculpted him. And yet, he's so gentle, caring and considerate. He literally satisfies my every need.”

“And his…” Leonie wiggled her finger.

She smiled. “More than adequate.”

“God, I knew it. You're such a lucky bitch. Now, whatever you do don't have kids with him. It’ll wreck everything. I’m serious. Before we had the devil spawn, we used to bang every five minutes. Steve was a demon. He took me in the kitchen, the bathroom, the laundry, it didn't matter. He just wanted me twenty-four seven–”

One of the girls screamed, interrupting her tirade. The youngest had grabbed a fist full of her sister’s hair and was yanking it.

Leonie rose from the bench. "And then, these little angels arrived."

Ali watched as her sister untangled the girls and kissed each on the cheek. She smiled to herself as she reflected on what a great father Mike would make. He was patient, kind and gentle. The way he treated Axe also proved he was compassionate. However, his underlying financial issues were concerning.

"Hey, lover girl. What's on your mind?"

"Huh, nothing."

"Come on. We don't keep secrets from each other. What's up?"

"It's Mike, he's got himself in some financial trouble. Forget to pay some bills when he was away on a mission."

"How much trouble?"

"I'm not sure. A debt collector came to his apartment this morning and told me they were going to take his truck."

"You're kidding me. Ali, that's a bit of a red flag. Surely a Navy SEAL can sort out his finances?"

"I know. The problem is I think I'm falling for him. He's so gentle and thoughtful, Leonie. He's a gentleman, an amazing lover and he even cooks. You know he disarmed a mugger the other night?"

"Oh shit, the full package."

"Yeah. But it isn't all smooth sailing. Since I started seeing him I feel like I'm constantly being challenged. First there was the mountain climb and the night of sickness and now this. It's as if the universe is conspiring against us."

"Look, Ali. If there's one piece of advice I can give you it's to follow your heart. There were plenty of things that got in the way of Steve and I. But we still made it through and now look at us. Two beautiful terrors… and no sex."

Ali wrapped her arms around her sister. "I know I don't say this enough, but I love you so much."

"Me too, bubs. I just want to see you happy. So, SEAL or no SEAL, if this guy breaks your heart I'm going to break his perfectly sculpted legs."

"Well, if it makes you feel better we're going to one of his team-mates for dinner tomorrow night and they've got two little boys. Mike says they're horrendous."

"Oh, joy. What's that? Date number five and the most romantic of all. Dinner with hyperactive midgets."

"At least, he's introducing me to his friends. That's got to be a good sign, right?"

"Definitely. Military guys take introductions to their buddies very seriously. But, if you have to drop your keys in a bowl on the way in, run like hell. But first, text me the address."

Ali punched her gently in the shoulder. "You and your one-track mind."

***

Ramirez was the only spectator at the training session. He watched as his son intercepted the soccer ball and dribbled it toward the goal. "Go Carlos!" he screamed as the boy lined up and kicked. The ball went wide, hitting the side post, and ricocheted off across the boundary.

"Good try, son," he shouted encouragingly as the boy, shoulders slumped, trotted toward him. "It is better to try and miss, than never try at all."

The boy shook his head and joined the back of the lineup as another child attempted the drill.

Ramirez's phone vibrated. He pulled it from his jacket. "Hello."

"When are you going to kill the fucking SEAL?"

He coolly held the phone away from his ear until the Butcher's tirade was finished. Then he brought it closer and spoke. "Many of the pieces are already in place. I am waiting on the last of my men to have the necessary documentation and then we will move."

"I want it done as soon as possible."

"These things are better not rushed. They require meticulous planning and rehearsals to ensure they are successful."

"Do you remember what happened to the last man who failed me?"

Ramirez paused. "I've never failed you before, why would I now? You forget who I am, Vicente Barbosa. I am the man that people go to when they want the impossible done. I am the man who can kill anyone… for the right price. I'm not a man you want to threaten."

Barbosa fell silent for a full ten seconds. "I have never given you a task more important than this. My family's honor is at stake. When you are successful, I will double your fee."

"Your kindness is appreciated. If things go according to plan, in forty-eight hours you will have your revenge."

"I want to see the pain on his face as he watches his woman die. Then, bring me his head."

"It can be arranged so you can watch."

"The Americans are trying to capture me. I cannot leave Mexico."

"You will not have to leave the safety of your home. Their deaths will be broadcast over the internet to your computer, for a nominal fee."

"Excellent, I look forward to the show."

"I will make the necessary arrangements." He terminated the call and turned his attention back to his son's soccer training.

His wife approached with a drink in each hand. "Was that work?"

"Yes."

"And?"

He turned to her, unable to hide his grim expression. "I'm sorry, but I'm afraid I can't make the game on Sunday."

She shook her head and turned away.

Ramirez fought the urge to curse. Instead he focused his attention on his phone. If he was going to be sleeping on the couch, then he may as well spend the night with his mistress.

Chapter Fifteen

Mike stood outside a three-story brick structure stenciled with the letters MOE. The Method of Entry building's many walls were adorned with every type of window or doorway that the SEALs were likely to encounter. The teams spent hours perfecting the art of bashing, chopping, cutting, and blowing their way into the building. Then, overnight, a team of maintenance staff would return it to its original condition, so they could attack it again.

TJ and the rest of the squad were in one of the explosives preparation bays, hidden behind a bank of dirt. Not wanting to talk to them, Mike had volunteered to set up the house. Seething he lifted a wooden door and made to slot it into its retaining brackets. TJ and the others had made him look like an idiot to Ali. He'd never borrowed a dime in his life, paying cash for his truck and everything in his apartment. Not to mention, Ali didn't have a gold digging bone in her body. The door failed to slide into the bracket and he gave it a solid kick.

TJ appeared holding a breaching charge attached to an extendable pole. "You all good?"

He managed to shove the door in place. "No, I'm not good." He spun and spotted Ernie and Rick joining them. "Which one of you assholes dumped the late notices at my place?" The sheepish look on Rick's face confirmed his suspicions. "I want my spare key back. None of you assholes can be trusted."

There was an awkward silence, then TJ spoke, "So, how was your day off?"

"Apart from Ali thinking I'm an idiot?" He paused. "Yeah, good I guess. I hope you enjoyed your little repo man cameo."

"I was pretty convincing, yeah. Although I'm surprised she hasn't dumped you."

"Why would she?"

Ernie laughed. "Because you're broke, holmes."

"Well I ain't saying she's a gold digga, but she ain't messing with a broke nigga," added Rick.

"Did you seriously just quote Kanye?"

Rick grinned. "You know I did, brother."

"You're enjoying this, aren't you," snapped Mike. "You're putting this woman through hell and you're enjoying it. You're all enjoying it." Their silence confirmed his assessment. "I thought as much."

All three men broke into righteous laughter.

"Come on, bud. Remember this is for your own good. And I gotta say, so far this girl is kicking selection in the butt," said Rick.

"We'll see," grumbled TJ. "Yeah, so far so good, but this next phase is the moneymaker." He held up his explosive charge. "Let's test this bang."

"Hang on, what do you mean by another phase?" Mike asked over his shoulder as he grabbed his helmet and eye protection. He joined the Chief at the door he'd installed. "She's been through enough. I think she's proven her mettle."

TJ pressed himself against the wall with the pole at arm's length, the charge resting against the door. "Not yet she hasn't. Eyes and ears, take cover!"

Mike checked his gear and tucked in behind TJ. "Ready."

Ernie and Rick did the same.

"How many more phases are there?"

TJ held up two fingers. "Fire in the hole."

A deafening explosion shook the building, covering them in dust and smoke.

"So, what are the final phases?"

"You already know the next one, *essé*," said Ernie as they inspected the door.

The charge had split it neatly in two, throwing both halves inside.

"I'd call that a clean breach," said TJ.

"I don't know what the hell you're talking about, Ernie."

"Family, bro, it's all about family."

TJ nodded. “Damn straight it is, Ernie. Behind every SEAL there should be a strong wife, capable of running the household in his absence.”

“Yeah, and you don't get a household crazier than this motherfucker’s.” Rick gestured to his offsider.

Mike shook his head. “Oh shit, you're not going to…”

Ernie slapped him on the shoulder. “Hell yeah we are, frogman. Dinner. My place. Seventeen hundred. Make sure she doesn't wear anything real nice. The boys have taken to throwing poop.”

“You're shitting me?”

“Oh, they'll shit you alright.” Rick grinned. “From head to toe.”

***

“So, you work with Ernie, right?” Ali asked, as Mike pulled his truck into the driveway of the Ernesto residence. Located a few miles from the San Diego River, the home was a large single-story, stucco hacienda painted white with a red tiled roof. The front garden was tastefully landscaped as a desert setting, complete with cacti and red boulders.

“Correct, he's in my squad. His wife, Maria, is probably the best Mexican cook in San Diego.”

“And, they’ve got two boys that are out of control?”

“Yeah, but don't mention that to Maria. She thinks they’re total angels.”

“Most mothers do.”

He knocked on the door. A moment later it opened and Ernie greeted them with a broad smile, welcoming them inside. Maria, a pint-sized brunette with a huge bosom, appeared from the kitchen and embraced him in a bear hug. “Mike, how's that beautiful dog of yours doing?”

“Great, thanks to the skills of this amazing woman. Maria, this is Alison.”

“Oh, the new girl. Ernie has told me a lot about you. So you're the one who's finally managed to rope my adopted son?”

Mike shot Ernie a questioning look.

"She doesn't know," he mouthed back.

"I don't know about roping him." Ali laughed.

"Well, you're the only one he's ever brought around here, so that makes you pretty special. Now, excuse me, I've got to finish preparing dinner. Ernie, get them a drink and take Ali out back to meet the boys."

"Yes, Maria."

A moment later, with ice-cold *Pacificos* in hand, they walked outside onto a wide deck overlooking a beautiful garden.

"Looking good, brother," said Mike as he surveyed the lush green lawn.

"Thanks, finally got it finished last week."

Ali spotted the boys playing in the sandbox under their stilted cubby house. A few feet away, on the grass, a Border Collie watched them intently.

"James, Ryan, come and say hello to our guests," called Ernie.

The two boys crawled out of the sandbox and trundled across the grass toward them. Dressed in matching sets of coveralls, Ali put their age at around four and five. They were adorable and resembled their parents, with dark hair, brown eyes and olive skin.

"Hey, guys," said Mike as they ran toward him and latched on to his legs.

"Mike, where's Axe?" one of the boys asked.

"He's not feeling great at the moment, Ryan. When he's better I'll bring him around."

"Who's that?" asked the younger of the two, James. He hid behind Mike's legs, peeking around at Ali.

"Oh my god, they're so cute," she said.

"This is Doctor Ali, she's helping Axe to get better," said Mike.

"Is that your girlfriend?" asked Ryan. "Mom says you can't find a good girlfriend."

Mike reached down, grabbed him by the coveralls and tossed him over his shoulder. "Is that right? Well your mom wouldn't know, because she's too busy bossing your dad around." The boy squealed with delight.

"Michael Saunders, I heard that." Maria was standing in the doorway to the living area with her hands on her hips.

"You're in trouble," sang James as he clapped.

Mike lowered Ryan to the ground and grinned sheepishly. "Every man wants a strong woman, Maria."

"Dinner is served," she growled.

"Dad loves it when Mike comes around," said Ryan as they walked inside.

"Why is that?" asked Ali.

"Because he never gets in trouble when Mike's here."

"Is that right?" She glanced at Mike and he shrugged.

As Ali entered the dining room, she gasped. Maria had prepared a veritable smorgasbord of Mexican cuisine. There were tortas, tamale, tacos, quesadillas, pambazos and a range of other dishes that Ali couldn't identify, but that looked and smelled amazing. Triggered by the colors and the aromas her stomach announced itself, loudly.

Maria pushed a full plate in front of her. "Mike, get some food in the woman before she starves."

For the next half hour Ali ate her fill of the amazing cuisine as she was bombarded with questions from Maria and the two boys.

"It's rude not to eat it all," whispered Mike as Maria ladled another serving of tamale onto her plate.

"Please Maria, your food is amazing but if I eat anymore, I'll burst."

"Nonsense, a skinny little thing like you should eat much more."

Thankfully, the ring of Maria's cell phone ended the ladling of food. She excused herself and moved into the kitchen to answer it.

Ali spooned some of the food onto Mike's plate. " You've got to help me with this."

"Nooo, I can't eat anymore."

Maria reappeared, shaking her head. "Mike and Ali, I'm so sorry to do this but I've got to duck away and help out a friend."

Ernie rose from the table. "Is everything OK?"

"One of the girls is having a bit of a cooking crisis. Tomorrow she has a school baking day. I shouldn't be very long. Will you be fine with the boys?"

"Not a problem," said Ernie.

"Will you two still be here when I get back?"

Mike grinned. "If you promise to bring back some of whatever you're baking."

"Of course, darling. Ali, make sure you've got room for dessert."

Ali managed a sickly grin as Maria left.

Once she was gone Ernie gestured outside. "Well, I think we should head back out to the deck and catch the last of the sun."

"Do you want us to help clean up?" Ali asked as they rose from the table.

"No, we'll sort that later."

A moment later they were sitting in deck chairs drinking beers while the boys played in their sandbox.

"This is the life," said Mike as he relaxed. "Not a care in the world." As he spoke his and Ernie's phones started buzzing. He pulled it from his pocket and checked it. "You've got to be shitting me."

"What is it?" asked Ali.

"We've been recalled," said Ernie.

"Recalled for what?" she asked.

"Not sure." Mike placed his beer on a side table and rose. "We've got to report to the base. Ernie, do you need a lift?"

"I can't leave the boys."

"Yeah right, I forgot."

Ali stood and joined them. "I can watch them till Maria gets back. She said she wasn't going to be long. Then I can get a cab home."

Mike frowned. "You sure you're OK with that?"

"Yeah, I look after my nieces all the time."

"These two can be a bit of a handful."

"Oh please, they're four. What could they possibly get up to?"

He shook his head. "Don't ask."

***

As Mike backed his truck out of the driveway he shot Ernie a glare. “This is the test, isn't it? You're going to see how she fares with the boys.” He dropped the truck into drive and took off toward the base.

“If she can manage those two after the amount of sugar they've had, she can handle anything.”

“Sugar? Did Maria agree to this?”

“In theory.”

“So, you told her about the Girlfriend Selection Course.”

“Not exactly. In fact it was TJ who convinced her it was a good idea.” He gestured to the side of the road. “Pull in here.”

Mike brought the pickup to a halt behind a gray van and they got out. He followed Ernie who opened the side door revealing Rick in a camping chair, eating popcorn. “Hey boys, you got here just in time for the show.”

The inside of the van was lined with monitors and there was a bench with a row of laptops. He recognized it as a surveillance setup. “Where the hell did you get this?”

“TJ borrowed it from a buddy with the Feds.” Rick directed Mike to a chair. “Ernie and I spent the afternoon wiring the house for sight and sound.”

Mike sat and watched the screens. Sure enough, they showed images from a half dozen cameras around the Ernesto residence.

“Your girl's got her hands full.” Rick pointed at one of the screens.

The boys had abandoned their play in the sandbox and were now pursuing separate activities. Ryan was in the kitchen with the dog and James was on the dining room table pushing leftovers around with a toy bulldozer. Ali was frantically attempting to talk him down, while at the same time catching plates as they spilled off the end of the table.

“Damn, Ryan’s a straight up mountain goat,” said Rick. In the kitchen, the four year old had pulled out drawers and was using them to climb up onto the counter.

"Maria's going to kill you, and Ali's going to help her hide the bodies. Things are getting a little out of control," said Mike.

"This is nothing," said Ernie as Ali grabbed James off the dining room table, tucked him under one arm and searched for Ryan.

"All things considered, she's not doing too bad," added Rick. "I mean, they haven't started throwing poop yet."

Mike pointed at one of the screens. "What the hell is Ryan doing?"

The preschooler was sitting on the counter with his back to the camera and was concentrating on something in front of him. Suddenly, a flame shot into the air above his head and he dropped a lit cooking blowtorch onto the floor.

Mike jumped from his chair. "Are you shitting me? I'm going back in there."

"Ernie, I think your dog's on fire."

Mike turned back to the screen and watched in horror as the Collie's coat ignited.

Suddenly, Ali appeared and extinguished the dog with a wet dishcloth. She recovered the burning torch, turned it off, and grabbed Ryan off the counter, in the space of a few seconds.

"She's fast, but not fast enough."

On another screen, James had climbed back onto the dining room table and was sliding through the remnants of dinner.

Ernie laughed. "Maria is so looking forward to them being big enough to help around the house. Something tells me this is not what she had in mind."

"Guys, seriously. This isn't funny. One of the boys could get badly injured."

"You kidding me? They're indestructible, *essé*. They'll burn the house down before they get hurt."

"And that doesn't bother you?"

"Ali's got it in hand, bud," said Rick. "See, she's got the boys under control… sort of."

She had the two boys outside now and they were running around on the lawn chasing the dog with a hose.

"Mike's right, Ernie. Maria's gonna kill you."

"Like hell. She said this was a good idea. I quote, 'I don't want Mike dating anymore of those vacuous, narcissistic, princess bitches." He imitated Maria's high-pitched voice perfectly.

"She said that, she actually said that?" asked Mike.

"Hey, you can't argue, it's true, buddy. That Stacey chick was hot as hell but damn, she was a selfish bitch," said Rick.

"Rick's right, *essé*. You've picked some *loco* women."

"Thanks guys, we've been over this, remember."

"The good news is this one's a bit of a kid whisperer." Rick pointed up at the screen where Ali had the boys sitting on the grass. She'd found a book and was reading them a story.

"That's impossible," said Ernie. "I jacked them up on so much candy they should be bouncing off the walls. Now they're eating out of her hand. Mike, don't let this one go. She is a goddess."

He managed a smile. "It would seem so. Well, I guess she passes this phase. Only one to go."

Rick shook his head. "TJ isn't gonna believe this."

"You know, if we head back now we might be able to clean the place up before Maria gets home," said Mike.

Ernie jumped out of his chair. "Good idea, you know what they say. 'A Happy wife, a happy life'."

Rick stuffed another fistful of popcorn into his mouth. "Nah, 'no wife, happy life'. You cats have fun, I'll see you at the beachfront tomorrow for training."

"You're such a dick, Rick."

"That's what she said."

Mike slammed the door of the van. "What are we going to tell Ali?"

"Same old story. False alarm," answered Ernie.

Chapter Sixteen

"I have to admit, Mike, that girl of yours is impressive," said TJ as he led the squad on a run along Coronado beach.

"That's what I've been telling you the whole time," said Mike as he avoided a patch of seaweed.

"Hey, let's not pin the trident just yet boys," said Rick. "There's still one more gateway."

Mike sighed. "What's that Rick, some kind of idiotic opportunity to cause her even more discomfort? You going to test her ability to carry five tons of shopping over an obstacle course?"

"Hey, that's not a bad idea. But no, this phase is all about pleasure. I call it the honey Rick."

Mike scowled. "The honey Rick?"

"Yeah, it's like a honeydick except…" He held his arms wide and pointed to his chest as he pranced through the sand.

"What the fuck is a honeydick?" asked TJ.

Mike shook his head. "The opposite of a honeypot."

Ernie grunted from the back of the squad. "You know, how an attractive woman uses her sexuality to seduce a man and gain information. Well a honeydick is the male version."

"I know what a honeypot is, dipshit. Mike, Rick seems to think he's a goddamn lady slayer. So tonight he'll try to charm Ali."

"What!" Mike stumbled and almost fell. "And I'm supposed to agree to that?"

Rick turned and ran backward, facing the rest of the squad. He stripped off his tank top. "You afraid I might succeed? You afraid she might succumb to the body of Adonis?"

"I'd be more scared of Axe stealing her."

Rick flexed his arms. "Good thing she's a vet, because I'm going to be bringing out these sick puppies."

"Sweet beard of Zeus, that's bad." TJ gave the Rick a shove, sending him tumbling backward into the sand. "Mike, I think your girl's pretty safe. Let's get this last phase wrapped up so we can start planning the bachelor party."

***

As the squad trained Ali was finishing up a rehabilitation session with Axe. The dog now walked normally and showed no sign of his previous behavioral issues. She was immensely proud of what she had achieved in such a short period of time.

"Is that the stud's beast?"

Grinning, she glanced back at her sister who handed her a coffee. "Yes, it is. This is Axe."

Leonie sat on the grass. "He's a handsome fella, just like his dad."

"Yeah, we're almost ready to take him to the next level."

"You talking about Axe or Mike?"

She joined her sister on the patio as Axe stretched out at their feet. "Mike's in the dog house."

"Really?"

She shook her head. "No, not really. But, last night's dinner did prove interesting."

"How so?"

"Everyone got called away to an emergency and I was left looking after two hyped-up preschoolers."

"Worse than my two?"

Ali rolled her eyes. "The girls are angels compared to these two. Leonie, they set fire to the dog."

Her sister's coffee splashed, almost spilling on Axe. "Holy shit, that's serious. I tell you what girl, from the amount of drama that comes with this boy he better be hung like a rogue bull."

"Tell me about it. I feel like the first five dates have been some kind of test. Every time we're together I come up against some kind of obstacle or problem that I have to solve."

"Babe, that's just life. It likes to throw you a shitload of curve balls. You like this guy and he likes you. Go with the flow. It'll all work out in the long run."

"I'm just wondering what else life's going to throw at me."

"When's your next date?"

"Tomorrow night, we're going to a show in town."

"Well, that sounds pretty straightforward. I'm sure it will be fine."

"Yeah, we'll see. What are your plans for the day?"

"I was going to do some shopping then pick up the girls from preschool, excitement plus. What about you?"

"I've got a full day here, then I might have an early one."

"Shall we do lunch on Thursday?" asked Leonie as she rose.

"Yes, let's."

She kissed Ali on the top of her head and said, "You can tell me all about your date."

When her sister was gone. Ali leaned down and scratched Axe between the ears. "Well, handsome man, how about we get you inside for some breakfast?"

Once in the clinic she poured him a bowl of dried food and checked on two other canine patients. As she finished filling their water, the phone in her office rang.

"Hello," she answered.

"Is this Ali?"

The voice was familiar, but she couldn't place it.

"It's Ernie's wife, Maria."

"Oh, of course, I'm so sorry. I didn't recognize your voice."

"I'm sorry if this seems out of the blue. Ernie's mother had your number and I wanted to ring and apologize again for the other night."

Ali smiled, Maria was such a sweetie. "That's no problem at all. I'm just glad that we got everything cleaned up."

"You did an amazing job with the boys. They can be a real handful."

"They're actually very sweet."

"Yes, well you more than passed the test."

Ali frowned. "Test?"

Maria chuckled. "Yes, it was the boy's idea. You see Mike keeps dating the most inappropriate women. They thought it would be a good idea to see if you were family material. I stupidly agreed to their silly plan. Poor Mike didn't even know."

"I see."

"After meeting you last night. I know that he's in fantastic hands. You're divine, my dear."

"Thanks, Maria. And thanks again for a wonderful meal. I look forward to seeing you and the boys, soon."

"You too Ali, have a great day."

As she hung up a tsunami of anger crashed over her. Now everything made sense. The mountain hike, the sickness, and, most recently, the chaos with Maria's boys. They were running some kind of test to see if she was worthy of a SEAL. The sheer arrogance of it made her cringe.

What if she'd failed one of the tests? Would Mike have discarded her despite what they had? Hell, she hadn't dropped him when it turned out that he had financial problems. She shook her head in disbelief. How stupid was she? Mike probably wasn't broke at all. More likely, they had staged it all as part of their stupid selection process.

Reaching for her phone, she started to message him, then stopped. No, that was letting him off lightly. She tossed the phone on her desk and folded her arms. Failing the next test would be a suitable gauge of Mike's commitment. If he was willing to let a stupid test destroy what they had then it wasn't worth keeping.

***

The border guard took the stack of passports from Ramirez and checked them individually before handing them to a colleague. "You're all from Castle Insurance?"

"Yes, that's correct. We're all here for the big event in San Diego. We're pretty excited to be attending the fifteenth Annual Home Insurance Conference." He handed the officer actual tickets to a conference that was being held in the city that week.

The officer checked the documents and handed them back. Then he peered in through the windows at the freshly-shaved men inside. All of them were dressed in dull business suits and wore bored expressions.

"The next one yours as well?" He pointed to the matching gray minivan behind them.

"Yes sir, there are twelve of us. We're the best in the company at what we do, that's why–"

"Sir, I don't give a shit how good you are at selling insurance. You just need to answer my questions. Then I can get you on your way."

"Yes, very good."

The guard walked to the second vehicle and inspected the men inside, along with their luggage, as the passports were processed. Once that was complete he handed them back to Ramirez. "Have a good time."

It was a short drive from the border crossing point to a quarry located a dozen miles from the outskirts of the city. Situated in an isolated valley the site was accessible by a single dirt track.

They parked the vans in front of a cluster of buildings that included the quarry's offices and equipment sheds. Ramirez stepped out into the dry hot desert air and surveyed the location through mirrored sunglasses. The metallic smell of crushed ore hung in the air.

The quarry made for a good ambush location. The access road entered the valley and crossed a large cleared area dominated by steep sides. Around the clearing were piles of gravel. There was a single front-end loader parked alongside a conveyor-fed crusher.

"Mr. Cortez." The voice came from the buildings.

His man in San Diego, Eduardo, was an unremarkable looking Latino who blended easily in a crowd. For that reason he was Ramirez's number one fixer.

"Eduardo." Ramirez shook his hand. "I trust everything is in order."

"Of course. It's all inside." His eyes narrowed as he watched the men alight from the two vans. "You brought a lot of guys this time."

He placed his hand on Eduardo's shoulder. "We're killing Navy SEALs, not gang bangers."

"Understood. I was able to find everything you wanted."

"Show me." He followed the man into the quarry's office. A smile formed on his lips as he surveyed his agent's work.

A map was stuck to the walls with locations marked by red pins. Around it were photos of a woman, a veterinary clinic and a quaint house with a picket fence. He pointed at the home. "Is this where she lives?"

"Yes. It's the best location, a long way from any police stations or military bases."

"Good. Show me the equipment."

"In the workshop." He directed Ramirez through a side door and into a large shed. Laid out on the floor was an arsenal of weapons and equipment, which included assault rifles, combat vests, two sniper rifles and half a dozen single-shot rocket launchers.

"What about the camera?"

"It's in the office. There is an internet connection and a laptop. All the gear is new and will be destroyed once we are done."

"And the bodies?"

"We have barrels of acid."

"You've done well, Eduardo. Show the men where they're staying. Then we'll conduct a reconnaissance with the kidnap team. I also want men providing continuous security."

"Yes, boss."

As his fixer went about his tasks, Ramirez returned to the office and studied the photo of the woman. The girl was pretty. He traced his finger across the photo. It would be satisfying to watch her die in front of him.

Chapter Seventeen

Ali felt the eyes of a dozen men on her as she walked into the Brassy Saloon. Her dress, a full-length, backless, black and white floral print, hugged her curves. And to ensure Mike got the message, she wore bright red lipstick, three inch, open-toed heels, and her hair hung loose across her bare back.

As she approached the bar a handsome black man in a well-tailored suit flashed a friendly smile.

She ignored him and took a seat.

"What are you having, gorgeous?" asked the bartender.

She smiled. "I'm waiting for someone. I'll order when he arrives."

He winked. "Lucky guy."

She felt her phone vibrate in her purse and fished it out. It was Mike. Here we go, she thought as she answered.

"Hey, babe. I haven't been able to get away from work yet. I'm going to be at least another forty-five minutes."

Ali shook her head. He actually sounded disappointed. "You know that's when the show starts?"

"I know, I'll meet you in the foyer. I promise I'll make it."

"OK, I'll see you then." She tossed her phone in her bag.

The handsome man moved to the seat next to her. "Your date running late?"

"It seems that way." She gestured for the bartender.

"Mine too. It sucks to be the dependable one. Seem to spend half your time waiting around."

"Tell me about it." The bartender appeared and Ali ordered a Manhattan.

"Make it two and let me get it," the man said.

Ali smiled. "No, I can't let you do that."

"Sure you can. You get the next one. I mean we've got an hour to kill till the show starts."

She managed a smile. "You're going to see the ballet?"

"Yes, I am." He extended his hand. "My name is Richard."

"I'm Alison. It's a pleasure to meet you, Richard." As she shook his hand she noticed how well he was dressed. He wore a finely cut gray suit with a light blue shirt, opened at the collar. On his wrist was an Omega, similar to the one Mike wore.

"So Alison, are you a local or a visitor to our fine town?"

"A local, I run a small veterinary clinic out at Iron Canyon. What about you?"

"I'm in banking. Well, I used to be in banking. I'm semi-retired now. I sit on a few boards, but most of the time I write."

"Really, what sort of writing?"

The drinks arrived and Richard paid for them. "Oh, a bit of poetry and the like. Nothing serious. Just dabbling really. Do you have any artistic pursuits?"

"Not really, my work takes up most of my time."

"I guess when you have a job as important and fulfilling as helping heal animals you don't need a hobby."

Ali smiled. She was enjoying talking to Richard, not that she believed he was a retired banker. She'd joined the dots quickly, the coincidence of him being at the bar, the Omega watch and the name Richard. On Mount Otay Mike had blamed his illness on his team-mate, Rick. This had to be another stupid test. And if that was the case then she was going to run with it. Plus, even if he was acting, Rick was a good listener and seemed genuinely interested in what she had to say. They ordered a second round of drinks and before they knew it forty-five minutes had passed.

Ali rose and made to leave. "I guess your date hasn't made it either."

"She's notoriously unreliable. A good friend, but not one for timings. Do you mind if I walk with you?"

"That would be lovely." The idea of arriving with the handsome Rick appealed to her. It was a short walk from the bar to Spreckles Theater, where the ballet was showing. The Chicago-style building was over a hundred years old. A marquee over the entrance displayed the performance name in bold, black letters on a white background.

As they reached the doors Richard smiled. "Would you like me to wait with you?"

"If you like, it would be nice to introduce you to Mike." She pulled out her cell and checked the time. He was already ten minutes late. The phone buzzed as a text arrived.

I'm so sorry I can't get away. Enjoy the ballet and we'll grab a bite to eat after.

Glancing up she saw Richard watching her. "Bad news?" he asked.

"Mike can't make it. I guess I'll be watching the show alone."

He checked his watch and frowned. "No, we can't do that. Look, Clarissa is clearly not coming and I've got director's circle tickets. Join me."

"Thank you, but it wouldn't be right."

"Alison, I simply wish to enjoy the ballet in the company of a new and interesting friend."

"Alright, but first let me send Mike a reply."

Richard waited at a respectful distance as she typed a response.

Don't worry. I'm going to head straight home after the show. I will see you tomorrow.

The performance lasted nearly two hours and Ali watched in rapt attention. Her gaze never left the dancers as they twirled to the notes of a full symphony orchestra. When it was finally over she sighed and slumped back in her chair.

"That was amazing," said Richard.

"It was, wasn't it."

"I think it was made even more enjoyable due to the company. You should have seen your face."

"It was delightful. I really wish Mike could have been here."

"His loss, I'm afraid."

They waited for the crowd to thin before leaving the theater.

"Would you like to get a nightcap? There is a great little bar not far from here."

"No, I'm afraid I'm feeling a little worn out. I'm going to head straight home. Thank you so much for a wonderful evening, Richard."

"My pleasure. Look, Ali, I wouldn't usually do this but I was wondering if I could give you my number."

"Richard, you're an amazing guy but I'm already seeing someone."

"I understand. Well, I have had a fantastic time. Thank you again, Alison." He pecked her on the cheek.

Ali smiled as she turned and walked away. It had been a lovely evening despite Mike's absence. That thought reminded her. She still needed to fail the test. Turning she chased after Rick. "Richard!"

He turned. "Yes?"

"Your number. I changed my mind."

She registered the look of surprise on his face followed by what could have been a glimmer of sadness. Then he managed a smile. "That would be fantastic. He took a card from his wallet and handed it to her. Give me a call anytime."

She took the card, found a pen and scribbled her number on the back. "How about you call me tomorrow."

Rick watched her walk down the street and hail a cab. Then he turned and strolled slowly in the opposite direction. A block further along the road he ducked into a pub and sat next to Mike. He placed the business card on the bar.

Mike stared at it for a few seconds before he picked it up and crushed it in his fist.

***

Ali sat in the back of the cab staring at her phone.

A few minutes into the trip the driver glanced at her in the rearview mirror. "You don't look happy, Miss,"

"I'm not. I just found out my boyfriend has been secretly testing me to see if I'm worthy."

"And that upsets you?"

She narrowed her eyes at him in the rear-vision mirror. "No woman would be happy with that."

"That's the difference between men and women. A man would see it as a challenge. Whereas, a woman might see it as a man not loving her for who she is."

"Exactly."

"So, did you fail on purpose?"

Ali frowned. "How could you know that?"

"Lady, I've been married for thirty years and that's exactly what my wife would do."

"Yeah, well that is exactly what I did."

"And now you're hoping he'll call you anyway."

She sighed. "Yeah, I guess so."

"Well, if he loves you he will. Now, this is you." He pulled the cab up in front of her home.

She paid and tipped him before stepping out onto the grass curb and kicking off her heels.

"Good luck," said the cabby through the window as he drove off.

As she was about to walk up her drive her phone vibrated and she glanced at the screen. It was a message from Mike.

Hey, I'll be around tomorrow to pick up Axe.

"Message received loud and clear, Michael Saunders," she murmured fighting back tears as she began to write a text.

Mike, sorry your little tests didn't go to plan. I will see you tomorrow.

She didn't see or hear the gray minivan as it stopped on the street. Staring at her phone she reread the message, wondering if he was as hurt as she was. Maybe she should let him stew on it for a few more minutes before she hit send. Fumbling with the lock she opened the door as she heard footsteps on the gravel behind her.

Turning, she called out in a loud voice. "Who's there? Mike, if this is another of your stupid tests…"

She caught a glimpse of two masked men then suddenly they were on her. A hand clasped her mouth as she was lifted from the ground by strong arms. The keys slipped from her grasp, as she struggled. Her heels fell off. A hood was slipped over her head plunging the world into darkness.

Chapter Eighteen

Mike sat in his truck outside the clinic, contemplating how best to handle Ali. He felt betrayed, but also disappointed. She had fooled him. She was just like all the other women he had dated, always looking for a better deal.

Now, he had to decide how to end it. Hell, she hadn't even replied to his text about Axe. Finally, he climbed out of the truck and entered the clinic.

The assistant behind the counter greeted him with a smile. "Are you here to see Axe?"

"Yeah, I'm here to take him home."

"Oh, in that case I'm going to have to call Ali."

Mike checked the clock on the wall. It was nearly ten in the morning. She should have been at work hours ago. "Does she have the day off?"

"No, she just hasn't been in yet." She lifted the phone to her ear. "That's weird, it's not connecting."

"Try her home number."

She dialed again and waited. "No one's answering."

Mike frowned. Was it possible she'd taken his text to heart and was avoiding him? No, that wasn't like Ali.

"Hey, how about I take Axe and go around and check that she's OK?"

The assistant shrugged. "I can't see a problem with that. I'll grab him for you."

As Mike waited, he tried using his cell to call her number. It immediately went to voice mail.

The assistant handed him Axe's lead. "Here he is."

The dog barked loudly and immediately sat next to Mike's leg. "Good boy. Hey, can you email through my final bill."

"Sure, I'll do it now."

As they left the clinic, Mike was amazed at Axe's strength. He moved as if he had never been injured. No matter what he thought of Ali, her skill as a vet was undeniable.

Axe jumped into the truck with ease. A moment later, they drove through Iron Canyon and headed to Ali's suburb. As he pulled into her driveway, he spotted the open door. He sprinted from the truck and almost tripped over a pair of heels. Her keys and purse were next to them. "What the hell."

Checking the garden, he found no sign of her. He slipped inside and quickly searched every room. Nothing. She wasn't avoiding him. Someone had taken her.

***

Ramirez sat at a desk in the quarry office, drumming his fingers against the chipped laminate surface. His kidnap team had returned with the bait. Now he needed to set the trap.

Eduardo stuck his head through the doorway. "Boss, she's ready for you."

"About time." He followed the fixer into the equipment shed through to one of the quarry's storerooms. Inside the woman was tied to a chair on a sheet of plastic facing a camera on a tripod. Ramirez gestured to the armed guards. "Is she really that dangerous?"

"She keeps trying to escape."

Chuckling, he stood in front of her and tugged the hood from her head. What greeted him was not the terrified victim he expected. Instead, he faced the fierce glare of a woman enraged.

"Where is Mike?" she snarled.

"Your boyfriend? You will see him soon enough."

Her eyes darted around the room. "What are you guys supposed to be, Mexican gangsters?"

Ramirez frowned. "We are not supposed to be anything. I don't think you understand the gravity of this situation."

"I don't think you understand the gravity of this situation, buddy. I'm over this shit and I'm over Mike. Get him in here now and I'll tell him myself."

Ramirez dropped the hood back over her head and gestured for Eduardo to join him outside. "What the hell is she talking about?"

He shrugged.

"It doesn't matter." He took his phone from his pocket and dialed Barbosa. The cartel boss answered after a few rings. "You wanted to know when we had the girl."

"Excellent, call me once you have the SEAL and I will make sure I'm at the computer."

He terminated the call. "Are the men in position?"

"Yes, they are ready."

"And her phone?"

He reached into his pocket and produced Ali's cell phone. "They turned it off like you asked."

"Good, but now we want Mike Saunders to know exactly where she is." He powered up the device, stepped back into the storage room and tore the hood off his prisoner's head. "What's your password?"

"Why don't you ask Mike? I'm sure he already knows it."

He clenched his fists. "I'm not screwing around. Give me the password."

She laughed. "Why, so you can see if I called that guy from last night? Is this some final test to see if I'm worthy? You know what, fine. The code is two-three-six-seven. Oh, and Mike, if you're listening, I think you're a pathetic, misogynist asshole."

Ramirez unlocked the device. On the screen was a text message. He smiled as he read it out loud. "Mike, sorry your little tests didn't go to plan. I will see you tomorrow."

Ali cocked her head to one side. "See, I worked out your little game."

"I guess you won't mind if I hit send then." He transmitted the message as he left the room and waited. Seconds passed before the phone rang. The name Mike was displayed on the screen.

"Ali, I just got your message. Look, I want to apologize." The man's voice was edged with concern.

"Listen to me very carefully, Mike Saunders," Ramirez growled.

"Who is this? Look if you've–"

"Shut up and listen. We have the girl and if you want to see her again come to the Atlas Quarry, alone. If you bring anyone with you, she dies. If you call the police, she dies. If you are not here within the hour, she dies. Come alone and she will live." He terminated the call, turned off the phone and handed it to Eduardo. "The trap is set."

Chapter Nineteen

Mike skidded his truck to a halt outside of the team building and sprinted inside, leaving Axe in the cab. Reaching his locker he grabbed his low-profile body armor and stuffed it in a gear bag. As he turned to leave, he locked eyes with TJ who was sitting on a bench seat working on paperwork.

"Mike, you OK, brother?" asked the Chief.

For a split second he contemplated not telling TJ. But the squad was his family and if anyone knew what to do it would be TJ. "No. Some Mexicans grabbed Ali and they want an exchange in…" He checked his watch. "Forty-five minutes."

"Exchange for what?"

Mike sighed. "Me. It has to be linked to Barbosa's brother. This is the revenge the Lieutenant briefed us on."

TJ pulled open his locker and grabbed his gear. "Right, and they gave you a deadline?"

"Yeah, an hour. Don't call the cops and come alone."

TJ slipped into his rig. "Motherfuckers don't know who they're messing with."

Rick entered the room with Ernie. "Who doesn't know?"

"No time to explain. Grab your gear and meet me at the armory."

"We got a job on?" asked Ernie.

"Yeah, I'll explain on the way. Mike, you got a location?"

He held up his phone. "Atlas Quarry, only ten miles away. It's got high ground all around it."

"Rick, you're on the sniper rifle," said TJ as he ducked out of the team room.

Three minutes later Mike pulled the truck in front of the armory. TJ had already unlocked the secure building. The boys grabbed their weapons and climbed into the bed of the pickup with Axe. TJ tossed in a bag of preloaded magazines they kept for contingencies and joined them, securing the cover.

"OK, let's do this," he broadcast over the secure radios they wore.

Mike checked his watch as they sped across the causeway that linked Coronado to the mainland. They had thirty minutes to make the timings dictated by Ali's kidnappers. Flooring the accelerator, he sent the truck screeching around a corner.

"Steady, brother," transmitted TJ. "I'm trying to study Google earth back here and come up with a plan."

"We've got a plan," said Mike. "We're going to kill them all and rescue Ali."

"Good plan. I'm keen to flesh it out a little."

"Well you better hurry because we've got less than half an hour to get there."

***

Ramirez sat smoking, watching the clock on the wall above the woman's head. Uneasy, he switched between the clock and studying his captive. The woman still believed this was all some kind of test that her boyfriend had organized. Why he would do such a thing baffled him. "Do you still think this is a game?" he asked, exhaling a stream of smoke into her face.

She coughed as her eyes darted from the armed guard in the corner of the room to the camera set up on the tripod.

"Your boyfriend, Mike, killed someone important to my client. Someone he loved dearly. Because of that, he has asked to watch Mike lose someone close to him. Unfortunately, that someone is you."

He watched as realization set in followed by mounting panic. "You don't understand. He won't come. He thinks I wanted to cheat on him."

"He will come. I sent him your angry little message." He laughed as she struggled against her bonds. Then, somehow she managed to tip the chair over backward. There was a loud crack as her head struck the concrete.

"Shit." He leaped to his feet. The last thing he needed was for her to die before the target arrived. "Get her upright," he barked at the guard.

The man grabbed the chair and yanked it onto its legs. Her head lolled forward against her chest.

Ramirez checked her vitals. She was breathing and had a strong pulse. Inspecting the back of her head he found a rapidly expanding lump. She would live, for now.

The sound of the door opening caught his attention.

"There's a truck approaching."

"Is it him?"

"Our snipers have confirmed there's only one person in the vehicle."

"Good. Let's go out and meet him." He turned to the guard watching over the woman. "Make sure nothing happens to her."

On his way out of the equipment shed Ramirez drew his pistol and checked it was ready. Then he joined the four men waiting to provide him with security. The rest of his people were already in their ambush positions.

***

Mike slowed the truck as he drove through the gates at the quarry. A battered sign read, *Atlas Resources*. He inched the truck forward, scanning the terrain for any sign of an ambush.

"Rick, you got anything?" he asked through his earpiece. They'd dropped him on a back road with access to the hill behind the quarry. He'd sprinted to get into position in time to cover their arrival with his sniper rifle.

"Negative," he managed between breaths.

"OK, we're going in." He drove the truck into a clearing in front of a cluster of buildings. Stopping in line with a huge ore crusher, he opened the door and stepped out into the dust.

Dry, hot air assaulted his senses, sun reflecting off the sheer rock walls of the quarry. Through his sunglasses he spotted movement. "We've got five tangos pulling CPP on a single primary. Gotta have at least a sniper pair in overwatch." His lips barely moved as the five men escorted a single, seemingly unarmed individual dressed in a suit and aviator sunglasses. As they got closer Mike identified he was Latino, they all were. There was no doubt about it. They had to be the Butcher's men.

"Rick?"

"I've got eyes on one sniper, looking for others."

Mike glanced at the high ground dominating the quarry then focused on the men. "Where's the girl?" he yelled.

Aviators stepped forward. "She's inside. Surrender yourself and I'll release her."

"Like hell!" yelled Mike. "You bring her out here and show me she's alive. Then we'll talk about what happens next."

The man laughed as his security detail aimed assault rifles at him. "The way I see it, you're coming with us, no matter what."

"Taking down the first sniper," reported Rick.

Mike thought he caught a glimpse of movement high on the lip of the quarry as he raised his hands. "Fine, I'm coming."

"Target down. I'm going for number two," said Rick.

Suddenly a shot rang out from high on the quarry wall. A bullet shattered the windshield of Mike's truck.

"Shit, sorry guys," said Rick. "Fucker got a round off. He's neutralized."

As Mike dropped to a knee, he whipped a pistol from the back of his pants. Blasting away at the group of men he saw one fall before the others returned fire. He sprinted for cover. Bullets churned the dust around him

From the back of the truck, Ernie and TJ appeared, their carbines spitting lead.

Axe leaped from the bed onto the gravel and dashed to Mike's side as he found cover behind the gravel crusher.

"Covering," Rick reported from the crater wall above them.

Ernie slid in next to Mike, tossing him a spare carbine and assault rig. It took him a second to throw it on then they fired in the direction of the buildings as TJ sprinted toward them.

"What the hell happened with Rick?" Mike asked as he shrugged on the rig. "Is he OK?"

"Yeah, when he nailed the sniper, the prick got a shot off," said TJ. "We've got to fight through before they kill Ali."

Ernie returned fire then yelled, "That's going to be a problem. We're outnumbered." A volley of bullets clanged into the crusher sending the men ducking for cover.

"Rick, what have you got?" TJ transmitted.

"I'm taking heavy fire, guys. I'm going to have to move. We've taken out three guys. I think there's at least ten more."

More rounds hit the crusher forcing them further back. Mike searched for Axe but couldn't find him anywhere. "Guys, have you seen Axe?"

"Negative," responded TJ.

"He was here a second ago," said Ernie.

For a second Mike forgot the raging gun battle and searched for the dog. He was nowhere to be seen. Clearly he was still suffering from PTSD, because despite being trained to work in a gunfight, he'd run away.

"Team," TJ's gruff voice snapped him back to reality. "We need to flank these fuckers. Mike, can we climb up through the crusher and over that mound of rubble?"

Mike peered up through the rusted steel beams. "Yeah, but that's going to take us further from the buildings. That's where they'll be holding Ali."

"It's our only option, bud. If we stay here we're going to be dead and of absolutely no use to her."

Mike clenched his fists in frustration. "I'll lead."

Chapter Twenty

Ali's heart raced as the sound of gunfire echoed through the flimsy walls of the storeroom. She fought the tape that held her arms to the chair. By wriggling her fingers she'd managed to loosen the bonds, ever so slightly. Thankfully, the boss with the sunglasses hadn't replaced the hood and she could see, albeit barely. The blow to the back of her head had left her with blurred vision and a splitting headache.

Suddenly, bullets punched through the thin sheet metal to her left. She screamed, toppling the chair over and onto her side. Her heart felt like it would explode as she fought her mounting panic.

The door opened. A blurry figure entered. She assumed it was the guard. She felt his hands grab her shoulders and push her back upright. "Don't move, bitch."

At that moment, she spotted a second, smaller shape at the doorway. A shape she knew well. His low guttural growl filled Ali with hope.

"Axe, it's you?"

She flinched as he leaped toward her. The guard screamed as Axe slammed into him. His weapon clattered to the ground. He fought back but Axe's attack was brutal. As Ali's vision finally cleared she saw the guard dash from the room, his mauled arm dangling uselessly.

"Good boy, Axe."

The dog nuzzled her then sat next to her, watching the door like a hawk.

Ali worked her taped wrists back and forth, managing to loosen them enough to free one hand. Then she pulled the tape from the other. Gunfire still raged outside as she stripped the tape from her legs, wincing as it tore her skin.

Barefoot, and still wearing her dress from the night before, she padded across to the door and peered out. No sign of her guard, she spotted a number of gunmen firing out toward the quarry.

There was an enormous front-end loader parked in the shed, obscuring the others.

"Where do we go, Axe?"

The dog led her out through a back door and away from the gunfight. He followed the shed before stopping at a corner. Ali made her way cautiously over the gravel and stopped alongside him. "Hey, we need to get out of here, buddy."

Axe whined as he stared intently in the direction of a rusted ore crusher. Ali spotted Mike's shattered pickup a short distance away.

"He's out there, isn't he?"

Axe's eyes never left the crusher.

"If we go out there we're dead, Axe. But, there might be another way. Come on, boy. Let's see what we can do."

***

"RPG!" yelled Mike when he spotted a plume of smoke spiraling out from the enemy position. The rocket screamed toward them and slammed into the pile of concrete drainage pipes they were using as cover. It exploded, showering them in dust and shrapnel. He felt a searing burn on his upper arm as hot steel sliced through his shirt.

"Everyone good?" bellowed TJ as he jumped to his feet and returned fire.

Mike checked his wound. "I'm good."

"I can't see shit," reported Ernie.

Mike registered the sound of another rocket launching. It streaked away from the equipment sheds and detonated high up on the cliffs. "Rick, you OK, buddy? That was a bit too close for comfort."

"Guys," Rick's voice was weak. "I've been hit. I've taken some shrapnel to the leg. Bleeding badly. Gonna try to get a tourniquet over it."

Mike turned to TJ and took in his grim expression. "We better call 9-1-1. We can't do this alone."

"Agree. We're pinned here. Without backup they're going to–" Another rocket exploded against the cement pipes. "-Pick us off one by one." He pulled out his phone and made the call.

Without Rick's covering fire the barrage hitting their position intensified. Mike tried to get a shot off but nearly lost his head as bullets snapped past inches away.

"TJ, Mike, Rick, I want you to know that it's been an honor serving with you. You're my brothers. And if we go down here, I'm proud it's with you," said Ernie.

"Fuck that," yelled Mike. "We're not going out like this." He leaned out from the pipes and fired full automatic in the direction of the sheds. "We can make a break for the office buildings."

"Negative, Mike," yelled TJ. "We wouldn't make it ten yards. We sit tight and wait for the cops."

"And what about, Ali?"

"Mike, if she's still alive, us running out there and getting killed, isn't going to help."

"She's alive, TJ."

"I don't doubt that, bud."

Mike fired another burst. He heard yelling coming from the gunmen.

"Ammo check!" yelled TJ.

"Two mags," replied Mike. "And, I think they're forming up for an assault."

"I've got two and a half," said Ernie.

"I've got two and Rick's out of the fight," confirmed TJ.

Mike didn't need him to outline exactly how dire the situation was. Their only hope was that the police arrived in time to turn the tide of the battle.

***

Ramirez knew he had the SEALs on the ropes. With their sniper down the rest were pinned behind a stack of concrete piping. He'd moved up with his men and was using a cluster of shipping containers to command the assault.

"Bring up the remaining rockets," he commanded Eduardo. "Have three of the men fire on them from here. The others will assault from the right flank. We need to move quickly before the authorities arrive."

Men dashed forward to their new positions. Then Ramirez waved them on with his pistol. The men providing covering fire unleashed a hail of bullets and rockets that smashed into the concrete piping. Ramirez grinned as he pictured the SEALs cowering, while his assault force leapfrogged from cover to cover on the flank. In a matter of minutes, they would be on top of the Americans.

He felt his phone vibrate in his pocket and he checked the screen; it was Barbosa.

"I've been sitting in front of this computer for ten minutes!" the Butcher screamed.

"There's been a change of plans. The SEAL brought friends," Ramirez yelled over the gunfire.

"You better kill them all or you're dead!"

Ramirez gritted his teeth. "For all of them the price has tripled." Barbosa didn't need to know that he had every intention of killing them for free.

"Fine, but I want evidence. I want photos of them and the woman too."

The girl, Ramirez had forgotten all about the girl. "It'll be done." He terminated the call and turned to his fixer. "Eduardo, kill the girl. Get photos."

"Yes, boss."

He turned his attention back to the battle. His men were less than a hundred yards from the Americans now. Soon it would be over. He'd abandon the team and slip away before the police arrived.

"Boss!"

At Eduardo's panicked scream, he glanced back at the equipment sheds. He heard a rumble and froze. The massive front-end loader plowed through a cloud of diesel smoke. A second later the mechanical monster gained speed and swung toward them. "Shit!" It was the woman behind the controls. As he raised his pistol the bucket lifted, blocking his shots. Diving to one side, he managed to avoid the wheels as it rumbled past.

The men firing on the SEALs were fixated and didn't see it in time. The blade lowered smashing them into the shipping containers, crushing them. Then the tractor backed off the wreckage and turned toward his assault force.

Ramirez fired his pistol into the back of the cockpit to no effect as it trundled forward. Screaming with rage, he ran after it, ducked between the wheels, grabbed the ladder to the cab, and started climbing.

***

"You hear that?" Mike yelled. The rate of fire from the cartel gunmen slackened as the rumble of a powerful diesel engine echoed off the quarry walls.

He peered around the crumbled concrete pipes but couldn't identify the source of the noise.

TJ and Ernie joined him as he spotted a group of gunmen forming an assault line. "They're trying to flank us," he said firing the last of his ammo at the men. The Mexicans dove for cover as two of their force were hit.

Mike dropped his carbine and snatched his pistol from its holster. "I'm out."

"Me too," added Ernie.

The gunmen retaliated, unleashing a hail of gunfire. Then, sprinting forward in pairs, they began assaulting, using piles of gravel for cover. Mike fired his pistol, to no effect. Just when he thought it was over, the diesel engine's noise intensified. A huge front-end loader smashed through the rubble, sending the gunmen scattering in all directions.

As the earthmover turned toward him, he spotted Ali at the wheel. She was handling the twenty-ton juggernaut like a seasoned pro. He spotted a figure at the top of the access ladder; it was the aviators wearing boss. Raising his pistol, he took aim. "Damn." He couldn't get a clear shot.

A rifle blasted close to his head. He caught a glimpse of one of the shooters toppling over.

"Get your hands up!" TJ screamed at the remaining men.

Mike ignored them as he sprinted after the earthmover. Out the corner of his eye he spotted a gunman aiming at him and flinched. The man went down.

"I've got you, brother," Rick said softy, over the radio.

Gaining on the front-end loader, he saw the cartel killer wrench open the door and aim his pistol. Then a flash of fur and teeth hit him, knocking him from the ladder. Man and dog plunged between the massive tires, disappearing in a maelstrom of dust and smoke.

"Axe!" Mike screamed as the earthmover came to a shuddering stop.

Heart pounding he peered under the earthmover, into the dust.

Ali appeared from the cabin. "Mike, is he there? Tell me he's alive."

As the dust dissipated Mike spotted a mangled and bloodied corpse. "Oh god, no."

A whimper cut through the air. Axe appeared, bloodied, battered and covered in soil.

"Axe, buddy, are you OK?" The dog walked toward him and licked his face. Mike wrapped his arms around him. "Yeah, you did good boy, you did good."

Tears streaming down her face, Ali stepped off the ladder and limped across to them. "Is he hurt?"

Mike turned to her. "He's fine. How are you?"

She nodded, smearing the tears from her face with her hands. "Battered and bruised, but overall, good. Is everyone else OK?"

"Rick got hit. It's bad."

The wail of sirens filled the air and a helicopter roared over the quarry. Mike turned and watched as a police SWAT van skidded in the gravel. Black-uniformed officers swarmed from the vehicle, their weapons aimed at the few remaining gunmen who had already surrendered to TJ and Ernie.

"Looks like the cavalry arrived just in time."

More police cars arrived, followed by a fire engine and an ambulance.

"Guys, if you're not using those paramedics I could do with a hand," transmitted Rick over the radio in a weak voice.

"I'm on it," replied Mike.

"Negative, we've got this. You take care of that girl," TJ said as he and Ernie trotted past with medics in tow.

Mike turned back to Ali. Barefoot, clad in last night's torn and filthy dress, with diesel soot smeared across her face, she'd never looked more beautiful to him. "Do you think you could bring it upon yourself to forgive me?"

"For ditching me last night or your childish selection course?"

He grimaced. "Both."

For a split second, her jaw clenched and he thought she would slap him.

"You know you're an idiot, Mike Saunders?"

He nodded. "Yeah, I know."

"You don't have to do everything your team-mates tell you to do. Sometimes you can trust your own instincts."

"They meant well."

Ali glanced up at the quarry wall where TJ was overseeing the movement of Rick back to the ambulance.

"They're good guys, Mike, and so are you."

He grinned sheepishly. "So, does that mean you like me?"

She shook her head. "You're such an idiot. I've known about your crappy test since yesterday morning. Maria called and let the cat out of the bag. I also worked out that Richard was the Rick you blamed for the food poisoning. Oh, and you both wear the same watch. Pretty slick operation you're running, not." Her eyes narrowed. "When I found out I literally wanted to kill you."

"But, now?"

The kiss surprised Mike. She stood up on her tiptoes and despite his assault rig and rifle, landed it directly on his lips.

As she pulled back, he clasped her close and deepened the kiss. Their mouths still locked he swept her off her feet and into his arms. "We need to get you checked out. You've been through a lot."

She laughed. "Really? You think after your crappy selection course I'm going to be phased by a kidnapping and a gunfight?"

"No. You're probably pretty well prepared for anything now. But this is for my peace of mind." He carried her through the gathering crowd of vehicles to a newly arrived ambulance and sat her on a stretcher. A paramedic immediately began inspecting her for injuries.

TJ and Ernie appeared carrying Rick on a stretcher. Bloodied and battered with a bandaged wound to his thigh he still wore a grin.

"Hey Ali, sorry, I was meaning to call."

"Hello Richard, how's the poetry going?"

"You know, hit and miss." He gave Mike thumbs-up as they loaded him in the ambulance next to Ali.

Mike frowned. "So you failed on purpose?"

She nodded.

"Why?"

The paramedic dabbed at the wound on the back of her head and she flinched. "Because I was angry. I let you into my life, Mike. I got to know you. And, you still wanted to run me through your stupid tests."

"Ma'am, I need you to lie down. You've suffered a concussion," said the paramedic. "We need to get you to hospital and have it checked out."

Mike nodded. "It was pretty stupid."

"Yeah, it was."

The paramedic grasped her shoulder. "Ma'am."

"Fine."

As she lay Mike climbed into the back and Axe jumped in after him.

"Sir, we can't have a dog in here."

Mike shrugged. "Sure, but you're going to have to tell him that."

The paramedic took one look at Axe's teeth and relented.

"You guys really like me, don't you?" Ali grinned.

Mike tucked a stray hair behind her ear. "I can't speak for Axe. But I can say… I've fallen for you."

Chapter Twenty One

Mike knelt in front of Axe and looked the dog directly in the eye. "Buddy, this is probably going to be our toughest gig ever. Yeah, I won't lie. It's going to be brutal. It's going to be tough. We've trained for unconventional warfare. We've fought cartels and terrorists. But this is going to take it to the next level."

Axe cocked his head to one side as if he understood exactly what Mike was saying.

"I know, brother, I'm scared as well. But we've got to do this. I mean come on, you're a decorated war hero."

Ali walked into the living area of her sister's house and stood with her hands on her hips. "Are you boys hiding in here? Come on team. You've got thirty screaming preschoolers out there and they want Mike the clown and his circus dog, Axe."

Mike sighed, rose and adjusted his costume.

"Come here, honey, you've smudged your face." Ali took the theatrical paints from the coffee table and used scarlet to outline his mouth. Then she adjusted his red nose and rainbow-colored wig. "There, now you look the part."

She glanced down at Axe. The dog was wearing a rainbow colored ruffle around his neck and had tiny bows in his fur. "You look very cute as well, Axe." She tousled his ears. "Well boys, this is only day two of husband selection, so get out there and charm those princesses."

"Surely this makes us even?"

"Not even close, lover. Now get rolling."

Mike grabbed a basket filled with treat bags and walked slowly through the sliding doors, into the backyard, with Axe at his side.

As thirty satin-clad, wand-waving fairy princesses spotted them, their screams hit him like a blast from a sonic weapon. An army of over-excited Disney characters, they descended upon the pair, demanding balloons, magic, and candy.

Mike held them at bay with the treat bags, but Axe wasn't so lucky. Girls swarmed all over him, pulling his ears and aggressively patting him. The Military Working Dog took it in his stride, sat calmly and looked up at Mike with eyes that said, why?

Deep in the folds of his costume Mike felt his phone vibrate. He fished it from his pocket and checked the screen.

Butcher located-rolling in 30.

He dropped the basket and made a beeline for the house. Safely inside, he stripped off the clown outfit revealing shorts and a T-shirt. His wig was tossed onto the lounge along with the red nose.

"Where do you think you're going?" demanded Ali from the kitchen where she was enjoying a coffee with Leonie.

"I've got a job on."

"Barbosa?"

He nodded.

"Go get him, honey."

As he made for the front door he heard the rattle of claws on the wooden floor. Glancing over his shoulder, he saw Axe had followed him. The dog sat and tipped his head, his lopsided ear flopping forward.

"You want in, don't you?"

Axe let out a sharp bark.

"OK, come on."

"Just remember, the selection process isn't over," yelled Ali from the kitchen. "I'm not saying yes till you pass all five stages."

"Maybe we'll stay in Mexico, hey Axe," he mumbled.

"I heard that." Ali appeared and wrapped her arms around him. "Be safe."

He kissed her, smearing red paint on her mouth. "I will. Axe has my back."

"You look after each other."

"That's what we do."

Chapter Twenty Two

"Cut-off is in position," reported TJ as he crouched next to Mike and Axe. The squad had parachuted into an area close to one of the Butcher's many haciendas. It was still a few hours before dark and they hid in the thick vegetation surrounding the home.

"And intel's still got him in location?" asked Mike.

"Correct," reported Ernie. "They've got multiple sources confirming his presence."

"Then what are we waiting for?"

"A green light from command," said TJ.

"He's going to slip away again."

"No he's not," replied Ernie. "We just got our green light. We're on point. Bravo and Charlie are backup and we've got snipers in position."

"Mike, you and Axe have lead," ordered the Chief. "Let's take him down, for Rick." The Corpsman was still in hospital.

"For Rick." Mike stepped out of the bushes with Axe by his side. TJ and Ernie followed, and behind them, the rest of the platoon. He moved quickly across the freshly mowed lawn, his weapon held ready.

Rounds snapped through the air as snipers engaged the guards on sentry around the facility.

Mike made it to the front door and tested the handle. It was unlocked. Pushing it open he slipped inside. "Axe, hunt."

The dog made a beeline for the staircase to the second level as the rest of the SEALs cleared the ground floor. Mike and his squad followed the dog.

Upstairs, Axe stopped before a doorway, staring intently at it.

Mike sniffed. The scent of tobacco hung thick in the air. Music blared loudly from down the hallway. He waited for TJ to tap him on the shoulder before swinging into the corridor.

Two cartel guards standing ten yards away saw him. They went for their guns. It was the last move they made. TJ and Mike dropped them with silenced shots.

Axe worked his way down the corridor before halting at another doorway. Rock guitar blasted from behind the thick wooden paneling.

"This is it?" asked TJ.

"Yeah. Axe looks pretty excited."

"OK, let's do this."

Mike scowled as he turned the handle of the door and pushed it gently open. The music increased in intensity as he peered through the gap.

The room inside was lavish. Through the haze of smoke he spotted a large bed. A naked woman sat astride an overweight male with her back to him.

Mike smirked, reached out and killed the stereo.

"What the fuck!" Barbosa pushed the girl off him. Sitting up he spotted the two SEALs. "No, no, don't kill me!" he screamed as he stared wide-eyed at Mike.

At Axe's low vicious growl, the girl screamed. Wrapping herself in the sheets she stumbled from the bed, leaving the naked cartel boss cowering.

"No, not the *payaso*. Not the *payaso*," he sobbed. "Not the *payaso*."

"Cover me," TJ grunted. Lowering his weapon, he flipped the naked man onto his stomach and flexi-cuffed his hands behind his back. "Find something to cover this turd."

Mike tossed him a robe from the back of the door.

They escorted the cartel kingpin to the front lawn where Commander Conner waited with a Blackhawk helicopter. He greeted them with a broad smile. "Job well done, guys." He frowned at Mike. "You come straight from a party or something?"

"Yes, sir. A kid's birthday party." He frowned. "How did you know that?"

The Commander winked and gave the dog a nod. "Good to see Axe back in the field."

The loadmaster grabbed the senior officer by the shoulder, informing him that prisoner had been loaded.

"OK boys, we need to get this guy to the FBI. I'll see you back at the strand."

The Blackhawk powered into the sky leaving them to wait for their own ride.

Mike turned to Ernie. "What's a *payaso*?"

"A clown."

"Why would the Butcher scream that when we captured him?"

TJ and Ernie stared at him with raised eyebrows.

"Have you seen your face, Bobo?" grunted TJ.

Ernie handed him his smartphone with the camera flipped. "Who knew the butcher is afraid of clowns."

Mike glanced at the screen and saw that he was still wearing most of the stage makeup that Ali had applied. "You guys could have said something."

A Blackhawk thundered into view and flared onto the lawn.

"Where's the fun in that?" yelled TJ as they climbed onboard. "Plus, Ali scares the crap out of us and we promised her we wouldn't interfere with the selection process."

Mike shook his head as he secured Axe's harness to a strap. "You do know that you guys got me into this mess."

TJ gave him thumbs-up. "Yep, but goddamn it's been worth it."

As they lifted off, Mike reached down and ruffled Axe's ears. "Yeah, I guess it has."

The dog rested his head on his thigh.

Mike sighed. "I can't wait to see what Ali's got lined up for us next."

THE END

SEAL the DEAL

Chapter One

Jennifer Reynolds leaned against the hood of her Ford pickup and sipped from a banana, acai and mango smoothie. Tall with a slim athletic build she cut an attractive figure in the khaki and green uniform of an Oregon Parks and Recreation Department Ranger. Her pale blue eyes watched the road out of town from beneath a felt campaign hat. Not one for sunglasses she tended to squint. Which, combined with her upturned nose, full mouth and high cheekbones, gave her a country girl next door look.

A passing pickup tooted its horn and Jenny, as her friends called her, raised her hand and waved. Oakridge, Oregon born and bred she'd left the small town after high school to pursue a career in law. Ten years later she was back having abandoned a corporate salary to pursue her childhood dream job.

As she finished the smoothie an SUV pulled out of the parking lot behind her and stopped alongside. The window lowered revealing a blonde woman in her late fifties.

"Hi Darlene," said Jenny.

"Afternoon, darlin'," replied the woman in a southern drawl. "Is class still on at five?"

Jenny nodded. "Yeah, but next month it changes to six. Sam is switching up the rosters."

Darlene smiled. "Don't you go canceling on us. Those classes are just the dandiest. I've got two new girls comin' along tonight."

"The more, the merrier."

"I haven't felt this fit since I was running track at Oklahoma State." She leaned out of the window and whispered. "And, ever since I got that home pole, Steve and I have been at it like jackrabbits."

Jenny laughed.

"No, seriously. It's done wonders for my confidence. I never thought pole dancing could be so therapeutic."

"I'm glad to hear that."

The radio on Jenny's equipment belt crackled. "Reynolds, you there?"

She recognized her boss Sam's voice. "Darlene, I have to take this."

The woman waved. "I'll see you tonight."

Jenny watched her drive away as she lifted the radio to her mouth. "Sam, Reynolds here."

"Jenny, can you shoot over to the Country Club. They've got a bear stuck in one of their dumpsters."

"Again? Seriously boss, do they ever fasten them?"

"Clearly not. Brian says it's only a little fellow. You'll be able to handle it, right?"

"I'll get over there right now." Jenny stowed the radio and climbed inside the pickup.

She grinned as she drove through the sleepy town and out onto the 58 toward McCredie Springs. A year ago she'd been part of a takeover of a multi-million dollar company. Now, she was speeding through the rolling tree-covered hills of Lane County to rescue an overly inquisitive black bear. She'd always dreamed of being a park ranger, but she'd been swept up in the pressure to attend college and join the corporate world. Long hours, dealing with endless greed and a failed relationship had been the catalyst to move home and pursue that dream.

The McCredie Springs Country Club was located on the outskirts of the Willamette National Forest, the one and a half million-acre park that Jenny helped manage. Technically it was outside of her jurisdiction, but when it came to wildlife that didn't perturb rangers.

She left the highway and drove along a pine-lined lane and into the opulent grounds. White colonial style villas dotted a landscape of vines, woods, golf greens and fairways. The heart of the estate was a southern mansion that housed the restaurant, day spa and offices. Turning off the main road she passed the swimming pool and stables, heading toward the equipment sheds.

A hundred yards out she spotted one of the bright green

police cruisers of the Sheriff's Department. Two uniformed officers were talking to Brian Douglass, the property manager. She parked a distance away and walked across to join them.

She recognized the officers; Ed and Harold had attended the same high school as her, albeit a few years later.

"Well if it ain't Jenny the bear wrestling lawyer from New York." Ed was the mouthier of the two. His hulking partner Harold didn't say much.

Jenny ignored the jibe and approached the manager. "Hi, Brian."

He gave a warm smile. "I'm sorry, Jenny. One of the staff forgot to fasten the latch. Came out here this morning and found the little fella inside." He gestured to a large dumpster positioned under a tree. "These boys were passing by, but they haven't been much help."

Ed spat in the dust. "Come on, that ain't right. I offered to shoot the damn thing."

Jenny glared at him as she walked across to the dumpster. Lifting the lid she peered inside. A snarl startled her and she dropped it with a clang. Instinctively her hand moved to the butt of the pistol she wore on her belt.

Ed laughed. "What's wrong Jenny? You scared of the little bear?"

Harold laughed.

Jenny exhaled and lifted the lid again.

In the bottom of the steel dumpster sat a young black bear. She guessed its weight at a little over eighty pounds, most likely a female. The shredded remains of trash bags surrounded the animal. It had evidently climbed in looking for food and couldn't grip the smooth sides to get out.

She flipped over the lid triggering aggressive roars from the bear. "Brian, I think it might be the same one as last time."

"Yeah, I figured as much. Once they work out where the food is they keep coming back."

Jenny strode to the bed of her truck where there was a large metal cage. She dropped the tailgate and hefted the cage to the ground. Then she grabbed a pole with a cord on the end of it and a long piece of two by four. "I'm going to relocate her to the park."

Brian took the timber from her. "Good idea. I'd hate to have to destroy her."

Ed watched from a distance. "Be easier to shoot it. There are plenty of bears in the park and this is a nuisance animal."

Jenny fixed him with an icy look.

"Hey, if I want to shoot it I can. This is Lane County jurisdiction, not National Forest."

She gestured for Brian to join her at the bin. "Shoot it, Ed. See what happens if you do."

"Don't threaten me, Missy," growled the deputy.

She turned to him and smiled. "That's not a threat, it's a promise. You try and destroy that animal and I'll push this pole sideways up your ass." A jiggle of the noose emphasized the point.

Ed scowled and Harold chuckled.

"Shut up idiot," he snapped.

Jenny turned her attention to the bear. "Brian, drop that log in so she can climb it."

The rancher followed her instructions and a moment later the head of the bear appeared over the lip. Jenny hooked the noose over its head and pulled the animal to the ground. Then with Brian's help, she maneuvered it into the transportation cage.

Ed watched from a safe distance, hand resting on the butt of his pistol.

"Don't just stand there. Help us lift the damn crate onto the truck," bellowed Brian.

The deputies helped out but didn't hang around for long. With the bear secure they continued their patrol, leaving Brian and Jenny sharing a Bud Light.

"Useless as all hell. Don't know why the administration staff called them," said the former rancher.

Jenny finished her beer and tossed it in the dumpster. "Well, this little lady shouldn't give you any more trouble." She checked her watch. "I've got enough time to get her back to the station, tagged and out into the park." She climbed into her truck.

"Till next time," Brian shot through her open window.

"Keep those bins closed."

"Yes, ma'am."

***

Jenny unwrapped her legs from the floor to ceiling pole and lowered herself slowly to the ground. "OK ladies, last move," she shouted over the pumping music.

Around her a dozen women dressed like her, in crop tops and leggings, attempted to replicate the move to varying levels of success. When they had all touched down she killed the music.

"Well done, a great effort by everyone. Let's run through some stretches and wrap it up."

She'd been instructing the small class at a dance studio in Jacksonville for the past six months. In that time it had grown from a few friends to classes of up to twenty women. Word had spread fast. If it continued she was going to need a bigger premises.

Once the warm down was complete Jenny pulled on a pair of track pants and a hoodie.

"Another fantastic session," gushed Darlene as she made to leave.

"You've really progressed," she replied, tying her laces. "Like I said, getting a pole at home was a smart move."

"Jenny, when are you getting more portable poles?" asked another of the women.

"Yeah, I want one too," added another.

Grinning she grabbed her gear bag. "They should arrive later in the week. I'll update my Facebook page as soon as they're in."

She left the dance studio and crossed the parking lot to where she'd left her car. On her way she spotted a massive truck parked alongside her Chrysler. A tall figure leaned against the door of a shiny new Ford F-150 Raptor.

She recognized Lieutenant Carter Brown by his trademark Stetson hat and square stubble covered jaw. Dressed in jeans, boots and a check shirt he wore a pistol on his belt. He was the senior officer at the Oakridge Sheriff's station and a former classmate of Jenny's.

He tipped his hat as she approached. "Miss Reynolds, how are you this evening?"

She managed a tight-lipped smile as she took out her keys. "I'm good thanks, Carter."

He stepped away from his truck. "Jenny, look, I dropped by because I wanted to apologize for the way my men acted today. Old man Douglass rang my office and gave me a heads up."

Jenny turned to the handsome police officer and shrugged. "It was nothing. Boys will be boys."

He laughed. "True, but I would like to make it up to you by taking you out to dinner."

"That's a lovely gesture, Carter, but totally unnecessary. I appreciate the courtesy of a face-to-face apology. Thank you, from one professional to another."

He took a step closer and placed his hand on the car door. "Look, all I'm asking for is dinner. We'll grab a steak, my treat. It'll be good for intra-agency relations."

Jenny put her key in the lock. "In that case, you should drop by the ranger station and catch up with Sam and the rest of the crew. Bring Ed and Harold, we'll put on coffee and donuts."

A scowl split his granite features. "I'm not someone you want to make an enemy of."

"No one's trying to make an enemy of you, Carter. I'm just declining your invitation to dinner. As far as I'm aware, that's not a declaration of hostile intent."

"You threatened one of my officers today. I could bring you in for that."

She turned to face him with hands on her hips. "Really? You're going to arrest me based on a flippant comment that was made in jest." She held her wrists out. "Take me in, big shot. I'll take great pleasure in destroying your fantasy in court."

"Just watch yourself, Jenny."

She smiled. "I will."

He turned, opened the door of his pickup and climbed in. The rig rumbled to life and he backed clear before roaring off down the road.

Jenny frowned as she watched the Ford disappear. The Raptor was an expensive truck. Not something a police wage would easily buy. Pushing the thought from her head she climbed into her sedan. She needed to get home, feed her cat, put dinner on and get to bed. The team had an early start in the morning.

***

A dozen miles out of Oakridge a battered pickup with a bloodhound in the bed was parked beneath a tree on a dirt track. Two men sat inside. Hank, the older of the two, wore jeans, a denim shirt, battered cowboy boots and a ten gallon hat. Carl wore woodland camouflage pants and a stained USMC T-shirt.

Hank held a cell phone to his ear. "Yeah, no worries we'll get it done." He ended the call and slid the phone into his shirt pocket. Pulling a revolver from his belt he popped the chamber and checked it was loaded.

"So, what's the deal?" asked Carl.

"Travis reckons he's been stealing dope and selling it on the side."

"Shit, that's low. Real low." Carl took out his Glock pistol, cracked the slide and eyeballed the brass cartridge in the chamber. "He want him dead or fucked up?"

"Smith's got kids. So, just a few broken bones to get the point across."

Carl smirked, holstering his pistol as he pulled an extendable baton from the pocket of his combat pants. "Been waiting to try this sucker out."

Hank frowned as he started the truck. "Where the hell did you get that?"

"I bought it online. Got me a sweet deal on a whole bunch of stuff."

"More useless military junk." He dropped the pickup into gear, turned on the headlights and planted his foot on the accelerator.

The truck bounced along the rutted track its lights illuminating thick woods on either side. After half a mile they passed a fence, turned right and stopped in front of a rundown farmhouse.

"I'll handle this. You back me up," said Hank as he killed the engine and donned a pair of thick leather gloves.

"Why am I always the backup?" whined Carl.

He turned with a frown. "Because you're a goddamn fuck up." Climbing from the truck he strode toward the house. As he approached the door opened and a figure clutching a shotgun appeared in the porch light, Andrew Smith.

"Who's out there?"

"Hey, it's Hank and Carl," Hank said as he climbed the steps to the porch, fists clenched by his side.

Smith relaxed and lowered the shotgun. "Oh, hi guys. Thought you might be rustlers. Someone tried to steal some gear outta my barn the other night."

Hank nodded. "Seems to be a lot of that going around." He swung a savage right hook as he reached out and ripped the shotgun from Smith's hands. His fist caught the man on the jaw and he went down like a sack of potatoes.

"Nice punch," said Carl as he joined him.

"Help get him around behind the barn." He lifted the unconscious man by one arm.

Carl took the other and they dragged him past the truck out of the light cast by the porch and behind a dilapidated barn.

They sat him against a wall and Hank slapped him. "Wake the fuck up."

It took a moment for the man to come to. When he did, he tried to climb to his feet. Hank jammed the revolver under his chin. "Sit tight, boy."

"What's this all about?" the man stammered.

"Why don't you tell me?"

Smith stared across at Carl with pleading eyes. "Look, I haven't done anything wrong, I promise."

"That's not what Travis is saying."

The fear dropped from his face, replaced with a look of contempt. "That fat fuck's a liar. What the hell has he told you?"

"Said you've been stealing dope," added Carl.

Hank turned and silenced his partner with a glare. Then he turned his attention back to Smith. "Leg or arm?"

"What?"

He clenched his jaw and hissed through his teeth. "Leg or fucking arm."

Smith stared him in the eye. "You'd take Travis's word over mine?"

"Carl, do both." Hank stepped back, his pistol still aimed at Smith's face.

"Really? You mean it?"

"Just do it."

His partner flicked the extendable baton from his pocket and stepped in over the top of Smith.

"Carl, we've been friends for a long time–"

The sickening crack of his leg snapping cut him off. A blood-curdling scream filled the air as Carl lifted the baton and smashed it into his arm, crushing more bone.

Hank pushed his partner out of the way. "Shut the fuck up. Shut up or I'll shoot you in the goddamn head."

Smith managed to clench his jaw and stifle his cries.

"You see that, Hank? You see that? Barely had to swing the bastard. Did all the work for me."

He turned to his partner. "Shut the hell up and get the truck." Waiting till his partner disappeared he leaned in close. "You tell anyone who did this and you're dead."

The man nodded with his jaw clenched.

"Andy, where are you?" a female voice called from the farmhouse.

"You've paid for your transgression. Things are square. Don't do anything you or your family is gonna regret."

He shook his head. "It wasn't me, Hank."

Hank left him whimpering against the barn strode across to the truck and climbed inside.

"That was fun," said Carl as they drove back down the track.

"You're a sick fuck," he murmured as he took a pinch of chewing tobacco from a tin and stuffed it into his lip.

"Goddamn thief deserved what he got."

"So we're told."

Carl turned to him with a confused look on his face. "If he hasn't been stealing the dope, who has?"

Hank spat into an empty coke bottle. "How the fuck would I know?"

Chapter Two

The beat of rotor blades penetrated the Plexiglas windows of the cockpit and reverberated through Mike Saunders' chest. The square-jawed twenty-nine-year-old wiped his hands on his knees. His palms were sweaty despite the frigid air inside the helicopter. He glanced out the window at the snowcapped mountains and exhaled slowly.

A Navy Special Warfare Operator, the grey-eyed SEAL was a veteran of two major campaigns and a dozen covert operations. He'd spent hundreds of hours in helicopters flying over mountains, jungles, deserts and the ocean. However, never in his career was he ever this nervous. The plan was elaborate. There were so many things that could go wrong.

"How you doing bud?" asked the pilot over his headset.

He raised an eyebrow at the man and gestured over his shoulder at the other passenger.

"You're all good. She can't hear us."

"What's our ETA?" asked Mike.

"Couple more minutes. The guys on the ground have everything ready. They're standing by for your arrival." He made an adjustment to the aircraft's controls. "So relax and stop looking so damn nervous." He nodded ahead. "OK, we're coming up on our landing zone."

Mike looked through the windshield at the approaching landscape. A boulder-speckled glacier between two high peaks rapidly approached.

He glanced over his shoulder at the passenger in the rear. Ali's green eyes sparkled from inside the hood of a North Face jacket. She wore a broad smile on her elfin features.

"Wow," she mouthed.

Her expression went a long way to easing his nerves. He and Ali had been dating for over a year now. In fact, for the last two months they'd been living together. Mike had never felt this way about anyone. He was totally and utterly in love with the beautiful veterinarian. She was intelligent and kind, but also independent enough to deal with his military career. What's more she adored his dog, Axe. This holiday to the South Island of New Zealand was his way of thanking her for everything she had done for them both.

Smiling he turned his attention back to the terrain ahead. The glacier loomed and a moment later the pilot touched the skids down on the hard packed snow, killing the turbine. "OK kids, this is it. Welcome to the Franz Josef glacier."

Mike stepped from the cabin, opened the rear door for Ali and surveyed the surroundings. Snow-capped mountains stretched out in every direction. In the distance, he could see the coastline and bright blue Tasman Sea.

"It's stunning, babe," she murmured.

Feeling her arms around his waist he turned, wrapped her in a hug and kissed her. The view lost its magnetism as their lips touched.

A moment later they parted and Mike turned to see the pilot at the nose of the helicopter pretending to inspect the windshield. He looked up, saw they were done and smiled. "OK, lovebirds. If you come with me, I'll show you the best view this side of the equator."

As they followed him across the glacier toward a rocky outcrop Mike's keen eye spotted fresh tracks in the snow. He glanced sideways at Ali; her attention was fixed on the horizon. She turned to him, grinning like a child at Christmas. Then she frowned and cocked her head. "Mike, can you hear that?"

He took her hand. "No, what can you hear?"

Her eyes sparkled. "Music."

Mike's pulse quickened as they rounded the outcrop and the notes of a violin reached his ears.

"You're kidding me." Ali stopped dead in her tracks and squeezed his hand.

A pair of deck chairs sat in the snow. Between them was perched a silver champagne bucket beside a platter of fruit, cheese and caviar. A few yards away a violinist dressed in a tuxedo was playing.

The pilot gestured to the chairs. "Please, take a seat."

Ali sat and the pilot turned waiter, placing a blanket over her legs. Then he poured them each a glass of champagne before disappearing behind the outcrop.

Mike turned to Ali and raised his glass. "To the most incredible person I know."

A tear formed in her eye as she lifted hers. "You're so sweet." She gestured to the view. "This is unbelievable."

His heart raced as he glanced at the violinist. The man nodded and changed the song.

It took a moment for Ali to recognize the tune. "That's 'My Heart Will Go On'." She turned to the musician.

Mike felt like a squadron of butterflies would burst from his stomach as he reached into his pocket. He slipped out of his chair, took her hand and knelt.

Her eyes went wide as he raised the velvet case and snapped it open. "Alison Charlotte Taylor," he said with a waver. "Will you make me the happiest man alive and marry me?"

Tears filled her eyes and she nodded. "Yes, yes. Of course, I will."

As he slipped the diamond ring onto her finger, she leaned forward and kissed him. Their lips touched and Mike felt all the anxiety of the last twenty-four hours replaced by elation. He was going to be marrying the love of his life.

***

It was the next day when Mike eased himself into the warm water of the Japanese style hot tub and joined Ali on the submerged wooden bench. His fiancé wore a sleek black one piece that accented her luscious curves. They'd spent the day hiking, and now were taking a well-earned soak in a luxury outdoor spa overlooking the Shotover River.

"Mike, this place is heaven," she purred as he wrapped his muscular arms around her waist and manhandled her into the middle of the pool. He pressed his lips to hers and kissed her passionately as he caressed her chest.

"Easy boy," she murmured, sliding her hand down to his groin. "We've only got this tub for an hour."

"More than enough time," he slipped her breast from the bathing suit and kissed the nipple.

Ali slapped him playfully. "Is that right? You put a ring on my finger and the romance disappears?" She backed away from him adjusting her suit. Then with a wry grin she reached out and stabbed a button on the spa's control panel.

A cold stream of water shot out of an opening on the roof drilling him between the shoulder blades.

"Cool off, big boy."

Mike grunted and dropped underwater.

Ali turned off the water and waited for him to surface. A split second later she felt his hands on her hips. They worked their way up her stomach to her breasts and then his face emerged.

"So, cold water and frustration. Is that what I can expect as a married man?"

She kissed him again. "Of course. You knew that, right?"

Glancing over her shoulder he spotted a bright star above the mountains beyond the river. "Look, babe, first star I see tonight."

Turning she took two glasses of champagne from the tray next to the tub and handed one to him. "Make a wish and toast it."

He raised the glass then snuggled in behind her so they could both watch the horizon. "Life doesn't get any better than this."

"No it doesn't," she murmured.

They stared out at the darkening sky, watching as more stars appeared. It was Mike who broke the silence. "So, when do you want to get married?"

She shrugged. "I'm not picky. As long as the people I love are there, I'm happy. I vote for a low-key affair. No stress, just friends, family and Axe."

"I thought we could all hike up to Mount Otay and–"

"Stop right there. You're not turning this into some kind of military operation. I passed the Girlfriend Selection Course. No more shenanigans."

"Babe, I'm so over shenanigans."

She turned and kissed his cheek. "Me too. I don't even want a bachelorette party. Just a small ceremony."

"Well, then I'm not having a bachelor party."

"Mike, you can't do that to the boys. Rick will be heartbroken."

He sipped from his glass. "It's OK, I'll tell him it was your idea."

Ali snorted into hers. "You will not. They know we're engaged, right?"

"Um, well, TJ kinda does," he said, referring to his SEAL squad leader.

"You didn't tell them you were going to propose?" Ali reached out of the tub and found her phone. "We're going to tell them, now."

"Really, now?"

"Yes, I want to check on Axe." She dialed TJ and propped the phone against the bottle of champagne.

As the call connected they ducked down so only their faces were visible on the screen.

"Hello, Ali can you hear me?" TJ's voice came over the speaker, but the screen was pink. The camera was pointing into his ear.

"TJ, it's Mike. It's a video call. You need to take it away from your head."

The image changed to the inside of the squad's team room at Coronado in San Diego. They caught a glimpse of a shirtless heavily muscled African American seated on a weights bench, Rick the squad Corpsman. Then the camera revealed the craggy features of Chief 'TJ' Lines. "Hey, how are the lovebirds doing?"

"Is that Mike?" Rick bellowed in the background. A moment later he appeared alongside TJ. "Hi, Ali." Rick frowned. "Are you guys in a hot tub?"

"Yes, we've had a big day. How's my boy, Axe?" asked Ali.

"Hang on," said TJ as he moved the camera.

Axe, Mike's Military Working Dog was sitting in a chair staring at a cartoon playing on a laptop. Mike whistled and the Belgian Malinois snapped his head toward the screen. The top of his right ear flopped forward as he tilted his head.

"How's my beautiful boy?" gushed Ali.

Axe cocked his head the other way.

"He's so confused," Mike said with a laugh.

TJ appeared on the screen. "He's been a bit mopey, but apart from that he's good. The cartoons seem to help. So, what's news with you guys? Having a good time in Middle Earth?"

"It's been OK." Ali held up her hand so the Chief could see the engagement ring.

He squinted and then a broad grin split his craggy features. "Goddamn, that's fantastic news. Rick, our boy popped the question. Mike and Ali are getting married."

There was a clang as a dumbbell hit the ground. "Job well done, Frogman." Rick's face appeared. "Way to go and congratulations to you little lady." Then the expression on his face changed, as if a bolt of enlightenment had struck him. "Fuck yeah, this means we're gonna throw a bachelor party."

"Whoa there, Rick. Ali and I have decided to keep this real low key. A small ceremony and that's it."

TJ's face appeared. "Probably a good idea."

"What the fuck?" Rick exclaimed in the background. "That's so damn selfish."

TJ rolled his eyes. "OK, you kids enjoy the last few days of your vacation. We'll see you on Tuesday."

"Thanks, TJ. Pass on our best to Ernie and let him know the news," replied Ali.

They could still hear Rick ranting as the call terminated.

Ali kissed Mike's neck. "You think he'll be over it by the time we get back?"

He laughed. "Definitely not."

***

"I can't believe he's not going to have a bachelor party," Rick said as he hefted a dumbbell from the floor.

"Who's not having a bachelor party?" a short Latino asked as he entered the team room. Ernesto, or Ernie as his friends called him, was the SEAL squad's communications specialist. Together with Mike, Rick, TJ and Axe, they formed an elite fighting team.

"Mike, he and Ali are getting hitched," said Rick.

"Really, when did that happen?"

TJ ruffled Axe's ears. "Today, in New Zealand. He popped the big one and she said yes."

Ernie grinned. "That's fantastic news."

Rick dumped the weight on the floor. "Except the selfish bastard isn't having a bachelor party."

"What, that makes no sense. You can't get married without a bachelor party."

"Mike can," grumbled Rick.

"You ladies done?" snapped TJ. "You know bachelor parties were never meant to be tequila swilling strip fests. The origin of the tradition stems from the Spartans, they held a feast to toast the groom and farewell his singlehood."

Rick yawned. "Boring. We need to take Mike to Tijuana and get him fuuuucked up."

TJ's eyes narrowed. "No. We need to take him on an epic adventure. Get him out in the woods away from the big smoke and back in touch with nature."

Rick shook his head and turned to Ernie. "You down with redneck shit or are you up for tequila and titties?"

The Latino's eyes narrowed. "Essé, I'm not going anywhere near Mexico with you. The Chief's idea sounds good. We get out in the woods. We drink a little bourbon around a fire and we chill."

"I've got a place in Willamette National Forest up in Oregon. We'll head up there for a weekend."

Rick sighed. "Great idea. Except for one thing, Mike and

Ali have already laid down the law. No bachelor party."

TJ gave Axe another pat. "You leave that to me. In the meantime, we've got boats to clean."

Rick and Ernie let out a simultaneous groan.

"Why is it we only wash boats when Mike's away," moaned Rick.

TJ smiled. "Because I like him more than I like you."

Rick frowned. "You're supposed to like us all the same."

The Chief chuckled. "This is a SEAL team, not the goddamn Brady Bunch. Get your ass off that bench and get down to the sheds."

Chapter Three

Mike laughed as Axe let out an excited bark and danced around on the beach like a hyperactive puppy.

"I guess he missed you," said TJ with a chuckle as the team jogged along the beach.

"Wait till he sees Ali," said Mike as they reached the turnaround point and headed back toward the Navy base.

The four SEALs ran shirtless in the warm morning sun. Their bodies were covered in sand and salt from the rigorous training program the Chief had run to celebrate Mike's return. They'd started with pushups and crunches in the surf followed by a half mile swim and finally a three mile soft sand run.

Throughout the session Axe never left Mike's side. Over eighteen months had passed since the dog had been shot and thanks to Ali's veterinary skills he showed no sign of injury.

"So, how did the proposal go down?" asked TJ between breaths as they reached the end of their run.

Mike gave the boys a move-by-move breakdown of the entire operation as they stretched in a park.

"That's pretty slick essé," said Ernie when the story was complete.

"An operation that'd make any SEAL proud," added TJ.

"Not bad at all kid," said Rick. "Kicks all my proposals in the ass."

Mike frowned. "You've only been married once."

Rick shrugged. "I went through a phase of asking chicks to marry me. No big deal."

The other three men shared looks of disbelief.

"Anyway," he continued. "We need to talk about your bachelor party."

Mike grabbed a stick and tossed it across the park. Axe dashed after it. "Yeah, Ali and I are keen to keep this low key. We don't want a repeat of the Girlfriend Selection Course."

"You two wouldn't even be together if it wasn't for

selection," said Rick. "Come on, brother. One last hit out with the team."

Axe dropped the stick at Mike's feet and looked up at him, tongue lolling from the side of his mouth. "One last hit out? I'm getting married not going to prison. The decision is final. No bachelor party."

"Does that mean you're not having a best man?" asked Ernie. "Because technically it was me who introduced you to Ali in the first place."

"The fuck! How you figure that?" snapped Rick.

"I recommended the vet. Even said she was pretty."

TJ finished stretching and sat on a bench seat. "That's true."

"Well, what about selection?" asked Rick.

"That was TJ's idea."

Rick frowned. "Yeah, well it was my element that let you SEAL the deal," he said accenting the words with his fingers.

Mike laughed. "Guys, I could never choose between you. You're all family. Plus, it was actually Axe who brought Ali and me together."

TJ grunted. "He's right, but you can't have a dog as your best man."

"True, and that's why I've asked my brother, Dean."

Rick frowned. "What the hell? I thought you were an only child?"

"That's because you're the world's worst listener. You're only interested in tits and ass," said Ernie.

"That's not true."

"Really? What's the Chief's wife's name?"

He frowned. "That's not fair. We never see her."

"Emily. Her name is Emily," answered Mike.

He shrugged. "I knew that."

TJ rose from the bench. "Rick, Mike and Ali want a low key event. We will respect that."

Rick scowled as he nodded. "Yeah, got it."

"Right," TJ continued. "Let's get back to work. We're running mask drills in the kill house."

***

Leonie's squeal of delight filled the café turning heads and earning a scowl from an elderly woman reading a paper. "Ali, it's freaking beautiful."

She blushed as her sister clutched her hand, inspecting the engagement ring.

"Holy shit! He must have dropped a bomb on this."

Her sister, a blonde middle-aged mother of two had a real way with words. Ali's father always accused her of having a mouth dirtier than a railway worker's coveralls.

"And you said he proposed on a glacier with a violinist and a bottle of Dom?"

Ali smiled. "Yes, he did. It was the most romantic thing I've ever experienced."

"That's panty dropping right there. I'm wet just thinking about it."

She giggled. "Leonie!"

Her sister took a sip from her coffee. "That boy's a goddamn dreamboat." Her eyes shone as she smiled. "I am so happy for you." She lowered the cup to the table. "OK, so let's talk wedding. When you were little, you always wanted the whole nine yards: unicorns, carriages, doves, an orchestra and white lace. Yards and yards of white lace."

"Oh, that's right, I remember. No, Mike and I have agreed on a small intimate affair. I'm thinking one of the vineyards out near Swartz Canyon."

"Yes, with a string quartet and a reception under the vines. Big weddings are so passé."

"I knew you'd understand." She paused. "That's why you have to be my Maid of Honor."

Leonie smirked. "Please, who else could do the job?" She clapped her hands. "This is going to be so much fun. I am going to throw you the best bachelorette party this city has ever seen."

Ali scrunched up her face.

"What?"

"Mike and I kind of agreed we would keep things low key."

The happiness slid from Leonie's face. "You're kidding, right? No bachelorette party?"

Ali shook her head.

Her sister's jaw dropped. "Why would you do that? You know the bachelorette party isn't actually for you. It's for people like me. Ladies who haven't been drunk in months. Ladies who haven't felt the hot hard abs of an athlete since… Well, since ever."

"You're being a little dramatic."

"No, I'm not. You're entirely selfish." She folded her arms.

"OK, OK, maybe we can have a small gathering. Just a few girls, but it's not a party."

Leonie winked. "Got it. Let's call it pre-wedding drinks and…" She raised her hands and used her fingers as inverted commas. "Activities."

Ali frowned. "Minimal activities."

Her sister downed the last of her coffee. "Yeah, yeah whatever. OK babe, I've got to run." She leaned over and kissed Ali on the forehead. "I'm so happy for you. Give my best to Mike and Axe. I'll see you at the planning brunch on the weekend."

Ali drank the last of her latte as her sister left the café. She couldn't help but feel she was going to regret agreeing to a 'small' gathering. Still, Leonie was an amazing sister and a terrific mom to her nieces. If she needed to let down her hair a little who was Ali to say no?

***

The wedding planning team occupied a long table at Mike and Ali's favorite café, the Spanner Shop. The converted mechanic's garage was a short distance from her veterinary clinic and served the best coffee, sandwiches and muffins in a ten-mile radius.

Mike and Ali sat on one side of the table with TJ, Leonie and Mike's younger brother Dean, opposite.

The junior Saunders bore a close resemblance to his older brother. He had the same gray eyes, chiseled jaw and blonde hair. However, unlike his SEAL brother Dean had not followed their father into the services. He was a software engineer who spent most of his time perched behind a computer. As a result his hair reached his collar and he carried a little extra weight.

It was Mike who started the meeting. "Guys, firstly Ali and I would like to thank you for taking time out on a Saturday to help us wade through all this wedding stuff."

"You're the best," added Ali.

"It's also a chance for TJ, who's agreed to be the master of ceremonies, and Leonie, Ali's sister and maid of honor, to meet my brother and best man, Dean."

Leonie leaned across and whispered to Ali. "He's just as handsome and he's younger."

Ali shook her head and laughed as Mike continued. "I'm going to reemphasize that this is going to be a very low key event. About thirty guests and the bridal party."

"And a string quartet," added Leonie.

"Of course."

"Have you chosen a venue yet?" asked TJ.

Ali answered, "We've narrowed it down to three. Mike and I are heading out to Swartz Canyon after this to check them out." She glanced at her watch. "In fact, we're going to have to leave soon."

Leonie clapped her hands. "OK, venue aside we need to get to the most important part, the fashion. Ali, have you picked out a dress?"

"No, I thought you and I could do that next week."

"Lock it in. I'll get something to wear at the same time. Right, now for the boys."

"I thought I could wear dress uniform," said Mike.

TJ coughed into his fist. "Wear a tux."

Dean nodded in agreement. "Hey, bro. Proud of your

service but this isn't about the military. This is for you and Ali."

Ali placed her hand on his. "I don't mind. It's up to you."

"Uniforms are sexy," added Leonie.

"Buy yourself a nice tuxedo. Every man should own one," TJ said. "Sure, get a few photos in your dress whites, but trust me, get married with class."

"Did you?" asked Mike.

TJ winked. "Damn straight I did. I wanted Emily to know she was marrying a man not a sailor. A man that would put her first over the service at the drop of a hat."

Mike nodded. "Tuxedo it is."

The Chief turned to Dean. "I've got an A-grade tailor that will sort both of you boys out. We'll hook it up for next week."

"Sounds good," replied Dean.

"Well that's the fashion," said Leonie. "Next we need to talk through decorations, music, invitations, food, gifts and timings. Oh, and most importantly, an engagement party."

Mike groaned.

Ali squeezed his hand. "Do we need an engagement party?"

Leonie shrugged. "Maybe not a party, just a sit-down dinner. I know Mom and Dad would love that."

Ali nodded. "OK, can you come up with some options? Mike and I need to get going."

They rose from the table and Ali hugged everyone. Then the pair disappeared out the front door leaving TJ, Dean and Leonie at the table.

"A buddy of mine owns a restaurant in town. Mike took Ali there on one of their first dates so it might be a good venue," said TJ.

"Just 'n' Thyme?" asked Leonie.

"That's the one."

She rolled her eyes. "It took me three months to get a table."

"Yeah, he tells me it's doing well. I'll make a call and let you know, but right now we get down to the real business."

"Which is?" asked Dean.

"The bachelor and bachelorette party."

Leonie's eyes lit up. "Oh hell yeah. Tell me more, Mr. SEAL."

Chapter Four

TJ's buddy had insisted on closing one of his dining rooms to host Mike and Ali's engagement dinner at his restaurant, Just 'n' Thyme. Thirty-five of their closest friends and family joined them in the romantic setting. Ali's parents had flown in from Nebraska, Mike's mom had come down from San Jose, and of course the team was in attendance along with their Commanding Officer.

The meal was a sumptuous three-course affair that started with oysters, progressed to lobster and rack of lamb, before concluding with a delicate adaptation of the classic, tiramisu.

When dinner was finished, Mike rose and thanked everyone for attending. He quickly told an abridged version of the proposal and professed his undying love for Ali. She added a few words of her own before they handed over to TJ, the master of ceremonies.

"Ladies and gentlemen, firstly I want to thank my old friend James for putting on a fabulous dinner." He gestured to the owner who was standing in the corner.

The room broke into applause.

He waited for silence then continued. "Most of you, if not all, are aware of the events that brought Ali and Mike together. One very special dog, who unfortunately couldn't be here tonight, but sends his regards, plus a series of challenges that myself and two other people in this room may or may not have played a role in concocting."

There was nervous laughter from Rick and Ernie's table.

"Needless to say, Ali came through. Not only for Mike and Axe but also Rick, Ernie and myself. In fact, we, like Axe, owe her our lives." He raised his glass. "Ladies and gentlemen, I'd like you to be upstanding."

The room rose and lifted their glasses.

"To Ali, a beautiful person and a killer teammate."

The room echoed his toast.

"Now, before we wrap up I would like to present a small gift to Ali and Mike from the rest of the team. It's not much, but it may go a small way to make up for the trauma of the Girlfriend Selection Course." He took an envelope from under his jacket and handed it to Ali. "You kids have a great time."

***

Later that night, in the townhouse he shared with Ali, Mike measured a scoop of dog food and emptied it into Axe's bowl. The hound looked up at him with a furrowed brow. "OK, fine." He sighed and added another half scoop to the bowl. "Don't blame me if you start getting fat."

Axe let out an excited bark and started eating.

Mike washed his hands and left the kitchen.

"Mike, you have to see this," Ali's voice sounded from the bedroom.

He pushed open the door to find his fiancé sitting on the bed in sleek satin underwear. She had an envelope in her hands and a smile on her face.

Mike stood in the doorway a moment and ran his eyes over her voluptuous body. Damn she was sexy.

"The boys got us a weekend away in a five-star resort in Oregon."

Mike removed his shirt and hung it on a chair. "They have resorts in Oregon?"

Ali nodded as she flicked through a pamphlet. "Yes and it looks amazing. It's got a day spa, restaurant, golf course, horses and it's set in the most beautiful forest." She held up a handwritten note. "And TJ knows the manager so we can take Axe."

"Of course he does. TJ knows everyone." Mike tossed his pants over his shirt, lowered himself onto the bed and slid toward her. "Sounds too good to be true. What's the catch?" He kissed her stomach.

"They booked us tickets. It's the weekend before the wedding."

He worked his way up her body to her cleavage. "Isn't that a bad time to go?" he murmured.

She moaned softly. "No, everything should be arranged by then. It's going to be the perfect time to relax."

"Sounds great." He kissed her neck and then nibbled her ear.

Her hands traced their way down his hard body as he reached under and unsnapped her bra with a deft touch. Their lips met as she reached down and squeezed gently. "We're going to have the best time."

"Now or at the resort?"

"Both."

Chapter Five

Rick drummed his fingers on the steering wheel as he drove Ernie's minivan through Las Vegas on Interstate 15. He shook his head as the black-glass pyramid of the The Luxor Hotel flashed past. "This is the cruelest shit I've ever heard of. Driving through Vegas to get to a redneck bachelor party in the mountains. That's ruthless as fuck, TJ."

In the passenger seat the Chief looked up from the book he was reading. "Trust me, it's the best way."

Rick glanced up at a huge sign announcing the Bellagio Hotel. "Come on. We're here. Surely we can stop overnight. Maybe catch a show at the Spearmint Rhino."

TJ shook his head. "Negative, we need to be in Fallon by lunchtime."

Rick glanced in the rear-view mirror. The other two passengers, Dean and Ernie were fast asleep. "Is that where we're changing teams?"

"Yeah, why? You getting tired?"

He yawned. "A little." Rick had been driving since they left San Diego five hours earlier.

"OK, pull into the next gas station and we'll grab some coffee and switch."

Twenty minutes later Rick sat in the passenger seat with a can of energy drink in one hand and his phone in the other. TJ was now behind the wheel, and Dean and Ernie were awake.

"Are you kidding me?" Rick exclaimed as he stared at the phone.

"What's wrong? Already run out of Tinder matches?" asked Dean.

"No, worse. There are literally zero strippers within a hundred miles of Oakridge, Oregon."

"Oh no, essé. What are you going to do? You might have to dress up and give Mike a lap dance," said Ernie.

"You'd like that, wouldn't you? You sick little midget."

"No need to get racist," replied the Latino.

"What, how is midget racist?"

"You were implying that Mexicans are much shorter than black men."

Rick turned with a cocked eyebrow. "Brother, you've got a serious complex." Returning his attention to his phone he missed the wink that Ernie shot Dean.

"OK, looks like your crappy little town has a pole dancing studio. That's pretty much stripping, right?"

TJ shook his head. "It used to be such a quaint place."

"Is that where you grew up?" asked Ernie as Rick thumbed an email on his phone.

"No, used to visit a lot. My grandfather built the cabin when I was a kid. We'd head up there most summers. Swim in the lake, raft the river and hunt deer. Some of my best times were had in those mountains."

Rick continued on his phone.

"What about you, Dean?" asked TJ. "You and Mike get out in the wilderness much?"

He nodded. "Yeah, we grew up on Navy bases though, so we spent more time in the water. The old man was posted to Pearl for a few years. We got up in the mountains there a fair bit."

"Mike doesn't talk much about his dad," said Ernie.

Dean nodded. "When dad died he took it pretty hard. They were real close. Mike idolized him. I was always closer to mom."

"Jackpot!" Rick punched his fist in the air.

"Tinder match?" asked Dean.

"Better, we've got ourselves a pole dancer for tomorrow night."

"You could turn a nun's picnic into a gangbang, couldn't you Rick?" growled TJ.

He grinned. "What can I say, it's a gift."

***

Ali's face was glued to the window of their hired sedan as it turned off the highway and entered the McCredie Springs Country Club. "Oh Mike, it's beautiful," she exclaimed as he drove them along a tree-lined laneway. They'd flown up from San Diego mid-afternoon and driven the sixty miles from the city of Eugene to their destination.

Mike parked the car in front of a grand southern-style mansion. As they stepped outside a man in his fifties dressed in jeans, boots and a McCredie Springs embroidered shirt appeared from inside.

"You must be Mike and Ali," he declared in a deep voice.

"That's us." Mike shook his hand. "Oh, and we've got Axe in the back."

"The hero, right?"

Ali smiled. "The one and only. Thank you so much for letting us bring him along."

"Hey, it's no problem at all. We've got a villa set aside for people with dogs. My name's Brian and if there's anything you need, you let me know."

"Thanks, Brian. I tell you what, this has to be the prettiest place I've ever seen," said Ali.

"We try. Now, I'll show you to your villa. The boys will bring your luggage along momentarily. Mike, if you leave your keys in the car, they'll park it for you and drop them off with the bags."

They let Axe out of the sedan and followed Brian down a stone pathway that weaved between tall birch trees. Birds flitted among the branches, their calls filling the air.

"You're welcome to let Axe run in the forest. However, we've got horses in the bottom paddock. They're fine with dogs, but Axe might not like them." He gestured to a velvet smooth green. "Mike are you much of a golfer?"

"I certainly am."

"Good, because I find that nine holes take about the same time as the deluxe spa treatment. Which, I might add is included with your room."

Ali grasped his arm. "You mean you won't be joining me?"

Mike laughed. "Hey, someone has to look after Axe."

She kissed his cheek. "So that's why you wanted to bring him."

They reached a quaint weatherboard cottage perched in the woods. Two stories with a deck it was framed with vine-laden trellis. As they climbed the steps to the porch Ali spotted a hot tub nestled in the garden.

"Mike, this is the best."

Brian swiped an electronic lock and pushed open the bi-fold doors revealing an opulent living area. There was a kitchen, dining setting, couches and a chandelier hanging from the ceiling.

"There are two bedrooms upstairs, both with their own bathrooms." He reached out and ruffled Axe's ears. "If you need anything just holler." He slipped away outside leaving the three of them alone.

"The boys have outdone themselves," said Ali as she climbed the stairs to the second floor.

Mike followed her and Axe upstairs. "The selection fiasco didn't exactly set the bar high."

"OK, now this is nice," announced Ali.

The master bedroom opened up onto a balcony with views out over the valley. White gauze curtains danced in the breeze. He turned around and was confronted by a dazzling white bathroom with an enormous brass-footed bathtub.

Ali was standing in front of it smiling. "I think we're going to be very comfortable here." She frowned and nodded toward the bed.

Mike looked over and saw Axe sprawled on the duvet. "Someone already is. Axe, off."

The dog jumped down and disappeared downstairs.

He turned back to Ali as she slipped her summer dress's shoulder straps off and let it drop to the floor. Beneath it, she wore lacy white underwear. She pouted her lips and pointed to his pants. "Mike, off."

***

It was early morning when TJ parked the van in front of a log cabin nestled among the trees on the shore of a lake. He stepped out, took a few paces, lifted his arms wide and sucked in a lungful of crisp mountain air.

The other three occupants of the van were a little slower to gather themselves. Dean and Ernie climbed out of the back of the van and stretched. Rick continued slumbering in the front passenger seat.

TJ opened his door. "Rise and shine cupcake, it's time to get this place ready for action."

Rick opened one eye. "You sir, are an asshole."

The boys unloaded their bags and boxes of supplies as TJ unlocked the cabin. He swung open the door and childhood memories came flooding back. The bunkhouse was exactly how he remembered it. It consisted of a single open room with bunks across the back and a massive fireplace at one end. At the other was the kitchen with its lake facing windows and an old cast iron cooker.

"Wow!" Rick let out a low whistle as he entered carrying a carton of Bulleit Bourbon. "Hey Pops, you shoot that?" He placed the booze on a rough-hewn table in the center of the cabin and gestured to a stuffed black bear in the corner of the room.

TJ shook his head. "Nope, grandma killed that one with her bare hands."

Rick frowned.

"Chief, this is a pretty special place," said Ernie as he and Dean entered with cartons of food.

"Yeah, man. Thanks for bringing us up here," added Dean.

"My pleasure, boys. Right, Rick, you check the raft. Should be in the boatshed. Dean, you get those rations stowed." He pointed to the shelves in the kitchen. "Ernie, lay the map on the table. I'll fire up the stove and get some coffee on. Full mission briefing in fifteen."

The men snapped into action like a well-oiled machine. Exactly fifteen minutes later with mugs of coffee in hand they gathered around the map that Ernie had pinned to the table.

"OK boys, we're here." TJ used the tip of a bowie knife to show their location. "Eugene city is over here." He pointed off the map. "McCredie Springs is here." He tapped the tip on the edge of the National Forest. "And the river is here." He traced a thin blue line that ran through the middle of the forest from north to south.

"Looks pretty remote," observed Ernie.

"It is. Twenty-two miles of untouched wilderness."

Rick unscrewed a bottle of bourbon and sloshed it in his coffee. "We're taking guns, right?"

"We're on the river. What are you going to shoot, fish?"

"The guns are for protection. Haven't you seen Deliverance?" Rick exposed his teeth in his best impersonation of a hick. "Hey boy, you squeal like a pig?"

TJ rolled his eyes. "This is Oregon, not West Virginia."

"Same shit. We need guns."

TJ tapped the bourbon bottle with his blade. "You going to be sober at any stage of this activity?"

Rick considered his point. "Nope."

"Then no guns." The Chief checked his watch. "I need to be at the airport in two and a half hours. I'll drop you boys at McCredie on the way through. You get eyes on the target and when I get back we'll make the snatch."

Rick raised his hand. "Question."

"Shoot."

"Can I stay here and get things ready for tonight?"

"Sure, but don't wander off into the woods. The bears are pretty active this time of year."

"Bears? What the fuck TJ, what hellhole have you brought us to? This is supposed to be a bachelor party not the god damn hunger games."

TJ spun the Bowie knife in his palm and flicked it into the wood. "Rick, stop being such a pansy, you'll be fine." He gestured to the others. "Get your gear sorted. We roll in thirty."

***

Leonie grabbed her bags from an airport conveyor belt and joined the women waiting at the exit. It was nine in the morning and they'd caught the first flight up from San Diego. As maid of honor she was responsible for the group of six. The bachelorette party consisted of two of Ali's friends from college, her assistant Naomi, a girl she played tennis with and Ernie's wife, Maria.

"OK ladies, is everyone ready?"

They let out a resounding cheer and Leonie led them out of the arrivals lounge. She spotted TJ standing alongside a minivan. She waved and he strode over.

She gave his cargo pants, checked shirt and baseball cap a once over. "Look at you, all rugged and outdoorsy."

He frowned at her bulging bags. "You do know you're only here for two nights."

"It's not all for me. I've packed vital party supplies."

He let out a grunt as he lifted the bags. "Lead pipes?" Lowering them into the trunk he slammed it shut. "We've got a little over an hours drive. There's a liquor store on the way. Is there anything else you ladies need before we reach the resort?"

Leonie glanced around the group. Everyone looked to her expectantly. "Sounds good."

The girls clambered aboard and soon they were on the highway heading south.

"So how come Mrs. Chief wasn't available for this little foray?" asked Leonie from the passenger seat.

"Emily was keen, but she's away on a business trip."

"Ah, that sucks. What line of work is she in?"

"She's a food critic."

"Get out of town."

TJ laughed. "What, too civilized for a sailor?"

"No, just not what I expected."

"I was a chef before I joined up."

"Do you clean as well?"

"Huh, I guess so. Why?"

"It's the ultimate package. Cooks, kills and cleans. You're Casey goddamn Ryback." Leonie reached into her handbag and removed a hip flask. "OK ladies, let's get this party started."

The van filled with laughter and TJ shook his head. He pressed the accelerator a little harder. The sooner he got to McCredie the sooner he could offload the six women.

Chapter Six

Mike tipped his head and cracked his neck before adjusting his stance and grip on a golf club. He drew back the five iron and drove through the ball.

"Oh yeah," he murmured as it sailed down the fairway and bounced toward the green. "You see that?" He turned to where Axe was lying on the grass chewing a bone. "Nailed it." The dog paid him no attention. "Yeah, I thought as much."

He returned the club to his bag and grabbed the handle. "OK, buddy. Let's roll."

Axe picked up his bone and trotted down the fairway alongside him. Mike checked his watch and smiled. He had enough time for a few more holes before meeting Ali at the villa. His thoughts turned to the wedding and how simple Ali was making the whole process. He had literally been to a coffee date, the engagement dinner and a suit fitting. In fact, everyone including his SEAL squad were being super helpful. Hell, he was getting married next week and here he was strolling along a fairway at a five-star resort with his best friend; life was good.

He reached his ball, selected a pitching wedge and lined up. The green was beyond a small rise. He could barely see the top of the flag. Chipping high he watched with satisfaction as the shot sailed toward the pin.

Axe chewed his bone as Mike scanned the green for the ball. There was no sign of it. Hoping for a birdie, he checked the hole; no ball. "You're kidding me," he mumbled, searching the grass at the edge of the green. He made his way into the undergrowth. Axe joined him as he poked in the pine needles.

The dog gave a bark and disappeared into the bushes with his tail wagging. "You found it?" he asked, following.

"Looking for this?" Ernie's voice startled him as he pushed through branches and saw his teammate holding the ball. Axe jumped up and licked the Latino's face.

Mike frowned. "What the hell are you doing here?"

"I'm here for the party."

There was a rustle to Mike's flank and TJ appeared holding a pair of plasticuffs. "We can do this the easy way or the hard way."

There was another noise to his right and Dean emerged clutching a black hood.

Mike glanced down at Axe who was sitting with his tongue lolling from his mouth. "Are you kidding me? You're not even going to try and protect me?"

The dog cocked his head and his ear flopped forward.

"Does Ali know about this?" Mike asked as he handed his club to Ernie and held his wrists together.

Dean slid the hood over his head as TJ cuffed him.

"By now she's got problems of her own," TJ replied with a laugh.

"Seriously, if this involves cartel hit men I'm going to be pissed."

***

Ali felt amazing. Her skin had never felt smoother in her life. Three hours of pampering at the day spa had been exactly what she needed. The planning for the wedding hadn't been particularly stressful. Leonie and TJ had taken care of most of the details, but it was still good to relax in the hands of a talented masseuse.

She strolled along the path to the villa enjoying the sunshine and the warm breeze on her face. Stepping onto the porch, she spotted Mike's golf clubs and smiled. He would have enough time to enjoy her smooth body before dinner.

Axe greeted her at the stairs and she stopped to pat him. Her smile widened as she spotted the drawn curtains. It looked as if Mike had something similar in mind.

Pushing open the doors she ducked through the gossamer material. "Mike, babe, I feel fantastic!"

"Surprise!" The screams of six female voices nearly sent her diving back outside. Leonie stood at the front of the pack with a huge cocktail glass in her hand. She thrust the beverage and its penis-shaped straw toward Ali.

"Welcome to your bachelorette party, little sister."

She gave the villa an uneasy scan, noting the phallic-themed decorations strung across the ceiling. Rows of alcohol bottles and cocktail glasses filled the kitchen bench top. Then it dawned on her. The resort and the day spa were all an elaborate plan.

She smiled, took a slurp from the cocktail and winced at the taste of tequila. "You are so devious."

The girls circled her lifting their glasses in the air. Axe joined them jumping up and down with excitement as they whooped and hollered.

"So what's the plan?" asked Ali. "What happened to Mike? I'm guessing the boys grabbed him?"

Leonie topped up her cocktail. "Correct, we're meeting up with them tomorrow afternoon. However, till then we're going to party like it's 1999."

Maria, Ernie's wife, joined them. The short buxom Mexican hugged Ali and planted a kiss on her cheek. "Tonight we've got a beautiful dinner. Then your sister can continue with her depraved plans."

Leonie shrugged. "She insisted."

Ali smiled. "Maria, I am so glad you're here to add a touch of class."

Her sister laughed. "Class? Sweetheart, we're drinking from cock straws."

The villa filled with laughter and Ali grinned. Maybe a bachelorette party wasn't such a bad idea after all.

***

Mike felt the van come to a halt and heard the door slide open. He was bundled outside and then the hood was ripped off. He'd guessed they were on their way to TJ's cabin and he was correct.

The Chief released the cuffs from Mike's wrists. "Welcome

to paradise."

"TJ, this is great," he exclaimed, examining the rough-hewn log building.

"Yeah, been in the family a long time."

At that moment the cabin door swung open and Rick appeared on the deck with a glass in each hand. "Mikey boy, welcome to the last day of your FREEEEEEEDOM!"

Mike laughed. "Rick, are you already wasted?"

The African American embraced him in a hug. "Not yet, but the night is young. Fellas, come inside, I've got someone I want you to meet."

"Here we go," said TJ as Dean and Ernie followed him into the cabin.

In the few hours that they'd been gone Rick had made some minor adjustments to the interior layout. The kitchen table had been moved to the far end of the room and served as a well-stocked bar. The couches had been shoved into each corner and the open space was now occupied by what looked like half a dozen stripper poles.

In front of the fireplace Mike spotted a tall woman dressed in leggings and a crop top. She had the body of a dancer and a girl next door face that was painted with a broad smile.

She waved at them. "Hi guys, my name's Jenny. Are you ready to get started?"

TJ turned to Rick. "What the hell's going on here?"

Rick shrugged. "It would seem that pole dancing is not the same as stripping." He downed one of his drinks and gestured to the bar. "Let's give it a go."

Mike doubled over with laughter. "Rick, you're a champion." He poured himself a bourbon and downed it. "Come on boys, let's get into it." He moved across and grabbed a pole. "Right, Jenny, I'm Mike. Exactly how do we do this?"

***

The staff at the Country Club had set aside a private dining area for the girls. The room was decorated with bouquets of white flowers, the tables laid with crisp linen and fine silver cutlery. Classical music played from a stereo in the corner as the women enjoyed an exceptional dining experience.

Ali, dressed in an elegant lace dress sat at the head of the table with a plastic tiara perched on her head. The other women, equally as resplendent, sat around her.

As dessert was served Leonie interrupted the conversation by striking her champagne glass with the back of the knife. It subsequently shattered unleashing its contents on the table. "Oh, fuck."

The girls broke into laughter as Maria used her napkin to abate the tidal wave of sparkling white.

Leonie tapped the stem of the shattered glass. "OK ladies, calm down. As usual, Maria has it under control." She paused as the girls clapped. "I'd like to take the opportunity to thank her for organizing this beautiful dinner."

The girls all cheered.

"Now, we all know that my baby sister is the reason we're here. Next week she marries a guy who may well be the sweetest dreamboat in the history of single men. And God knows after the dick weeds she's dated, she deserves him."

Ali smiled. "Thanks, sis."

"But, married is next week. Tonight she's going to party hard." Leonie nodded to a girl positioned next to the stereo system. "So ladies, I hope you've left enough room for another round of dessert, because here come the sweetest treats you've ever seen."

Classical music was suddenly replaced by a thumping beat and the doors to the dining room burst open. At first, no one appeared. Then, as the music peaked, two handsome twenty-something men dressed as a fireman and police officer strutted into view.

"Woo, hoo. Happy bachelorette Ali!" screamed Leonie as the strippers danced their way into the room and circled the ladies like hungry sharks.

Ali blushed as they made their way to the head of the table

and danced suggestively on either side of her. The fireman was the first to disrobe, letting his jacket fall to reveal a rock hard body.

The girls whooped and cheered as the police officer followed his cue and ripped open his shirt. The scantily clad men took it in turns to rub their sculpted torsos on either side of Ali. She giggled, trying hard not to burst into laughter as they took her hands and traced them over their abs.

"Leonie, you're so dead," she mouthed.

Her sister raised a fresh glass. "Live it up baby, this is your night."

***

Meanwhile, less than twenty miles away the boy's night was progressing somewhat differently. Mike, TJ, Dean and Ernie had abandoned their attempts at pole dancing and had resorted to drinking as they watched an inebriated Rick try to follow Jenny's instructions.

"OK, Rick. Let's move to something more advanced." Jenny hauled herself up the pole, flipped upside down, wrapped her legs around it, released her hands and slowly spun around the pole to the ground.

Perched on a stool, TJ poured himself another bourbon. "You're pushing shit uphill, Jenny. That big ox will never be able to do that." He turned to Mike and winked.

"What the hell, granddad. I don't see any other motherfucker out here trying this pole shit." Rick stripped to his briefs revealing muscles that would put a professional athlete to shame.

"And the fish takes the bait," said Ernie.

Mike laughed. "Every time."

Rick hauled himself effortlessly up the pole, flipped upside down and wrapped his legs around it.

"I just realized why you're so good at this," said TJ.

"Because I'm strong," yelled Rick as he contemplated releasing his hands.

"No, because you're the only one who shaves his legs. It's a matter of friction."

Mike snickered into his drink and bourbon shot from his nose. He hunched over coughing as the others burst into laughter.

"Serves you right, bachelor boy. Should be you up this damn pole," yelled Rick from where he was hanging.

Standing in the corner, Jenny suppressed a smirk. "Come on Rick, they all gave up. You can do this."

"Damn straight I can. I'm a frogman." He released the pole and slowly spun around it toward the ground.

"He's actually doing it," yelled Dean. "He's actually doing it."

Ernie started the chant. "Rick, Rick, Rick."

In a matter of seconds everyone, including Jenny was yelling the pole dancing Navy SEAL's name.

Then, as he got closer to the ground he started gathering speed. Then he lost traction and dropped like a rock, landing on his head with a thump. His legs unlatched from the pole and he collapsed into a motionless heap.

The room fell silent.

Suddenly Rick jumped to his feet. "Nailed it!" He sprinted across to Mike, snatched his drink, downed it and grabbed the bachelor in a bear hug. "I did it for you, Mikey, because soon you're going to be locked in the prison of monogamy."

TJ slapped him on the shoulder. "Way to go, bud."

Jenny joined them at the makeshift bar. "That was pretty good. I've got girls I've been training for months who can't pull off that move."

Rick turned to face her. "That's because they're not SEALs."

She met his gaze and then lowered her eyes slowly over his body. "No, they're most definitely not." Then she looked away. "OK, well things look like they're going to get pretty messy here. So, I'm going to leave you to it."

Rick frowned. "You sure we can't convince you to take off–"

Jenny silenced him with a raised finger. "You were doing so good, pretty boy. Now help me pack these poles."

Mike suppressed a grin as Rick helped her pack the equipment.

"Well I'll be damned," said TJ. "I ain't ever seen a lady put that boy in his place."

"Must have been the bump to the head. He's gone all loco," added Ernie.

"Right, show's over." Dean took a pack of cards from his pocket. "Do you guys know how to play asshole?"

Mike snorted. "Hell yeah, we do. We're the guys it's named after."

TJ pulled a box of cigars from a drawer. "Dean, you smoke?"

"Cubans or reefers?"

The Chief's eyes narrowed.

"I was joking. Cubans are cool."

As Dean dealt the cards Rick carried the bags containing Jenny's poles out of the cabin. He placed them at the back of her car and quickly ducked into the bushes to pee while she went in to say goodbye to the team.

As he relieved himself he heard something rustling in the bushes. Squinting he tried to identify the source. There was a loud growl and he caught a glimpse of long white fangs in the moonlight. Zipping his fly, he backed away then turned and ran. As he burst from the bushes he almost collided with Jenny.

"Bear! There's a bear," he whispered.

She smiled. "Really, where?"

Rick turned and pointed. The animal lumbered out of the bushes, saw Jenny and rocked back on its haunches. In the glow of the cabin's lights he could see its teeth. It seemed to be eyeing him hungrily.

Jenny fumbled in her bag and pulled out a flashlight. She shone it on the bear's face. The animal let out a low growl.

"Don't do that. You're making it angry."

She shook her head. "She's tagged. I know this bear." Jenny put the flashlight away, clapped her hands and took a step toward the beast. It reared up to its full height. "Off you go, Nancy. Stop being a little trash pig."

The bear let out a grumble then turned and disappeared into the bushes.

Jenny unlocked her car. "If she comes around again make some loud noises and chase her off. This time of year they're looking for easy food. Trust me, she's more scared than you."

Rick managed a weak nod.

"Was nice meeting you all. I might see you around the park." She climbed inside, started the car and drove off, leaving Rick standing in the dark.

"Hey pole dancer," bellowed Ernie. "You going to stay out there moping or you going to join the party?"

"Yeah, coming." Rick climbed the stairs and took the drink Ernie offered him. "What did I miss?"

"We're playing asshole and Mike's winning."

Rick cracked his knuckles. "Well, it's time to turn that around. Let's get this pretty boy bachelor messed up."

Chapter Seven

Rick lay on a patch of sun-soaked grass. He was dressed in a full-length wetsuit, buoyancy vest, backpack and a helmet. Mike and Dean, dressed in a similar fashion, sat on a log a few feet away. All three were nursing monster hangovers.

A dozen yards away on the bank of a river TJ was lashing a cooler to the center of a blue inflatable raft. Ernie sat on the side of the rubber boat, using a foot pump to inflate it.

"What the hell did I drink last night?" asked Rick. "My head feels like I landed on it."

Dean laughed. "That's because you did. You don't remember the pole incident?"

He sat up. "No, but I do remember a bear and a beautiful woman."

Mike sighed. "Jenny, the pole dancing instructor. I don't remember any bears."

"There was one outside. She chased it away. The woman is goddamn Tarzan." He stretched out his arms and lay down. "I think I'm in love."

TJ tossed a paddle and it landed on his chest. "You fall in love every week. Now, everyone get your asses on the raft."

The three hungover men rose to their feet and walked slowly to the boat.

"All hands on," ordered TJ once Ernie had the pump stowed. They grabbed a handle each.

"Prepare to lift, lift."

They heaved the boat up and slid it across the rocky bank into the river. TJ took the back right spot as the others clambered in. Rick positioned himself in the center alongside the cooler.

"Y'all know how this works?" asked TJ as he guided the raft toward the middle of the river.

Dean shook his head.

"Pretty simple. I'll tell you when and what direction to

paddle. Try to stay in the boat. If you get thrown out go feet first through the rapids and then swim to the raft. We'll pull you back in or meet up with you on the other side. Don't swim toward large rocks. They're bad news."

The men nodded in unison.

"We've got a half-dozen smaller rapids before we hit the big stuff. So you better get your shit together. Rick, you might want to join the rest of us on the tubes."

Rick waved his hand. "I'm good."

"OK, suit yourself. Right, forward paddle."

The splash of the water, warmth of the sun and comfort of the rubber raft soon lulled Rick into a slumber. He faintly registered the roar of water rushing over rocks as they progressed downstream.

"Back paddle!"

TJ's yell woke him and he opened his eyes, raising his head to see what was going on. As he did the raft bucked under him.

"What the fuck?" he bellowed as he fell and bounced off the ice chest.

"Woo hoo! Hell yeah," yelled Mike as he rode the raft like a bucking bronco.

Rick struggled to his knees as they hit the next rapids. He looked up and caught a wink from TJ.

"See you later, bud."

He lunged for one of the rope handles as the raft bucked again throwing him head first over the side. Ice-cold water drove the air from his lungs. A rock smacked his hip as he fought his way to the surface and sucked in a breath of air. Then he shot head first over a small waterfall.

Suddenly he felt like he was in a washing machine. Surrounded by foaming white water he was tumbled like dirty laundry. Right as he was starting to panic the hydraulic action released him, spitting him back into the river.

Gasping for breath he looked downstream, searching for the raft. He spotted it a dozen yards away. Concerned faces scanned the river for him.

"There he is!" yelled Dean as Rick swam toward them.

TJ held a paddle out and he grabbed it, dragging him toward the boat. "Got yourself a solid recirculation there, buddy." The Chief chuckled as the team hauled him into the raft.

"God damn!" bellowed Rick. "Now I'm awake."

Laughter echoed off the water as he grabbed his paddle and joined the others, sitting on the edge of the raft.

"Did it clear your hangover?" asked Dean.

"Hell yeah, it did."

Mike's brother grinned. "Good, then I'm going in on the next one."

"There's a soft set coming up. You can swim them safely. I wouldn't recommend hitting a grade three like Rick."

"You could have warned me."

"Pretty sure I did."

The next mile of rafting went smoothly with the boys taking it in turns to slip from the craft and ride the white water, except TJ who stayed at the helm. Soon they were past the first series of rapids and floating gently downstream.

"Anyone else sore from that pole dancing?" asked Dean as they cruised through a pristine stretch of forest.

Rick cracked his neck. "I'm the only one who should be sore. The rest of you pansies skipped out soon as it got tough."

"We're not as streamlined as you," said Ernie. "My package was getting in the way."

"Yeah and we weren't trying to impress Jennifer," said Mike.

"Trying? Please, she loved my action," replied Rick.

"Is that before or after she had to save you from the scary bear?" asked TJ.

"There was a bear!"

"I don't doubt it. The woods are full of them, but they're completely harmless and terrified of people."

Rick scowled. "That's not true. Grizzly bears eat people all the time."

"That may well be, but there ain't no grizzlies in these woods, only black bears. And they're not dangerous."

"Yeah, well when you've got your Johnson out anything with teeth is a threat."

"That's a fair point," said Dean.

As they cruised slowly around a curve in the river the dull roar of more rapids reached their ears.

"Time to stop thinking about broads 'n' bears and focus," barked TJ. "This is our first set of grade four rapids. Stand by for my command."

***

The smell of eggs and bacon assaulted Ali's nose, waking her from a drunken slumber. She stretched out in the crisp white sheets of her king sized bed and let out a groan. The aroma of coffee wafted through the bedroom and her stomach rumbled.

As she sat up her head throbbed. She reached for a glass of water from her nightstand and tipped it down her parched throat.

Then she heard claws rattling on the wooden floor and a damp nose snuffled its way over the edge of the bed into her hand.

"Morning, Axe," she croaked as she stepped out of bed and wrapped herself in a robe.

Stumbling downstairs she found Maria in the kitchen. She greeted Ali with a vibrant smile. "Good morning. How are you feeling?"

Ali sat on a stool and leaned on the counter. "Terrible."

Maria placed a mug in front of her and poured piping hot coffee into it. "Well, that's what happens when you drink too much, but it's OK. Aunty Maria will sort you out."

Ali smiled and sipped the coffee. "What are you making?"

"Mexican omelets. I make them every time Ernie goes out drinking. Chases a hangover straight out the door." She returned to the stove and checked a frying pan. "Almost ready."

Axe placed his head on Ali's knee and she ruffled his ears.

"So, what's on the cards today?"

"Today we have a girly day. Day spa, high tea and then a picnic dinner at the river with the boys."

"That sounds perfect."

"Maria tipped an omelet onto a plate and slid it in front of Ali. "You get stuck into this, and I'll go and wake the others." She removed her apron and left the villa.

Ali took a bite of the omelet. It tasted incredible. Sipping more coffee, her thoughts turned to Mike. According to Leonie, the boys were spending the day white water rafting. She grimaced, she couldn't think of anything worse than paddling with a hangover. Nope, a day spa and high tea sounded far more civilized.

***

"Paddle hard, boys!" TJ bellowed as he steered the raft around a massive boulder and down a narrow chute.

The team hollered with excitement as the raft bounced over rocks, surging through the white water into a fast flowing channel.

"Hell yeah. That was wicked," announced Rick as their speed subsided.

"Not a bad way to spend the day," agreed Mike.

"Better than Vegas strippers?" asked Ernie as TJ directed the raft toward the bank.

Rick dipped his paddle propelling them forward. "Let's not get too excited."

"OK boys, paddle hard." TJ aimed the nose of the raft at a pebbled beach.

The team dug deep, propelling the craft out of the current and onto the bank. Ernie leaped from the front, grabbed a rope and tied it off to a log.

"Let's have some lunch," said TJ as they carried the cooler ashore.

Fifteen minutes later the Chief had a fire roaring under a skillet layed with minute steak. The cooler was open and Ernie was hard at work slicing tomato, cheese and pickles. Rick, Mike and Dean had positioned themselves on a log with beers in hand.

"Yeah, this is the life," said Rick. "I could get used to this. Get me a little cabin and invite Jenny around for some dancing, drinking and loving."

"You'd want her around all the time if you lived out here," said Mike.

"Hell yeah, she is one sexy lady."

"No, I mean to save you from the scary bears."

The boys broke into laughter.

Rick shook his head. "I knew I shouldn't have told you."

"It's OK essé," added Ernie. "We all know you can't 'bear' to keep a secret."

More laughter filled the beach.

TJ rose from the fire with the skillet in hand. "OK boys, meat's up."

The log served as a table as they lined up with beers in one hand and rolls in the other. They sandwiched the tender beef in crusty bread, layering it with relish, pickles, cheese and tomatoes.

"This is real good, TJ," complimented Dean. "What's the meat?"

"Venison shot in these very mountains."

"Tastes great," said Mike. "Guys, I just wanted to say thanks for putting this together. It's been awesome to get on the gas with you, even if I did have to watch Rick spin around a pole in his underwear. TJ, I know this was all your idea. Thanks for being a great team leader and an even better friend."

The others raised their beers in agreement and they sat in the sun, enjoying the meal.

Ten minutes later TJ tossed his empty into the cooler. "OK, let's get back on the damn river before Rick starts bitching again. We've got the afternoon to cover twenty miles of class five rapids. This is the bit that separates the men from the pole dancers."

Chapter Eight

Revitalized by breakfast and a morning at the day spa Ali stepped out of the minivan into a picturesque park. Lush green grass met the waters of a wide slow-moving river lined with majestic swaying trees.

"This is magical," said Ali as the other girls joined her.

A loud bark sounded and she spotted Axe running toward them with a bright red ribbon around his neck. The dog made a beeline for her, barking excitedly. She dropped to a knee and he licked her face. "Hey buddy, you smell good. Have you had a bath?"

Leonie gave him a pat. "Maria organized a groomer. He spent the morning getting pampered. OK Axe, are you going to show us the way?"

The dog let out a bark and trotted off through the park toward a thick grove of trees. The girls followed.

"Is this where we're meeting Mike and the boys?" asked Ali as they followed a path into the woods.

"Yeah, in a few hours. There's fun to be had before then."

A row of ribbon tied trees lined the path as they approached a clearing. Ali let out a squeal of delight as she spotted a table laden with cakes and teapots. Around it strewn on the grass were croquet mallets, a ring toss, lawn balls and other games. A smaller table adorned with long-stemmed glasses stood next to a steel tub filled with champagne bottles.

In among the fairytale setting stood Maria in a beautiful summer dress. "Ladies, welcome to the bachelorette's delights."

She pressed a remote control and music filled the garden setting.

"Maria, this is beautiful," gushed Ali as she wrapped her arms around the buxom Latino.

"We couldn't have Leonie running the whole event. Like I said last night, someone had to bring a touch of class."

The other women gathered around the table.

Leonie pointed to a tree of cupcakes. "Oh look, little cock cakes."

Ali leaned closer and saw each of the hand-made cakes had an iced penis drawn on it.

"Wait till you see the lawn games," Maria said with a chuckle.

After the ladies enjoyed the afternoon snacks their host directed them to the equipment. "Ladies, high tea in the forest isn't complete without penis-themed games."

Ali started off with the ring toss, and threw an oversized plastic ring at the dildo serving as a peg. She missed. "Damn it."

Leonie stepped up for her go. "I really hope you're better at that with Mike."

"I generally don't throw anything this large at Mike's penis," replied Ali.

Leonie giggled and tossed, missing by yards. "It's harder than it looks."

Ali shook her head, laughing. "This has been a fantastic few days," she said as Maria joined them. "Thank you so much."

"My dear girl, it's our pleasure," said Maria.

Leonie nodded in agreement and then gestured to where Axe was enjoying a bone. "Even the hound is having a good time." She tossed another ring, missing again. "Screw this, I'm out." Dropping the rings, she downed her champagne.

Ali made a throw. "I wonder how the boys are doing?"

Leonie topped up her glass. "They'll be having a great time on the river." She checked her watch. "Only an hour till they arrive."

Ali tossed another ring. "I feel like we should organize some food for them."

Leonie raised her glass. "Already done. Maria has chow and coffee ready to go."

She tossed another ring. This time it fell directly on the rubber dildo. She jumped up and down in excitement. "I did it.

I landed one."

***

Rick strained to hear TJ's orders over the roar of the hundreds of thousands of gallons of water smashing over and around massive granite boulders. The little raft bucked and twisted as they maneuvered it with deft strokes.

Then as suddenly as the wild section of the river started, it ended and they found themselves in calm water.

"Damn, that's hectic," yelled Rick as he leaned back against the raft and held his paddle across his knees.

"That was a grade four," said TJ. "There's two sets of grade five-plus in the next stretch. If you guys don't move a little faster when I give commands we'll end up in the drink."

"Keep your pants on, old man," said Rick. "We've been handling it like pros. Plus it's not like we can't swim, we're SEALs."

"The Meat Grinder doesn't give a crap what you are. You go in and you're in serious trouble."

"The Meat Grinder?" Dean sounded a little uncertain.

Rick laughed. "He's just trying to scare you."

"We'll see."

They cruised with the flow of the river for a few minutes before the familiar roar of rapids could be heard.

Rick readied himself for the onslaught. The roaring increasing in intensity as they approached a bend.

"Right side forward!" bellowed TJ.

He dug his paddle and the raft made its way to the outside of the bend narrowly avoiding a large rock. As they rounded the corner the rest of the rapids came into view. "Oh shit," murmured Rick as he surveyed the raging torrent of white water forcing its way between two huge boulders.

"Forward!" yelled TJ.

Together they paddled as the Chief aimed them for the gap.

Through the torrent Rick could see a crest of water then

more boulders and rapids. He felt the raft gain speed as it was sucked into the chute. Water lashed his face and the craft bucked wildly as they entered the maelstrom.

"Right back!" screamed TJ over the noise.

Rick paddled hard spinning the raft. They dropped over a small waterfall into a whirlpool where they surfed for a moment before TJ angled them clear.

"Left back."

He paddled frantically before realizing he'd messed up. They bounced off a massive boulder and slipped down a crevasse slightly narrower than the boat. It wedged firm and tons of water tipped them downward. TJ disappeared under the raft and then it broke free, flipping end over end.

Caught beneath it Rick managed to keep his legs up as the raft bounced through the rapids. Then suddenly it was gone and he was jetting through the rapids alone. He fought to keep his head above water as he was pumped through another set of small waterfalls. A boulder dealt him a solid blow, robbing him of feeling in his right arm.

The pummeling felt like it went on for minutes, but in reality it was a matter of seconds before he was clear of the rapids.

"Rick!"

He turned toward the voice and spotted Mike towing Dean toward the bank. Striking out with his good arm he kicked toward them. Behind him, another voice called out.

"Where's TJ?" Ernie caught up with him. "I can't see the raft or TJ."

The two men reached the shore together where Mike was supporting a coughing Dean. "Everyone OK?" he asked.

Rick wriggled his fingers. The feeling was slowly returning to his hand. "I'm good."

Dean coughed the last of the water from his lungs and gave thumbs up.

"TJ is gone." Ernie scanned the river with a concerned expression.

"He was first in. So he's probably further downstream.

Don't worry, the old man knows the river," said Rick.

Once they were all out of the water Mike led them along the river, scrambling over boulders in search of TJ. As they hunted Rick spotted something blue ahead. They got closer and he saw it was their cooler. The Chief was sitting on the bank next to it. The raft was nowhere to be seen.

Rick crouched next to him. "TJ, you alright?"

"I would be if you listened to instructions," growled the veteran SEAL. "Caught my ankle under a rock." He gestured to his naked foot. The ankle looked red and swollen. "Lost my bootie and twisted it pretty bad."

"Thought we'd lost you," said Ernie.

"In this pissy river?" scoffed TJ.

"But, the meat grinder," added Dean.

The Chief laughed. "I made that up. It's actually called The Chute. Level four plus." He turned to Rick. "I don't suppose you've got a med kit, Corpsman?"

Rick shrugged off the backpack he wore over his life vest. Inside were his water bladder and a small medical kit. He never went anywhere without one.

"So what now?" asked Mike as Rick strapped TJ's ankle.

"Well, without a raft we've only got one option. We walk out."

"Follow the river downstream?" asked Ernie.

TJ shook his head. "No, the terrain gets worse. It would take us all night." He pointed up the bank. "We head due west till we hit one of the fire trails."

"Why don't we call for help?" asked Dean as he fished a plastic bag out of his life vest. Inside was his cell phone.

"No coverage up here, son." TJ selected a branch from a pile left by the river. He snapped off the end and used it to help him climb the riverbank. "We get going and we might be out of here by nightfall."

***

"Leonie, do you think something has happened to them?"

Ali sat with a blanket wrapped around her shoulders on the bank of the river. "I mean, they were supposed to be here two hours ago, right?"

The girls had finished their high tea and moved to the agreed meeting point to receive the boys. Maria had organized their food on picnic tables in anticipation of hungry mouths.

"Something might be holding them up," said Maria. "You know TJ, he always plans for everything. They'll be along soon."

Ali turned to where Axe was sitting watching the river. The dog seemed to have a sixth sense when it came to locating Mike. His tongue lolled from his mouth and he wore an unconcerned expression. "Yeah, I'm sure everything is OK."

As they waited, the girls recounted the antics of the last twenty-four hours. Before long they were all giggling as they drank champagne left over from the high tea.

Another fifteen minutes passed without their arrival. Ali turned when she heard the sound of a car pulling into the parking lot. Her heart skipping a beat when she saw it was a park ranger's truck.

A tall female ranger walked across the lawn toward them. "Hi guys, I take it the rafters haven't arrived yet?"

Ali rose to greet her. "You don't have any news?"

The woman shook her head. "No, I met the boys last night when I ran a class for them. TJ told me they'd be arriving around now."

"You ran a class for them?" asked Ali.

"Sorry." She held out her hand. "My name's Jenny. I run a pole dancing fitness class in town as well as being a park ranger."

Ali took her hand and introduced the other women.

"I'm confused, pole dancing?" said Leonie.

She laughed. "Yeah, I think Rick was a little confused too. He thought he'd hired a stripper, not a pole dancing instructor."

"Tell me you made them try it."

Jenny flashed a cheeky smile. "Of course I did. Rick

decided he had something to prove."

"I hope someone got it on camera," said Ali.

"What happens at pole camp stays at pole camp." She took out her phone and showed them a picture of Rick inverted.

"Do you think they're all right?" asked Ali when the laughter had subsided.

"There's any number of reasons they might have been delayed."

"But, they're now two hours late."

"I'll radio into headquarters and find out if anyone has seen them. The river usually has a little traffic this time of year."

"Thanks, that would be great."

"In the meantime, you should sit tight. I'm sure the boys will be along shortly."

Chapter Nine

"TJ, that ankle's not looking good," Rick said as they rested. He had removed his life vest and rolled his wetsuit down to his hips. His helmet now hung from his backpack. They'd been on the move for an hour, but had made little progress.

The Chief sat on the ground opposite his wetsuit unzipped and swollen ankle raised on a log.

Dean, Mike and Ernie had also ditched their safety gear and were in various states of undress.

Rick passed his water bladder to TJ. Sweat was streaming down the Chief's face, his features contorted with pain.

"We should think about sending guys ahead to get comms and organize an evac. Because at this rate, we're not going to be back in time for the wedding."

TJ grabbed his stick and used it to stand. "I can walk."

"Sure you can, Gandalf. Guys, this isn't workable. I propose you head up to the spur and find the track. I'll stay with the Chief and we'll make our way up slow time."

Mike shook his head. "We should stay together."

TJ took a tentative step and grunted. "No. For the first time ever, Rick's right. I'm not going to be able to walk out anytime soon."

"You sure?" asked Ernie.

"Yeah, look it's easy to find the track. Keep heading uphill. Then turn right and follow it down till it hits a road. You should be able to get a call out there or flag someone down. You need to contact Leonie or Ali." He glanced at his watch. "We've missed our RV by three hours. They're going to be a little concerned."

Mike nodded. "Yeah, Ali is going to be stressed if we don't make contact soon. OK boys, let's move fast."

They left Rick and TJ sitting in the shade of a tree and began climbing the steep slope toward the ridgeline. The going was tough, hampered by thick vines and shrubs. Mike led the way, pushing a path through the undergrowth. They'd managed half a mile when he halted for a break.

As they sat, Ernie clawed at the crotch of his wetsuit. "Is anyone else getting chafed?"

"Like a bastard," said Dean as he fanned his face with his hand. He peered through some bushes and frowned. "Hey, what's that? Looks like some kind of netting."

Mike scanned the undergrowth. He didn't see anything until the wind picked up and he spotted what looked like a camouflage net, flapping in the breeze.

"Might be a camp," said Dean. "We should check it out." He pushed into the bushes with Mike and Ernie close behind.

The vegetation suddenly thinned and they found themselves standing in a plantation of tall bright green plants.

Mike looked up and saw that there were camouflage nets strung high in the trees.

"Wow! That's a lot of weed," said Dean.

Mike turned to Ernie who wore a concerned expression. "We need to get the hell out of here."

"It's a little late for that."

The voice came from behind them. They turned and found themselves staring into the barrel of a pump-action shotgun. The man that held it wore a denim shirt, dirty jeans and a ten-gallon hat. A fierce scowl adorned his face. "What the hell are you doing in our fields?"

"Look, our raft capsized on the river. We're hiking out to the track so we can get home."

The corner of the man's mouth lifted in a snarl. "Bullshit."

"Hey, essé we don't usually go hiking in wetsuits," snapped Ernie.

His eyes narrowed. "You better come with me." He used the barrel of the shotgun to direct them through the plantation.

Mike caught Ernie's eye and the Latino clenched his fist. He shook his head. There were too many variables. They didn't know if there were other men in the plantation. "Hey bud, we're not looking for trouble. We just need to find our way out of the woods so I can get to my wedding next week."

"Yeah, well you'll have to ask Travis."

"Who's Travis?" said Mike as they walked through the marijuana crop.

"You'll find out soon enough."

The plantation was sizeable. Nothing like the scale of the operations Mike had seen in Afghanistan, but still at least a dozen acres of plants hidden under camouflage netting.

A minute later they arrived at what he guessed was the caretaker's cabin. It was smaller than TJ's, run down with a sloping verandah that looked on the verge of collapsing. To one side was a large steel cage with a doghouse inside. He glanced around but couldn't see any dogs.

"Hold it there," said their captor. "Travis!" he bellowed.

A thumping sound emanated from the cabin and the door swung open revealing a morbidly obese man wearing coveralls. "Who the fuck are these guys?"

"I found them in the crop."

Travis scrutinized them through squinted eyes. "They look like cops."

Mike shook his head. "We're not cops, we're rafters who capsized on the river. If you'd point us in the direction of the closest road, we'll get out of your hair."

The fat man's forehead creased as he frowned and pulled a pistol from under his singlet. "Put them in the cage. Carter will know what to do with them."

"What? Are you kidding me?" Mike took a step forward. "You can't lock people up–" He felt a sharp pain in the back of his head, and his legs buckled. The last thing he remembered before he blacked out was hitting the ground face first.

***

The light was fading fast as Jenny pulled her pickup into the parking lot of the ranger station. Ali rode alongside her. "Is the Malinois yours?" she asked as they left the vehicle and walked into the building.

"He's Mike's, my fiancé."

Jenny held the door open for her. "He's a beautiful dog. I used to have Shepherds when I was a girl."

Ali's phone beeped as they walked through the foyer of the log-walled station into the operations room. A single ranger sat behind a bank of computer screens with his feet on the desk.

The message was an update from Maria who was still at the park. The other girls had returned to the resort with Leonie.

"Jenny, that was Maria. The guys still haven't arrived."

"OK." The ranger turned to her colleague. "Ben have we had any news?"

He lowered his feet and checked a screen. "No, nothing since this morning. Some guy called TJ rang in at 0930 to log his rafting trip. Nothing heard since."

"OK, I think it might be time to contact the Sheriff's Department." She reached for a phone and hit a speed dial button.

Ali waited as Jenny spoke to someone on the line passing on the details of the rafting expedition. She tried to reassure herself that Mike and the others were safe. Something may have happened, but Mike and the team were highly trained professionals. What's more, Rick was an experienced medic. None of it stopped her from worrying.

Jenny wore a glum expression as she returned the phone to its cradle. "Sheriff's department won't take any action until they've been missing for at least 48 hours."

"48 hours!"

"Yes, they're hamstrung by policy. Look, we can't do a lot tonight. Tomorrow I can organize a helicopter to give the river a once over. That's if they don't turn up before then."

"You sure there's nothing we can do?"

Jenny placed a hand on her shoulder. "The terrain in there is too rough for vehicles. We'd have to hike in and we can't do that when it's dark."

Ali considered her options. "Can we go at first light?"

"Hike in?"

"Yes, surely there's a spot where we can start looking."

Jenny walked across to a map pinned to the wall. "We could hike in to Granite Hut and then down to the five-mile rapids. If they've gotten in trouble, that's where they'll be."

"Then that's where we need to go. I'll bring Axe, he can find Mike anywhere."

"OK, if they don't turn up by dawn we'll hike in and locate them." She ran a critical eye over Ali's summer dress and flats. "You got any outdoor gear?"

"Yes, I came prepared to hike."

"Good, I've got everything else we'll need. I'll drop you back at the resort. Ben will call if he gets anything."

Ali scribbled her number on a slip of paper. "Thank you so much Jenny, you too Ben."

"It's all part of the job. I'm sure we'll find the boys safe and sound tomorrow."

***

Rick pulled his wetsuit back on and sat with his back against a tree, shivering. "Surely they would have made it out by now."

TJ was sitting a few feet away trying to light a fire using the battery from his cell phone and a chewing gum wrapper. "They'll have only just reached the road. It might take some time for them to organize a recovery team. I think we're going to be spending the night here."

"What! TJ, I'm starving." He watched as the Chief fiddled with the phone. A glow emitted from his hands and a second later he had a flame. It quickly took to a small ball of dried moss, gaining intensity. TJ fed it branches as it increased in size. Happy it was established he grabbed an energy bar from his pack and tossed it to Rick.

"Thanks, brother." He snapped off half and made to toss it back.

TJ waved him off as he fed logs into the fire. "I've got a few more."

"OK, so what do we do now?" he asked between

mouthfuls.

The Chief inspected a piece of wood carefully and tossed it into the darkness. "Well, you need to find some dry wood, so we don't freeze to death."

He finished the bar and climbed to his feet. "That I can do."

"Don't go too far, it's easy to get lost out here."

"Yes Gandalf, I won't wander too far into Mirkwood."

"What the hell are you talking about?"

"Lord of the Rings."

"The movie?"

"No, the books." Rick shook his head. "Never mind. OK, I'll head uphill. At least then I know down is the way back."

"Good plan. You're full of surprises tonight."

Rick laughed. "Because I know how to avoid getting lost?"

"No, I didn't think you could read. Now go get some wood before this fire burns out."

Rick grinned. "Asshole."

He pushed his way through the bushes then waited for his eyes to adjust before searching for dry wood. With so many trees it shouldn't be that hard. He found a large dead log and started pulling pieces from it. The rotten wood came away in his hand. It was damp and moldy.

Walking another twenty yards up the hill he remembered back to the survival course he'd attended in fleet. One of the instructors had mentioned something about dry bark on the leeward side of trees.

He picked a large elm and searched around the trunk. Sure enough one side of it was completely dry. It took him a few minutes to collect an armful of the thick bark. Then he made his way back to their makeshift camp.

As he got closer he heard voices. He stopped and listened; someone was talking to the Chief. Voices carried in the cold night air. It was two men and they sounded angry.

He lowered the bark and crept forward until he could see the figures in the glow of TJ's fire.

"Are you alone?" snapped a deep voice.

"My friends went for help. They should be back soon."

If TJ was lying about Rick being nearby, there was a damn good reason for it. TJ had identified the men as a potential threat.

"What happened to your foot?" asked the voice again.

"I already told you. Our raft flipped and I got caught in the rapids. Look, I don't know what your problem is, but where I'm from you offer an injured stranger help. Not threats."

"There's no help coming for you. We've already got your buddies," said another in a nasal voice.

"Shut up," the deep voice ordered.

Rick's heart sank as he realized Mike and the others had been captured. He caught a glimpse of a shotgun in one of the men's hands.

The deep voice barked again. "Get on your feet. You're coming with us."

"I can't walk."

"It wasn't a goddamn question."

Rick crouched in the darkness with his fists clenched, watching as one of the men hauled the Chief to his feet. The other stood with his weapon held ready.

The way he saw it he had two options. One, he could attack the men and risk them killing TJ, or two, he could follow from a distance and look for an opportunity to free the Chief and the others. He opted for the latter.

***

Rick tailed TJ and his captors from a distance. Thankfully the woods were damp and he was able to move silently through the bushes and vines.

They pushed the Chief into a thick grove of plants. It wasn't till he was among them that the pungent smell of marijuana filled his nostrils. "Holy shit, pot growing rednecks," he whispered.

He crept through the field, following the voices of the men as they yelled for the injured SEAL to move faster. Soon he saw lights from a dwelling.

Lowering to his stomach he crawled forward till he spotted a low-slung cabin. There was a large metal cage to one side of it and in the glow of the single bulb under the verandah he spotted Ernie, Dean and Mike. They were locked inside. "Fuck."

The two men directed the Chief to sit on the cabin's deck. Then the front door opened and a horrendously overweight man waddled out. He reminded Rick of a redneck version of the *Star Wars* character, Jabba the Hutt.

"What the hell, another cop?" the man bellowed. "Carter is going to lose his shit."

Rick made a mental note of the name.

"Put him in the cage with the others."

He watched as they manhandled TJ into the cage and locked it with a thick chain.

"You keep watch. I'm going to call Carter." Jabba waddled back inside.

Rick now knew there was a phone in the cabin. He just needed to come up with a plan to lure the yokels away, immobilize Jabba, and free the guys. Not too hard a job for a SEAL.

"Hey, you guys better let us go!" The voice was Dean's. He stood, gripping the bars. "These guys are Navy SEALs and there's still another one out there."

"Dean, shut the hell up," mouthed Rick as Mike grabbed his brother and silenced him.

The taller of the two, with the deep voice, strode across to the makeshift prison and aimed his shotgun at them. "I don't give a fuck who you are, shut the hell up."

The second man bashed on the door of the cabin. "Travis, there's another one out there."

Jabba reappeared and stared out into the plantation with beady eyes. "Carter's sending up the boys. If there's another one we'll find him."

Rick's heart skipped a beat. He needed to get the hell out of the park and find help ASAP. He wiggled backward into the plantation. First things first he had to orientate himself and locate the track out of the park. Pushing out of the dope farm into a clearing he searched the sky. Finding the big dipper he traced a line through the top two stars to the North Star. Now at least he knew which way to go.

Chapter Ten

Rick pushed through thick vines cursing under his breath as he extracted himself from their clutches and checked his watch. He'd been moving uphill for the better part of five hours. Sitting in a clearing he wiped the sweat from his brow. Surely he should have hit the fire trail by now. In the starlight he noticed that the clearing extended away from him to the west. A turn of his head confirmed it did the same in the opposite direction. Finally, he'd found TJ's damn track.

He rested for a moment longer and then started off along the overgrown trail. Without the thick undergrowth he was able to break into a slow jog. The chafing from his wetsuit restricted his movement to more of a fast hobble.

As he jogged he ran through his plan in his head. He would get to town, alert the local authorities, and of course Ali, and then contact his boss, Commander Conner. The SEAL officer had contacts in the DEA. They would sort these pot-growing hicks out in no time.

Fixated on justice he almost missed the distant snarl of a small engine. There was a flash of lights and Rick leaped off the track into the bushes. Seconds later the first of two buggies roared past. In the headlights of the second vehicle he spotted a bloodhound sitting in the bed of the ATV. Other buggies raced past with more men, some wielding firearms. Jabba had assembled a posse of hunters.

Rick now faced a major dilemma. If he stuck to the track the dogs would be able to easily sniff him out and the buggies run him down. As much as he hated the thought he needed to use the cover of the woods.

A glance at the sky identified the North Star and orientated him. Then he shoved his way into the bushes and started walking. Behind him he heard the buggies roaring into the distance.

***

Mike and the others sat huddled together in the filthy cage in an attempt to keep warm. The rubber of their wetsuits gave them a little insulation, but not enough to ward off the temperature drop that came with early dawn.

All four men turned when the sound of engines reached them. They watched as two ATVs arrived at the front of the cabin. Gun-toting hicks climbed from the vehicles and reported to Travis, the obese caretaker. A dog gave a long howl from the back of one of the buggies.

"I'm sorry guys," managed Dean between chattering teeth. "I should have kept my mouth shut."

TJ grasped his shoulder. "Not your fault, bud."

They listened as Travis addressed his posse of four gunmen. "Good thing y'all got here quick. Because we got ourselves a major problem." He gestured to cage. "These assholes stumbled on the crop. They've got government written all over them. There's one more out there trying to get out of the park." He held up a life vest. "Carter wants him alive." Tossing the flotation device to the men he waddled back inside the cabin.

One of the men released the bloodhound from the Polaris. It jumped down and sniffed the vest.

"Oh shit," murmured Mike.

The dog let out a howl and dashed toward the cage. It sniffed the air, circled and then darted into the drug plantation. A moment later it let out a blood-curdling bay.

"What the hell does that mean?" asked Dean.

"It means he's got Rick's scent," Mike whispered.

"He'll get away, though, right?" asked Dean.

"Damn straight he will," said TJ.

"He's a SEAL essé," he'll run rings around these yokels," added Ernie.

In the gloom, Mike caught the grim look on TJ's face. They needed to come up with an escape plan.

***

Ali gripped the Ford pickup's grab handle as it lurched over rocks and struggled for grip. Behind the wheel Jenny activated the diff lock and eased the truck forward. Spotlights illuminated the track in front of them, revealing a heavily rutted trail.

"Your sister and Maria are great," said Jenny as they bounced over another boulder.

"Yeah, they're the best."

Jenny had picked her up at the resort at a little past four in the morning. Leonie and Maria had already been up packing sandwiches and coffee. They'd dropped the two women at the ranger station where they had insisted on helping man the phones in the operations room. The women knew they would be a liability in the field but that didn't stop them from helping.

The truck rocked sideways and there was a bark from the rear of the dual cab.

"I don't think Axe likes my driving."

"Yeah, well I do. The further we go in the truck the less we have to walk, right?"

"Exactly." Jenny changed gears as the track smoothed.

"I know I've said this a dozen times, but thank you."

Jenny turned and smiled at her. "Hey, it's nothing. I love getting out in the park. Your guys looked capable. I'm sure they've camped up for the night. We'll find them in no time."

Ali nodded. "Yeah." She sat silently as they wound their way up a hill. Minutes passed before a wide clearing appeared in the spotlights.

Jenny brought the truck to a halt and killed the engine. "This is far as we can drive."

They climbed out of the cab and Ali snapped a lead onto Axe's collar. Jenny handed her a backpack before reaching for her own.

"Base this is Jenny, over," the ranger spoke into her radio.

A moment later Maria's voice replied. "Go ahead, Jenny."

Jenny smiled. "Wow, already on the airwaves." Lifting the

radio to her mouth, she replied, "Base, we've reached Whistler's clearing. My handheld will probably drop out soon. We'll check in at Granite Hut no later than zero nine hundred."

"No problems," replied Maria. "The chopper will be flying through at zero six thirty."

"Copy that, Jenny out." She adjusted a headlamp then took a pump action shotgun from the truck and strapped it to the side of her bag. "Right, let's get moving."

Ali activated her own light and gripped Axe's lead tight as she followed the ranger along a track into the woods. The dog stepped out in front, pulling eagerly.

They only needed their lamps for another half hour. Soon the soft glow of dawn penetrated the forest and it came alive with the call of birds.

"It's so beautiful," said Ali as they descended a steep ravine.

"Beats the hell out of working in an office."

"You said you were a lawyer, right?"

"Worked corporate law in New York for almost ten years. Came out here to escape."

"And is there a Mr. Park Ranger?"

She shook her head. "No. I had a guy in New York. He turned out to be a thief and a cheat."

"Oh, so sorry to hear that."

"My fault for dating a banker."

They reached the bottom of the gully and Jenny unslung her backpack. "How about we have a short break? Coffee and a sandwich?"

"Sounds good." Ali's stomach had been grumbling for the last fifteen minutes.

Jenny poured coffee from a flask as Ali unwrapped the sandwiches. Axe licked his chops as he sat at her feet.

"So, was Axe a military dog?" asked Jenny as she sipped.

"Still is, he and Mike are teammates."

Jenny reached over and ruffled his ears. "He's a handsome boy."

As they ate Ali heard a faint sound in the distance. The

noise grew louder and she identified it as a helicopter.

Jenny unhooked her radio. "That'll be the search chopper." She checked the channel guide taped to the back and made an adjustment. "Fire Spotter, this is Jen."

Ali looked up through the forest canopy for the helicopter as she listened.

"Jenny, this is Ed. You down there?"

"Yeah, we're on our way to Granite Hut."

"Roger, look we spotted what we think is a raft on Whistler's Bend. No sign of any bodies though."

Ali's heart leaped as she locked eyes with Jenny.

"OK, Ed. Look, we're not far away. We'll go down and take a look."

"Roger, I'll do one more pass and then I'm heading back to base."

"Thanks, bud." Jenny reattached the radio to the shoulder strap of her backpack. "Ali, this is a good thing. If they got separated from their raft they'll be trying to walk out. No mean feat in this terrain. We'll head down to the bend and check it out. Any luck, we'll meet up with them on the way."

***

Rick skidded down a steep slope, snagged a branch on his wetsuit and lost his footing. Tumbling through the bushes he rolled off a ledge and hit the ground with an almighty thud. On his back he stared up through the forest canopy. "Fuck my life."

As he lay motionless a chopper thundered overhead. He jumped to his feet ignoring the chafing between his legs and ran in the direction of the aircraft. A moment later, realizing how futile the gesture was, he sat on a boulder and gathered himself.

Things had gone wrong when he was forced to abandon the track and make his own way through the thick forest. ATVs racing along the trail had pushed him further and further off course until he was well and truly lost. He knew he was somewhere between the river and the ridgeline.

Taking his phone from his backpack he powered it up; still no reception. His stomach growled loudly, reminding him that he hadn't eaten since the night before.

He sipped water from the bladder in his pack and slung it over his shoulder. Then as he was about to set off there was a rustle in the bushes.

Turning slowly he spotted a large black shape among the foliage. A bear emerged from the undergrowth and sat on its haunches. It inspected him through small inquisitive eyes.

Rick's pulse raced as his brain screamed orders to his legs to turn and run. "Jenny said you were more afraid of me than I am of you. In which case, you must be scared shitless," he mumbled, fighting the urge to bolt.

The bear ambled forward and sat a few yards from him. Yawning it scratched its belly. Rick's heart rate dropped as he studied the animal. Jenny was right it didn't seem to be a threat. He spotted a tag in its ear and recalled that she'd said they were after easy food.

"Hey, I'm sorry. I haven't got anything to eat. In fact, I'm starving. So if you could point me in the direction of a Jack in the Box that would be killer."

The animal turned its head away from him, angling its ears up the hill.

"What can you hear?"

Suddenly the bear rose and dashed past Rick, disappearing into the bushes. A moment later the baying of a dog reached his ears. "Oh shit." He turned and sprinted after the bear.

***

Mike inspected the lock on the heavy chain that secured the cage as he rubbed the lump on the back of his head.

"What's the prognosis?" asked TJ.

He sighed. "Nothing serious, just a bruise."

"No, the lock."

"Oh, not good. This is high-grade and the chain's

tempered steel. We need to find another way out."

The sound of the cabin door opening caught his attention. He watched as a tall square-jawed cowboy appeared. He wore a Stetson, jeans, checked shirt and a pistol on a belt with an oversized buckle. At a guess, this was the boss, Carter.

The man swaggered across to the cage and stood in front of them with his thumbs tucked behind his buckle. "So, these are our nation's finest." He sniffed and spat in the dust. "Y'all gonna tell me what you were doing sniffing around my business?"

"Looking for Bin Laden?" replied TJ, deadpan.

"Hilarious. Didn't you guys already kill him?"

"That's what the government wants you to believe," added Ernie.

"Regular fucking comedians, aren't ya."

"We try," said TJ. "Now, how about you let us out before you find yourself in a whole lot of trouble that you don't need."

Carter flashed a broad smile. "Yes, sir. Right away. While I'm at it, I'll whip you up some eggs for breakfast." He took a step closer. "You smart ass city boys better enjoy your last few hours. Because, as soon as I find your friend I'm gonna let the river finish what it started."

Behind him, Travis appeared carrying a water jug and a funnel with a length of hose attached to it. The overweight caretaker dumped the items alongside a chair.

"Y'all get some rest now." Carter turned and returned to the cabin.

"What the hell is that for?" Dean gestured to the funnel and hose.

"They're going to fill us full of water and dump us in the river," replied TJ. "That way, everyone will assume we drowned."

Mike rattled the bars in frustration. "Four SEALs drown in a river. Are they stupid? No one is going to believe that."

"Don't count on it. This river has killed far more experienced rafting crews."

He turned from the bars with his jaw clenched. "And you

thought it would be a good idea to bring a team of first timers out on it, the week before my wedding."

"Relax, we had it well in hand."

"Apart from the whole losing the raft and ending up in a drug baron's prison thing."

"I think baron is a long bow to draw. He's more of a weed growing yokel. Compared to Barbosa, he's *los bajos fondos*," added Ernie.

"Barbosa, I'd forgotten about that piece of shit. Why is it that every time you guys interfere with my love life it ends up involving a criminal?"

"To be fair, this hasn't got anything to do with your love life. It was just an excuse to get away and bond," said TJ.

"Yeah, well it's working. You don't get a better bonding experience than being locked in a POW cage on a dope farm."

Dean managed a chuckle. "True, I mean you couldn't plan this shit."

Mike turned to TJ. "Now would be an excellent time to tell us this is all a hoax."

The look on the veteran SEAL's face told him it wasn't. They were actually facing death and it looked as if their only hope was Rick; a man who hated the outdoors even more than he hated his ex-wife.

Chapter Eleven

Ali and Jenny found the raft lodged between rocks on a bend in the river. From high on the bank the deflated craft resembled a discarded garbage bag submerged in a puddle.

They climbed over boulders to get a closer look. Fixated on the boat Ali slipped on the slimy surface. She threw an arm out to brace herself, but missed and toppled into a shallow pool, drenching her bag and clothing.

"Ali, are you OK?"

She grimaced in pain, clutching her arm to her chest as Jenny helped her from the water. Axe bounded across and licked her face as she sat on the bank. "So stupid."

"Show me your arm."

Ali extended the injured limb toward the ranger who inspected it.

"Wiggle your fingers."

She complied.

"Now clench your fist."

Pain shot through her forearm, but there was no impingement to the movement.

"It's not broken. However, it's pretty badly bruised."

"I'm so sorry, Jenny. I'm not usually this clumsy."

The ranger looked at her with kind eyes. "Hey, it's not your fault. You've got a lot on your mind." She took a map from her pocket. "The good news is there's no sign of the boys. So, I think they're walking out. If TJ is half the woodsman he seems to be they would have pushed up this ridgeline and down the track." She used a twig to show the route. "That means they would have reached Granite Hut. It's not far from here. We'll head over, get you dry, take another look at that arm and radio HQ. You think you're going to be right to walk?"

Ali nodded. "Yeah, I might be clumsy, but I'm not soft."

"I didn't think so. OK, let's get a move on."

***

It took Ali, Jenny and Axe a little under an hour to reach Granite Hut. The eight-bunk outpost got its name from an outcrop that was visible from the porch. Popular with climbers and hikers it was the main access point to the east of the park.

Jenny unlatched the door and placed her backpack on the table inside. Soon she had a fire lit in the iron stove and a kettle heating. "I've got a dry sweater in my pack."

Ali sat on a stool with her arm held across her chest. "Thanks, any chance you have some pain killers?"

Jenny pulled clothing and a medical kit from her pack. "Of course. How's the arm feeling?"

"Starting to swell."

Jenny tipped pills into the cap of a bottle, poured a cup of water from the cabin sink and handed them to Ali. "This should help."

She took the medication before struggling out of her wet T-shirt and slipping Jenny's sweater over her head. As she warmed in front of the stove Axe explored the cabin, sniffing every corner.

"Mike hasn't been here," she concluded when he sat at her feet.

Jenny strode across to a large steel cabinet and unlocked it with a combination. Inside were a radio and shelves loaded with search and rescue supplies. She turned on the radio, adjusted the frequency and spoke into the handset. "Base, this is Jenny at Granite Hut."

There was a pause then a hiss of static and finally a reply. "Jenny, good to hear from you. How are things going?"

Ali didn't recognize the voice.

"We found the raft near Whistler's Bend. No sign of the guys."

"OK, the chopper spotted movement about three miles due west of your location. Had to return to base before he could check it out."

Jenny turned to Ali and nodded.

"I'll take a look. Ali's injured her arm so she'll be staying here at Granite."

She shook her head at the ranger.

"Anything serious?"

"No, but I think it would be a good idea to have someone here in case they make it this far. Plus, I can use her as a relay back to you guys."

"Good idea."

"OK, well I'm going to go check out that sighting. Ali will radio in on the hour."

"Good luck."

Jenny secured the handset as the kettle whistled. She lifted it from the stove and took two mugs from a cupboard. "I think it's better if you stay here. I need you to operate the radio in case I have to get in contact with the station. I'll be back in a few hours."

Ali winced as she raised her arm to take the coffee. "You're right. I'm only going to slow you down. I'm sorry." She glanced down at Axe who wore a concerned expression. "Take, Axe. If Mike is out there he'll find him."

"You sure he will be OK without you?"

The dog walked across to the door and scratched at it.

"I guess so," Jenny said as she grabbed her backpack.

Ali followed her out onto the porch. "You two be careful and please, bring the boys home."

Jenny embraced her in a hug. "With Axe's nose there's no way we won't find them."

Ali watched the dog and the ranger walk across the clearing. Axe turned at the edge of the woods and stared at her before letting out a reassuring bark. Then he disappeared after Jenny. She stood for a moment, staring after them. Then she returned to the cabin to man the radio.

***

Rick leaped over a log landed heavily and rolled. Jumping

back to his feet he wiped the sweat from his brow and paused to listen.

A few hundred yards away the dog bayed. Then for the first time, he heard voices. The hunters were getting closer.

He started off through the woods, wincing as a rock punched through what remained of his dive booties. The shredded rubber footwear barely clung to his feet. His legs ached, he'd run out of water and the inside of his thighs were chafed to the point where he could feel the sting of raw flesh against the rubber.

Despite all that he wasn't going to stop. The rest of the team depended on him. He needed to get to a phone and get help.

The baying of the hound turned to frantic barking. With each outburst he could hear it getting closer. The men's shouting was also louder, accompanied now by the sound of them crashing through the undergrowth.

A wise man had once said, 'Don't run you'll only die tired'. It was a motto that Rick embodied. He was all about lifting iron, fighting hard and kicking his enemy in the teeth. Skidding to a halt, he tore a branch from a tree to use as a club. He took deep breaths, slowing his racing heart rate. Whatever happened next he was going to go down swinging.

The dog was the first to appear. It charged out of the bushes and spotted him, baring its teeth. Rick waved his homemade cudgel at it. "You want a piece of me?"

Snarling it charged forward, snapping its jaws.

Rick swung and the dog jumped clear. He didn't want to hurt the animal, but he saw no other way to escape.

"Hold it right there, muscles." He glanced in the direction of the voice and found himself looking down the barrel of a pump action shotgun. The man holding it wore camouflage pants and a USMC T-shirt.

A second man appeared. This one carried a lever action rifle and was dressed in a denim shirt, jeans and cowboy boots.

"You're pretty fast for a gym junkie," said the guy with the shotgun. "Now lower the stick or I'm going to blow your head off."

Rick's jaw was clenched, his muscles taught and ready to leap into action. However, he knew he could never cover the dozen yards that separated him and the gunmen. His only hope was to jump behind a tree and sprint for cover.

"I know you're thinking about running. You do that and old Bones here will run you down," said the cowboy.

At the mention of its name the dog let out a savage growl.

Rick lowered his cudgel and came up with a new plan. He'd let the men get close then disarm one of them, knock out the other, deal with the dog and escape. The odds weren't in his favor, but it was better than giving up.

Suddenly, there was a low snarl from the bushes. The noise sent a shiver racing up his spine. Bones dropped his tail then whimpered and cowered on the ground.

The shotgun swung in the direction of the commotion.

"What the fuck is that?" asked the other man. "Doesn't sound like no bear."

"RICK, DOWN!" a familiar female voice yelled.

As he dropped to the earth a shotgun boomed. He caught a glimpse of a brown shape as it streaked from the bushes.

The hound yelped wildly and the men bellowed in terror as Axe attacked. The SEAL dog went directly for the camouflaged gunman. Axe ripped the shotgun from his hands then latched onto his arm. The man in the cowboy hat fled after his dog.

"Axe, stop!" screamed the woman's voice.

Rick watched as the dog released the hunter. The man turned and fled, crashing through the foliage. The shotgun boomed again, blasting leaves above his head.

"Damn, am I glad to see you," said Rick to Axe as the Malinois set upon him with a slobbery tongue. He let the dog lick his face as he turned to identify the shooter.

Jenny, the pole-dancing ranger, stepped from the bushes dressed in cargo pants and a green uniform shirt. She looked like someone from the Wild West with a pistol on her hip and a shotgun in the crook of her arm. "You look a little worse for wear, sailor."

Rick climbed to his feet, grinning.

"You're a god damn angel," he croaked from a parched throat.

"Axe is your angel." She took a canteen from her backpack and passed it to him. "He led me straight to you."

She gave him a moment to drink then handed him granola bars. He devoured two in a matter of seconds.

"We need to get help," he managed as he chewed.

"Is someone injured? Where are the others?" she asked, reloading her shotgun. "And who the hell were those guys?"

He took another sip from the bottle and then recounted the past sixteen hours to her.

She shook her head in disbelief. "That's crazy. I can't believe they've got an entire plantation growing up there. We need to get back and let the police know."

"More like the DEA. Do you have a radio?"

She nodded and unhooked it from her shoulder strap. "Ali, this is Jenny do you read me?"

"Ali's up here?"

She nodded as she listened for a reply. When she heard nothing, she tried again. There was still no response. "There could be interference. Are you right to walk with me to the hut?"

"Can we contact the authorities from there?"

"Yes, Ali's manning the radio back to my station."

"Excellent, let's get a move on then." He climbed to his feet and took a few tentative steps.

"Are you, OK?" she asked.

Rick screwed up his face. "Not really."

"Your feet?"

He shook his head. "My groin. The wetsuit has rubbed me raw."

She rummaged in her pack and produced a jar of Vaseline. "This works for me."

"You're an angel. This is literally the third time you've saved me."

She winked. "The bear doesn't count. Now hurry up and

get lathered up so we can get out of here before those assholes come back." She strode across and recovered the shotgun the gunman had dropped. When she turned back he was screwing the lid on the jar. She waved it away when he offered it to her. "You keep it." Then she handed him the other gun. "Just in case we run into them again."

He checked the breech of the weapon. "I'm counting on that."

Chapter Twelve

Carter grabbed a half bottle of bourbon from a rickety table and tossed it against the wall. It smashed, dribbling the liquor down the grimy wood.

"How did you mess this up?" he screamed into his radio. "How did you let an unarmed wetsuit-wearing tourist get the drop on you?"

There was a hiss of static and then a sheepish reply. "He had help."

"From who? Yogi the damn bear?"

"No, a park ranger."

Carter turned and stared at Travis who was sitting wedged in a tatty recliner. "Just one?"

"Yeah, tall chick with a crazy dog. Came out shooting and the dog tore Carl up pretty bad."

He scowled at Travis. "I only know one tall female ranger, Jenny." He spoke into the radio. "Where are you now?"

"Back with our ATVs up on the ridgeline. I've bandaged up Carl's arm."

The deputy sheriff stormed across to the wall where a map of the park was nailed. He traced his finger from the ridgeline down to the main road out of the park. A few miles from Carl and Hank's location pointed at a small square, Granite Hut. He knew from experience that it was the only place you could get radio reception out to the ranger station. "They're heading to Granite," he spoke into his handset. "You need to get there first and stop them from getting a call out."

"What do you want us to do with them?"

"Whatever you have to, just bury the bitch deep."

"I was hoping you'd say that."

He tossed the radio on the table.

"We should kill those fucking SEALs," Travis said with a snort. "They're working for the man."

Carter's eyes narrowed. "Don't start that conspiracy crap

with me. Until we have the other one we keep them alive. We get in a situation and they're the only bargaining chip we have."

"They're a liability, Carter. They've seen too much."

He glared at the fat man. "You're a god damn liability, Travis. If you had've taken care of this in the first place, I wouldn't be here cleaning up your mess."

"That's not fair."

Carter made for the door. "Life's not fair." He stepped out into the bright sunshine and squinted, donning his sunglasses. He turned and checked on his caged captives.

"Things not going your way?" asked the old guy with the busted ankle. "You know, if you let us out and show us to safety we'll forget any of this happened. You can be the hero that saved some lost rafters."

Carter eyeballed the man. "That's not how things work up here."

***

Jenny was impressed. Despite his injuries and lack of sleep and food Rick was moving fast. He was right on her heels as she jogged through the woods in the direction of Granite Hut. Axe, keen to return to Ali was scouting out in front.

As she jogged she found herself comparing the handsome SEAL to her ex in New York. Sam, a cocksure banker had been utterly full of himself. He'd continually boast about making mulit-million dollar deals and holding people's jobs in his hand. Yes, he was handsome and yes, the sex was fantastic, but in the end it couldn't make up for his utter lack of humility and empathy.

Rick on the other hand was a man who had reasons to be proud. He was an elite operative and a decorated veteran. Yet, there was vulnerability about him. He might be a bit of a show boater, but he didn't take himself too seriously. He'd proven that with his attempt at pole dancing. He also had an undying loyalty to his friends and loved ones. Of course it also helped that he was about as chiseled and handsome as a man could get.

"Jenny, you hear that?"

Rick's voice snapped her back to their current situation. She paused and over her breath she heard the snarl of ATVs. "They're heading for the cabin."

She broke into a run. Ahead, Axe disappeared into the undergrowth. The dog seemed to sense that Ali was in danger.

Suddenly, Rick dashed past her with the shotgun held ready. He plowed through the undergrowth like a bulldozer. She tried to match his speed, but fell behind.

The noise of the buggies grew louder and then started to fade as they pulled ahead. Jenny guessed they would reach Granite Hut in a matter of minutes. Meanwhile, she and Rick were at least fifteen away. She slowed and talked into her radio. "Ali, this is Jenny. Do you read me?"

There was a burst of static.

"Ali, this is Jenny, if you can hear me you need to get out of the hut. I say again, you need to get out of the hut."

***

Ali abandoned her attempt to reply to Jenny over the radio, stuffed her things in her backpack and slung it over her shoulder as she made for the door.

She'd heard rather than saw the buggies that arrived outside. Frantically searching the cabin for a hiding place she dropped her bag and slid in under one of the bunks. Pressing herself against the wall she fought to control her panic.

The door creaked as it opened. From her hiding place she could see two pairs of boots as they clumped inside. Cowboy boots and a pair of battered combat boots. The cowboy wore jeans with frayed cuffs. His partner wore camouflaged cargos not unlike those Mike wore to work.

The men moved around the cabin, searching.

"There's no one here," drawled a gruff voice.

The cowboy poked her backpack with the toe of his boot. "There was."

Her heartbeat sounded like a brass drum as she fought to keep her breathing low and shallow.

The combat boots strode across to the radio cabinet. "The handset's still warm."

Panic overwhelmed her and she pushed harder against the wall, willing it to open and swallow her.

"You going to come out from under there?" drawled the cowboy as he stood in front of the bunk. "We ain't gonna hurt you."

"Yeah, we just want to talk to your friends."

"Shut the fuck up, Carl. Look, don't be scared. My friend's a bit stupid, but he's harmless."

Both pairs of boots were now standing a few feet from the bunk and pointing directly at her. Her only option was to crawl out and make a run for the door. "If you step back I'll come out."

There was a pause. She pictured the two men looking at each other, questioningly.

"OK."

The boots took a step back. She took a deep breath then crawled out from under the bed.

The men looked exactly how she pictured them. Cowboy wore a denim shirt and held a rifle. Camo Guy had a pistol clutched in one hand. The other was heavily-bandaged.

"What happened to you?" she asked in a soft voice.

"Bear," the man grunted.

Cowboy silenced him with a glare. "We're the ones asking the questions. Where's your ranger buddy?"

Ali feigned ignorance. "I don't know who you're talking about."

His eyes narrowed. "Don't fuck around with us, Missy."

She could tell by the look that he meant it.

"She left, I don't know when she'll be back."

"She's lying," said Camo Guy.

Cowboy spat on the floor. "Tie her hands. We'll take her back to Carter. He can decide what to do with her."

The pistol was thrust into her face and a moment later they

spun her around, binding her wrists with tape. Camo Guy shoved her through the door as Cowboy smashed the radio.

Outside two buggies were parked side by side. A morose looking Bloodhound sat on the back of one of them. Camo Guy gestured for her to climb into the passenger seat of the other. As she did the dog started whining.

"Bones, what the fuck's wrong with you?" said her captor as he climbed into the driver's seat.

There was a menacing growl from the opposite side of the buggy and the hound's whining intensified.

Ali recognized the sound instantly. She turned and saw Axe, hackles raised and teeth bared, standing a few yards away.

"Aw, shit." The man raised his pistol.

She shoved him with her shoulder and the gun went off, hitting the dirt.

Before he could recover Axe leaped onto the hood and pounced through the open roll cage, clamping his jaws on the man's bandaged arm. He screamed and the pistol was flung clear as the dog shook his arm, tearing flesh.

"Carl, get down!" yelled Cowboy from the porch. He had his rifle aimed at Axe.

Ali screamed. "No!"

The boom of a gun echoed off the mountains. A chunk blew out of the cabin wall next to Cowboy's head. As he ducked Ali turned and saw Rick storm out from the bushes. He had a shotgun held firm in his shoulder the barrel aimed unwaveringly at Cowboy. A tattered wetsuit covered his legs the top half hanging from his waist. He looked like he'd been through hell.

"Next one's on you," he bellowed.

Cowboy stood staring at the SEAL, his rifle held low.

Rick stopped ten yards short with the shotgun aimed directly at his chest. "I see that gun move and you're dead."

Axe had released the other man's arm and stood on the hood of the buggy, teeth bared and eyes fixed on his throat.

There was a rustle in the bushes and Jenny appeared with her gun raised. "Drop the rifle."

Outmatched, Cowboy let his weapon drop on the porch. "You people don't know who you're fucking with. Carter is going to be pissed."

"Carter? Lieutenant Carter Brown?" asked Jenny as she approached.

Cowboy realized he'd already said too much and buttoned his lips. Rick stepped onto the porch, kicked the rifle away, reversed his shotgun and drove the butt into the man's stomach."

He doubled over and dropped to his knees, groaning.

Rick bent down to whisper in his ear. "If anything's happened to my friends you're going to wish you never lived."

Jenny freed Ali and then found the roll of tape Carl had used to secure her. They bound both men's hands behind their backs and dumped them on a bunk with their feet taped.

"We can't get a call out," said Ali as she joined them with Axe by her side. "They smashed the radio."

Rick inspected the cabinet as Jenny poured him a mug of cold water from the sink. "Can you fix it?" she asked, handing the mug to him.

He prodded the shattered control panel with his finger. "Ernie could. I don't have the skills."

"We need to get a message out and alert the authorities," said Jenny.

Ali's gaze fell on the two buggies parked outside. "I could go."

Jenny shook her head. "No, we shouldn't split up again. We should all go."

"I'm not leaving without the others," said Rick in a low voice.

"You and Jenny can help free Mike and the others. I'll drive a buggy back to the main road and get help." She inspected one of them. "I had a Polaris on dad's farm. It'll be a piece of cake."

Rick nodded. "I think it's the best option."

Jenny frowned. "The forest is a maze of trails. You could get lost."

"This buggy's got a GPS. I can follow it straight out of the park."

Jenny considered the plan. "OK, let's do it."

"You girls sort that out," said Rick as he eyeballed the two men on the bunk. "I need to get out of this wetsuit."

Ali grabbed her backpack, carried it outside and tossed it in the buggy. She realized that the Bloodhound was missing. It must have run off into the woods.

The GPS was an expensive touch screen model with high-resolution maps. It took Jenny a matter of minutes to program a route for Ali.

As she finished Rick appeared from inside the cabin. He'd relieved Carl of his camouflage pants, hacked them off below the knee and somehow managed to squeeze into them. He'd also borrowed a USMC T-shirt that looked two sizes too small. With a pistol belt around his waist and a shotgun slung over his shoulder he looked like a cross between Rambo and a WWE wrestler.

"I'm going to start calling you Rickbo," said Jenny with a laugh as she climbed out of the buggy.

He managed a grin. "We need to get moving. We'll go on foot. They'll have the tracks leading to the plantation covered."

Ali started the buggy. "Axe should go with you. He'll find Mike and he's good in a fight."

Jenny nodded. "He's saved the day twice already."

"Just take care of him. I'll be back with help as soon as I can." She spun the buggy's wheels and took off into the woods.

Jenny turned to Rick who was rummaging through the other ATV. He stuffed a roll of tape, gas stove canisters and other items into his backpack along with boxes of cartridges for the pistol, shotgun and rifle he'd taken from the gunmen. He had one of the men's radios hooked to his belt.

"What's the plan?" she asked.

"Recon followed by direct action."

She watched him shrug the backpack over his broad shoulders and gather up the guns. The man oozed masculinity and confidence from every pore of his muscular body. Despite the seriousness of the situation she couldn't help but feel a little excited.

"What's up? Have I got something on my face?" he asked.

Realizing she was staring she blushed, turned away and started off up the hill. Axe fell in alongside her. "Come on, Rick. Let's get a hustle on."

Chapter Thirteen

Carter stood on the cabin's rickety porch with his radio held high in the air. Travis sat in a rocking chair next to him with a shotgun across his knees.

"That ain't going to help. Radio waves don't work that way."

"Oh, so you're an engineer all of a sudden. How about you shut your mouth and watch those prisoners."

Travis frowned and turned away from him.

"Yeah, sulk while I solve this damn problem." As he turned his attention back to the radio he spotted movement on the trail that led through the plantation. It was a dog. To be more precise it was Bones, Hank's dog. Something must have happened. That was why he wasn't getting a response on the radio.

"Fuck."

The dog made its way across to Travis and sat at his feet. "Carter, Bones wouldn't leave Hank."

"No shit." He changed the channel on the radio and called his deputies. "Ed, you read me?"

"Yeah, boss," came through immediately.

"I need you to get to Granite Hut. Is Harold with you?"

"Yeah, we found a truck down at Whistler's Clearing. It's one of the rangers."

"Goddamn Jenny," he said to himself. He depressed the transmit button. "Immobilize it and then get up to Granite. Something's happened to Carl and Hank."

"Yeah boss, you can count on us."

Carter stepped off the balcony and strode across to the cage where he locked eyes with the grizzled old SEAL, if that's what he actually was. "If your buddies killed any of my boys I'll slit your throat."

The man stared defiantly at him. Carter spat in the sand, turned and tossed his radio to Travis. "Watch them and keep an ear out." Then he disappeared inside.

A moment later the older guy called out from the cage. "Travis, I don't think he respects you very much."

The overweight yokel racked the action of his shotgun. "Shut the hell up."

"Just an observation. Looks like you do all the work around here and Carter gets to call the shots."

Travis pried himself from the chair and waddled across to the cage. "I know what you're trying to do G-man. Divide and conquer and all that stuff. I know exactly how you work, but it ain't gonna work on me."

"Hey, I'm just making an observation."

"Yeah, well keep them to yourself."

***

Ali slowed the buggy and came to a halt at a fork in the track. The GPS was struggling to keep up. She guessed it was because of the dense forest coverage. Idling she waited for the dash mounted device to update.

She didn't hear the two ATVs that appeared on the opposite track. The noise of her engine masked their approach. They blasted around the corner, nearly collided with her as they shot past. She watched in the mirror as they skidded to a halt in a cloud of dust.

The idea of asking them for help dissipated as quickly as she spotted a weapon in the mirror. One of the ATVs turned toward her. The other zoomed off in the direction of the hut.

Ali dropped her Polaris into gear and floored it. The thousand cc engine roared, wheels spun and she rocketed down the trail. Branches slapped the roll cage as she accelerated, her eyes watering as she hit forty miles an hour. A glance in the mirror confirmed that one of the buggies was in pursuit.

She gritted her teeth and pushed the throttle harder. People were depending on her. Mike depended on her.

Spotting a sandy section ahead she backed off the gas. Then as she entered a corner she put the Polaris into a controlled slide narrowly missing a tree as the road snaked back into the woods.

Gunshots rang out and bullets cracked past her head. One ricocheted off a roll bar punching a hole in the plastic roof.

Ali checked the mirror. Her pursuer was only a few yards behind, close enough for her to see it was one of Carter's deputies, Ed. "Son of a bitch." She braced and slammed on the brakes. The other buggy hit hers with a thud.

The driver wasn't prepared and was flung forward against the steering wheel. Over her shoulder she saw a pistol fly through the air.

She rode the impact, accelerating away. The track was rocky and she tried to check the GPS as the buggy bounced down the ridgeline. A spinning icon told her it was useless.

The track took a hard left and dropped away. She wrenched the wheel and jumped on the brakes, wincing as it jerked her injured arm. Sitting high in the seat she peered over the hood. It was steeper than anything she'd attempted in her dad's farm buggy.

An engine roared behind her.

"Here goes nothing." She gripped the steering wheel tight and released the brake.

The little buggy gained speed as it slipped and skidded down what felt like a nearly vertical slope. Ali kept her foot clear of the brake, letting the gearbox manage the speed the best it could.

In the mirror she spotted the other ATV at the top of the slope. Ed handled the steep descent with skill. In a matter of seconds he was back on her tail.

The only saving grace was that he'd lost his weapon. Now he had to rely on his driving skills to stop her. What's more, from a glimpse of his machine she'd deduced it was an older Yamaha, inferior to the Polaris she'd borrowed. That didn't stop him from milking everything he could from the engine.

At the bottom of the descent the track dipped into a muddy stream. The wheels of Ali's buggy spun and she slid sideways off the path onto the opposite bank. The bushes were sparse so she ran with the alternate route. Snaking around rocks and logs she felt barely in control of the snarling vehicle. A glance over her shoulder confirmed that the Yamaha was still on her tail.

As the scrub thickened she was forced to slow. Her buggy roared shoving its way through the thick undergrowth. Free to follow in her tracks the pursuer was soon right on her bumper.

"Pull over!" Ed bellowed over the engine.

Ali ignored him, working the steering wheel in an attempt to gain momentum. Through the branches she spotted a clearing. With a thump from behind her ATV's nose lifted. She didn't need to turn to know that the driver had jumped from his vehicle onto the back of hers.

As the Polaris burst out of the bushes into another clearing she gunned the engine, swinging the wheel from side to side. They fishtailed across wet grass, the knobby tires throwing up plumes of mud.

"Stop the damn buggy."

She felt a hand grab at her hair and ducked forward. Through the trees ahead she spotted the river.

Ali gave the thousand cc engine its head.

"Fucking stop!" screamed Ed as he clung to the roll cage.

"Go to hell."

At the last safe moment she spun the wheel and jammed on the brakes. Her intent was to throw the man into the river. However, she didn't anticipate the slick grass.

The Polaris spun like a top, flinging the man clear. With the engine still racing it flipped and rolled down the embankment, tumbling into the river.

Ali clung to the steering wheel as the Polaris dropped through the cold clear water. It hit the rocky bottom upside down and rolled with the current, coming to a halt against a submerged log. She didn't panic until she tried to leave the cabin and found her foot wedged under the accelerator.

With water pushing against her she couldn't free her hiking boot. She lost her grip and the flow of the river grabbed her, twisting her torso out of the cabin. Panic escalated as she fought the current, her foot trapped. Her lungs burned, her injured arm screamed with pain as she desperately tried to pull her leg free. She spun back and forth, wriggling her toes in one last futile attempt to break free.

Blackness filled the edges of her vision as she looked up through the water at the light above. It was so close and yet so distant. Then, as she felt her strength ebb her foot slipped from the boot and she was free.

Her head broke the surface in a maelstrom of white water. She sucked in a lungful of air before being pulled back under. Managing to roll onto her back she lifted her legs and rode the rapids.

Minutes later the river calmed and she was able to swim to the bank. Lying on a pebbly beach she sucked air into her aching lungs. She allowed herself only a moment's rest before climbing to her feet and checking her surroundings.

She'd floated at least half a mile downstream from where the buggy had sunk. That was faster than she could move on foot. The river was her best chance of getting help, quickly.

At the far end of the beach she spotted a plastic drum wedged in a pile of debris. Digging it out she checked the lid was tight and waded out into the freezing water with it clutched to her chest. When her feet left the bottom she let the current grab her and she floated downstream.

With the sun low on the horizon it wouldn't be long before it disappeared completely, taking with it the last traces of warmth. Already she could feel the river sapping her body's heat. She needed to find help before she succumbed to the cold.

***

As Ali fought hypothermia, Rick and Jenny were dealing with the other end of the spectrum. The pair was drenched in sweat and short of breath as they took a break so Rick could orientate himself to the ground.

"We're close to the plantation. I remember this tree." The

SEAL pointed to a pine that had been split by lightning.

Jenny waited patiently as he scanned the terrain. Axe sat by her side, watching with his head cocked.

He pointed to a thick grove of trees. "This way."

They set off and a moment later the dense underbrush parted revealing rows of planted marijuana.

Jenny looked up at the camouflage netting strung in the trees. "Holy crap. They've been growing this right under our noses."

"Pretty slick little setup. Must be a couple of thousand plants under here. I wouldn't be surprised if there are more plantations spread out in the forest."

She nodded. "Could be. Apart from a few ATV operators no one comes out here. They usually camp at Granite Hut and then head west into the park."

"That's why Carter and his buddies chose this spot."

"So what do you think? Should we wait for Ali's help to arrive?"

"No, might be too late. We're going to free the guys, but before we do that we need to even the numbers a little."

"Lure them out?"

"Yep, and into a trap."

"Do you have something in mind?"

He frowned. "Not really. I was hoping we might crack it together."

"Teamwork, yeah I think we'll be able to come up with something." She shot him a coy smile.

There was a moment as they stared at each other. Jenny caught herself thinking about how good his lips would feel pressed against hers.

"Right." He broke eye contact. "What gear do we have?" Rick emptied the contents of his backpack. There was a water bladder, a roll of tape, gas cylinders, a coil of nylon rope and ammunition.

Jenny did likewise adding more rope, a hand saw, bivy sack, small shovel, fire starters, medical kit, toilet paper and some rations.

They both sat silently staring at the gear.

"OK, MacGyver, I think I've got an idea," said Jenny.

"Good, because all I've come up with is an exploding toilet paper bomb."

***

Ali could no longer feel her hands and feet as she kicked ashore, released the drum and crawled up onto the beach. She lay there for a moment, gathering herself before she managed to climb shakily to her feet.

The sun had set and the light was fading as she climbed the riverbank. She recognized the park from where they had waited for the raft the day prior. Remembering the way to the road she hugged her arms around her body and hobbled toward it.

She waited beside the road for ten minutes without a car appearing. Shivering uncontrollably she started walking in the direction of the ranger station.

It wasn't long till a flash of headlights warned her of an approaching vehicle.

She stood in the middle of the road waving her arms. A pickup stopped with a screech of tires.

A door opened and an agitated voice yelled out at her, "What the hell are you doing in the middle of the road, woman? I could have killed you."

Ali staggered toward the truck. "I need help. I just came off the river. My friends are in trouble."

The elderly driver was a sixth generation mountain man and immediately recognized the onset of hypothermia. He grabbed his jacket from the truck, threw it over her shoulders and bundled her into the cab. Moments later, with the heater blazing they drove toward town.

"I'm going to get you to the hospital."

"No, no," Ali managed through teeth chattering like a machine gun. "My friends need help. Please, take me to the ranger station."

He frowned. "You sure? Those lips of yours are pretty

blue."

She nodded.

He reached across and popped the glove compartment. "Have a look in there. Should be something to keep you warm."

She found a hip flask nestled among dog-eared manuals and paperwork.

"Best bourbon in Oregon."

She unscrewed the lid, gave it a sniff and took a sip. The smooth liquid warmed her throat and then her stomach. "Thank you."

"Tom, name's Tom."

"I'm Ali."

"Pleasure to meet you, Ali. Now, we're about twenty minutes from the ranger station. How's about you tell me what happened to you and your friends."

Ali took another sip then began the story.

***

Darkness had set in early under the thick forest canopy. Working more by touch than sight Rick hauled on a rope, looped it around a branch, pulled it tight and tied it off. "That's a wrap."

"Impressive," said Jenny from the darkness. "Let's hope it works."

Rick made his way across to where she was consolidating their supplies. Axe sat next to her, watching intently.

"No reason it shouldn't. Your plan is good."

She handed him a granola bar. "I think your knots are the key."

He unwrapped the snack. "Knots are all I've got. I'm a SEAL out of water."

"You've done pretty well so far," she murmured as she glanced up at the sky. "Rick, it's getting dark. Should we wait for morning?"

"Yeah, I was thinking we attack at the crack of dawn.

They'll be up all night, tired and more likely to make mistakes." He chewed the bar.

"Makes sense." Jenny opened a packet of jerky and fed some of it to Axe. "How long have you been in the navy?"

"Twelve years now. I started in the fleet and moved across to the SEALs about eight years ago. What about you? How long have you been a ranger?"

She offered him a piece. "Not long."

He waved it away. "Axe needs it more than me."

"I was a lawyer in New York, hated it. Threw it all in to move out here and become a ranger."

"And part-time pole dancing instructor slash torture consultant."

She laughed. "Yeah, that too."

"So, is there a man in your life?"

"No, I left a guy in New York. Not about to go jumping back into a relationship. What about you?"

"I got married a few years back."

Jenny felt disappointment wash over her.

"Worst decision of my life. It lasted a little over eight months. Fortunately, we didn't have kids."

Axe let out a sigh as he lay next to Jenny. She turned and ruffled his ears, hiding her smile. "Too much time away?"

"No, she wasn't a good match for me. TJ would call it a poor life choice."

"Is TJ your boss?"

"Yeah, he's in that cage with the rest of my team. Best friends a guy could have."

"Ali said you guys were a tight crew."

"She's part of the family. Even passed selection."

"Selection?"

Rick's teeth flashed in the darkness. "You know, we should get some sleep. It's going to be an early one."

Jenny pulled a Gore-Tex bivy and a sleeping bag from her backpack and passed them to Rick. "I'll keep the first watch."

"No need. Axe has the best nose and ears in the business. Anyone comes within a hundred yards and he'll wake us. I'll take the bivy. You'll stay warmer in the sleeping bag."

"That thing's not going to keep you warm."

"It's OK. I'll snuggle with Axe."

"Don't be silly. The best way to conserve body heat is to share it. Stuff the bag full of pine needles, it will insulate us from the ground.

Rick did as he was told and when the bag was full he handed it to Jenny who laid it on the ground. Then she unzipped the sleeping bag. "Sorry, you're going to have to be the big spoon."

"I've got to warn you," said Rick as he placed his shotgun within arm's reach, "I smell pretty bad." He lay and Jenny wiggled in front of him. Axe lay alongside her.

"Hey, at least you're not wearing that wetsuit anymore."

He draped the sleeping bag over her.

Jenny was overcome with a sense of well-being. She felt safe lying next to Rick. It was a sensation she'd never experienced with her ex.

A strong arm reached over and pulled her in tight. She could smell his sweat mixed with the damp of the forest. A smile formed on her lips as she realized this was the first time she'd laid with a man since moving to Oregon.

"Are you comfortable," he asked softly.

"Yeah, the smell isn't too bad. What about you?"

"Remarkably so."

There was a moment's silence. It was Rick who broke it. "Brown bears, mild concussions, gunfights, hostages and shotgun-toting yokels aside, this has been a very rewarding trip. I sure am glad I met you, Jenny."

"Let's keep it professional," she murmured as she drifted off to sleep.

"Yes, ma'am."

***

Less than half a mile away inside Travis's cabin Carter had assembled his men. Ed, Harold, Hank and Carl, with his arm bandaged, sat around the table. Travis had been relegated to guarding the prisoners.

"So, let me get this straight. You idiots let an unarmed man, two women and a dog get the better of you?" growled Carter.

"One of the women drowned," said Hank.

"Oh, that makes this so much better." Carter fixed him with a steely glare. "That SEAL bastard and that bitch, Jenny, are still out there. I want them found."

Ed frowned. "Boss, we go out there now and we're going to blunder around in the darkness till we run into them." He gestured to Hank and Carl. "And, thanks to these two they've got guns."

He considered the point. "We go at first light." He turned to Hank. "That hound of yours going to be any use?"

"He can track them, but we need to put a bullet in that mongrel of theirs."

"Well, I'm sure between the four of you, it won't be a problem. Travis and I will hold the fort. I've got two of my deputies patrolling the main road in case they try to make a run for it. They'll hand 'em over no questions asked."

"They'll have to walk out. I fixed that ranger's truck good," said Harold.

Carter nodded. "There are only two of them, they've got no comms and they don't know this area like we do. It shouldn't take you long to wrap them up. Get some sleep. We roll at dawn."

"You want us to swap with Travis?" asked one of the men.

"No, that slug has been sitting on his ass all day. I'll take over from him in a few hours."

"And the prisoners?"

"Tomorrow they go in the river, with or without their buddies. Then we'll harvest the crop, burn this place to the ground and get the hell out of here."

"Why don't we burn them with the cabin?" suggested Hank.

Carter's lip turned up in a sinister smile. "Yeah, I like that idea. Fire will rip through this area. By the time they find the bodies we'll be long gone."

"That means we can shoot the nigger and the girl?" asked Ed.

He nodded. "And the mongrel. Kill all three of 'em."

***

Maria poured fresh coffee into Leonie's cup and patted her shoulder. "It's going to be OK."

"We haven't heard from them in…" She glanced up at the digital clock on the wall. "Five hours. Something has happened. We need to get a search party out there, right now."

Ben, the ranger, looked up from his workstation. "The search party's heading out at first light. You shouldn't worry. The radio probably went down at Granite Hut. It can be a bit patchy. I wouldn't be surprised if Jenny has them all there."

"I shouldn't worry? My kid sister's out there along with her fiancé, their dog, Maria's husband and the rest of their team. If something's happened to them I won't be able to live with myself."

"We're doing everything we can," said Maria as she offered the pot of coffee to Ben.

Leonie sighed and turned her attention back to the computer monitor that showed all the incoming communications traffic. The last message from Ali at Granite Hut had been received at lunchtime.

An alarm chimed telling them that someone had opened the front door. Leonie glanced at the monitor that displayed a video feed from the reception area. She instantly recognized her sister wrapped in a jacket. There was a man with her. She leaped from her chair. "It's Ali!"

Dashing through the office she burst into the waiting area and wrapped her sister in a hug. "Oh god, I thought I'd lost you." She immediately noticed how cold Ali was. "Maria, we need coffee and blankets."

She bundled Ali through to the living area at the back of

the station and sat her on a bunk.

Maria appeared with a pile of blankets and piping hot coffee. "Let's get her out of those damp clothes."

Ali waved them away. "No, first we need to contact Commander Conner."

Ernie's wife frowned. "Why? What's happened?"

"The boys have been captured by drug growers. They're being held in a cabin in the hills." Ali took a sip of coffee.

Leonie's eyebrows rose. "You're kidding me?"

She shook her head. "No, they flipped their raft. Tried to walk out and ran into a dope plantation. Rick and Jenny are still up there. We need to get them help."

"Seriously, those boys could stir up trouble in a cemetery." Leonie turned and bellowed through the open door, "Ben, we've got ourselves a situation. I'm going to need a direct line to the DEA."

"I'll call Conner," said Maria. "You get a warm shower. Jenny's locker is over there. Her clothes should fit. Don't you worry about any of this, Leonie and I will sort it out."

Ali followed them into the command room and watched as the two women snapped into action. Suddenly overwhelmed with fatigue, she sat in a chair and sipped her coffee. Finally, she felt like she could rest. Help for Mike and the others was on the way.

Chapter Fourteen

Jenny's lips felt soft and warm as they pressed against Rick's cheek. He sighed turning his head until he could kiss her full on the mouth. Her tongue pressed against his then ran its way across his face leaving a wet trail. "What the hell?"

His eyes darted open as Axe's whiskers tickled his nostrils. The kiss had been a dream. All except the part with the tongue. He shoved the dog away. "Thanks, bud."

He remembered he was lying next to Jenny and gently eased himself away so he could wipe his face and check his watch. It was a little after five in the morning.

"Good morning," said Jenny as she sat up.

"Sleep well?" he asked.

"Surprisingly." She gathered up the bedding, emptied out the leaves and stuffed it back into her pack.

Rick rose and checked the traps they'd built the night before. Everything was still intact. He picked up the shotgun and rifle then shouldered his backpack. "You ready for this?"

Jenny handed her pistol to him and checked her shotgun. "Let's do it."

They followed Axe through the woods until they reached the edge of the drug plantation. The sun was rising casting a soft glow across the crop.

"You sure about this?" he asked. "I can do it alone."

She turned and placed a hand on the side of his face. Leaning in she kissed him softly.

For a moment Rick was somewhere other than the drug plantation. The location was irrelevant, all that existed was the taste and feel of her lips and mouth.

"We're a team now," she said when they parted. "Now, let's rescue your friends."

He grinned. "Fuck yeah."

She kissed him again. “Get into position.”

Rick left her at the edge of the plantation and made his way between the rows of waxen green plants. He felt elated, partially because of the pending action, but mostly because Jenny liked him. He felt like a teenager giddy with first love as he stalked through the marijuana crop. Pausing he exhaled and focused. This wasn’t about him. This was about freeing Mike and the boys and then exacting a little revenge on the criminals holding them.

***

Harold and Ed led the hunting party. Hank, without his dog, and Carl, with his arm bandaged, had been relegated to supporting roles. The four men left the cabin at first light armed to the teeth with shotguns, pistols and two AR-15 assault rifles. Ed had a walkie-talkie attached to his belt.

“We’ll skirt the plantation,” said Ed as they paused at the edge of the clearing. “Harold can track a field mouse through a parking lot. Shouldn’t take us long to pick up their trail and run them down.”

“What if they legged it out of the park?” asked Hank.

“Then our buddies would have picked them up. Damn, do you two just play stupid or are you actually thick as shit,” snapped Ed.

Harold stood peering into the forest as his partner ripped into the other men. “Guys, I think I see something.” He pointed through the bushes.

Ed raised his AR-15 and peered through the scope. In the soft morning light he spotted something fluttering in the breeze. “This way.” He gestured for the others to follow.

The four men moved swiftly into the thick undergrowth that bordered the camouflaged plantation. Harold took the lead, scanning the soft ground for footprints.

He found a food wrapper stuck in the branches of a bush. Plucking it free he rolled the plastic between his fingers and sniffed it. “This is new.” He dropped to a knee and examined the ground. A trail of boot marks led into the forest. "They went this way."

The path their prey had taken became even clearer to the tracker as they moved deeper into the woods. His experienced eye was drawn to broken twigs, scuff marks in the leaves and indentations in the soft soil.

Ed was the first to spot their quarry. "Down there," he whispered, gesturing through a gap in the trees. A figure was walking slowly away from them. It disappeared into a thick patch of bushes.

Weapons held ready they gave chase, sliding through the leaf litter that covered the steep slope.

Ed spotted their target again, long brown hair and a feminine build revealing it was the park ranger. She turned, saw them and started running.

A weapon fired alongside his ear and a bullet blew a chunk out of a tree.

"What the fuck!" Ed screamed at Hank who held the smoking rifle. "It's just the girl. If we bring her in alive Carter might let us have some fun with her."

Harold pushed ahead, sprinting through the scrub like a dog on the scent of a rabbit. Ed wasn't far behind his eyes peeled for any sign of the SEAL or the dog.

"She's on her own," hollered his partner.

They covered a hundred yards through thick undergrowth, closing the gap between them and the girl. She wore a backpack, but as far as Ed could see she was unarmed. He raised his AR-15 in the air and fired.

Terrified the girl slipped, fell to the ground and clambered back to her feet.

"Hold it right there sweetheart!" yelled Ed.

She was a dozen feet in front of them when she stopped and turned. "Please don't hurt me."

Ed eyeballed the empty holster on her belt as he came up alongside Harold, who had her covered with his shotgun. "Where's your SEAL buddy?"

Hank and Carl caught up, skidding to a halt behind them.

"He went for help," she managed through her tears.

The four men stood in a semi-circle not more than ten feet from their quarry. Like a pack of hyenas confronting a lioness they tentatively edged forward. Ed's eyes darted from side to side as he searched for any sign of the SEAL or the dog.

The ranger swayed slightly, reached out and grasped a tree.

Hank lowered his weapon. "She looks like she's gonna faint."

She pulled at something and suddenly a rope snaked through the leaves alongside them. Ed frowned as his eyes followed it. Then a noise behind him caught his attention. He turned at the same time as the others.

"Fuck," was all he managed as a three hundred pound log swung down toward them. It hit Carl and Hank with a sickening crunch as he dove sideways. The two men and log slammed into Harold, knocking him off his feet. It caught Ed a glancing blow sending him sprawling, his rifle flung from his hands.

He hit the ground with a thud, pain shooting up from a bruised thigh. He rolled over to see the park ranger standing over the crumpled heap of the other three men with a pump action shotgun in her shoulder.

"You fucking whore," he said as he reached for his rifle.

A savage growl filled the air and he froze. He found himself staring directly into the bared fangs of a mean looking dog.

"I wouldn't move if I were you," said the ranger. "That's a trained attack dog. One word from me and he'll tear out your throat." She tossed something into his lap.

He glanced at the roll of tape and then at the men lying under the suspended log. Hank and Carl were out cold. Harold stared silently into the barrel of her shotgun.

She flashed him a smile. "Now, how about you crawl over here real slowly and tape up your buddies."

"How about you go to hell."

The dog let out a loud bark and another savage growl.

"Pardon me?"

Ed swallowed, picked up the tape and slid slowly across to the others. The dog followed him its eyes locked on his throat.

Behind him in the leaves, his radio hissed. “Ed, what the hell’s going on down there?” demanded Carter.

Chapter Fifteen

Rick's adrenaline was firing, his heart pounding as he sprinted through the marijuana plants in the direction of the ambush. He'd heard a single gunshot and then nothing, a sure sign that Jenny was in trouble.

As he reached the edge of the plantation another shot rang out followed by a second and a third. He skidded to a halt and exhaled. That was the signal he'd given her. The ambush had been a success. Now, he could focus on rescuing the team.

He made his way back through the plantation, searching for his backpack. Locating it he rummaged inside and removed a gas stove and spare canister. Placing the burner under a plant he lit it and sat the canister on top.

Leaving the bag he continued through the plantation with the lever action rifle in one hand and the shotgun in the other. He had Jenny's Glock stuffed into the back of his shorts.

Reaching the edge of the marijuana plants he slid to his stomach and crawled forward till he could see the cabin.

He was on the opposite side to the cage that held his friends. Between them were the porch and two ATVs. An overweight figure sat in a rocking chair with a shotgun across his knees watching the cage. Rick lined him up with the rifle.

A second figure appeared from the cabin. This guy was tall with a Stetson, cowboy boots and a pistol belt. He stormed across to the cage and aimed his pistol at the group of captives. Rick assumed that this was Carter, the guy in charge.

"I know you're out there," he bellowed. "Show yourself or I'm going to start killing your buddies."

Rick didn't have a shot from where he was lying and if he did and missed it could hit the others. What's more he didn't have much faith in the old lever action's accuracy.

"I'm not messing around. You've got five seconds before I

shoot this old bastard in the face," bellowed the man.

Rick contemplated calling his bluff. However, something told him that Carter had the will to kill TJ.

"Four."

He dropped the rifle and stood.

"Three."

He walked slowly toward the cabin.

"Two."

The fat bastard on the porch nearly fell out of his chair. "He's here! Carter, he's here!" he said as he stood and aimed his shotgun.

Carter turned as Rick stopped alongside the ATVs. "Travis, you got him covered?" he asked.

"Yeah, he as much as smiles and I'll blow his head off."

Carter holstered his pistol and took a pair of handcuffs from his belt. "Where are the woman and the dog?" He tossed them onto the ground in front of Rick.

"I don't know."

"Sure you don't. Put the damn cuffs on."

As Rick bent down to retrieve the handcuffs there was a loud explosion in the plantation; the gas canister. He dropped to one knee, snatched the Glock from the back of his shorts and aimed it at Carter.

A shotgun boomed from the porch. He barely registered the sting in his buttocks as pellets ripped into his flesh.

Carter dove for cover as Rick fired rapidly. His shots struck a pile of drums where he had disappeared.

Movement near the cage caught his eye and he spotted Jenny emerging from the marijuana her shotgun held ready, Axe by her side.

The report of a gun reminded him that Travis, the fat bastard, was still on the porch. He popped up over the ATV and snapped off a shot hitting him in the torso. The morbidly obese redneck didn't flinch and racked his shotgun. "I'm a gonna kill you."

Rick heard a pistol shot and felt the bullet crease his shoulder as he fired another round into Travis. He spun and saw Carter running toward one of the other ATVs. Jenny's shotgun boomed and buckshot impacted the ground around the man as he leaped into the vehicle. Rick tried to raise the Glock but his arm was unresponsive.

Jenny fired again and pellets sprayed the ATV as it started and took off with a roar. Axe sprinted after it, barking frantically.

Rick checked to see that Travis was down as he climbed into the remaining buggy.

"Shove over big boy," said Jenny as she made to jump into the driver's seat.

He grinned and slid sideways, transferring his pistol to his good arm. A glance in the wing mirror confirmed that she had freed Mike and the others.

Jenny gunned the ATV and sent it power sliding around the corner. He was impressed; she handled the powerful buggy like a rally driver. In a matter of seconds, they'd caught up with Axe.

Rick let out a whistle and the dog pulled to one side of the road. Jenny slowed and he leaped onto the rear seats. "Good boy," said Rick as the dog licked him. "Now, let's get this Carter dickhead."

Jenny floored the throttle and sent the Polaris soaring over a rise in the road.

As they landed with a bounce Rick spotted Carter's buggy ahead. He gripped the handle in front of him with his bad hand and clutched the pistol with the other. "I'm going to shoot out his tires."

As she closed the gap between the two ATVs Rick fired a volley of bullets. They went wide. He tried again, striking the tailgate.

Hearing the shots Carter swerved his buggy from side to side, kicking up dust. Jenny closed the gap to a few feet. In the maelstrom of dust Rick couldn't get a clear shot.

"Hold on!" Jenny said as she rammed the back of Carter's ATV.

The impact jolted him forward and he braced himself,

wounded shoulder burning. Then he felt Axe jump from the rear seat past his head onto the hood of the buggy. With a flash of fur he disappeared through the dust, leaping into the back of Carter's ATV.

Brake lights flashed and they slammed into the buggy again. Jenny fought to keep control as they skidded.

Carter's screams filled the air as his ATV slowed, angled off the track and bumped into a large tree.

Rick jumped out pistol in hand. As the dust cleared he saw Carter's predicament.

Axe had the crooked policeman by the back of his neck, his teeth sunk into the shirt collar. Fortunately for the military working dog the crooked cop had also lost his pistol. It lay out of reach in the foot well on the passenger side.

"I don't think he likes you," said Rick as he aimed the Glock.

"Get him off me. Please, get him off me," whimpered Carter.

Rick ordered the dog to release and gestured for Carter to climb out. "On your knees, hands behind your back."

Jenny produced a pair of handcuffs and soon Carter was sitting cuffed in the back of their buggy with Axe sitting alongside him, teeth bared.

"Way to go, sailor." Jenny gave his hand a squeeze.

He reached out, grasped her waist and pulled her in close. "Hey, it was all you, ranger girl."

They locked eyes for a moment and then Rick tipped his head forward and they touched lips. He forgot the pain in his shoulder and the pellets in his buttocks and legs as her mouth parted and they kissed long and hard.

Her body felt firm and muscular pressed against him as their tongues touched. Blood rushed to his groin and he felt it harden against her stomach.

"Steady on big boy," she murmured as their lips parted, "you're injured, remember."

As he held her he heard a faint yet familiar sound. The dull thud of helicopter blades grew louder. They both looked skyward as a black chopper thundered overhead.

"The cavalry has arrived," said Rick.

Jenny kissed him again. "No, our backup has arrived."

Rick laughed. "Good point. Shall we get back and see how the boys are doing?"

***

When they pulled up outside the cabin a squad of camouflaged operatives met them. A DEA team had rappelled in from the helicopter and secured the site.

Mike, Dean, Ernie and the Chief all sat on the porch drinking beers they'd raided from Travis's stash. The overweight pot grower was lying bandaged on a stretcher under the watchful eye of a DEA paramedic.

Axe leaped from the ATV and made a beeline for Mike. He knocked him backward spilling his beer as he licked his face. "Hey buddy, good to see you too," Mike said with a laugh.

All four men rose as Rick stepped from the ATV. Ernie was the first to reach him. The Latino threw his arms around his SEAL teammate. "You came through, bro. I thought we were dead. Then you come out all guns blazing like Rambo."

"I had help. Jenny's the one who found me."

Ernie looked confused. "You mean you had to find a pole-dancing instructor to save us."

Rick elbowed him. "She's a park ranger."

Ernie shook his head. "No, essé, she's a hero." He ran across and embraced the ranger.

Mike shook his hand next. "Thanks, brother."

"That dog of yours. He's pretty damn amazing."

Mike nodded in the direction of Jenny. "Pretty good matchmaker too." He headed over to thank the ranger.

"Looks like you learned something out there," said TJ as he approached.

"Yeah, I learned I'm sticking to boats. This forest crap is bullshit."

TJ placed a hand on his shoulder. "And here's me thinking you'd found a little humility." He grinned. "You did good, son. We'll make a woodsman out of you yet."

Dean was the last to offer his thanks to Rick. Then they all retired to the porch to drink beers as the DEA team secured Carter and his cronies. Jenny found a medical kit and inspected Rick's wounds between sips of her ale.

"Hey Rick," said Ernie. "How come you're the one who always gets shot?"

"Because, unlike you I'm not small enough to hide behind every bit of cover."

"That's so racist," declared the Latino.

"How is calling you a midget racist?" Rick winced as Jenny applied a dressing to his shoulder.

"Rick's right. He's a heightist," said the Chief.

"Well, if you didn't work out so much there wouldn't be so much of you to get shot," quipped Ernie.

Jenny snickered as she finished bandaging his wound.

"Oh, you think he's funny?"

She shook her head. "I think you're all crazy. Do you have many adventures like this?"

"Too many," lamented Mike. "From now on TJ is banned from planning any group activities outside of work."

"Amen to that," echoed Ernie and Rick.

As they laughed and drank one of the DEA agents approached. "Guys, we've prepared a landing zone a little way up the road. If you take the ATV's up there the helicopter will be able to lift you out to the ranger station. There's a paramedic team waiting there for you."

The Chief raised his beer. "Thanks, bud."

***

Mike was the first off the chopper when it touched down in a field behind the ranger station. With Axe by his side he ran straight into the arms of Ali, who was waiting with Maria and Leonie.

"I'm so sorry, babe. You must have been worried to death."

She nodded with eyes filled with tears. "Yes, I was."

He hugged her again and then she knelt and wrapped her arms around Axe. "I don't know what I would do without you, bud. You're the only thing keeping everyone in this family alive."

Axe licked the side of her face and wagged his tail furiously.

"That dog's a damn good SEAL," said TJ as he and the rest of the team joined them. Ernie already had his arms wrapped around his wife.

"OK team," said Ali's sister. "Maria and I have whipped up some coffee and breakfast inside. If you've got any injuries you should head over and see the medics." She pointed to the ambulance parked a dozen yards away.

"You're unbelievable, Leonie," said Ali.

She shrugged. "It's nothing. I mean, as of next week all you special kids are going to be family. Like it or not I'm lumped with you."

Jenny laughed as she helped Rick limp across to the back of the ambulance.

"It's a pretty crazy family," he said as one of the medics pulled out a stretcher and he eased himself up onto it.

"They're a pretty tight bunch," she said. "You're lucky to have friends like that." She turned to the medic. "He's got a gunshot graze to the right shoulder and buckshot wounds to the buttocks and legs."

"Got it, make yourself comfortable, sir."

Rick lay down with a pillow under his face.

"How's our hero?" he heard TJ ask.

"He'll be okay once the medic pulls the buckshot out of his butt," replied Jenny.

"Can I have some goddamn privacy?" bellowed Rick.

"Sure thing." The medic slid the gurney into the back of the ambulance. "Is the lady allowed to stay?"

"Yeah, someone has to hold my hand."

The doors of the van closed and Jenny sat opposite.

"You attached to these shorts?" asked the medic.

"Not particularly," replied Rick. He jolted as the medic used shears to cut away his shorts and underwear. "Steady there, bud."

"You've got a lovely butt," Jenny said with a chuckle. "Well except for the buckshot."

He felt the medic examining his wounds with a metal probe.

"What are you doing next Wednesday?" he asked.

"Look, we just met," quipped the medic.

Rick shook his head.

"I'm not sure, why?" responded Jenny.

"I need a date for Mike and Ali's wedding."

"You're asking me to go to your teammate's wedding with you? Isn't that kind of a big deal?"

He turned and smiled. "Yeah, it is."

She leaned forward and kissed him. "I'd love to go."

"Sir, this might hurt a little."

Rick felt a sharp pain in his buttocks as the medic used a pair of forceps to pluck shot from the flesh. "Son of a bitch."

He twitched as the wound was squirted with antiseptic then sponged dry and dressed. "You're real lucky these didn't go very deep."

"That's what she said," joked Rick as the medic removed another pellet. "Holy shit. What are you doing back there?"

Jenny kissed him on the side of the face. "Come on. I thought you were a big tough SEAL."

His eyes narrowed. "And I thought you were a sensitive park ranger."

A wicked smile flashed across her face. "You've got a lot to learn." Then she turned to the medic. "Any chance I can take over?"

Chapter Sixteen

A little over a week later and Rick, TJ, Ernie and Dean sat in a row of chairs in a picturesque vineyard nestled in the rugged hills of Swartz Canyon, San Diego. All four were dressed in dark blue suits with matching silver ties.

In front of them under a vine covered arbor adorned with flowers stood Mike. Dressed in a tailored tuxedo he wore a smile a mile wide. Next to him sat Axe, his coat freshly groomed and a bowtie fitted to his collar.

Mike turned and Rick shot him a broad smile and a wink. A feeling of pride swelled through his chest as his teammate waited for his bride to be.

Glancing over his shoulder he spotted Jenny sitting with Leonie and Maria. His date looked beautiful in a silver dress with an exposed back. She wore her hair high with sprigs of white flowers in it. He grinned, she looked more elegant than any woman he'd ever laid eyes on.

She caught his eye and smiled. It was the look that a woman reserved for the man she loved. It was subtle, but Rick felt it like a hit of morphine. A warm sensation flooded his body and he smiled back.

Suddenly, music filled the air and he rose with the others. Everyone turned to face the red carpet that ran from the lush green vines between the rows of chairs to the altar.

Ali stepped into view on her father's arm and the crowd let out a collective sigh. She looked stunning in a simple yet elegant off-the-shoulder dress that barely touched the ground. Like Jenny she wore her hair up, except hers was adorned with white roses.

He turned back to Mike and saw the look of pure bliss on his SEAL buddy's face. A little over a week ago he wouldn't have truly understood how Mike felt, but since meeting Jenny that had changed. "He looks so happy," he whispered.

Ernie gave a quiet chuckle. "Bro, you haven't seen the shit eating grin on your face."

He frowned. "What's that supposed to mean?"

"It means you're in love, essé."

Rick leaned down so his mouth was close to Ernie's ear. "You might be right, but if you tell anyone I'm going to kick your ass."

He straightened up as Ali's father passed her across to Mike. Then a priest joined the two of them.

The service was short and sweet. Axe supplied the ring. Then the priest declared them man and wife. They kissed and cheers filled the vineyard.

While the newlyweds and Axe disappeared for photos the wedding guests, under the guidance of Leonie, gathered inside the winery for drinks.

Rick and Jenny joined Ernie, Maria and TJ at the bar.

"What a beautiful wedding," said Jenny.

"Ali looked amazing," added Maria.

The boys ordered beers and stepped away leaving the ladies talking.

The Chief raised his beer. "So, Rick. The last man standing."

"Once stung, twice shy," he replied.

"You seem pretty smitten with your ranger," said TJ.

"You're in love, bro," added Ernie.

Rick shrugged. "Maybe." He took a sip of his beer.

TJ grinned. "Maybe? Maybe it's time to run another Girlfriend Selection Course."

Rick snorted into his beer. It sprayed froth over the three others. "Nope. I ain't doing that shit." He coughed up amber liquid.

Jenny and Maria glanced over.

TJ laughed, relieving Rick of the overflowing beer. "Relax. I think it's safe to say that Jenny can skip selection. I mean hell, she rescued our asses."

Ernie stepped over to the bar and grabbed another beer.

"What am I, chopped liver?" said Rick.

Ernie handed him a bottle. "Hey, we know you helped out. You make a pretty good sidekick."

Rick glared as the girls joined them and Jenny kissed his cheek. "What are you boys talking about?"

TJ smiled. "We were just reminiscing about how Mike and Ali met. Rick was saying how much he enjoyed the selection course."

She grinned. "Oh, yes. He mentioned that up in Oregon, but never got to explain it."

Maria grasped her by the arm. "That's not a story you want to hear without champagne."

As Ernie's wife directed her back to the bar Jenny flashed Rick a smile. He returned it staring intensely into her eyes.

"Oh, she's got you bad," TJ said.

"Signed SEAL'd and delivered," added Ernie. "This time next year we'll be doing it all over."

"If, and I mean if I ever get married again, there will be no bachelor party, no secret plans and no damn shenanigans."

TJ lifted his beer. "Here's to shenanigans."

***

It was well after three in the morning when Rick and Jenny arrived at the villa he'd rented a short Uber ride from the wedding venue. As he fumbled with the front door he felt Jenny's arms around his waist.

"You look so damn handsome in that suit," she murmured as her lips caressed his ear.

He abandoned the door, turned and met her lips with his own. The kiss was long, passionate and sent fire coursing through his veins.

When, after minutes their lips finally parted Rick was breathing heavily. "You, you're something else Jenny. I've never met a woman like you before."

She grinned, her hands traveling from his waist to his groin where she squeezed him gently through the fabric of his suit. "So, you think I could pass your selection course?"

His brow rose. "Ah, Maria spilled the beans."

"Yes, she also told me I'm the first woman to tame the untamable Rick."

"Tame me? That's fun–"

She squeezed him again and pressed her mouth against his. They kissed like teenagers as she unzipped his fly and slipped her hand inside his pants.

He let out a soft moan and moved his lips to her neck as he slid the thin straps of her dress over her shoulders and unzipped the satin material. The garment slid to her waist revealing her pert breasts.

"Are you going to do something about the door," she murmured. "Or are we going to make love on the porch."

It took Rick a matter of seconds to open it.

Jenny stepped inside, pushed her dress down her hips and let it slide to the floor. She stepped out of it and walked slowly along the hall in just her panties and heels.

Rick stood in the doorway his eyes glued to her lithe body.

She glanced back at him. "You going to stand there gawking or come in?"

"Huh, yeah." He closed the door, shrugged off his jacket and followed her into the bedroom.

She lay back on the bed as he shed his clothes. His eyes never left hers as she watched him intently.

When he was completely naked she smiled. "God you're a hunk of a man." She beckoned with her finger.

He started at her feet. Softly kissing her legs, thighs, stomach and breasts, he slowly made his way up the bed. Finally, when their mouths touched he felt her hand grasp his manhood. She pushed aside her underwear and slowly guided him in as they kissed.

Epilogue

Vicente Barbosa sat on the plush mattress he'd had smuggled into his prison cell and studied the cards in his hand. The poker game had become something of a tradition. Every Friday three of the most influential men in the maximum-security facility joined him for a game.

On his immediate left sat Enrique a Hispanic gangbanger and mass murderer from MS13. Next to him was a hulking African American with a shaved head; Trey an enforcer from Detroit. The brute was rumored to have murdered an entire family with his bare hands. The third man, arguably the most influential in their current environment was Jules Deveron, the prison's head guard. At six-foot-five with the build of a professional wrestler he was a man who demanded and received the utmost respect from all but the stupidest of prisoners.

The guard pushed the last of his cigarettes into the center of the table and narrowed his eyes. "OK, Vicente. Show us your cards."

Barbosa shrugged and tossed his hand on the table, a pair of aces.

"You shitting me?" exclaimed Enrique. "Two lousy aces. You got balls essé. Big brass balls."

"Yeah, but balls or no balls that's still a shitty hand." Deveron tossed a straight flush on the table and grinned. "You can have the cigarettes, divvy them between yourselves." He rose from the plastic stool. "I've got to get back to my reports."

He made for the cell door where two of his guards were waiting. As he was about to leave he stopped and turned, reaching into his jacket. "Almost forgot. Mail for Mr. Barbosa." He tossed a letter toward the former cartel kingpin. "Same time next week, gentlemen. Stay out of trouble."

He disappeared and the guards gestured for Trey and Enrique to follow.

Barbosa waited until they were gone and his cell door locked before he opened the envelope.

The hand written letters were a coded report from his men in Mexico. They informed him of shipments, earnings, thefts and actions taken to remedy problems. He noted that profits were up; his second in command was doing well.

Among the reports was a letter from his wife. His son had made the state soccer team and his grades had improved.

The final item in the envelope was a single piece of paper with a photograph printed on it. The glossy shot was a wedding photo. A man and a woman stood in front of a priest with a dog by their side.

He sat staring at the picture, channeling hatred at the people and animal that had put him in this shit hole far from his family and his beloved Mexico.

Scrunching the paper into a ball he tossed it at the wall. "I'm going to destroy you, Michael Saunders. I'm going to wait till you have a family of your own and then you're going to watch them die."

THE END

SIGNED SEAL'D AND DELIVERED

Chapter One

Mike Saunders lay on a deck chair under a tree in the front yard of his house. A warm breeze rustled the leaves above as he stretched his muscled arms high and folded them behind his head. The corners of his mouth turned up in a smile and the edges of his grey eyes crinkled as he watched his son playing.

The two-year-old charged around the lawn with Axe, Mike's recently retired military working dog. The Belgian Malinois adored Junior and was closely supervising the toddler's activities.

Mike watched as Junior made a break toward his wife's rose bushes. Axe leaped into action, gently blocking his progress.

Junior clutched the dog's long fur, and the hound guided him back to the middle of the lawn. When the toddler was safe Axe sat on his haunches and looked toward Mike. One of his ears flopped over and his tongue lolled from the side of his mouth.

"Who needs a nanny when you've got Axe?" said a soft voice from behind.

He turned and watched his wife cross the lawn from the porch of their townhouse. Alison Saunders wore a floral print dress that hugged her curves, putting an even broader smile on his face.

His wife, a veterinarian, had bright green eyes, a button nose and plump lips that were perpetually turned up in a smile.

"What would we do without him?"

Ali reached the deck chair, hitched her dress and straddled him, leaning forward to kiss him. "Not as much of this."

Mike slipped his hands around her waist as she nibbled his lip. He felt the blood rush into his shorts as she ground down on him. "Spring is in the air?" he murmured.

Ali turned her attention to his ear, soft lips brushing the lobe. "It's a pity we've got an audience," she whispered.

Mike turned and looked directly into two pairs of bright inquisitive eyes. Both his son and dog were watching intently. "Isn't it time for Junior's nap?"

Ali nibbled his ear. "A huh, and if you put him to bed, we can have a nap of our own."

Mike slid his hands under her dress and along her thighs. "I'm heading out on an exercise. I'm not interested in napping."

She sat upright, shifting weight on to his crotch as she traced her fingers down his granite hard abs. "I suggest reading him *Bish the Adventure Jug*; it's his current favorite."

He groaned as she slid off him and walked toward the house. The dress did nothing to hide the lines of her butt as she climbed the porch. "Anytime now," she said with a chuckle as she disappeared inside.

Mike grinned to himself as he rose from the chair and crossed the lawn. He had to be one of the luckiest men alive, with a stunning wife, vibrant young son, great teammates and a killer job. He ruffled his dog's ears, a loyal best friend. Life was good.

Scooping his son from the grass he carried him toward the front door. As he reached for the handle, he sensed something was off and turned back to the yard.

Axe stood, staring past the rose bushes and through their white picket fence. Hackles raised and ears angled forward, it was body language that Mike knew from their time in combat.

"What's up boy?" Mike scanned the street as he bounced his son on his hip.

There were a half-dozen cars parked opposite, and he scanned each one. He spotted a white sedan in the shade of a leafy tree, and his eyes narrowed. Three years earlier, a similar car had played a role in the abduction and attempted murder of Ali. Shaking his head, he drove the idea from his mind; Barbosa was rotting in a maximum-security prison with eight life sentences.

Axe let out a half-hearted bark before joining him on the porch. The dog looked at him with intelligent brown eyes.

"What's up bud, squirrel?"

Axe cocked his head, and his right ear flopped forward. Mike reached down and ruffled his ears. Then he left the porch and walked through to Junior's bedroom. Axe's claws rattled on the floorboards as he followed. The toddler struggled to keep his eyes open as Mike tucked him into bed.

"Dadda, Axe," he managed between yawns.

"He's right here, bud." Mike kissed Junior on his forehead as the dog jumped onto the bed and curled up alongside his son.

He stroked Axe and kissed Junior again. Pausing a moment at the door, he smiled as his son reached out and placed one hand on the dog's paw. From the moment that Ali had introduced their son to his dog, the two had become inseparable. The former military working dog had taken it upon himself to watch over Junior and keep him safe.

"They're so cute," whispered his wife as she slipped an arm around his waist.

"Yeah." He turned and dipped his head to kiss her.

What started as a tender embrace rapidly escalated to heated passion as he maneuvered her into the hall. Items of clothing dropped to the floor as they continued along the passage into their bedroom. Mike removed her bra with a deft flick of his wrist and lifted her off the ground. She wrapped her legs around him as they kissed. Then he lowered her gently onto the bed.

"Can't TJ cancel the exercise so you can stay at home?" Ali purred.

Mike chuckled. "That ain't gonna happen. The old man spends all his time at the office."

"Trouble at home?"

He kissed her neck, gently brushing his lips against her skin. She moaned as he caressed her breasts. Slipping his fingers into the sides of her French cut briefs he slid them along her thighs as he continued kissing his way down her body.

Outside, less than fifty yards away in a white car, a man sat hunched over a tablet. On the seat next to him was a compact camera with a long lens.

On screen, he sorted through photos of Mike and his family as they relaxed in their yard. Selecting four images, he transferred them into an encrypted email account and hit send. Then he fished a phone from the pocket of his jacket. Holding the device to his mouth he recorded a message.

"I've sent you the pictures. Let me know what the next move is," he said in Spanish.

A moment later the message was sent and he awaited a reply. It came less than thirty seconds later in the form of text.

Maintain observation.

***

Ali took a sip from her coffee before slotting it into the cup holder on the handle of Junior's stroller. Her son was attached to his father's leg as Mike tossed a gear bag into the back of his pickup.

"Dadda, no go," he wailed.

Mike scooped him into his arms. "Hey bud, dad's got to go to work. I need you to stay here and look after mom and Axe."

"Nooo," he said shaking his head.

Ali thought her heart would break as her son buried his head into her husband's shoulder and clung to him like a koala. Feeling pressure against her leg she glanced down and saw that Axe was sitting alongside her. The dog had an uncanny knack for sensing emotions and offering support. She reached down and stroked his head.

"Hey bud, I gotta go look after my team. I'll only be gone a few days. Axe and mom need you here."

Axe barked, gaining Junior's attention, then jumped up on Mike so he could lick the boy's leg. The toddler's mood changed instantly. He giggled and reached for the dog's ears. "Dadda, down."

Mike lowered him, and he immediately wrapped his arms

around Axe's neck.

"He's distracted, you need to go now," said Ali.

Mike nodded, stepped across and embraced her, kissing her softly. "I'll be back in a few days." Then he checked to make sure Axe and Junior were well clear of the pickup before jumping inside and pulling out of the drive. He gave Ali a wave as he drove away.

Once the truck had disappeared, she gathered her giggling son from the ground and placed him in the stroller. Axe stayed closed, continuing his role as the distractor.

"OK, boys. Let's get rolling."

Ali pushed the stroller across the lawn and out the gate. Axe fell in by her side. He was more than familiar with the routine of delivering Junior to daycare. The dog waited patiently as she secured the gate and handed her son a juice box. Then, with coffee in hand, they started the half-mile stroll.

For the last two months Ali had been working three half-days a week with Junior going to daycare and Axe joining her at the clinic. It was good for both of them. The toddler got to socialize, and she was able to return to the job she loved.

The walk was made even more enjoyable by the pleasure that Axe got from it. The dog's nose worked overtime as they passed houses and then shops. Ali had worried that he would miss working with Mike and the team. However, he seemed more than content in his role as Junior's guardian. He trotted alongside the stroller, sticking his head in every now and then to check on his charge.

Ali had finished her coffee when they arrived at the daycare center. She unstrapped Junior, and he took off at lightning speed, heading straight for the jungle gym. She smiled. He was so much like his father, always charging off on another adventure.

She checked in with the staff before starting home with Axe and the stroller. The dog wore a worried expression, glancing back over his shoulder every few feet.

"It's OK, Axe. He's going to be fine."

As they moved across the parking lot Axe's attention

returned to his surroundings, and Ali's thoughts turned to her day at the clinic. Today, she was expecting a broad range of patients: two Labradors, a Cocker Spaniel and a Chihuahua.

Axe interrupted her thoughts when he stopped dead and let out a low growl. Ali turned in the direction he was looking and wound his lead in a little tighter. "What is it, boy?"

There were a handful of cars in the parking lot and no pedestrians. Axe seemed to be fixated on a white sedan that had pulled in only moments earlier. The vehicle drove slowly, seemingly searching for a park. It passed two empty spots then exited onto the main road. Once it was gone Axe relaxed and sat on his haunches.

Ali knelt beside him and stroked his neck. "You didn't like that car, did you, buddy?"

He licked her cheek, and Ali chuckled. "OK, let's get to work." The rest of the walk home was uneventful, and soon they were on their way to her practice. She considered ringing Mike and telling him about the incident in the parking lot. But, she quickly pushed the idea from her mind. Axe had been through a lot in his life; he was allowed to have a little outburst every now and then.

***

Meanwhile, a little over twelve miles away at Halsey Field, Coronado Naval Base, Mike and his teammates, Rick and Ernie, were dressed in combat fatigues as they checked their equipment. Behind them, sailors were preparing an eleven-meter Rigid Hull Inflatable Boat (RHIB) for parachute insertion.

The SEALs had laid their gear out on the floor of a hangar so they could double-check their mission essential kit. Parachutes, wetsuits, combat harnesses, fins, radios, weapons, NVGs, batteries and helmets were inspected and accounted for.

Rick, a muscle-bound African American, checked his watch as he sipped from a can of energy drink. "Where's TJ?

Not like pops to be late."

Chisel-jawed with a shaved head, Rick was the team's Corpsman. The former ladies' man had found love when Mike's bachelor party had gone badly wrong in the wilds of an Oregon forest.

"His wife was dropping him off," added Ernesto, or Ernie as his friends called him. The compact Latino was the team's comms guy and a family man with two boys.

"Deborah is going to drop him off at work?" asked Mike, as he adjusted the straps on his gear bag.

"I know, essé. Been on team with the guy for six years and I think I've met his wife twice."

"Doing better than me, I've never met her," added Rick as he finished the energy drink and crushed it.

"I met her once," said Mike.

"In my mind I picture her being statuesque," said Rick.

Mike shook his head. "Statuesque? Since when do you use words like statuesque to describe a woman?"

Rick tossed the can in the trash. "What? I just picture the Chief with someone empowered and yet elegant."

Mike and Ernie started at him in disbelief.

"There's something wrong with you." Mike finished with his gear. "I'm going to check the team rooms. The Chief might have gotten caught up."

Ernie gestured to the RHIB, where the riggers were making the final adjustments to the boat. "As soon as these guys are done we're supposed to be airborne."

Mike nodded and strode out of the hangar toward the team rooms. As he rounded the corner he spotted TJ unloading bags from a Mercedes sedan in the parking lot. A tall woman in an elegant suit stood at the driver's door of the car, Deborah.

Mike paused as TJ slung his bag over his shoulder and slammed the trunk. He watched as the veteran SEAL walked to his wife and stopped two feet from her. Mike couldn't hear what was being said, but from Deborah's body language it wasn't a fond farewell. She had her arms folded in front of her chest and was tapping her foot impatiently.

Feeling like he was intruding, Mike turned and returned to the hangar.

"You find him?" asked Ernie.

"Yeah, he's on his way."

"How's Junior and Ali doing?" asked Rick as he joined them.

"Good, bud. Junior's in daycare now and Ali's back at work."

"How's Axe handling that?"

"He's been heading to the surgery with Ali."

"I bet he's missing team life," added Ernie.

TJ appeared at the hangar entrance with his gear bag slung over his shoulder. With a square jaw and craggy features the Chief looked every bit the veteran operator that he was. A team guy through and through he'd been kicking doors and driving boats for over twenty years.

"How's it hanging, Chief?" Rick asked as TJ dumped his gear on the floor.

The squad leader fixed him with an icy stare. "What the hell is that supposed to mean?"

Rick swallowed. "Nothing, just wanted to know how you're doing."

"I'm fine. Got all your gear?"

"Team's fully accounted for," replied Ernie. "Your stuff is over next to mine."

"And the boat?"

"Riggers are finishing up now," added Mike.

"Good, soon as they're done load up and we'll get going." TJ strode across to his own equipment, leaving the boys to check on the boat.

"What the hell's wrong with him?" asked Rick in a low voice.

"He probably missed his coffee, you know how he gets," answered Ernie as he checked the shackles that attached the bundle of parachutes to the rubber boat.

"Yeah, grumpy as hell."

"Hey, how's Jenny going at her new job?" Mike said steering the conversation away from TJ.

Rick grinned. "She loves it. Very different to up north, but still plenty of critters to look after." His girlfriend was a park ranger.

"And the apartment, how you going with a woman in the house?"

He shrugged. "All good."

"All good?"

"OK, OK, I like it. She's great company and damn can she cook."

Mike turned to Ernie and smirked, the Latino winked and started whistling a tune. It took him a moment to realize it was Beyonce's *Single Ladies.*

"Quit grab-assing and get that damn boat loaded!" bellowed TJ from the other side of the hangar.

"Jeez, he is shitty," added Rick as he waved a cargo loader forward.

"Yeah," murmured Mike as he watched his squad leader stuff gear into a dive bag.

"Well, let's hope he chills out on the flight. Otherwise, this is going to be a long job."

Chapter Two

Vincent Barbosa sat cuffed with his hands shackled to a stainless steel table in a prison visitor's cell. The former cartel kingpin, known as *The Butcher*, wore a bright orange jumpsuit. A thick mustache adorned his face along with a smug look as he stared up at the security camera in the corner of the room.

"What's the holdup?" He shook his chains and spat into the corner.

A moment later there was a rattle from the room's steel door and it swung open, revealing a middle-aged man dressed in an ill-fitting suit, clutching a brown suitcase. Past his shoulder Barbosa caught a glimpse of a burly prison guard.

"You've got five minutes," barked the guard.

Barbosa's lawyer knew the drill. He scurried into the room and sat in the chair opposite, opening the briefcase to remove paperwork and a pen. "Sir, I've got some documents for you to sign."

"The usual?"

"Yes." He took an envelope from the case. "I also have a letter from your wife and children. I spoke to them this morning. They are well and send their love." The lawyer shot a look at the camera in the corner of the room as he slid the pen and documents across.

He took the pen and scribbled his signature in the required places.

The lawyer watched, glancing up at the camera every few seconds.

Barbosa leaned forward so he could tuck the letter from his family into the top pocket of his jumpsuit. "How is the plan progressing?"

The lawyer held up his hand as he rechecked the camera. As he did, it swiveled until the lens was facing the wall. He checked his watch. "OK, now we can talk. We've got two minutes before they start recording again."

"And?"

"Of course, the plan. Yes, it's progressing well. According to my sources, you will be transferred to another maximum security prison in Arizona."

"Do you have the date and time?"

The lawyer nodded. "Arrangements are being made."

Barbosa smiled. "Good, and what about my friends in San Diego, how are they?"

The lawyer swallowed. "My associate tells me they are in good health."

"Even the dog?"

"Yes, the dog is still with them."

His lip curled into a half snarl. "So nice to hear that nothing has happened to them."

The lawyer adjusted his tie. "Are we to proceed?"

"As planned."

"Very good." He checked the time. "There are other matters we must discuss. One of your men is suspected of being an agent for the Sinaloa cartel."

"Who?"

"Eduardo Salcido."

Barbosa stared intently at the lawyer, who glanced up at the camera. "I never liked that worm. Have Duvan take care of him."

"Yes, sir." He checked his watch. "That's all we've got time for today."

The camera swiveled to face them.

The lawyer gathered up the papers. Then he rose and tucked his suitcase under his arm. "I'll see you soon."

Barbosa snorted. "I'll try to be here."

There was a familiar rattle, and the door opened. "You're done," ordered the guard.

Barbosa sat, quietly reflecting on the conversation as he waited for the guards to arrive and return him to his cell. Finally, after three long years, he was going to see vengeance for the wrongs against him. Finally, his brother Juan would get the justice he deserved.

***

A bell chimed as Ali pushed open the door to her favorite café, The Spanner Shop, a former garage that had been converted into a funky eatery. She spotted her sister, Leonie, at the rearmost table. The curvy brunette was sitting with a taller woman who had her back to the door, Jenny.

Athletic with almost jet-black hair, the park ranger had been dating Mike's teammate, Rick, ever since she and Ali had saved his SEAL team from red neck drug growers. She'd subsequently moved to San Diego and had become one of her closest friends. The three of them, Ali, her sister and Jenny met weekly for lunch or coffee at the café.

"Hey you," exclaimed Leonie as Ali took a seat.

"Hi guys."

"We've ordered you a coffee," added Jenny.

"Thanks, after this morning I need it."

"What's up?" asked Jenny.

"That gorgeous boy giving you trouble?" asked Leonie.

Ali shook her head. "Not at all. He's an angel, just like his dad. No, I had a rehabilitation session with a young Labrador. Eighty pounds of fur, tongue and slobber."

"Sounds like fun," said Jenny. "Where's Axe?"

"Christine took him for a walk," she replied, referring to her assistant at the practice.

A waiter arrived with a tray of coffees and placed them on the table.

"So, what's news with you?" Ali asked Jenny.

Jenny smirked as she reached out and grasped her coffee with her left hand. As she did Ali spotted a glint of light reflecting from a stone on her finger.

"No way," she squealed.

It took Leonie a split second to realize what was going on and add her own delighted screams to the cacophony. She leaped out of her chair and barged around the table. Stepping past her sister, she wrapped her arms around Jenny's athletic frame and almost crushed her. "Oh my god, that is so exciting. I'm so happy for you."

Ali managed to squeeze in and join the hug. "Congratulations, gorgeous."

When the excitement had subsided, Ali asked, "So, how did he do it? Give us all the details."

"Yes," added Leonie as she returned to her chair. "Every sordid morsel."

Jenny shot them a sheepish look as she sipped her coffee.

"What?" asked Ali.

"Oh god, don't tell me he tied it to his dick with a ribbon," exclaimed Leonie.

Jenny nearly spat out her coffee. "No, he certainly did not."

"Well come on then, spill the beans. How did San Diego's most eligible bachelor drop the question?"

"Well… he kind of didn't."

Ali gave her a sister a questioning look before turning to Jenny. "What do you mean?"

Jenny wore a cheeky smile. "I may or may not have asked him."

"Get out of town," bellowed Leonie.

"No way," added Ali. "And he said yes?"

Jenny nodded. "He even cried."

"That's adorable."

"But you can't repeat that, he'd be mortified if the boys knew. I mean they're going to give him hell when they find out we're engaged."

"They don't know?" asked Ali.

She shook her head.

"Hold the farm," said Leonie. "If you proposed, where did the ring come from?"

"He already had it."

Leonie tipped her head back and laughed. "So you got the drop on Mr. Muscles. That's the best thing ever. Now, give us the deets. You take a knee and slip a ring on his finger?"

"No, I took him out to dinner and gave him a watch."

"How did you ask?" said Ali.

She shrugged. "I just asked him if he wanted to get married."

"And?"

"And then he took a knee and said yes."

"And cried!" added Leonie.

"There was a tear or two."

"That's so damn romantic… and also kind of empowering. So, when's the date?"

"July 22, we want to get married up at the cabin."

"Back where it all began," said Ali. "It seems like yesterday we were up there saving the boy's asses."

"Seems like yesterday they were putting you through that crazy selection course," added Leonie. "Which reminds me. Did Rick pass anymore of your challenges?"

Jenny shook her head. "No, he failed the Home Depot challenge with flying colors. We both got kicked out after he wore a lamp shade as a hat."

Leonie and Ali laughed.

"That's when I realized he was the one."

***

Mike slipped his combat rig over his head and adjusted the side straps. Then he climbed into his parachute harness and tightened it. As he did, he glanced sideways to where Rick and the others were doing the same.

The team and their gear were squeezed in alongside the RHIB that had been loaded into a C-17 transporter. A little under an hour from their target, TJ had given them the order to suit up.

Rick was struggling to get his broad shoulders into his harness. Mike shuffled over to help him. As he yanked the straps over the Corpsman's shoulders and passed him the ends, he noticed a shiny watch on Rick's wrist.

"New bling?" he yelled over the hum that filled the cargo hold.

Rick flashed a shit-eating grin. "Jenny bought it for me."

"That's a pretty expensive gift. You guys getting serious, hey?"

"Show me that thing," demanded Ernie from where he'd appeared. The Latino hadn't started rigging up yet, having checked the boat with the loadmaster. He grabbed Rick's wrist and pulled the watch up in front of his face. "Omega Seamaster; brother that's an expensive gift. That woman's put her mark on you."

Rick snatched his arm back.

"Quit screwing around, we've got forty minutes till we're on target," TJ yelled from down the line.

"What's up his ass?" mouthed Rick.

Mike shrugged and turned his attention back to his equipment.

Thirty minutes later the team stood ready for action. TJ moved along the line, checking each of them. Then, as second-in-command, it was Mike's responsibility to inspect the Chief's gear.

He stood in front of TJ as he ran through the checklist of safety and mission essential equipment. As he inspected the clips that attached the parachute to his squad leader's shoulders, he noticed a distant look in his eyes. "Chief, you OK?"

"Yeah, I'm good. We done here?"

He gave a thumbs-up and moved back in behind him. Looking forward he focused on the loadmaster.

The ramp of the C-17 lowered with a whine that was barely audible over the rush of air that whipped inside. Mike could now see the ocean, reaching out to the horizon behind the aircraft. He checked his watch. It was 1733 hours. They were still on schedule to get the boat in the water before dark.

The helmeted loadmaster pointed at the team and held up his palm, then gestured to the boat and raised a thumb.

A red light flashed green and the loadmaster tossed a drogue chute over the ramp. It hauled a second parachute that yanked the RHIB free of the jet. Mike watched as the massive parachute blossomed above it and the aircraft banked.

It took less than four minutes for them to loop back around. In that time the loadmaster confirmed that the boat was afloat. Then, as they leveled out, the call of thirty seconds was made.

Mike shuffled forward with his equipment braced against his legs. His pulse pounded in his ears, his breathing was shallow and muscles taut. No matter how many times he jumped, it still terrified him. Previously he'd always had the comforting bulk of Axe strapped to his front. The dog had jumped with him on more than a dozen missions and it never bothered him.

The light turned green and the loadmaster gave them the chop. Mike lurched forward after the others and stepped off the ramp into the buffeting tornado of the slipstream. There was a roar and then silence as the aircraft disappeared behind him. Free-fall was short, only a few seconds. Mike activated his chute and braced for the jerk as it deployed. Then he glanced up to check the canopy before grasping the toggles and steering for clear air.

The rest of the team was also under canopy and heading toward the boat a half-mile distant. Mike aimed toward it and enjoyed the sensation of unpowered flight. Then, as he got closer, he cut his equipment away. It dropped to the end of its tether and hit the water.

Seconds later he splashed in and cut away his parachute. Bobbing to the surface he struggled out of his harness, detached his fins from his belt, slipped them over his boots and kicked toward the boat.

When he arrived everyone was still in the water. Rick was the first to drag himself into the RHIB. He helped the others inside and like a well-oiled machine they went to work preparing to get underway.

Minutes later they were blasting over calm waters with the sun setting behind them. TJ stood at the center console, controlling the twin marine diesels that propelled the craft at breakneck speed across the ocean. Mike stood braced against the machine gun mounting in the bow, using his sleeve to wipe the spray from his Oakleys.

After a half hour of travel TJ throttled back the engines before killing them.

"This is our rally point. We wait here till dark and then head to the beach RV." He glanced at his watch. "Sunset is fifteen minutes away. Use that time to check your kit."

Rick threw out a sea anchor then he and Ernie sat in the bow going over their gear. Mike took the opportunity to move to the stern where TJ was studying a nautical chart.

"TJ, you doing OK?"

The Chief glared at him. "Why wouldn't I be?"

He shrugged. "Just asking."

TJ turned his attention back to the map.

Mike sat on the inflatable gunnels and checked the pouches on his combat rig.

"Deb wants a divorce," TJ stated.

The news hit Mike like a punch to the chest. TJ never talked much about his home life, but when he did it was with nothing but admiration for his wife.

The Chief's brow furrowed as he continued to look at the chart. "She says we've been apart too much. Doesn't know who I am anymore."

Mike was lost for words. He'd never seen his squad leader so vulnerable. "I'm sorry to hear that," he managed. "Have you thought of taking some time off, heading somewhere to reconnect?"

TJ nodded. "Yeah, I suggested all that. Told her we could see a counselor. She said none of it would help. It's too late."

"It's never too late. You're not going to give up are you?"

TJ looked up at him with sad eyes. "Bud, I still love her as much as the day I married her, but I don't know what I can do."

Mike leaned forward and placed a hand on his friend's shoulder. "If there's anything Ali and I can do, just ask."

"Yeah, thanks bud." The veteran SEAL glanced at his watch, then over at Ernie and Rick, who were finalizing their gear in the bow. All vulnerability disappeared from his craggy features as he thumbed the engine starter. "All right, let's get this show on the road."

***

The figure in the white sedan had been watching the house for a little over half an hour, ensuring that nobody was home. He wasn't expecting the woman, dog or the child to be there, having tailed them to what he assumed was her sister's house across town. However, the family did have a cleaner and he didn't want her interrupting his work. It had happened on a previous job and hiding the body had proven to be a time-consuming undertaking.

Confident that the house was empty he slipped from his sedan, crossed the street and made his way along the sidewalk.

The suburb was relatively well to do and he'd tailored his disguise accordingly. He wore tracksuit pants and a San Diego Padres hoodie. He held a dog leash and had a backpack over his shoulder. It was all part of his 'Have you seen my dog?' cover story.

As he reached the target house, he glanced up and down the street. There was no one in sight, so he slipped the latch and entered the yard. Walking across the lawn he squeezed down the side of the townhouse into a tiny courtyard. The front of the home was exposed. However, a high fence and shrubs hid the rear.

A sensor light clicked on as he approached the door, slipping a lock clicker from his pocket. He smirked as he quickly picked the deadlock and pushed open the door. His employer was paying top dollar for his skills and so far it looked like a walk in the park.

The intruder knew there would be an alarm and his intuition told him exactly where the panel would be. He started a countdown in his head as he padded through a modern kitchen into a central hall. The alarm panel was on the wall a short distance from the front door. His count reached five as he examined the high-end unit. It was one he was familiar with. Popping the cover, he punched in an override code and killed a flashing red light.

Checking his watch he moved swiftly through the three-bedroom townhouse, examining each room. He paused in the doorway of what looked to be the nursery. There was a cot on one side, toy box, wardrobe and the floor was littered with plush toys. He wondered what the boy's parents had done to anger the man who'd purchased his services. Not that it mattered to him. Cash was cash. He nudged a stuffed bear with his sneaker before turning and continuing his search.

He found what he was looking for in the third bedroom. A home office had been set up at the end of the bed. A shiny aluminum laptop sat on a stand over a wireless keyboard and mouse. A touch of the keyboard brought the screen to life. The computer was locked with a password, no surprises there. He took a USB drive from his pocket and connected it.

As the software worked, he flicked through a veterinary science catalog that he found on the desk. A minute and twenty-five seconds passed before the code he'd written successfully bypassed the security of the laptop, giving him access. He wasn't there to snoop. That would come later. Selecting a file from the USB, he dragged it onto the screen and installed an application. Then, as he deleted any trace of his presence, he heard the familiar sound of a key being inserted into a lock.

Ali balanced her sleeping toddler in one arm as she turned the key to the front door. Before she could open it, Axe let out a low growl, shoved his head into the gap and forced his way inside.

"Axe, no."

It was too late. He disappeared inside, bounding down the corridor. She cursed under her breath as she stopped at the alarm panel to disarm it. A frown creased her forehead as she realized it wasn't active. Hadn't she armed it when she left the house? There was a growl from the end of the corridor and she turned to see Axe pacing the hallway, his hackles raised and tail high. She'd seen that body language before. He was hunting.

Ali's pulse quickened as she fumbled in her bag for the can of mace Mike insisted she carry.

"Axe, Axe, Axe," murmured Junior on her hip.

"Yes, buddy, it's Axe," she murmured as she flicked the safety bail off the can and moved slowly down the corridor.

The dog appeared from her study with his ears up and moved through to the kitchen. Ali followed him with the mace held ready. Axe went straight to the back door and sniffed around it while growling. A quick glance through the window didn't reveal anything out of the ordinary, so she placed the can on the bench and let him out.

Axe bolted into the yard and made for the far corner where he sniffed around in the dirt. Ali watched from the doorway as he checked every inch of the garden.

"Squirra," declared Junior as he pointed at a tree in the backyard.

Ali spotted a rodent clinging to the trunk six feet off the ground and shook her head. "Yep, it's a squirrel darling." She closed the door, leaving Axe to continue his obsession with the rodent. "OK, little man. It's time to get you to bed."

Outside on the street the intruder pulled his car over to the side of the road and took a tablet from the sports bag on the passenger seat. Opening an application he waited thirty seconds for the device to connect to the implant on his target's computer. Then he confirmed he had access to the operating system before sending a short message to his client.

I'm in.

Chapter Three

"Hey bro, I think we should have turned up that last valley," whispered Rick as he knelt alongside Mike.

The SEAL team was a quarter-mile from their insertion point in some of the thickest jungle they'd ever experienced. They'd only been ashore overnight, and already they were covered from head to toe in mud, sweat and slime from the river where they'd stashed the boat.

Mike took a map from a pouch on his chest rig and checked it. A moment later he confirmed Rick's doubts. "I think you're right."

The Corpsman waved a mosquito the size of a small bird away from his face. "Other people come to Hawaii to vacation," he muttered. "So, what's up with the old man? His mind ain't on the job."

Mike shrugged. "Not for me to say."

"What's not for you to say?" Ernie appeared alongside.

"Nothing," said Rick. "Just bitchin' about these damn mosquitoes."

TJ joined them. "We need to backtrack a little, but we've got time for a short break." He slumped against a tree and took a sip from the hydration hose that hung over his shoulder.

Rick shot Mike a look before making himself comfortable next to Ernie.

Mike watched the Chief's face. Behind the thick layer of camouflage cream, he could see that his friend was hurting. He was dealing with a problem that couldn't be solved with tactical maneuver and firepower.

"I think we need to talk about the elephant in the room," said Ernie between bites of an energy bar.

TJ's eyes narrowed as he turned to Mike. "What elephant is that?"

"Rick's engagement watch."

Mike and TJ both turned to face the Corpsman.

"Engagement watch, is that even a thing?" asked Mike.

"Why else would she buy him a sweet-ass watch?" said Ernie.

TJ looked relieved that the attention was away from him. "Seems legit. So, what's the go Romeo? That woman of yours laid claim?"

Mike couldn't remember the last time he'd seen Rick embarrassed. The Corpsman fiddled with the sight on his assault rifle and avoided eye contact.

"Holy crap, it's true," said Mike.

Rick sighed. "Yeah it's true. We're engaged. She got a ring and I got a watch."

"Bro, that's awesome news," said Mike.

Ernie slapped his teammate on the shoulder. "Congratulations, essé. I guess this means you passed her selection."

"Good work, son," added TJ.

Rick smiled sheepishly. "So, you're not going to give me shit?"

"About what?" asked Mike. "This is great news."

"About the watch?" Rick replied.

"What about it? I mean it's a really good-looking watch. Has to be worth a few dollars?" said Mike.

"Come on guys, quit messing with me."

The three men stared at him blankly.

"The watch?" said Rick. "Ernie literally told you what it was."

The Latino shrugged. "An engagement watch?"

Suddenly, Mike got what he was saying. "Holy shit, she proposed to you, didn't she?"

Rick nodded sheepishly.

"Shit essé, that's straight up brutal. Did she drop to a knee?" added Ernie.

"OK, enough," grumbled TJ. "We've got a mission to roll." He rose, prompting the other men to do the same.

Mike offered Rick a hand and hauled him from the ground.

"What's up with the Chief, man? He didn't bat an eyelid

when he found out. In fact, he looked sad as hell," murmured Rick.

"He's got a lot going on."

"You don't say."

Rick started off after TJ while Mike waited to take his position at the rear. As they slid down a steep slope, back toward the river, he found himself thinking about the amount of time he spent away from Ali and Junior. If time away was what broke TJ's relationship then he was going to have to get better at work-life balance.

***

Mike and the rest of the team sat in thick jungle on the slope of a long-dead volcano as a pair of F/A-18 Hornets screamed up the valley. He watched through binoculars as each jet released two bombs before shooting near vertical into the sky.

Flashes and billowing balls of dust and debris marked the impact of the bombs on target three seconds before the sound of the explosion reached them. "Target destroyed."

Ernie repeated the confirmation into the radio, informing headquarters that the mission had been completed.

"Job well done," announced TJ as they packed up their gear.

"Evac bird is inbound to the LZ," added Ernie.

The four men finished stowing their equipment and hiked the final quarter-mile to a clearing at the lip of the former volcano. On arriving they dropped their packs and waited for the helicopter.

"This place isn't so bad when you're not slugging it out with the jungle," said Rick as they admired the view out over the training area to the ocean. The four men sat in silence, enjoying the serenity of the morning.

"I let you guys down today," TJ said breaking the silence. "My mind hasn't been on the job."

"We all have our off days, Chief," said Rick.

"Yeah, remember that time I forgot the radio batteries," added Ernie.

"You wanna talk about it?" asked Rick.

Mike caught the Corpsman's eye and shook his head. The last thing TJ would want was to share his problems with everyone else. He was amazed the Chief had even told him.

"Deb wants a divorce," said TJ, matter of fact.

The team was silent.

"I'm sorry to hear that, Chief," said Rick as the beat of a helicopter's blades reached their ears.

"No, I'm sorry for putting a dampener on your news."

"I think we all need a beer," said Mike as their ride thundered overhead.

"I know a good steakhouse in Honolulu," added Ernie as they gathered their gear. "When's our flight home?"

"Tomorrow at 0930," replied Mike.

"Chopper's going to drop us at the boat. We should be back in Pearl by lunchtime and wrapped up by 1600," said TJ.

"Then beer and steak it is," said Ernie.

***

A few hours later on the other side of the Pacific Ali had walked Axe to the daycare facility to pick up Junior. As she fastened him in his stroller for the walk home, her phone rang. She took it from her pocket and checked the screen. It was Mike. "Hey handsome, can you give me a few seconds?" Attaching a pair of buds and slipping them into her ears she took her place behind the stroller. "Hey, I'm back. What's up? How did the exercise go?" She began walking with Axe alongside the stroller.

"It was good, we're all done now. I just wanted to call and tell you and Junior that I love you both."

"And we love you. Are you still back tomorrow?"

"Yeah, can't wait to see you."

Ali thought she could detect something in Mike's voice. "Babe, is everything OK?"

There was a pause. "Yeah, I just wanted you to know how much I love you and appreciate the hard work you put in."

Ali frowned. "Thanks, babe… Are you sure everything is OK?"

There was a pause.

"Deborah wants a divorce. TJ's not taking it well."

"I'm sorry to hear that. Is there anything I can do?"

"No, we're heading out to dinner now. Hopefully, he'll open up a little over a few beers."

"Mike, I know you mean well, but sometimes people need a little space to work out their problems. I don't want you guys coming up with a harebrained scheme to try and help."

"When has that ever happened?"

"When has it ever not?"

There was a pause. "Good point. We'll keep it low key."

"Good idea. OK, love you handsome. I'll see you tomorrow."

"Love you too."

Ali ended the call as they reached the street before their block. While she checked for traffic, she found herself thinking about TJ and Deborah. She'd only met her a few times, but Deb was always lovely. What's more, TJ had made her feel like part of the team. He was the wise sage that she could turn to for advice on anything. It saddened her to think of how much pain he must be dealing with.

A loud bark from Axe drew her attention and she glanced across the street in the direction he was looking. There were some cars parked by the side of the road. She stopped and ruffled Axe's ears. "What's up, bud?"

The dog growled.

Ali checked across the street and spotted a figure sitting in a white sedan. "It's OK Axe."

Something about the car had spooked the dog and it left her feeling uneasy.

She returned to behind the stroller and pushed it quickly along the sidewalk. Axe fell into place but kept glancing across at the car.

As they progressed the dog seemed to calm. By the time they reached their townhouse he was a little less agitated. He stood watch by the front door as she opened it and bundled Junior inside. Her son was asleep, exhausted from daycare. She called Axe inside and locked the door.

Moving into the sitting room, she left Junior sleeping in his stroller. Axe was by her side as she peered through the blinds. A moment later her concerns were confirmed. The white car drove slowly past the house.

Ali checked on Junior as she took her phone from the stroller. Her finger hovered over the button to call Mike. Was she being paranoid? She decided against ringing him and stepped away from the window, glancing down at Axe. They were more than capable of looking after things until Mike got home tomorrow. In the meantime, she needed to get Junior fed and into bed before checking her emails.

***

Mike raised a beer-filled glass in the air and cleared his throat. "To Jenny and Rick."

The other members of the team followed suit, raising their drinks and echoing the words over the background noise of the bar. They'd followed Ernie's advice and ended up in a steakhouse called the Yard House. With over a hundred beers on tap, it was a perfect fit for the thirsty SEAL team.

"If I can give you one tip," added TJ. "Make Jenny the most important thing in your world. The teams will come and go. You're marrying her for life."

Mike could see the pain in TJ's eyes as he delivered his heart-felt advice.

Rick nodded solemnly.

"Shouldn't be a problem," added Ernie, with a wink. "She already wears the pants."

Rick shook his head as the others broke into laughter.

A waitress appeared and TJ ordered another round. "Thanks, guys. I needed this."

"That's what we're here for," said Mike.

"Yeah, although I'm not usually the one needing advice."

"No, that's true. It always used to be Mike and his latest girlfriend problems, or Rick and his latest STD," said Ernie.

There was more laughter.

"Oh, it's pick on Rick day is it?"

"Just wait for the bachelor party," said Ernie. "It's payback time."

The waitress returned with their beers.

"In all seriousness, though," TJ continued, "I don't know what to do. Deb won't consider seeing a counselor. She says it's too late. It's over."

All three men could see the pain on their squad leader's face.

"SEALs don't give in that easy, Chief," said Mike. "If you love her, you need to fight for her."

"Yeah," echoed Ernie. "And if we can do anything to help, just ask."

TJ nodded. "You can start by joining me in another toast." He gestured for the waiter. "Can we get five tequilas, please."

"Five?" enquired Mike.

TJ shot him a sly grin. "Two for Rick."

"Damn straight."

Rick slapped his palm on the table. "Hell, yeah. Let's get this party started."

Mike shook his head. It was going to be one of those nights.

Chapter Four

Ali handed Junior a piece of brown toast smothered in avocado and smiled as he attacked it with gusto. Her son had yet to master eating rather than wearing his food. As he continued to smear himself she walked through the house and glanced out the front window. Axe followed her and stood at the door.

There was no sign of the car from last night. She glanced at the dog and noticed that he was completely relaxed. If Axe didn't sense a threat then she had nothing to fear. A former SEAL working dog, he was the best bodyguard that she and Junior could have. Although it would be nice when Mike was back. Checking her watch she calculated the time difference between San Diego and Hawaii; he would land in the next few hours.

A delighted squeal sounded from the kitchen and she checked on Junior. As predicted, he'd smeared most of his avocado across his face. Seeing he was preoccupied she ducked into the home office to check her emails. First message in the inbox was an appointment reminder. “Oh, crap.” Junior was due for a checkup with the GP that morning.

Dashing into the kitchen she pried the excited toddler from his high chair, stripped him and ran him through the shower. Fifteen minutes later she had him in clean clothes and was strapping him into the booster seat in the back of her Prius.

As she closed the door Axe touched the back of her hand with his nose. She stooped to grasp his head in her hands and kiss the top of his head. “I'm sorry, bud. I can't take you to the doctor. Guard the house, we'll be back soon and so will Mike.”

Axe let out a soft bark at the sound of his master’s name. Then he turned and trotted across to the shade of a large tree where he sat watching Ali climb into the car. She gave him a wave, backed out onto the street and hit close on the gate remote.

As she drove she glanced in the mirror and caught Junior's reflection.

"Axe, Axe, Axe," the boy demanded.

She smiled and shook her head as he continued chanting the dog's name. In the last few months the two had become inseparable. She'd worried how Axe would deal with retirement from the SEAL team; but he'd taken to his new role like a fish to water.

As Ali's silver hybrid turned out of the street a set of eyes followed it. The man who'd broken into their home thumbed a message into his phone from where he sat in a rented yellow hatch and hit send. Then he pulled out from the curb and commenced tailing the Prius. His target had left the dog at home, making it the perfect opportunity to strike. Now, he just needed to wait for the go ahead from his client.

***

Barbosa lay on his bunk staring at the concrete ceiling of his cell. He knew every crease, every one of the dimples caused by air bubbles when the slab had been laid. For three years it had been the first thing and last thing he saw. Day after day, week after week, month after month, but not for much longer. A smirk formed on his lips as he imagined his return to Mexico. Yes, he would see his family, but more importantly, he would taste revenge.

A faint buzz sounded from beneath his pillow. He lifted his head and recovered his contraband cell phone. The obsolete Nokia had cost him more than a small car on the outside.

He checked the screen and smiled. There was a coded message from one of his most trusted men. He thumbed a response and waited for the confirmation. It came a moment later. The plan was in motion.

Slipping the phone beneath his pillow he sat on the edge of his bed and reached under for a small box. The battered container held the only personal items he was permitted to have in prison. He rummaged through the contents until he found the thing he was looking for. It was a photo of two men standing shoulder-to-shoulder with broad smiles on their faces. One of them was Barbosa, albeit much plumper. The other was his brother, Juan.

A vein in the side of his head pulsed as he remembered the night that an American SEAL team had come for him. He recalled, in vivid detail, the face of the man who'd fired the bullet that had killed his only brother. Mike Saunders' grey eyes and square jaw were etched into his mind.

"I will avenge you," he whispered then returned the photo to the box. He'd been planning this operation for three years, and today, it was finally going to be put into action. Mike Saunders was going to feel loss like nothing he could ever imagine.

***

A green van, with the words Royal Garden Services stenciled on the side, turned into the Saunders' street and cruised slowly past the houses. Inside, two men dressed in grey coveralls scanned the street numbers.

"This is it," said Hugo from the passenger seat. He was the taller of the two, broad-shouldered and in his mid-twenties.

His partner Antonio, at least ten years older and thirty pounds heavier, dipped his multiple chins in concurrence. "I'll park out front." He maneuvered the van with skill, parallel parking it directly in front of the picket fence that bordered the quaint home.

Hugo jumped out of the van and opened the side door. It was empty except for a large metal crate and plastic box. As his partner joined him, he took a paper-wrapped parcel from the box. Unrolling it he revealed a juicy pink fillet steak.

"You put enough on it?" asked Antonio.

"Yeah, enough to drop a dinosaur."

"It better not kill the damn thing. I don't want a repeat of that incident in Tijuana."

"That wasn't my fault. How was I to know the old lady was already jacked up on happy pills?"

"Just get on with it."

The two men stepped away from the van and approached the fence. They were an arm's length away when a loud bark startled them both.

"Good doggie," murmured Hugo as he flicked the steak into the yard. The Malinois launched itself against the fence and bared a jagged set of teeth as it growled.

"Holy shit," yelled Hugo as he backpedaled.

Antonio laughed. "Hombre, it's just a dog."

"It's a monster."

"Yeah, and soon he's going to be a sleepy monster."

The men returned to the van's cabin and closed the doors. From their elevated position they could see into the yard. They watched as the dog sniffed the steak.

"Yum, yum, eat it all up," said Antonio.

Behind the fence the dog gave the steak another sniff then moved to the porch where he had better observation across his domain.

The men watched for another fifteen minutes and yet still the Malinois ignored the meat.

"Eat the steak you bastard," said Hugo.

"He will," replied Antonio.

"Maybe it's not hungry?"

"Dogs are always hungry."

"You're always hungry. That's why you're so fat."

Hugo's phone vibrated. He pulled it from the center console and inspected the screen. "We need to move now. The woman's coming back to the house."

"We'll use the dart guns."

They alighted from the van and opened the side door. From inside the box they recovered two sleek black dart guns. Both men checked the weapons were loaded. Then Hugo made for the picket gate as Antonio stepped up to the fence.

"Where is it?" asked Hugo as he leaned over the gate.

"It was on the porch."

He scanned the yard but saw no sign of the dog. "You're kidding me." He reached over the gate and grasped the latch.

There was a savage growl and he screamed as strong jaws clamped on to his arm. Jagged teeth pierced his flesh as he wailed, "Help me, help me."

Antonio lurched forward, leaned over the fence and fired the gun. The dart shot past the dog, thudding into the lawn.

At the same time, Hugo managed to fire his weapon with his free hand. The dart lodged in the dog's shoulder but the animal growled louder, savaging his arm with a vicious shake.

"Shoot it again! Shoot it again!" Hugo screamed hysterically, bracing against the gate.

Antonio fumbled with his dart gun. Seconds passed before he reloaded, aimed and fired. The projectile flew straight and true, striking the dog in the flank. However, the two doses of sedative made no difference.

"Get him off me!" yelled Hugo as Antonio reloaded and fired yet another dart into the animal.

Finally, the attack dog released Hugo and fell back. He swayed and stumbled as he retreated to the porch.

"When he drops, you get him," said Hugo as he clutched his bloodied arm to his chest.

Antonio's eyes were wide. "I'm not going in there till he's out for the count."

Hugo found a sweater from inside the van and wrapped it around his arm to staunch the bleeding. It felt like the dog's teeth had reached the bone. "Just get the bastard dog. We need to get the hell out of here."

***

Junior was singing as Ali turned her Prius into their street. He had passed his checkup with flying colors. Mike was going to beam with pride when she passed on the news that he was significantly larger than other children his age.

The smile dropped from her face as Ali caught a glimpse of a man bundling a dark object into a van immediately in front of their house. The vehicle pulled away from the curb as she reached their drive. A glance out the window confirmed her worst fear. The white picket gate was smeared with blood and wide open. She jumped from the car. "Axe, Axe!" she screamed.

There was no sign of the dog.

Ali dove back into the Prius and stomped the accelerator to the floor. The little hybrid's tires chirped as it lurched forward. She aimed it down the street after the van that was turning the corner.

Her heart lurched as she lost sight of the vehicle and she urged the hybrid on. Behind her Junior squealed with delight as they zoomed around the corner, narrowly missing another car.

She'd closed the gap with the van to the point where she could read the plate number. Committing it to memory, she backed off the throttle. Mike had taught her the basics of tailing another car on one of their many road trips; one of the perks of having a SEAL as a husband.

As she drove she activated the car's entertainment system. "Dial 911," she ordered the voice recognition program.

A moment later the call connected. "Hello, you've reached 911 how may I help you?"

"Hi, look someone has abducted my dog. I'm in pursuit of a white van with the following plate number." She positioned the car so she could read off the license plate.

"Ma'am, are you in any way in danger?"

Ali shook her head. "No, someone has stolen my dog."

"Yes, ma'am I am aware and I have reported the incident. However, I need to know if your life or anyone else's life is in immediate danger."

"Yes, my dog's life is in danger."

"Understood ma'am. Officers will investigate the theft as soon as possible."

"I'm following them right now."

"Miss, that's not advised. You need to leave this to the professionals. I'll have officers get in contact with you as soon as possible."

"So that's it?" Ali thumped the steering wheel in frustration.

"Yes, ma'am. A BOLO will be issued for the van and officers will respond as quickly as they can."

Ahead Ali saw the van slow and indicate to turn left. At the same time, a pickup moved into the gap between them. If she wasn't careful, she was going to lose them.

"Ma'am is that all?"

"Huh? Yeah, that's all. Thanks for your help." She terminated the call and braked as the pickup slowed. "Get out of the way, idiot!"

"Idiot!" echoed Junior from the backseat.

"We don't say that, darling."

The pickup came to a complete stop, leaving a small gap that allowed her to squeeze around the corner. Accelerating she searched for the van. The street was empty and her heart skipped a beat. Then, she caught a glimpse of it on a side street. Slowing she turned across the opposite lane. A truck skidded to a halt, its horn blaring.

Ali whipped the hybrid into a tight U-turn and continued her chase. Further ahead the van was gathering speed. Traffic was heavier here and there was a danger that she'd lose Axe's dognappers in the afternoon rush.

A traffic signal changed to yellow as the van rushed through it. Ali gunned the engine. The light went red as the Prius belted forward. At that moment Ali realized the risks she was taking with Junior in the car. She slammed on the brakes, and the car shuddered to a halt a yard past the intersection. Ali's eyes never left the van as it escaped into traffic. Faintly, she registered the flash of movement to her right. Then there was an almighty bang as a car smashed into the Prius, flinging it sideways.

Chapter Five

Mike burst into the police station and stormed up to the counter. "I'm here to see my wife, Alison Saunders."

The elderly sergeant behind the counter looked up from his computer screen and gave the SEAL a once over. As he did, another man appeared at the door, TJ.

"Mr. Saunders, your wife and son are safe and sound in interview room one. I'll buzz you through."

As promised, Mike found Ali and Junior in an interview room with a female police officer. His wife leaped out of her chair and wrapped her arms around him. "Mike, they took Axe. I'm so sorry I couldn't stop them."

"Babe, it's OK. You and Junior are safe, that's what's important."

"You have to find him."

"Sir," said the police officer. "We've issued a BOLO on the vehicle. Our people are actively searching for your dog."

Mike nodded. "Thanks officer. Do you mind if I take my family home now?"

"No problem. We're all done here."

Mike picked up Junior and the three of them walked out to the reception area where TJ was talking with the sergeant. A moment later the Chief joined them in the parking lot.

"Cops ran the plates on the van and got nothing."

"What about the company name, Royal Garden Services?" asked Ali.

"Company's got a website, but it's not registered."

"It's a front?" asked Mike.

"Looks that way," said TJ.

"Why would someone target Axe?" asked Ali.

Mike and TJ shared a look.

"No, he's in jail. Barbosa can't possibly have done it."

"They'll try to get Axe across the border. We need to stake out the crossing points," said Mike.

"I'll get Ernie, Rick and some of the boys to help us out."

TJ took his phone from his pocket and started dialing.

"Mike, what can I do?" asked Ali.

"Babe, you've done enough. If it weren't for you, we wouldn't have a lead. TJ and I will get Axe back."

"Axe, Axe, Axe!" yelled Junior.

Ali looked up at her husband with tear filled eyes. "You have to get him back."

***

The Royal Garden Services van pulled into a rented warehouse and a sliding door clanged shut behind it. Hugo jumped from the cabin as the lights flickered on. He spotted their employer standing alongside a stack of barrels.

"Any problems?" asked the man who'd broken into Ali and Mike's home.

"All good, essé," replied Hugo.

"All good?" squawked Antonio as he climbed from the passenger seat, clutching his bloodied arm. "That dog is loco."

The man nodded. "I told you he was an attack dog. Why did you get so close?" He spat on the floor. "Actually, I don't care. Is it sedated?"

"Yes, we dosed him good."

"He better be alive."

"He is, we're not complete amateurs."

The man raised his eyebrows as he glanced at Antonio's arm. "If you say so." Then he gestured to a flatbed truck parked on the far side of the warehouse. The tray was stacked high with blue barrels. "Put the dog in a barrel and hit the road. The quicker we get you across the border, the better."

Hugo nodded and slid the door to the van open.

"We're going to need more money," said Antonio.

"Because you screwed up?"

"No, because the dog's loco."

The burglar shook his head. "You know who's paying the bills?"

"Do I care? Look at my arm."

"You know who the Butcher is?"

The color drained from Antonio's face.

"Yeah, I thought so. Now get the dog in a barrel."

***

Mike and TJ sat in the US Customs and Border Protection command post, staring at a wall of screens. TJ had called in a favor with an FBI colleague to get them access. When he'd explained the situation to the Border Guards, they'd been only too happy to help.

"We're chasing a needle in a haystack," said Mike.

"We've got Rick and Ernie at the other checkpoints," replied TJ.

On screen, Mike watched a large flatbed truck loaded with barrels passing through one of the checkpoints. "They could have changed vehicles a dozen times by now."

TJ nodded. "Mike, we need to start thinking about enacting a contingency plan."

"The priority is Axe."

"No, the priority is keeping you and your family safe. Barbosa knows where you live."

"He's always known where we live."

"Yes, but now he's taken action on that."

"You're right, we need to confront him."

"You sure you want to do that?"

Mike turned to the Chief with a look of anguish on his face. "Do we have any other choice?"

"If he took Axe it's because he wants to bargain, and you know the only thing he wants more than that dog is you."

"Yeah, but we're not gonna let that happen."

"I'll make the arrangements."

Mike continued to watch the flow of vehicles as TJ made a call. He and Axe had served together in Afghanistan, Mexico and Columbia. The dog had saved his life and the lives of his teammates on more than one occasion. Axe had also brought Ali and him together, and saved her life. There was no way in hell that Mike was going to rest until that dog was safe at home where he belonged.

***

The truck ground its way along a sandy track bordered on both sides by thick scrubby bush. Hugo and Antonio had driven their cargo down the Baja peninsula to the resort town of Cabo San Lucas before heading inland. Their destination was a shabby looking ranch nestled in the foothills of a steep mountain range.

"What a dump," said Antonio as the truck's brakes hissed, sending up a cloud of yellow dust.

Las Polvo had once been a horse ranch. Now it was a dilapidated collection of adobe buildings clustered around an open square. At one end a set of yards filled with tumbleweeds was slowly disintegrating in the harsh Mexican sun.

As Hugo stepped from the truck the front door of one of the buildings opened and a figure dressed in faded jeans, boots, a check shirt and a Stetson appeared. The dog snatcher noted the Glock pistol and spare magazines attached to the man's belt, and the submachine gun slung over his shoulder. The guy looked cartel, through and through.

"You guys made good time," said the man as a second, similarly equipped *sicario* wearing a baseball cap joined him.

"Traffic was light," said Hugo.

Antonio joined them and the men eyeballed the bloodied bandaged wrapped around his arm.

The man spat tobacco into the dust. "OK essé, where's the dog?"

Hugo moved to the side of the truck and released a strap. Grasping a barrel, he hefted it clear. As he dropped it to the ground a savage growl emanated from inside.

"Angry little bastard," said one of the men.

Antonio raised his injured arm. "You could say that."

"The pens are around the back."

The cartel guy's offsider appeared with a sack truck and

kicked it under the barrel. The growling continued as Hugo wheeled it behind the buildings to where there were four concrete floored pens.

Dog fighting was popular in Mexico and Hugo knew that the cartels controlled it. This must be one of the facilities where they held the dogs before the fights. As he pushed the drum into a pen he noted bloodstains on the floor, and scratch marks on the steel posts.

"Put it in the middle and undo the lid," said the *sicario.*

Hugo dumped the barrel and stepped away from it. "You do it." He left the cage.

"Pussies." The other man stepped forward and unlatched the lid. As he levered it free the dog broke into a volley of savage barks. He flipped the lid, backpedaled out of the cage and slammed the gate.

The Stetson-wearer grabbed a pole from where it leaned against the cage. Pushing it through the wire fence he gave the barrel a shove. The dog growled as it rocked. He gave it a harder shove and it toppled over.

A moment later their captive appeared, baring its teeth at the men with raised hackles.

"Shit, that's a mean looking *perro.*"

Stetson handed the pole to his partner and took a phone from his pocket. "Give him a poke." He started filming as the other man shoved the pole through the fence at the dog.

Axe savaged the end of the stick, tearing it from his hands.

"He's a real feisty one. Pity the boss has got other plans for him. He'd make us a fortune in the fights."

The dog retreated to the corner with the stick and proceeded to tear it to pieces. Stetson finished filming and placed his phone in his pocket. There was no reception at the ranch. He'd head into town to upload the video.

"Have you got our money?" asked Antonio.

"Inside." He gestured for his partner to get it.

"Do you know what the plan is for the dog?" continued Antonio as they walked back to the truck.

"Oh, that hound's gonna wish he was never born."

"Good." He gestured to his bandaged arm. "Make sure he really suffers."

Chapter Six

TJ grasped Mike by the shoulder as he made to enter the visitor's cell in the Supermax prison. "Hey, don't let your emotions get the better of you in there. Remember, Barbosa is a full-blown psycho and you punched his brother's ticket. He's out for revenge and getting angry is going to play straight into his hands."

Mike nodded. "Yeah, got it."

A burly looking guard opened the door and gestured for the men to enter.

Barbosa, *The Butcher*, sat shackled to a steel table. Mike paused in the doorway. If it weren't for the eyes, he would have sworn it was a different man. Prison life had been good for the former cartel kingpin. He'd lost at least thirty pounds of fat and gained some muscle in his chest and shoulders.

"Petty Officer Mike Saunders." Barbosa greeted him with a broad smile. "It's a real pleasure to see you."

"I'm sure it is," snapped Mike as he moved inside and TJ followed him.

There was a moment of awkward silence as the three men eyeballed each other.

"So, to what do I owe the pleasure, amigos?"

"Where the hell is Axe?"

Barbosa feigned confusion. "How would I know where your tomahawk is?"

"You know exactly what I'm talking about."

"Do I?"

"My dog, where is my dog?" growled Mike.

"Easy," said TJ.

The cartel boss shrugged. "I've got no idea what you're talking about."

Mike clenched his jaw so hard his teeth hurt. He imagined reaching across, grasping Barbosa's head and smashing his face into the table.

Barbosa smiled. “How's the family, Mike? Alison and the little boy, Junior, right? It must be so nice to be able to spend time with them. Family is so important, don't you agree?”

He stepped forward. “I'm going to kill you. Just like I killed your worthless brother.”

The smile dropped from Barbosa’s face and for a split second Mike thought he had gotten to him. However, rage was soon replaced by a smirk. “Have fun searching for your dog.”

“If you tell me where he is, I’ll make it quick.”

“OK, we're done here,” said TJ. He turned to the camera in the corner of the room. “Guard!”

“I'm sorry, TJ,” Mike said as they climbed into his truck having left the prison. “That bastard got the better of me.”

“Understandable.”

As Mike exhaled and inserted his key in the ignition his phone vibrated. He took it from the center console and examined the screen.

“What is it?” asked TJ.

“A blocked number just sent me a video. It's downloading.”

Mike’s heart shuddered when the video started playing and he recognized Axe savaging a broom handle behind a mesh fence. He watched the short clip twice then passed it to TJ.

“At least we know he's alive,” said the Chief.

Tears formed in Mike's eyes and he clenched his fists as he visualized Axe being tortured by Barbosa's men. “I need to go back in there and beat it out of him.”

“Bud, he's not going to tell you. But, if we get this video to the right people, they might be able to give us a lead.”

“Your guys in the FBI?”

“No. I think we need a little more clout.”

***

Deborah Lines sat in an expensive leather chair behind a glass desk in her corner office at Style Cuisine Magazine. The statuesque brunette wore an immaculately tailored two-piece suit, white blouse and had designer glasses perched on her pointed nose.

Rocking back in her chair she tapped the glass with a Mont Blanc pen as she read a report on her Apple laptop. According to one of the Agency's analysts, there was a vigilante organization actively targeting criminals and despots with impunity across the globe. It all sounded a little fanciful to her. However, the reason the document caught her attention was that it named a former work colleague of hers as one of the organization's founders. Vance and she had been close friends when they'd started out in the Agency. However, they had lost touch and he'd reportedly been killed in a terrorist attack in the UAE in 2003.

Her thoughts were interrupted when her cell phone vibrated. She picked it up and saw that it was a message from her recently separated husband, TJ.

"What does he want?" she mumbled as she opened the message and read the brief paragraph. Then she tapped the attached file and watched the short video.

"Son of a bitch."

Storming out of her office she weaved her way through an open plan workspace until she reached a door marked Archives. A thumb scanner gave her access to an airlock where a second device checked her retina. Finally, a door opened giving her access to a space the size of a small bedroom packed with screens and pieces of high-tech looking equipment.

"Deb, how are you?" asked one of the four people sitting at workstations in the room, a middle-aged woman with blonde bangs.

"I'm good, Lu. Look, I just emailed you a file. Can you bring it up?"

"No problems." Her fingers danced on the keys and the video TJ had sent appeared on screen. "What is this?"

"This, this is your priority. I want everything you can get me from this video."

"This got anything to do with TJ?"

Deb nodded. "Yeah, that's the dog from his team."

"The hero matchmaker?"

"The one and only. Allegedly he's been abducted and this is the only lead that TJ and his guys have."

"Ah, huh." Lu had already loaded the file into three different programs and had set a bank of supercomputers to work. "So, how are things going with TJ?"

"He's moved out."

"So, not well."

She sighed. "In the last five years we've spent next to no time together. I barely know the guy anymore. How long do you need to work this video?"

"Give me an hour."

"I'll be in my office."

Moments later Deb was sitting back at her desk gazing at a photo she'd taken from the bottom of her filing cabinet. It was a picture of her and TJ on a beach in Mexico. The ruggedly handsome SEAL operator had his arm around her waist and they both wore broad smiles; a happier time. Sighing she returned the photo to the cabinet and turned back to her computer. She'd help TJ find Axe and then she'd need to break off all contact.

Chapter Seven

TJ pushed open the door to the café and spotted Mike, Ali and Junior sitting in the far corner. The SEAL and his wife looked like they hadn't slept. He knew how that felt. He'd been up all night contacting buddies in the FBI, DEA and every other three-letter agency, trying to get some assistance in locating Axe.

"Morning, guys." He sat at the end of the bench seat next to Ali.

Almost immediately a waiter appeared with a coffee. "A triple espresso Americano!"

He shot Mike a nod of appreciation and took a sip. "OK, guys. I've got good news and bad news. My contact managed to rip some information out of the video Mike was sent."

"Do you know where he is?" asked Mike.

"We know the broad area where the video was uploaded."

"And?"

"It was down in Mexico on the Baja peninsula near Cabo San Lucas."

"Barbosa," growled Mike.

"TJ, is there any way we can get a government agency to help?" asked Ali.

"No one's going to stick their neck out for a dog."

"Even a decorated war hero?"

He shook his head.

"Momma, where Axe?" asked Junior from where he was sitting next to Mike.

TJ's heart lurched when he saw the look of concern on the boy's face.

"We could head down there and take a look around," said Mike, his voice cracking.

"Mike, you'd be playing right into Barbosa's hands."

"I can't just give up on him."

He faintly registered the jingle of the door behind him. The expression on Mike's face told him someone he recognized had entered the café.

"Ali, Mike, good morning."

TJ turned to face his estranged wife.

She smiled politely. "Terrance, do you mind if I join you?"

"By all means."

Deb sat and gestured for the waiter. "I hope you don't mind, TJ sent me the video of Axe. I had my people work on it." She ordered a latté.

"Your people?" Ali wore a confused look. "I thought you worked for a culinary magazine?"

"We have diverse interests. The bottom line is we managed to identify the device that recorded the video."

Mike nodded. "Yeah, TJ said. Axe is in Cabo, I'm going to head down and find him."

"Mike, that's not a good idea. The cartels have a strong presence down there. A military guy sniffing around is only going to draw heat."

"Look, Axe has saved me, Ali and TJ more than once. We can't hang him out to dry."

Deb nodded. "I get that, but you need to understand the risk."

"This lead's already 24 hours old. The risk is if we don't move now we'll lose him forever."

Deb's coffee arrived and she sipped it. Once the waiter had departed she turned to TJ. "What do you think?"

TJ locked eyes with Mike. "Axe is a member of my team. If Mike goes down there I'm going with him."

"I thought as much." She took another sip. "I'll make the necessary arrangements for equipment and accommodation. It's going to look strange if I head down with the boys." She paused. "Ali, how do you feel about joining us? With you we can pass for two couples on a holiday. It would go a long way to reducing our risk profile."

Mike shot his wife a concerned look.

Ali exhaled. "I can do that."

"Who will look after Junior?" asked Mike.

"Rick and Jenny," replied Ali. "You know how clucky she's been recently. Plus, it will only be for a few days right?"

"If we move fast," said Deb.

"Then we better get organized," said Mike.

"Give me a few hours to get some equipment together and then we'll meet at yours," said Deb as they bundled Junior into his stroller.

"This means the world to us guys," said Mike as they departed.

Deb finished her coffee and made to leave. She took two paces toward the door before turning back. "Terrance, don't get any funny ideas. I'm doing this for Ali, Mike and Junior."

He nodded. "Got it."

She left and TJ sat finishing his coffee. A plan was already forming in his head as to how they were going locate Axe. They'd need to set up a surveillance net and sweep the town with specialist equipment. Having Deb on board was going to make the job a hell of a lot easier. His thoughts wandered from the pending mission to his now estranged wife. They'd never worked together before. Maybe this was the opportunity they needed to reconnect. As quickly as the thought emerged he banished it from his mind and downed the last of his coffee. The mission was recovering Axe, and that was precisely what he was going to do.

***

The look of horror on Rick's face confirmed that he was terrified of the idea of babysitting Junior. "Can't I go to Mexico?" he asked.

Mike and Ali had driven their son around to his godparent's house as part of their preparation for the mission to rescue Axe.

"No you can't," said Jenny. "Remember when we agreed to be his guardians?" She arched an eyebrow. "That comes with certain responsibilities. You need to man up." Her voice softened. "Plus, think of it as a dress rehearsal."

"Dress rehearsal for what?"

Mike, Ali and Jenny all stared at him.

"Wait, Jenny, you're not..."

His fiancée shook her head. "No, you dolt. But, we did talk about having kids soon."

"Oh yeah, right." Rick shot Mike a look of relief. "In all seriousness, brother. If you need backup, I'm there."

"I need you here, bud. If anything happens to Ali and I... you and Jenny will be Junior's legal guardians."

Rick reached out and grasped his teammate's shoulders. "That's not gonna happen. We'll take good care of him, bud. You focus on getting Axe back."

***

Mike loaded his and Ali's suitcases into the back of his pickup while she locked the house. As he turned to see how she was doing he spotted one of Axe's favorite toys under his deck chair on the front lawn. In his mind, he could see his best friend playing on the grass with Junior.

"We're going to get him back," said Ali as she wrapped an arm around his waist.

The toot of a horn caught their attention and they saw a grey SUV pull to the curb. Through the windshield, Mike spotted TJ at the wheel and Deb in the passenger seat. The two alighted and joined them at the truck.

"You ready to roll?" asked TJ.

Mike managed a smile. "Yeah, let's do this."

"I've booked accommodation at a resort," said Deb. "The rooms are adjoining so we can coordinate the search." She gestured to the SUV. "We've got all the gear we're going to need."

"What about border control?" asked Mike.

Deb shrugged. "Taken care of."

TJ handed Mike a hand-held radio. "Crypto and frequency are loaded. We'll lead."

"OK then." Mike and Ali climbed into his truck and reversed out onto the road where TJ and Deb were waiting in their own vehicle.

As they started down the road, Ali spoke, "Something tells me that Deborah isn't a food critique."

Mike nodded. "She's CIA."

They drove in silence before Ali spoke again. "Mike, what if this is a trap. What if Barbosa wants you to come and try to rescue Axe?"

"Deb wouldn't have agreed to help if she hadn't accounted for that risk."

"Why do you think they're keeping him alive?"

He exhaled. "I don't even want to think about that. I just want to get down there and find him."

Meanwhile, in the vehicle ahead Deb and TJ were traveling in silence, TJ behind the wheel. "Remember that time we drove down to Tijuana for the night and you…"

"Terrance, there's no need for the nostalgia. Let's keep it professional."

To TJ the comment felt like a backhand to the face. He hunched forward and concentrated on the road.

"I'm sorry," Deb said softly. "I do remember that trip. You'd just come back from Iraq. We hired that little bungalow down on the beach."

He smiled. "Yeah and that dog you fed followed us home and snored like a freight train on the porch. I didn't sleep a wink." He paused. "You always had a soft spot for strays."

From the corner of his eye, he caught the faintest hint of a smile on her lips.

"Well, today we're not hunting strays. We're hunting for Axe. Now keep your mind on the job."

"Yes, ma'am." TJ maintained his composure but inside felt a glimmer of hope. Perhaps this trip would help them reconnect and maybe, just maybe, it could rekindle the spark that he desperately hoped was still smoldering in the depths of her heart.

Chapter Eight

Mike parked his pickup alongside TJ's SUV in the garage of the villa that Deb had booked in Cabo. He carried their bags up a short flight of stairs into an open plan living, kitchen and dining area. The ocean sparkled through the broad windows beyond a wide golden beach.

"Wow," said Mike as he dropped their bags.

Deb emerged from a door to his right and gestured to the room opposite. "Your suite is through there. We'll set up the gear in here on the dining room table."

Mike helped TJ bring some additional cases of equipment up from the SUV as Ali unpacked their bags in their room.

"Things can't be that bad if you're sharing a suite," said Mike as they retrieved the last of the equipment from the car.

TJ sighed. "Separate rooms."

By the time they'd brought all the gear up into the villa Deb had set up a laptop and laid out some of her specialist equipment. Mike identified smartphones, a small commercial drone and a bunch of other electrical devices. He shot Ali a questioning look.

"OK guys, here's the plan." Deb spun her computer so they could see a satellite image of the area on screen. "We know the phone that made the video has been active in Cabo. I've broken the town down into search sectors." She gestured to two phones that lay alongside black nylon pouches. "We'll use mustang surveillance devices to get a fix on the phone and then go from there."

"They easy to use?" asked Mike.

Deb nodded. "Yes, they're already configured. The antenna array is in the pouch; leave that in your car if you go out on foot. The basic unit has a range of about fifty yards."

"What happens after we locate the phone?" asked Ali.

"Then this goes from a find and fix operation to recovery,

and that just happens to be the boy's specialty."

"Damn, straight," said Mike. "Let's get out on the ground and find this dirt bag."

"Mike, I need to cover off on a few points." Deb's tone was stern. "You need to remember your cover story. We're not down here searching for Axe. We're down here on a couple's retreat. That means we at least need to look like we're having a good time."

Ali and Mike nodded.

"And if you get compromised the drill is to head straight back to San Diego. Make sure you keep all of your personal effects on your person."

"I take it the room can't be linked to us," said TJ.

"Correct."

"Is that it?" Mike asked impatiently.

"Yes, that's all."

Mike rose and took the mustang unit from the table. "I'll set up in the truck."

Ali waited till he was gone. "Deb, Mike and I appreciate this so much. You've gone above and beyond to help us find Axe and that means the world to us."

A smile appeared on Deb's face. "We all owe a lot to that dog."

TJ clapped his hands. "Agreed, let's go out and find him."

***

Mike drove the pickup along a wide street bordered on both sides by small blocks of faded stucco apartments. They passed a row of dune buggies parked in front of a bar and Mike turned to his wife, who was studying the mustang device. "Anything?"

"Not yet."

He slowed the truck and indicated to turn right. "We'll box around this suburb then move to another sector."

"Mike, aren't people going to get suspicious if we keep driving around? Not as many cars on the road as I expected."

They crossed the main highway and headed down a side street. "One last circuit and then we'll find somewhere to eat." Mike scanned both sides of the street as he drove.

"Deb is very efficient."

"Yeah, brutally so."

They drove in silence.

"I think she still loves him," Ali said as they reached the end of the block.

"What makes you say that?"

"Just a feeling."

"Yeah, well according to TJ there's no feeling left. That's the problem. She's gone completely cold on him." Mike turned the truck down another street. "Still nothing?"

Ali shook her head.

Mike smacked his hands against the wheel in frustration.

She reached across and touched his shoulder. "Babe, this was never going to be easy. We're going to find him. It's just going to take a little time. How about we get something to eat and check the bar area?"

He accelerated the truck. "That's a good idea. Barbosa's guys will be neck deep in booze and broads."

"I'm not going into a strip club."

Mike managed a chuckle. "With the mustang we don't have to. Keep it in your bag and we can walk past."

They parked the truck on a side street and walked through to Cabo's primary bar and dining zone, set a street back from the marina. The low slung concrete buildings, palm trees and wide roads reminded Mike of parts of Baghdad city. Only the streets of Cabo weren't pockmarked with bullet holes and Mike didn't have his full team behind him and Axe by his side. He swallowed hard as images from the video popped into his mind. By now Axe's captors could have severely injured him, or worse.

They walked the length of the street before Ali gestured to a bright painted cantina that had a sign declaring free beer with every plate of tacos. "How about this place?"

"Yeah, why not."

They took a table on the street.

Mike watched as Ali took the mustang from her bag and checked it. He could tell by the look on her face that they'd had no luck.

She reached across the table and took his hand. "Mike, we will find him."

"Yeah, hopefully TJ and Deb are having more luck."

Chapter Nine

A little over eight miles away the other pair was conducting their sweep of the outskirts of Cabo. Under Deb's guidance TJ had configured the antenna array to maximize the mustang's collection footprint. So far, like Mike and Ali, they'd had no luck in locating the phone associated with the video of Axe.

"Damn it's dry down here," said TJ as they finished a run along a dusty road and turned back on the main route into town.

"It is a desert," said Deb, with her eyes fixed on the locator.

"Yeah, the cactuses are a dead give-away."

"Cacti, the plural is cacti."

"You sure?"

"Yes, I'm a journalist, remember."

"Really, does food critique classify as journalism?"

She glanced up at him. "In what world does it not?"

"In a world where it's a cover story and not your real job."

"I'll have you know I won an AFJ award last year for one of my articles."

TJ shot her a questioning look. "An award?"

Her eyes narrowed. "Yes, an award. Is that so surprising?"

"Not at all. I just thought someone else wrote the articles for you."

Deb turned her attention back to the mustang.

He chuckled. "You won an award for someone else's writing."

"I edited the article."

TJ slowed the SUV as they arrived at the outskirts of Cabo.

"Take the next right," said Deb.

"You're actually a talented writer. Remember when you used to keep a journal?"

"I do."

"Used to read it to me. The words were always beautiful." TJ turned the truck onto a potholed laneway that skirted the edge of the town.

She looked up and smiled. "You're a good listener."

They held the gaze for a moment before TJ turned back to the road. "Deb, what happened?"

"You stopped listening and spent all your time in the teams."

"I never stopped listening… or loving you."

"We're not doing this now, Terrance. It's too–" A loud beep emitted from the tracking device. "We've got a hit!"

TJ slowed the truck. "Where?"

Her brow furrowed as she studied the mustang. "It's behind us."

He spun the wheel and turned the SUV in a tight circle, jumping the curb.

"It's approaching the intersection ahead."

TJ eased his foot onto the accelerator and they closed the gap with the main road. Fortunately, traffic was light with only three vehicles flashing past as TJ braked at a yield sign.

"Should be the next car," said Deb.

A battered Ford Bronco appeared to their right and drove past the intersection. TJ eased them in behind and accelerated to match the speed.

"Don't get too close," ordered Deb.

"This ain't my first rodeo, sweetheart," drawled TJ in his best southern accent. "You think we should contact Mike and Ali?"

"Not yet. Let's tail the Bronco and see where it leads. Once we've got some kind of confirmation, we'll update the others."

"Right on."

As they followed the Bronco Deb took a tablet from her bag and accessed a satellite imagery app. "Not much out here other than ranches."

"They're probably holding Axe at one of Barbosa's places. He's got properties spread across Northern Mexico."

"Not out here, well at least not that we know of. I pulled the company's file on your boy. His operations and real-estate are mainly focused in Sonora and Chihuahua."

"And they haven't been hamstrung by his incarceration?"

"Not that we can see. It's business as usual."

They followed the Bronco for another five miles before it slowed and turned off the road onto a gravel track.

"Keep going," said Deb as she checked her tablet. "That road leads to a ranch in the foothills. It could be where they're keeping Axe."

TJ continued a further quarter of a mile before pulling over to the side of the road. "You want to send in the drone?"

"Good idea. There's a trail a few hundred yards up. Leads into a small valley. It should hide us from the road and the ranch."

TJ followed her directions and a moment later they were parked in a dry streambed behind a low rise.

"We've got about an hour till sunset," said TJ as he unpacked a quadcopter from its soft case. "Probably a good idea to send an update to Mike."

Deb checked her phone. "I've got no cell or sat coverage." She glanced up at the imposing mountain range to their west. "This place is a black hole."

"That's probably why they go in to Cabo." He unfolded the arms of the compact drone and placed it on the hood of the SUV.

"Have you flown one of these before?" she asked.

"You bought me one for Christmas."

"Right, that may have been my assistant?"

"The same one that wrote your award-winning article?" TJ shot her a grin and was rewarded with a faint smile. He toggled the drone's controls and sent it soaring into the sky. Deb stood next to him so she could see the screen as he orientated it toward their target.

From two miles away they could only see a cluster of buildings in a clearing. He moved the craft forward and they slowly grew in size.

A waft of Deb's fragrance hit TJ's nose. It was the same one she'd always worn; a subtle scent that reminded him of far more intimate times. He realized that they were standing shoulder to shoulder. It pained him to realize that this was the closest he'd been to his estranged wife in the last few months.

"You're kidding me?"

The angry tone of her voice snapped him back to reality. The image on the drone's screen was blurring and distorting. TJ reversed its track and the picture cleared.

"Is that normal?"

"No. It's got a three-mile range. There's definitely some kind of serious interference out here. We're going to have to get closer."

He turned his head and found himself looking directly into Deb's eyes. There was an awkward silence before he spoke. "I'll go in for a closer look."

"Not by yourself you won't."

"It would be better if you stayed here and–"

She cut him off with a withering look. "There are binoculars and radios in the truck."

***

TJ led Deb through thorny scrub to a position just under a mile from the ranch, where they assessed the vehicle had stopped. He lowered the backpack he'd taken from their SUV and sat under a gnarled tree.

Deb joined him and he passed her a water bottle.

"We've got about thirty minutes of light."

She took a sip and returned the bottle. TJ took a mouthful and stashed it in his pack. He pulled out the drone and set it up on a rock. "I'm going to go forward with the binoculars. If you stay here, you can use the drone for overwatch and communicate with me via radio."

The look on Deb's face told him she wasn't happy with the plan.

"We can't both go. If something happens, you need to be able to get back into cell phone range and tell Mike and Ali."

"You're right. OK, let's get this done."

TJ clipped a radio to his belt and inserted an earpiece.

"Check, check," he transmitted.

"Lima Charlie," she responded over her radio as she grasped his shoulder. "Be safe."

TJ set off through the scrub at a trot. He'd cover as much ground as he could before finding a position where he could observe the ranch. With any luck he'd get eyes on the Bronco and then Axe.

The whirr of blades told him the drone was up. The noise faded as Deb sent it high to avoid detection.

"I can see you," she transmitted.

"How's the feed?"

"Grainy, but workable."

He slowed to a walk as he approached a rise that he estimated was less than four hundred yards from the ranch. Crouching low he used a bush for cover and raised his binoculars.

He spotted the Bronco parked in front of a low-slung hacienda. There were two men lifting bags from the tailgate. A third joined them to assist in carrying the supplies inside. TJ spotted a pistol on the hip of one of the men.

"You getting this?" transmitted Deb.

"Yeah, three men. At least one is armed."

"Not much of an indicator. Everyone around here carries."

TJ watched as the three men disappeared inside. He waited a few minutes and when they didn't reappear, he lowered the binoculars. "I'm going in for a better look."

"I can't get any closer. The image degrades."

"OK, just keep an eye on the front and let me know if they come out."

"Be careful."

"Yes, ma'am."

TJ slipped down the slope into the bushes that ran all the way to the edge of the clearing where the ranch was situated. He worked his way around the buildings to a weathered stockyard. Through the railings he could see chain-link fences behind the main building. They looked to him like cages. Cages like the one in the video sent to Mike.

He crouched low and worked his way along the outside of the yards. As he approached the cages, Deb transmitted a message.

"They're coming out."

TJ dropped to his stomach and slid in tight against the railing. Men's voices carried on the evening breeze as two figures appeared from the ranch house. They passed within yards of TJ as they made their way toward the pens.

He lifted his head slightly and watched them from behind the stockyard. One of the men was carrying a bloodied plastic bag. They stopped near the cage and flung something over the fence.

His heart skipped a beat when he heard a bark and a savage growl. He couldn't see the dog, but he instantly recognized the bark as Axe's. "He's here," he whispered into the radio.

"TJ, you need to get out of there." Even masked by the radio, he could hear the concern in her voice.

The men stood talking near the cages and then turned and walked back toward the hacienda. TJ lowered his head as one of them looked in his direction. He hugged the earth as the men's voices got closer.

"Don't move," transmitted Deb.

Savage barking filled the air and one of the men yelled out at the dog.

"Crawl back," said Deb.

TJ scrabbled backward along the edge of the stockyard into the cover of the scrub and rose to his knees. A glance over his shoulder confirmed that the men had moved to the edge of the yard. One of them looked to be studying the spot where TJ had been lying. As the man crouched to inspect the ground TJ backed further into the bushes, turned and ran as fast as he could.

"They're on to you," transmitted Deb. "The third guy just left the building armed with a submachine gun."

"Deb, head back to the truck. I'll meet you there."

TJ heard a shout from behind, spurring him on. He found

his tracks in the sandy soil and followed them between thorny bushes and cacti. It took him less than three minutes to reach the ridge where he'd left Deb. The only sign of her was the footprints leading back toward their SUV.

"I'm at the truck," she transmitted as he jogged after her. "All three men are following you. They're about two hundred yards behind."

She must still have the drone up, he thought as he dashed through the scrub. A thorn bush snagged his arm as he brushed past it. The long spines tore into his skin, but he pressed on. Finally, with lungs heaving, he burst from the bushes onto the track where the SUV was waiting with the passenger door open. He leaped into the cab and slammed it shut as Deb gunned the engine.

The SUV took off like a startled horse, she struggled to keep it centered on the sandy track. "Close call," she said as they hit the main road and gained speed. She wore a smile as she turned to TJ. "Well done, old man."

"You did well, Mrs. Smith." He chuckled, referring to the action movie starring *Brad Pitt* and *Angelina Jolie.*

TJ checked his phone for messages as they drove back into town. He kept one eye on the wing mirror, checking for anyone following. "Mike and Ali just got back to the villa. We can update them when we arrive."

"Sounds good," replied Deb as they reached the outskirts of Cabo.

"What happened to the drone?" TJ asked.

"I sent it over the mountains. It should be running out of batteries real soon."

"Good thinking."

"Not just a pretty face."

"That's why I married you."

He glanced sideways and caught an ever so slight smile on her lips. For the first time in months, he felt a glimmer of hope that he could save his marriage.

***

TJ bounded up the stairs and into the living area of the rented villa where a glum-looking Mike sat at the dining room table. "I think we found him," he exclaimed.

Ali appeared from the door to their suite at the same time that Deb entered the room.

"We got a hit on the phone and tracked it to a ranch outside of town," TJ continued.

"And you saw him?" said Mike.

"No. I heard him."

Mike took his phone from his pocket and pushed it across the table to TJ. A video was playing on the screen. The SEAL Chief positioned it so he and Deb could see. It was another video of Axe being poked through a chain fence with a stick. The dog was wide-eyed with his teeth bared and his fur matted with blood.

"Does this look the same?" asked Mike.

"The cage looks like a match. We spotted three men on target. I can confirm that at least one is armed."

"We need to hit the place tonight," Mike said in earnest.

"I agree." TJ swallowed. "Our recce may have been compromised."

"They saw you?"

TJ shook his head. "No, they saw my tracks."

Mike rose and stared out the windows at the sun setting over the ocean. "If they think someone's onto them they'll move him." He turned back with a look of steely determination. "Deb, what can you do about hardware?"

"No can do. You get caught with guns in Mexico and you're screwed. You'll do five to ten in one of the worst prisons on earth." She grabbed a black pelican case from the floor and opened it. Inside was a pair of night-vision goggles and a number of innocuous looking devices that included a phone, camera and a flashlight. She took the items from the case. "The phone, camera and light contain Tasers. They will be our last resort."

Mike frowned as he grasped the camera. "We're going to

go up against Barbosa's *sicarios* armed with Tasers?"

"It's doable," said TJ. "We lure them away from the ranch, grab Axe and get back across the border."

"It's our only option. You thinking a distraction?"

"Yep."

"What can we do to help?" asked Ali.

TJ nodded. "We're going to need to find a hardware store." He checked his watch. "We'll raid the ranch in the early hours of the morning."

***

Rick's brain throbbed as he sat on the edge of Junior's bed and attempted to distract the wailing toddler with his favorite stuffed toy. A glance at his watch confirmed it was just past midnight, meaning the toddler had been crying for two hours straight. Rick had no idea where the kid found the energy.

"Mom, mom, mom, mom," Junior chanted between sobs.

"I know bud. You're mom's going to be back soon with dad and Axe."

At the mention of the dog's name, Junior looked up at him with tear-filled eyes. "Axe," he murmured. "Where Axe?"

"He's looking after your mom and dad."

That seemed to appease the boy and he raised his arms toward Rick. The hulking SEAL picked him up and the toddler wrapped his tiny arms around his neck.

"Axe look after mom," Junior said.

Rick's heart nearly broke as he cuddled his godson. "Yes, he will."

As he comforted the boy, he reflected on the message that TJ had sent him. They'd located Axe and would be attempting a recovery within the next few hours. With any luck, Junior would be reunited with his buddy in no time.

"Oh you definitely pass the husband selection course," whispered Jenny from the doorway.

He glanced up at his fiancée. There was a smile on her face and her dark eyes shone brightly. "Huh?"

"He's asleep."

Rick turned his head slightly so he could see the boy sleeping against his chest. "Isn't this the dad selection course?"

She stepped into the room and kissed his shaved head. "One step at a time, big guy. Have you heard from TJ?"

"Yeah, they should be back tomorrow."

"They've got Axe?"

"Not yet. In a few hours."

Mike made to lower the boy into his bed. Junior mumbled something incoherent and clung to him like a baby koala. Rick sighed and made himself comfortable. "I guess I'm sleeping here tonight."

Jenny kissed him again before snuggling in alongside him. "We're both sleeping here tonight."

Chapter Ten

Barbosa sat on a bench in the exercise yard with a cigarette dangling from the corner of his mouth. He gazed up at the orange sky and exhaled a cloud of smoke into the air. Cigarettes and yard time were precious commodities in prison. Commodities he purchased with wads of cash smuggled into the prison by his agents.

"Time's up," barked a gruff voice.

He glanced up at the guard. "Not yet."

"What did you say?"

"NOT YET!"

Barbosa flicked the half-smoked cigarette at the exercise yard's chain fence and fixed his eyes on the concrete wall fifty yards distant.

"On your feet!" barked the guard. "On your feet or I'll break your god damn arm."

"What's the time?" asked Barbosa as he rose.

"Time for you to go back to your cell."

"I don't think so." Barbosa fixed the man with a dark stare.

The guard's lip rose in a snarl as he raised his baton.

A massive explosion reverberated throughout the yard, and the guard's face went from rage to shock in a split second.

Barbosa smiled as the air around him exploded in a cacophony of screeching metal. He turned and saw a garbage truck slamming its way through the prison's walls and fences. It made it through two layers of barriers before it ground to a halt.

Masked men flooded in through the breach as the hiss of gas replaced the noise of the crash. Gunfire filled the air as the guards in the towers fired at the truck. A rocket streaked over the wall and detonated against the armored glass of one of the towers. Barbosa covered his nose and mouth with a hand as figures moved toward him.

"Shit!" managed the guard before an AK rattled and he was cut down in a hail of bullets.

The roar of a two-stroke engine sounded as a circular blade sliced through the fence that separated Barbosa from the assailants. In a matter of seconds the exercise yard was breached. One of the figures thrust a gas mask into his hands and he donned it.

Gunfire raged as the men led him back to the garbage truck and out through the hole it had smashed through the prison walls.

Outside a half-dozen black GMC SUVs were parked along the fence. No less than twenty gunmen were blasting away at the towers with assault rifles and rockets. The wail of a siren rang in his ears as the men bundled him into one of the vehicles. Wheels spun and they accelerated away. Safely inside, Barbosa removed his mask and tossed it onto the seat.

As he gave the prison one last glance a massive fireball rolled into the air and the glass vibrated as the garbage truck detonated.

"A parting gift, boss," said the only other person in the SUV, the driver.

"Nice touch."

The convoy of black SUVs sped along a highway into the desert and onto a side road. They belted down a dirt track until they turned onto a small airfield. Barbosa's vehicle pulled in alongside a business jet parked under floodlights in front of a rusted hangar.

"Time to fly boss," said the driver.

One of his men opened the door and directed him into the waiting jet. As he mounted the stairs, a curvy stewardess in a tight outfit greeted him with a tumbler of his favorite whiskey on ice.

She closed the doors as the jet's turbines whined pushing them smoothly forward. He took the stewardess's cue and relaxed in a plush leather seat after downing the whiskey. The engines roared and they lurched off the tarmac and banked hard. Barely a minute had passed when the jet leveled off and the intercom buzzed.

"Sir, we've entered Mexican airspace."

Barbosa clapped his hands together. “Excellent, now bring me a phone. There's business that needs taking care of.”

***

“Dokka dokka dokka, here comes the helicopter.” Rick flew a spoonful of food around Junior’s head as the boy squealed with delight, flapping his arms like a deranged bird. The boy was secured in his high chair in the kitchen of their apartment.

“Open up. Here comes the SEAL team.” He shoveled the food into Junior’s mouth and the toddler swallowed it in a single gulp.

“More, more,” he demanded.

“OK, here it comes.” Rick saw his phone flash on the counter as he reloaded the spoon. “Babe can you grab that?” he asked Jenny who was preparing dinner.

“Sure thing,” she said, picking up the phone and checking the screen. “It’s a message from Ernie.”

Rick pushed another food-laden spoon into Junior’s mouth. “What’s it say?”

“Bravo has escaped and is at large.” She frowned. “Who’s bravo?”

Rick placed the spoon down. “Babe, you know how we discussed contingency plans?”

“Yes, is this–”

“An emergency? Yes. Can you look after Junior? I’ll grab our bags and meet you at the car.”

“Is Bravo the cartel guy?”

Rick nodded as he shrugged off the apron he’d been wearing to feed Junior. “Yeah, and he’s escaped. We need to get Junior to World’s End and wait for the others.”

“World’s End?” asked Jenny as she wiped the toddler’s face.

“More, heli bopper,” demanded Junior.

“We have to go on a trip. More heli bopper then,” said Rick. He turned back to Jenny. “World’s End is a safe house that TJ setup in case something like this happened. Ernie is going to meet us there."

"Do you think Barbosa is going after Mike?"

"Yeah, it makes sense. He's already got Axe."

***

TJ jammed the last of Deb's boxes into the back of the SUV and closed the trunk. He checked his watch. It was a little after midnight. They'd made good time in getting everything ready for the recovery op.

As the others came downstairs his phone buzzed. It was a message from Rick.

Barbosa has escaped. Taking Junior to World's End.

"Shit!"

"What's wrong?" asked Ali.

"We forget something?" said Deb.

"No, Barbosa escaped."

The look of horror on Mike's face reflected his own emotions.

"We need to roll on Axe now," he said.

TJ locked eyes with Deb who slowly shook her head. "No, it's too dangerous. You and Ali need to head back stateside and get to World's End. Ernie, Rick and the girls will meet you there."

Mike clenched his jaw. It was a look that TJ had seen before and it meant his teammate was about to defy his directions.

"I'm not going anywhere without Axe."

TJ was about to speak when Deb placed a hand on his shoulder. "Mike, you and Ali head back stateside. TJ and I will grab Axe and meet up with you there."

Ali shook her head. "No, we can't let you do that."

"You don't have a choice. You stay in Mexico and Barbosa will find you. He has no idea who I am."

"He knows TJ," said Mike.

TJ shook his head. "Deb can't go alone. Plus, we don't have kids. You and Ali have to think of Junior." TJ winked. "I mean, imagine if Rick raised the poor kid. He wouldn't stand a chance in life."

"So that's it then," said Deb in an authoritative voice. "TJ and I will recover Axe."

Mike looked like was going to object, then his shoulders slumped. "Fine, but don't take any unnecessary risks."

TJ let out a grunt. "Oh, that's rich coming from you." He reached out and shook Mike's hand. "We'll see you guys at World's End."

Chapter Eleven

The jet's stairs lowered and Barbosa, now dressed in a well-fitted suit, descended the steps. He paused on the tarmac and took a deep breath of the night air. "Oh how I love you, Mexico!" he bellowed before striding across to the man waiting alongside a silver Mercedes G-Wagen armored SUV.

"Juan Duvan, my friend." He embraced his deputy in a bearlike hug. "Your plan was brilliant."

The mustached enforcer slapped his boss's shoulder. "It's good to have you back."

The two men entered the vehicle and it drove off the airfield followed by four SUVs.

"Where is my family?" Barbosa asked. "I thought they would be here."

"They're at the fortress. I thought they would be safer there. The Cali Cartel has been pushing the boundaries of our friendship. I'm looking forward to having you here to deal with them."

Barbosa raised a hand. "That can wait. First things first. Where is the dog?"

"He's at a facility outside Cabo."

"And the boy?"

Duvan dropped his eyes. "We are yet to locate him or his parents."

Barbosa scowled. "Bring the dog to me and find the child." He managed a faint smile as he imagined the horror on Michael Saunders' face as he watched a video of his loyal dog tearing his son's throat out. Yes, vengeance was going to be sweet and he was going to enjoy every moment of it.

***

TJ placed the Improvised Explosive Device he'd constructed under a shrub and toggled the switch that armed it. He'd already set two other devices and this one completed an arc a hundred yards from the western side of the ranch.

Stealing through the scrub he worked his way around to the eastern side where he'd left Deb, watching the front of the hacienda. They were dressed in a similar fashion; jeans and dark pullovers to blend with the shadows. TJ was carrying a backpack loaded with equipment. The pair also had balaclavas rolled up on their heads and night-vision devices stowed in their pockets in case the half moon disappeared behind a cloud.

"Any movement?" he asked.

"No, it's dead to the world. How did you go with the distractions?"

"They'll blow if we need them." They touched as he passed her the garage remote.

Deb closed her hand around his and gave it a gentle squeeze. "Let's do this."

TJ smiled as he moved through the darkness toward the ranch buildings. Behind him, Deb was watching the front of the main hacienda. If anyone appeared she would detonate the charges, buying him time to grab Axe and withdraw.

He paused at the edge of the yards and fished the night-vision monocular from his pocket. A quick scan of the ranch buildings confirmed it was all clear, so he moved silently toward the location where he'd seen the cages and heard Axe's bark.

As he stalked forward a strange rumbling noise came from the hacienda. He paused and then almost laughed as he realized it was someone snoring. Creeping along the side of the building he stopped a few feet short of the metal cages.

"Axe, Axe, boy."

There was a low whimper from inside and TJ spotted a shape inside the cage. He moved across, pressed his hand against the wire and was rewarded with a warm nose and wet licks.

"Axe, buddy it's you. I knew it was you." TJ felt tears forming in eyes.

The dog growled.

"Hey, buddy–"

"What the hell are you doing?" snarled an accented voice behind him. "Turn around real slow."

TJ complied and found himself staring into the barrel of a pistol.

"Don't move gringo." The man turned his head slightly and yelled out in Spanish.

There was a grunt and then yelling from inside the hacienda before a light snapped on.

"Oh shit," whispered TJ.

"Oh shit is right, gr–" The *sicario's* eyes rolled back into his head as a Taser crackled. His arms dropped to his side and he convulsed as an electrical charge coursed through his muscles.

TJ grabbed the pistol as the man dropped, revealing Deb standing behind him with the flashlight Taser in her hand. "I'm sorry, he must have snuck out of a back door."

There was another shout from inside and the sound of a weapon being cocked. TJ shrugged out of his pack and grabbed the bolt cutters inside. Slipping them onto a chain he cut through it and opened the cage.

Axe bounded from inside and jumped on the Chief, licking him. TJ snapped a lead on his collar. "Let's get you out of here."

Deb led as they dashed from the cages to the yards. TJ and Axe were halfway across when a burst of gunfire stitched the sand in front of them. He felt a bullet tug at his shirt and nick his arm as he raised the pistol.

There was an almighty flash and TJ thought he'd been shot until he realized that Deb had detonated the bombs he'd planted.

In the light from fireballs he saw two men at the front of the hacienda. Both were fixated on the blast. TJ aimed the pistol and fired. He hit one and the other beat a hasty retreat into the building.

"Come on!" yelled Deb.

TJ fired one last shot and followed her into the scrub. Axe ran by his side as she led them along a trail they'd used on the way in. Behind them a gun barked and bullets hissed over their heads.

They were halfway to the truck when TJ realized the bullet that he thought had nicked his arm had actually gone much deeper. Blood drenched his side, and he couldn't raise his arm. He felt the pistol slip from his grasp as he ran.

By the time they reached the SUV he was feeling light-headed and short of breath. Deb opened the rear door and Axe leaped into the back seat.

"Deb, you'll have to drive." He winced.

"Are you hurt?"

"I'm OK," he said climbing into the passenger seat.

She started the engine and navigated the track back to the main road. Axe shoved his head between the seats and whined softly as he pushed his head up against TJ. He patted the dog's head with his good hand as his vision spun. "Good boy."

He felt the overwhelming need to sleep as his head rocked forward against his chest.

"TJ, stay with me."

He faintly registered Deb's voice as he fought to stay awake.

"Don't you die on me you selfish bastard. Don't you leave me."

"I won't. I can't. I love you," he managed before passing out.

Chapter Twelve

Barbosa snatched a heavy tumbler from the desk in his study and flung it against the wall. It hit the rosewood paneling with a dull thud leaving a dent and dropped onto the thick carpet. "How the hell did they find the dog?" he screamed at Duvan.

"I don't know, boss. They must have had help," his head of security responded tentatively.

"Of course they had help."

"My men hit one of them. There was a blood trail leading to a vehicle. I warned out our people all the way up Baja. We've got our police running checkpoints and people checking every hospital, doctor's surgery and pharmacy. They won't get far, we'll find them."

"You better." Barbosa took a new glass from a tray on his desk, added ice cubes and poured himself a new drink. "I want you to triple the bounty on Petty Officer Saunders and his family. Spread the word."

"You still want him alive?"

"Yes, I want him alive. He's going to pay for everything he's done to me. Now, get out there and find that dog."

Duvan left the office with his phone pressed to his ear. He had contacts in almost every US agency with interests in Mexico. If the dog was still on the peninsular his people would find out where he was being hidden.

***

TJ's eyes snapped open and he reached for a pistol that he wasn't wearing. As his eyes slowly focused he realized he was lying in a bed in a well-lit room with a white ceiling. He winced as he sat up so he could take in his surroundings. There was a single window with a blind and a door opposite the bed.

As the activities of the night before came flooding back he

went to raise his arm and found there was a tube running into the back of his hand. A sideways glance confirmed that someone had put an IV line in. A check of the opposite arm also revealed that his gunshot wound had been dressed.

There was a soft whine from beyond the edge of the bed and a wet nose gently nudged his hand. "Hey, Axe," he croaked.

The door to the room opened and he turned his head to see Deb carrying in a tray.

She placed it on a side table and sat on the edge of the bed. "You gave us quite the scare last night."

"Where are we?"

"An Agency safe house."

"Did you stitch me up?"

"It was the least I could do. I let you down last night. That first guy should never have gotten past me."

TJ reached over and placed his hand on top of hers. "You were amazing." He tipped his head toward his arm. "You saved my life."

She turned her hand and interlocked their fingers. "There was a moment there when I thought I'd lost you." A tear formed in her eye. "I realized I couldn't bear the idea of you not being in my life."

They locked eyes and TJ squeezed her hand. She edged forward on the bed and he leaned forward until their lips touched. His heart raced as the kiss gained in intensity. Deb's hands ran up his torso to his face and he took his good arm around her back and pulled her closer.

Axe whined from the side of the bed and made a beeline for the door. As TJ and Deb broke for air they spotted his tail disappearing out of the room and laughed. Then he kissed his wife again. This time her hands wandered south and for the first time in almost a year he felt her touch.

He winced and lifted his injured arm to pull the needle and IV line from his hand.

"You lost a lot of blood," Deb whispered.

"I almost lost a hell of a lot more." He managed to slip his hand under her shirt and release her bra.

"This isn't going to fix everything."

"No, but it's a good start, right?"

***

Rick skidded a Polaris ATV to a halt behind a rocky outcrop. Leaping from the seat he grabbed his M4 carbine and headed up a goat trail. It was a chilly winter's day, but he still managed to work up a sweat under his body armor. By the time he crested the ridge he was breathing hard. Pausing for a moment he took in the sweeping vista of desert that reached out to the horizon. World's End was a rural property that belonged to a close friend of TJ's. The owner, a former Agency man, had added some significant security improvements. One of those was the reason Rick was out patrolling the perimeter.

He made his way along the ridgeline to what looked like a cell phone tower. The structure was actually an array of sophisticated sensors that included thermal cameras, vibration monitoring gear and communications intercept modules. It was part of the broader security network that piped data to the ranch house, three miles away. This particular tower had recently reported an error message.

As he approached the tower he spotted the problem. An access panel had popped open in the wind and birds had built a nest inside. "Sorry guys." He stripped the debris from the hole and closed it.

A noise to the west caught his ear as he patrolled back to the ATV. He took binoculars from a pouch on his rig and lifted them to his eyes. Far out over the desert he spotted a cloud of dust.

"Alpha, this is Bravo, I've got a vehicle inbound," he transmitted over his radio.

"Alpha here," responded Jenny. "That call sign is friendly. Get your ass back to the ranch, lunch is on."

Rick scrambled down to the ATV and gunned it across the

desert. Insects bounced off his goggles and slapped into his face as he approached the ranch house. Parking, he joined Jenny and Junior under the sweeping verandahs of the renovated hacienda.

His fiancée was dressed in combat pants and T-shirt with a pistol on one hip and the toddler on the other.

"Looks good on you," he said, slipping out of his armor.

"Pistol or the kid?"

He kissed her on the cheek. "Both."

Behind them a glass door slid open. "Mike and Ali are inbound," reported Ernie as he entered.

"Any news from TJ and Deb?" asked Jenny.

"Yeah, they're in a secure location with Axe and will extract tonight. They should be here in the morning."

A horn sounded as the approaching vehicle passed the outer fence of the home block and drove up the gravel drive.

"Axe, Axe, Axe," chanted Junior as he recognized his father's pickup. It pulled in alongside the ATV. The doors swung open and Mike and Ali appeared. Ali made straight for the porch with her arms extended.

Jenny had already lowered the toddler and he took off across the grass still chanting the dog's name.

Ali swept him into her arms and hugged him tight as the others gathered around. "My darling boy. I missed you so much."

"Mom, where Axe?" he asked.

"He'll be back tomorrow," said Mike as he joined them. "Guys, thanks so much for looking after him." He hugged Jenny and shook hands with Rick and Ernie.

"It was our pleasure," said Jenny. "Come inside, we've got lunch on the table."

Mike updated the rest of the team on TJ and Deb's success in locating and extracting Axe.

"So, all going well, they should be here tomorrow?" asked Ernie.

"Yeah," said Mike. "Now, what do we know about Barbosa?"

"His people smashed their way into a maximum security prison, snatched him and detonated a massive IED to cover their tracks. They killed a half-dozen guards and at least thirty other prisoners."

"Brutal," said Rick.

"Axe's abduction had to be part of this plan," said Mike.

"I agree," said Ernie. "And so do the FBI. They want to put you all in witness protection."

Mike shook his head. "No. We're not spending our lives running and hiding. Once TJ and Axe are back we need to find a way to neutralize Barbosa. We need to go on the offensive."

***

The ring tone of Duvan's phone sent an involuntary shiver down his spine. He glanced at the screen, hoping it wasn't another call from Barbosa demanding an update on the search for the dog. So far his people had failed to locate any trace of the animal or the people who had snatched it.

This time it wasn't Barbosa.

He answered. "Tell me good news."

"I've got a tip off," his source replied. "The people you're looking for might be in a safe house near Los Barriles." He rattled off an address.

"Where did you get the information? Is it good?"

"It's from the inside. It's good."

"It better be." Duvan terminated the call and dialed Barbosa. The cartel kingpin answered immediately.

"Have you found them?"

"I've got a lead on a safe house in Los Barriles."

"Good, get as many men together as you can. I want the dog alive. Kill everyone else."

Chapter Thirteen

TJ managed to slide his wounded arm into his shirt and fasten the buttons with one hand. Then he left the room where he'd been resting and explored the CIA safe house where he, Deb and Axe were laying low.

He found Deb in the kitchen making dinner with Axe by her side. She was still dressed in the tactical outfit she'd been wearing the night before. "Hey gorgeous."

She turned and smiled. "Coffee?"

"Yes please."

"How are you feeling?" she asked as TJ sat at the kitchen table. Axe moved to his side and placed his chin on his thigh.

He stroked the dog's head. "Pretty good, thanks to you."

"Terrance…"

He winced at the sound of his given name, she only used it when she was about to deliver a lecture.

"What happened between us doesn't fix the problem." She poured him a cup of black coffee from a percolator on the bench. Turning she registered the pained look on his face. "Don't get me wrong, it was wonderful. It's just…" She passed him the mug.

"Yeah, I know. But I also want you to know that I'm willing to do whatever it takes to rekindle what we had."

"It's not that simple."

Axe growled.

"Clearly someone disagrees."

She smiled faintly. "Well, he is the matchmaker."

Axe growled again and headed out into the hall toward the front door. TJ noticed that his hackles were raised. "Have you got a weapon?"

"In the basement. What's up?"

He rose from the chair. "Probably nothing, but–"

Axe's bark was one that TJ had heard before. The dog was

alerting them to an impending threat. "Show me the basement, now!"

Deb dashed into the corridor and he followed her through a side door and downstairs. "Axe, come," he ordered as they descended into a small room filled with shelves of supplies. Deb gripped the corner of a rack of boxes and slid it sideways revealing a selection of weapons and equipment. TJ grabbed an ammunition-laden vest, wounded arm forgotten, dropped it over his head and fastened it around his torso. Axe stood at the top of the stairs, guarding the door.

Deb opened another hidden panel exposing a row of CCTV screens. She studied them intently as TJ geared up. "I can see two vehicles."

He joined her at the screens. The safe house was located a short distance from the beach and backed on to scrubby dunes. One of the cameras showed two pickups parked among the dunes. Gunmen were clustered around them, their attention focused toward the safe house.

"Why are they waiting?" asked Deb.

"They're waiting for more of their buddies. Once they have the numbers, they'll storm the joint. We need to get out of here and fast."

"If it weren't for Axe they'd have got the jump on us." Deb took a vest and submachine gun from the rack. "What's the plan?"

TJ loaded and cocked a rifle. "They'll have the road blocked. The beach is our best option."

"Good idea." She gestured to the screen where another vehicle had joined the others. "More of their friends."

TJ grabbed a backpack filled with ammunition and slung it over his shoulder. "I'm on point. You got the keys? "

She nodded. "What about Axe?"

"He knows his way around a gunfight, right bud."

The dog gave an excited bark.

TJ led them out of the basement and through the house to the porch that overlooked the beach. Their SUV was parked to one side. TJ figured they could get to it unobserved then make their escape. He checked Deb and Axe were close behind and descended the porch to the sandy lawn. Crouching at the corner of the house he peered past the SUV to where the cameras had revealed the massing gunmen.

"Cover me," he whispered to Deb.

"No." She placed a hand on his shoulder. "I'll drive. You shoot."

The stubborn look on her face told him not to argue. "OK, use the key not the remote, it will flash and draw attention."

She nodded and stole forward to the side of the SUV. As she inserted the key in the driver's door he moved forward to the passenger side. Opening the door he gestured for Axe to jump inside.

As the dog leaped in a burst of gunfire sounded from behind and bullets smacked into the side of the house. TJ spun and spotted figures approaching from the road. He returned fire as Deb started the SUV, and then clambered in.

Axe barked excitedly as they rocketed across the lawn, smashing through a white picket fence before bouncing over low dunes onto the beach.

The SUV fishtailed wildly as Deb turned and ran it parallel to the dark blue ocean.

"Steady on," grunted TJ as he climbed between the seats into the rear. Axe licked his face as he clambered into the cargo area. "Thanks, bud."

"What are you doing?" asked Deb as he found the lever to release the trunk door.

"Preparing for company." He braced his legs either side of the opening and aimed his rifle down the beach. They were a few hundred yards from the house when the first of the *sicario* trucks appeared.

"Right on cue," said TJ as he squeezed off a volley of shots.

"How far do you want me to go?" yelled Deb.

"Get us back on the road as soon as you can."

"OK."

TJ fired again as three pickups accelerated after them. Sitting on massive tires with powerful engines the trucks ate up the distance between them. He spotted muzzle flashes from above the cabins as men in the beds of the trucks fired. A bullet shattered a side window, spraying him with glass as he fired back.

"You OK?" he yelled between shots.

"Yeah, there's a track ahead. I'm getting us out of here."

He fired again and a jet of steam burst from the hood of one of the pickups. As he switched aim to another vehicle he was thrown sideways as Deb sent the SUV careening off the beach. Shrubs lashed the sides of the car as they blasted along a narrow track. Tires squealed as they turned abruptly onto tarmac.

"You OK back there?" yelled Deb.

TJ glanced over his shoulder and saw Axe calmly watching him with his tongue lolling and ears flapping in the wind.

"Yeah I'm good," he said, replacing an empty magazine with a fresh one from his vest.

"I'm going to contact my people and arrange an extraction," said Deb.

"Good idea." TJ turned his attention back to the road as they accelerated around a sweeping bend. "We need to stay off the main highway."

He fished his phone from his pocket and checked the screen, no reception. "Typical," he mumbled.

"How's the arm?" asked Deb as they turned onto a dirt track.

With the adrenaline of the gunfight and escape, he'd completely forgotten the injury. A glance confirmed that the bandage was intact and the wound wasn't weeping. "All good. Your stitches are holding."

"Who would have thought? I mean considering how crappy my sewing is. Remember that time in New Zealand when I tried to fix your pants?"

"How could I forget? I inadvertently exposed myself to a table of old ladies." He glanced over his shoulder and caught her looking at him in the mirror. Her eyes were shining and there were smile lines around them. She held his gaze for a moment before returning her attention to the road.

TJ turned to check if they were still being followed but couldn't see anything through the dust cloud trailing behind them. Despite their precarious situation Deb was softening, he was sure of it.

***

As TJ and Deb made their way north toward the border, Mike was pacing the living room at World's End. He hadn't been able to get through on the Chief's number. With every passing minute he was getting more and more worried. It was unlike TJ not to check in or make timings. Something had definitely happened.

He heard footsteps on the terracotta tiled floor and turned to see Ali approaching with a concerned look. "Any news?" she asked.

"No, nothing."

She wrapped an arm around his waist as Ernie and Rick appeared.

"You guys get through to TJ?" Mike asked.

"Negative," answered Rick.

"Well, let's hope that Deb can get her people to help out."

"Not sure how a fine dining magazine is going to help get them out of Mexico?" Rick said, with a confused look.

"She's Agency," said Mike.

"No shit!"

"I did not see that coming," said Ernie. "Although it does explain a few things."

"And it means she can get them out, easy. TJ and Axe are in good hands," said Rick.

"Unless something's happened to them. What if Barbosa's men caught up with them? We're literally sitting on our hands here," said Mike.

Rick grasped his shoulder. "Bud, you need to think of your

family. If you go charging down to Mexico, they could lose both you and Axe."

"And that's exactly what Barbosa wants," said Ernie. "Let's give TJ and Deb a little more time. I've got a feeling they're going to come through with the goods."

***

"We've got a tail!" yelled TJ over the wind rushing into the SUV as it tore along a desert road. He'd spotted the outline of a pickup in the thick dust they were throwing up behind them.

Bullets cracked past his head, tearing into the roof of the SUV and exiting through the windshield. His heart lurched as he turned and saw holes directly in front of the driver. "Deb!" he yelled.

Her head bobbed back into view. "I'm good. I'm good." More gunfire sounded and the SUV shuddered. "Can you do something about that?"

TJ blasted into the dust with his rifle. Remembering the backpack he dug into it and found a grenade. Tearing the pin free, he popped the handle and counted down.

"Five, four, three, two." He lobbed the grenade into the dust. "One, zero."

The bomb detonated with an angry flash in the dust. He raised his rifle and waited for the truck to reappear. Seconds passed without it emerging. "That'll slow them down."

"We've got a town coming up," said Deb.

As she slowed a loud scraping noise filled the cabin. "Ah, TJ. I think they hit something vital."

The noise increased in intensity as she limped the SUV into a dusty town and pulled in alongside a row of dune buggies and pickups parked in front of a bar.

"We need some new wheels," said TJ as he jumped from the back of the SUV. Axe joined him as he eyeballed the vehicles. He strode across to a pickup truck with huge tires and exposed shock absorbers. It had tools strapped to the hood, spare wheels in the back and on the cab roof. "This will do nicely." He opened the driver's side door and saw the keys in the ignition. "Deb, we've got a new ride." He tossed his backpack into the cab and whistled for Axe to join him.

"You couldn't find something less obtrusive?"

"We need to get off the roads and head through the desert."

TJ turned over the engine, and the high-performance V8 rumbled to life. As he backed the truck out onto the street a figure appeared from the doorway of the bar.

"Hey, what the hell are you doing?"

Deb waved at the man as they roared down the road. "You're crazy, TJ." She laughed as they raced out of town.

"Crazy is going to keep us alive." TJ glanced in the mirror and spotted one of the pickups that had chased them from the safe house. "We've got company. Time to head into the desert."

He bounced the off-roader over a ditch, pointed the nose north and gunned the engine. The custom machine spat sand from all four tires as it blasted across the desert, leaving their pursuers in its wake. Deb wrapped her arms around Axe as they bounced over rocks, smashed through shrubs and launched over dunes.

After five minutes of bashing their way through scrub TJ reached a track heading roughly north. A further hour and they'd progressed a significant distance up the Baja peninsula toward the US border, winding their way through rocky outcrops and clusters of cacti, as TJ now knew was the plural for the prickly plants.

"It's got a rugged, uncompromising beauty that takes your breath away," said Deb as they crested a low ridge, revealing a broad basin. The sun was low in the sky, and the shadows cast by the rocks and bushes looked like fingers clutching at the shifting sands.

"Sure does," he replied as they descended a rutted section of trail.

As they drove across the valley floor the big V8 missed a beat and spluttered. TJ frowned as he studied the instrument panel. The temperature needle wasn't in the red, oil pressure was good and the fuel gauge hadn't moved from full. He tapped the glass with his finger and the needle immediately dropped to zero. It had been stuck on full. "Son of a bitch."

"How far are we from the border?" asked Deb as the engine died.

"At least twenty miles."

"We could walk out."

He shook his head. "Not at night in this terrain. We need to get away from the truck and hole up. Your people can extract us in the morning, right?"

Deb hauled her satellite phone from her bag and checked the screen. "Yeah, as soon as we go firm I'll update our position."

Axe whined, and TJ jumped from the cab to let him out. He immediately relieved himself on a cactus before patrolling the area around the truck while TJ and Deb gathered their gear.

"They'll expect us to keep heading toward the border." He gestured to a rocky outcrop a mile or so to the east. "There might be a cave up there."

TJ found a bottle of water in the truck and stashed it in his pack. Then he led the threesome across the desert floor as the sun was setting behind them. In the distance he heard the snarl of engines, possibly dirt bikes. Their escape into the desert had bought them time, but it hadn't shaken Barbosa's men. They were still being hunted.

***

TJ crouched alongside a boulder with his rifle in hand, staring out at the pinpricks of light flashing in the darkness. Vehicles had been crisscrossing the desert all night, searching. He flexed his hand to get the blood moving through his wounded arm. The temperature had dropped with the sun causing it to ache. Satisfied that none of the lights were heading in their direction he turned and made his way back to the cave where Axe and Deb were camped.

"Are they still looking?" asked Deb from the darkness as he ducked inside.

"Yeah, but north like we thought." He gave Axe a pat and sat beside him.

"You mean like 'you' thought," she said. "You've done a pretty good job keeping us out of trouble."

"It's been a team effort."

"Just like staying warm. Come sit next to me."

TJ shuffled across till he was alongside his wife.

"It's so cold," Deb said as she snuggled in close, lowering her head to his chest. On her opposite side Axe lay facing the opening of the cave.

TJ sat silently, enjoying the intimacy.

"I'm sorry," said Deb.

"Sorry for what?"

"Putting my career before you. Not taking the time to build on our relationship."

TJ sighed. "I'm sorry for the same things. I'm sorry I put the team first when it should have been you."

Deb chuckled. "That was never going to happen. I married a man dedicated to serving his country and his teammates. I guess I just hoped that I would be a part of that team."

He slid his injured arm around behind her back and pulled her closer. "Deborah Lines, you are my team."

There was a soft growl from Axe.

"Oh, you too bud."

The dog rose from where he was sitting next to Deb and growled again.

"What is it," she whispered.

"Could be a coyote. I'll check it out."

She kissed his cheek. "Be careful."

TJ rose and followed Axe outside. The dog disappeared into the gloom as he emerged from the cluster of boulders and scanned the horizon. He could see more now that sunrise was less than an hour away. As he patrolled the ridgeline he was on edge, as every cactus resembled a human figure, a potential threat.

Confident that the coast was clear he made his way back. Deb had already updated the Agency on their location and extraction was due at daybreak. He checked his watch. That was only thirty minutes away. He needed to get Deb up and moving.

He was halfway back to the cave when a voice stopped him dead in his tracks.

"*Manos arriba, gringo.*"

He slowly raised his hands in the air, letting his rifle hang from its sling. A gunman stepped out from behind a boulder a few feet distant, aiming a submachine gun at TJ's face.

"You're going to make me rich *essé*," the man said.

A terrifying snarl sounded from atop the rock next to the *sicario*. The man turned and saw Axe poised to strike.

TJ snatched up his rifle and swung it in a tight arc, connecting with the *sicario's* temple. As the man dropped he sprayed a burst into the distance, gunshots echoing across the valley. A split second later shouting sounded from the west.

"Axe, come." TJ sprinted for the cave. Skidding into the opening, he grabbed his bag. "Deb, we've got to go."

"Are you OK?" she asked.

"Yeah, but we're about to have company."

This time it was Axe who took point, leading them down a boulder-strewn slope that offered good cover. TJ let Deb and the dog push ahead, turning every few seconds to check for pursuers.

He paused behind a boulder, and in the soft glow of dawn, he spotted a swarm of men scrambling over the hill where they'd camped. Lining one up he squeezed off a shot and was rewarded with a cry of pain.

Muzzles flashed on the hillside and bullets ricocheted off rocks as he turned and sprinted after Deb and Axe. He jinked from side to side to throw off the aim of the attackers. Breathing hard he skirted a cluster of cacti and nearly ran into his wife crouched behind bushes with Axe. "Deb, we need to keep moving."

She grabbed his leg. "Get down."

He knelt alongside them. "What's up?"

"Look." She pointed at a rise to the east, the direction they were traveling.

TJ spotted figures silhouetted by the orange sunrise. He counted at least six gunmen blocking their escape route.

Gunfire sounded from behind, and he spun, readying his rifle. The bullets struck to his right, cutting off another avenue of escape.

"What are we going to do?" whispered Deb, her weapon held ready.

TJ could hear the fear in her voice. "We go north as fast as we can, stay low." He grabbed her hand, and they ran together with Axe following behind. Shouting filled the air as the *sicarios* gave chase. Bullets hissed past and ricocheted off rocks as they weaved between cacti, bushes and rocks.

TJ knew it was only a matter of time before a bullet hit one of them or the men caught up. Strangely he wasn't afraid. He was overcome with a feeling of rage. Finally, he'd found a connection with his wife, and now these men were going to take that from him. "Keep going," he yelled as he spun and fired on the closest of the gunmen.

As they dove for cover he fired again and again, cutting down two pursuers. He tossed his two remaining grenades, turned, and sprinted after the others. A quick calculation in his head confirmed he was down to the last of his ammunition.

He found Deb and Axe hunkered down in a cluster of rocks. Deb greeted him with a grim look, her submachine gun held ready. "They've cut us completely off."

TJ took up a firing position behind a rock. He felt the reassuring presence of Axe and glanced down at the loyal dog. He and Deb could surrender, but he owed it to Axe to keep him out of the hands of Barbosa.

Bullets ricocheted off the rocks as the cartel goons moved in.

"TJ, you can't let him fall into their hands again. We won't get a second chance at finding him," Deb said softly as she stroked the dog's ears.

"I know." He choked back tears.

TJ could see a line of men approaching from the east. A glance around confirmed that the others were holding firm.

"It's now or never," he said softly.

Deb's eyes were rimmed with tears. "I can't watch."

"He won't feel a thing."

At that moment a ripping sound filled the air. It was a noise that TJ knew from his time in Afghanistan… it was salvation.

A black helicopter thundered overhead, spewing rounds from the machine guns poking from each side of its fuselage. It cut a lap above them before touching down in a clearing a hundred yards distant.

"Go, go, go!" bellowed TJ as he shepherded them toward the helicopter.

The door gunners waved them forward between bursts of fire aimed at the fleeing cartel gunmen. Deb clambered into the chopper followed by Axe who turned to make sure that TJ was close behind. He jumped in and slumped into one of the webbing seats as they lifted off. Locking eyes with Deb, he shook his head. "That was a close call," he mouthed.

"You were amazing," she replied.

"No, you were beyond amazing."

She smiled and took a headset from one of the loadmasters. She listened for a moment then leaned forward so he could hear her. "We're being transferred to a CIA helicopter in Hermosillo. They'll take all three of us up to World's End."

He gave her thumbs up as she slid into the seat next to him. On his opposite side Axe sat looking out over the desert with his ears flapping in the wind.

"How's your arm?" she asked.

He grimaced. "I think I may have finally torn your stitches."

She placed her hand on his thigh and gave it a squeeze. "As soon as we land I'll have a look at it."

Chapter Fourteen

Rick paused from where he was cleaning his rifle and watched as a white unmarked helicopter thundered in, cutting a tight lap around the World's End hacienda as the pilot surveyed potential landing zones. The lush green lawn at the back of the residence, beyond the swimming pool, was the selected spot.

Rotor wash lashed the vines that grew over the rear of the adobe building as he joined Mike, Jenny, Ernie and Ali, holding Junior, who were waiting to see who alighted.

The doors of the unmarked chopper slid back and a blur of brown and black dashed from the idling aircraft.

Axe rounded the pool at high speed and made a beeline for the group.

Mike dropped to a knee. "Axe, Axe, boy."

Rick choked back tears as his buddy wrapped his arms around the excited animal.

"Axe," cried out Junior as he recognized the dog. Ali lowered him to the ground and the toddler hugged his best friend as Axe licked his face.

"That's so sweet," said Jenny as she took his hand.

Ali bent and gave the ecstatic hound a quick once-over. "Looks like he's in good health."

Rick glanced back at the helicopter and spotted TJ and Deb. TJ's wife had her arm around his waist, and he looked to be wearing a sling.

Mike met them at the edge of the pool. "I can't thank you guys enough." He hugged Deb before turning to TJ. "What happened? You OK?"

The craggy SEAL nodded. "Yeah, Deb took good care of me."

Behind them, the helicopter's blades thundered as it took off into the setting sun.

"Let's get everyone inside," said Ali as she scooped Junior

from the ground. "Dinner's on the table and I've been saving a huge bone for Axe."

As they moved inside Rick noticed that TJ and Deb hung back. He nudged Mike and tipped his head in the direction of the couple. "Looks like Axe has done it again."

Mike nodded. "Cupid in a fur coat. Let's leave them to it."

TJ gazed out over the desert with one arm around his wife, the other hitched in a sling. "Deb, what you did for the team and me–"

She cut him off by grasping his face and kissing him. "You were amazing out there," she said breathlessly when they broke. "That was the Terrance I fell in love with; a man of action, a man of passion and power. That's the man I wanted to live the rest of my life with."

"I've always been that man, Deb."

"Yes, but not for me. I never get to see you. Both of us have been married to our jobs."

"For me, that's going to change."

"How? It's always been the SEALs first."

TJ shook his head. "Mike's a dad now, Ernie has his family, and it won't be long till Rick and Jenny get started. It's about time we all slowed down a little. I've requested the team be moved over to training."

Deb's eyes narrowed. "Training? You'll be bored in a week."

"Maybe." He leaned in and kissed her again. "But that's a risk I'm willing to take."

The kissed lingered for a moment before she pulled away. "I've got a better idea. How about I get the team attached to the Agency's South American Special Activities Division?"

"You can do that?"

Deb nuzzled in against his neck. "Of course I can. I'm the Regional Director."

"When did that happen?"

"About a month ago." She took his hand.

"Is this because of your journalism award?"

Deb laughed. "Yeah, that's it." She led him toward the

ranch house, from which the smell of roasted meat was wafting. "Now come on, I'm starving."

***

Hours later, with Junior in bed, the team sat on the porch of the ranch house drinking whiskey and smoking cigars. In the distance a coyote let out a mournful series of yips, triggering a low growl from Axe.

Mike ruffled the dog's ears. "Easy boy."

TJ took a puff of his Cuban and exhaled a ring of smoke into the air. "You know Barbosa isn't going to let up."

The others were silent.

"Till that guy's neutralized, Mike, Ali, Junior and Axe are always going to be in danger."

Rick nodded. "Always looking over your shoulder. You can't live like that, brother."

"So what are we going to do about it?" asked Ernie.

Mike sighed. "What can we do about it other than hiding? Barbosa's resources are next level. He's surrounded by guards, constantly moves and we can't hit him with an airstrike." He turned to Deb. "Can we?"

"No." She sipped from her whiskey. "However, a few years back someone took down a cartel operation in Chihuahua. High speed, clandestine type stuff. They cut down *sicarios*, corrupt cops and mercenaries like they were nothing."

"Agency guys?" asked Ernie.

"No, there were a bunch of corrupt CIA contractors involved. They didn't fare much better."

"And you think these guys could take down Barbosa?" asked TJ.

"Oh, there's no doubt about it."

"But, they're mercenaries and mercenaries cost money, right?" said Jenny.

"Something tells me these guys aren't motivated by money. Plus, if rumors are true, and they usually are, I used to work with one of them."

"Ex-CIA?" asked Mike.

"Correct. Vance was one of the Agency's best till he was presumed killed with his partner in a botched operation in the UAE. However, his partner turned up in Afghanistan three years later, wounded but alive."

"And you think they're running some kind of vigilante group taking down bad guys?" asked Rick.

"Knowing Vance, that's exactly what they're doing."

Mike locked eyes with his wife.

"We're running out of options," Ali said quietly.

"Can you get in contact with them?" he asked Deb.

"I think I know a way."

TJ rested his hand on Mike's shoulder. "OK, let's make it happen then."

Chapter Fifteen

TJ turned a battered Ford Explorer onto an equally neglected airstrip and brought it to a halt alongside the rusted hulk of an ancient Anderson aircraft hangar. "This is it."

Deb, dressed in tan cargo pants and a loose fitting green shirt checked her phone. "In position and on time."

"You really think these people can help us?" asked TJ as he un-holstered his pistol and confirmed there was a round chambered.

"I hope so, for Ali and Junior's sake. Jumping from safe house to safe house is no way to raise a kid."

TJ nodded as he took a handheld radio from the belt under his jacket and spoke into it. "Team, how we looking?"

"In position," reported Rick.

"Same here," said Ernie.

"Ready to rock," added Mike.

All three men were positioned around the airfield and armed with marksman rifles. They had infiltrated overnight to provide protection to Deb and TJ as they met with the shadowy organization she'd contacted through a former CIA operative.

"Team, I apologize for my tardiness," a strange voice emitted from the radio. "I'll be with you in a moment."

TJ turned to his wife. "That's an encrypted radio."

"And now it's compromised." Deb stepped out of the vehicle and scanned the horizon. It was less than an hour after sunrise and the sky was clear. "I can't see anything."

As TJ joined her they heard a sound like ruffling sheets above them. They glanced up and spotted a figure descending under a black parachute.

"These guys are pretty switched," said TJ.

The rest of the team was silent now that their radio network had been compromised. They watched as the parachutist cut tight turns, descending toward them. Then, a dozen feet above the ground, they flared and executed a controlled landing. The operative bundled the chute, removed their helmet and used it to weight the nylon fabric.

The operative rose and TJ saw it was a man. His guess was mid-thirties with a trim waist and broad shoulders. As he approached, he got a good look at his face. He had intelligent brown eyes, a strong stubble-covered jaw and a crooked nose, suggesting he wasn't one to shy away from a fight.

The man's equipment spoke to the sophistication of his unit. He wore a lightweight parachute harness the likes of which TJ had never seen before. It was the type of rig that the SEALs dreamed of using instead of the bulky setups the Navy supplied. Interestingly, he could see no evidence of a weapon or communications equipment.

The man extended a hand to Deb. "Hi, name's Bishop."

She shook it. "I'm Deb, this is TJ."

Bishop shook his hand with a firm grip. TJ thought he identified a slight twang to the man's accent, but he couldn't place it.

"Your buddies in overwatch. They going to join the party?"

Deb smiled thinly. "I like them where they are."

He shrugged. "Fair enough. Just so you know, my people have got them covered from above."

TJ glanced skyward; he could see no sign of an aircraft or drone.

"So, tell me everything you know about Barbosa," said Bishop.

Deb reached into her pocket and removed a flash drive, which she handed to the man. "This is everything that the Agency knows."

"But, you can't get to him?"

"I wouldn't be talking to you if we could."

Bishop nodded. "We'll look into it, but I can't make any promises."

"Got a lot on your plate?"

"You know how it is. No shortage of work."

"There's one piece of information that won't be on the

stick," said Mike as he rounded the SUV dressed in head to toe camouflage and carrying a sniper rifle. "The Butcher has a clown phobia."

The clandestine operative smirked. "I might have to crack out my Pennywise costume," he said, referring to the clown character from Stephen King's, *IT*. "You must be Mike."

Mike slung his weapon and shook the man's hand. "Yeah, pleased to meet you, Bishop. Look, I've got a favor to ask."

"You want in on the mission, right?"

"Yeah."

"Figures, if some guy was trying to kill my family and friends I'd want to be the one taking him down. Look, I can't promise anything, but I will run it past my people."

"Appreciated."

"OK, is there anything else?"

Deb's eyes narrowed. "How's Vance doing?"

"Not bad for a dead man. He sends his regards. Allegedly, he thinks very highly of you, or this meeting would never have happened." Bishop took a phone from his pocket and tapped the screen. "I guess this is where people would expect a speech about this meeting never happening." He slipped the device back into his pocket. "But, we're all professionals, so it's not necessary." He turned to Mike. "I'll be in touch."

TJ sensed warmth in the man's smile as he shook hands with each of them.

"A pleasure." Bishop turned and nodded toward the end of the runway. "That'll be my ride."

TJ turned and spotted a speck on the horizon. It rapidly grew into an aircraft that touched down in a cloud of dust. A parachute flared from behind and the sleek white business jet slowed with a roar of engines.

"Catch you on the flip side."

TJ shook his head as the man jogged across to the jet as a set of stairs dropped. He stepped inside and it closed. Then there was an almighty roar and the aircraft blasted off the dirt strip with twin jets of flame spewing from its turbines. Within seconds it was airborne and streaking away.

"God damn," said TJ.

"Impressive," added Mike as he watched it disappear.

"Did you see any markings on that jet?" asked Deb.

"No, but I think we're dealing with a very capable organization," said TJ as they moved away from Mike toward the SUV.

"The Agency made the exact same assessment."

TJ slipped an arm around his wife's slender waist. "So, tell me more about this Vance character."

She turned and kissed him on the cheek. "Don't be jealous, it was a purely professional relationship. We worked together on one of my first field operations."

"And he thinks highly of you?" TJ mimicked Bishop's accent.

She laughed. "Darling, he was compromised and abducted. I managed to tail his kidnappers and a paramilitary team recovered him before they could work him over."

"You saved his life."

"I guess you could say that."

"My wife the super agent." He kissed her on the lips.

"Hey, get a room guys," Rick's voice hissed over the radio.

Deb grabbed TJ's handset from his belt. "Need I remind you that these means have been compromised."

"I think we all know who's going to get compromised," replied Rick.

Mike laughed as he joined them.

Deb shook her head as they climbed into the SUV. "Your teammates."

"Correction, our," said TJ. "They're your teammates too."

***

Barbosa sipped his coffee as he listened to one of his lieutenants outline the reason that drug production from one of his labs had slumped. Allegedly, the farmers he forced to supply the cocaine had chosen to grow food, limiting their output of coca leaves. "How long has this been going on?" he asked as a servant brought in his breakfast of poached eggs on salmon, drizzled with pesto.

"About three months," replied his man. "There has been a drought–"

He cut the lieutenant off with a wave of his hand as he stuffed a laden fork into his mouth. "There are no excuses," he mumbled.

The man nodded.

He swallowed. "Take two families." He paused to sip his coffee. "And kill them."

"Even the children?"

Barbosa stared at him over his cup. "Children, grandparents, chickens, cats, dogs. Kill them all. Set an example for the others."

"Yes, boss."

"Actually, forget it. I'll look after it myself." He wiped his chin with a crisp white napkin. "Is my car ready?"

"Yes, boss," one of the bodyguards loitering in the background replied.

Barbosa downed his coffee and left the dining room. His wife farewelled him in the foyer of their luxurious home and he strolled out to where a convoy of three armored SUVs were parked.

His head of security, Duvan, was waiting at the middle vehicle with the door open. "I've got good news, boss."

Barbosa climbed into the rear of the SUV. Duvan slammed the heavy door and rode shotgun in the front passenger seat.

"One of our people got some red hot intel on the SEAL and the dog."

"Have they found them?"

"No, but we know they're going to be attending a wedding in Washington state, tomorrow, along with all their friends."

The cartel boss gazed out of the window as the vehicle started moving. "Get as many shooters as you can. Make it a bloodbath. Kill everyone and everything."

"I'll make the arrangements."

As the convoy left the heavily guarded estate Barbosa took

a tablet from a seat pocket to check his sharemarket portfolio. His forehead wrinkled into a frown as the device refused to link to the cellular network. He tried for a minute and then tossed it on the leather seat in disgust. Again, he tried on his phone where he encountered the same problem. "What the hell is wrong with the network?"

"Towers must be down," said Duvan.

Barbosa scowled as his car slowed and came to a halt. "What now?"

Duvan spoke into a radio before reporting to his boss. "There's a clown on the road."

"A what?"

"Some guy dressed as a clown. He's holding a red balloon."

"What the hell?"

"Yeah, weird shit. Stay here, boss, I'm going to check it out." Duvan opened the door of the armored SUV.

"No–"

Duvan let out a grunt and toppled over.

"No, no, no." Barbosa struggled through to the front seat and grabbed the door, pulling it closed. "Get us out of here!" he screamed at the driver.

There was a blinding flash. He glanced through the windshield and saw the lead vehicle engulfed in flames. "Go!"

The armored SUV rocked as another blast crippled the vehicle behind it. Then the driver angled the wheel and stomped the accelerator to the floor. Barbosa was flung sideways as the truck bounced over a curb and stalled.

"Get it going!"

His man struggled with the ignition, but the truck refused to start.

"Pump the gas."

Still, the engine refused to catch.

He caught a glimpse of movement through the side window. A figure was approaching through the smoke from the burning vehicles. As they got closer, he saw it was an armed man wearing a clown mask.

Barbosa fumbled for his pistol as the grinning clown approached the window. He winced as a gloved hand slapped a written card up against the glass. His blood ran cold as he read the neatly printed words.

This is for Axe, Ali and Junior. But... mostly Axe.

The figure tore off his mask and Barbosa found himself face to face with Petty Officer Mike Saunders, the man whose life he had pledged to destroy. Mike glared at him with grim determination and waved with a gloved hand.

There was a loud thump from under the SUV. Barbosa turned to the driver who was still trying to start the engine. "We need to get out." He crawled through to the back seat with his pistol in hand and fumbled with the door latch. It wouldn't open.

He turned back to the window where the message was stuck to the glass. There was no sign of the SEAL.

Barbosa, *The Butcher,* had a split second of remorse as the floor beneath him was super heated to a half-million degrees by a thermal charge. Then, he felt nothing as he was instantly incinerated.

A few hundred yards away Mike stood with a second clown, watching the vehicle burn. The other clown tore off his mask, revealing a crooked nose and brown eyes.

"Job done," said Bishop.

Mike felt like a massive weight had been lifted from his shoulders. With Barbosa dead his family would no longer live in fear. The cartel boss's reign of terror was finally over.

"Thank you," said Mike.

"No dramas. Dealing with scum like him is what PRIMAL does," replied Bishop.

"PRIMAL, hey. Well it's good to know that someone out there is willing to take out the trash."

Bishop laughed. "That's one way of putting it. Now, we need to get ourselves to a wedding."

***

"Does Rick look nervous?" TJ whispered to his wife. They sat with fifty other people on benches under the sweeping boughs of the forest that surrounded his family cabin. A string quartet played softly in the background as Rick and his best man, Mike, waited for the arrival of his bride.

She nudged him gently. "I do remember you being pretty nervous when we got married."

"That's because your father was carrying a gun."

Deb chuckled. "Terrance, he was a cop."

"That made it worse."

She took his hand a squeezed it gently. "Well, you didn't look nervous yesterday."

As a precursor to Rick and Jenny's wedding the two of them had held a small commitment ceremony for just the teammates and their friends. It was TJ's idea to reaffirm their vows and there hadn't been a dry eye in the cabin when they'd finished.

"Oh my god, that's so cute," gushed Deb.

TJ turned his head and saw Junior, dressed in a miniature tuxedo, leading Axe along the red carpet that split the rows of people sitting on benches. The little boy was grinning as he clutched the collar of the former Military Working Dog. He noted that Junior wasn't actually leading the dog. It was Axe who was guiding the toddler down the aisle. He smiled. Axe was wearing a bowtie on his collar.

The two of them stopped alongside Rick where he was standing with Mike. The groom wore a grin wider than the Golden Gate Bridge.

"This is to die for," whispered Deb.

TJ turned and kissed her on the cheek as the string quartet increased in tempo and volume. All eyes were drawn to the aisle as Jenny appeared from behind a massive sequoia tree. She was radiant in an elegant ivory off-the-shoulder dress with intricate beading around the bust. Her father wore a stern expression as he escorted his only daughter down the aisle.

TJ felt a tear forming in his eye. Then, he nearly laughed as he realized the quartet was playing a string rendition of Beyonce's *Single Ladies.* "Last man down," he whispered as the bride joined the groom.

An hour later, with the bridal party having photos taken in the woods, TJ found himself at the outside bar drinking champagne with Deb, Ernie and his wife, Maria.

"Wasn't that a beautiful ceremony," said Maria.

"Stunning," agreed Deb. "And it went flawlessly."

As small talk continued, TJ spotted a familiar face among the guests milling among the wine barrels and rough-hewn benches being used to hold food and drinks. The man from the meeting in Mexico, Bishop, was talking with a group of Jenny's friends from New York. "Deb, look who it is."

His wife didn't miss a beat. "Oh, how lovely he could make it." She excused herself from the group and they moved toward Bishop.

The clandestine operative broke from his own conversation and met them half way.

"What a surprise to see you here," said Deb as she offered her hand.

Bishop shook both their hands. "Deborah, you look stunning. TJ, good to see you again. I apologize for the intrusion, but our people got wind of a plan for Barbosa's people to target the wedding. We wanted to make sure that nothing happened."

TJ's eyes scanned the surrounding forest and he contemplated making a beeline for the gun cabinet in the cabin.

"There's no need to be alarmed," he added. "The key threats have been neutralized. We just wanted to make sure there were no residual elements in play." Bishop took a flash drive from his suit and handed it to Deb. "There are details of his known associates included with his jackpot card."

Deb shook Bishop's hand. "We owe you guys a debt of gratitude. Tell Vance he will always have a friend inside the Agency."

"Appreciated."

“Who invited this clown?” Mike appeared with Ali, Junior and Axe. The SEAL and his wife both wore carefree smiles. Junior greeted Deb and TJ with squeals of delight as Deb lifted him from the ground.

“Hello handsome,” she said as Mike shook hands with Bishop and introduced him to Ali.

The boy wrapped his arms around her neck. “Hello Aunty Deb.”

TJ bent and stroked Axe’s ears as his wife cuddled the toddler. He rose when a waiter brought a tray of drinks to the group and Ernie and his wife joined them. Behind them he spotted Rick and Jenny. Accepting a flute of champagne he waited for the couple to arrive. “Ladies and gentlemen, a toast.”

The others followed suit.

“To the newlyweds.”

They echoed the toast and everyone sipped. Then Rick raised his own glass. “Most importantly, to Axe. The best damn dog I’ve ever met.”

“Axe, Axe, Axe,” chanted Junior as the adults raised their glasses then drank.

“So, Mike,” said Bishop. “Any chance Axe has a girlfriend? Because if he ever sires pups I want one.”

“Me too,” said Ernie.

“Amen to that,” said Rick.

“I don’t think you’d have any problems homing them,” said Jenny. “We’d take two.”

Mike glanced down at Axe. “Seems only fair that we find him a lady, I mean, he helped me get mine.”

“Me too,” said Rick.

“Same here,” said TJ as he leaned across and kissed his wife on the cheek.

“What do you think, bud?” Mike asked his loyal friend. “You ready to be a dad?”

Axe let out a bark, rose up on his rear legs and placed his paws on the barrel.

“Looks like he’s interested,” Ali said with a laugh. “And I

just happen to know a very available and very beautiful Alsatian."

"Hang on," said Ernie. "Does this mean we're going to have to run a canine girlfriend selection course?"

THE END

AUTHOR'S FINAL WORDS

Well, that concludes the SEAL trilogy. I hope you have all enjoyed the journey as much as I have. Is this the end of Jack Silkstone's foray into lighthearted romance? Considering the overwhelmingly positive feedback I've had for this series, probably not. However, I do need to get back to the PRIMAL series, as I owe the fans book #10 before the close of 2018.

If you truly enjoyed the SEAL series please consider signing up to my email list here so I can let you know when I get back to romance. Or, if you really enjoyed my style you might consider giving PRIMAL a read. The series is filled with characters not unlike Mike, Ali and the rest of your favorites.

Cheers,

JS

BOOKS BY JACK SILKSTONE

PRIMAL Inception
PRIMAL Mirza
PRIMAL Origin
PRIMAL Unleashed
PRIMAL Vengeance
PRIMAL Fury
PRIMAL Reckoning
PRIMAL Nemesis
PRIMAL Redemption
PRIMAL Compendium
PRIMAL Renegade
PRIMAL Deception
PRIMAL Exodus
SEAL of Approval
SEAL the Deal
Signed SEAL'd and Delivered

ABOUT THE AUTHOR

Jack Silkstone grew up on a steady diet of Tom Clancy, James Bond, Jason Bourne, Commando comics, and the original first-person shooters, Wolfenstein and Doom. His background includes a career in military intelligence and special operations, working alongside some of the world's most elite units. His love of action-adventure stories, his military background, and his real-world experiences combined to inspire the no-holds-barred PRIMAL series.

jacksilkstone@primalunleashed.com
www.primalunleashed.com
www.twitter.com/jsilkstone
www.facebook.com/primalunleashed

www.ingramcontent.com/pod-product-compliance
Lightning Source LLC
Chambersburg PA
CBHW062303030626
46163CB00008B/223
9781983240027